Queenie

By the same author

Kimberley
CHAMBERS

Queenie

HarperCollins*Publishers*

HarperCollins*Publishers* Ltd
1 London Bridge Street,
London SE1 9GF

www.harpercollins.co.uk

First published by HarperCollins*Publishers* 2020
1

A catalogue record for this book is available from the British Library

ISBN: 978-0-00-814482-1 (HB)
ISBN: 978-0-00-820848-6 (TPB)

Typeset in Sabon LT Std by
Palimpsest Book Production Ltd, Falkirk, Stirlingshire

Printed and bound in the UK by CPI Group (UK) Ltd, Croydon CR0 4YY

MIX
Paper from
responsible sources
FSC
www.fsc.org   **FSC™ C007454**

This book is produced from independently certified FSC™ paper
to ensure responsible forest management.

For more information visit: www.harpercollins.co.uk/green

In loving memory of
Joyce Pauline Darling
July 1941—November 2017

ACKNOWLEDGEMENTS

As always, a big thanks to the fabulous team at HarperCollins for all your dedication and hard graft.

A special mention to my brilliant editor, Kimberley Young. My agent, Tim Bates, and my publicist, Felicity Denham. Also Sarah Shea, Charlotte Brabbin, Charlie Redmayne and Laura Meyer. Each and every one of you is a joy to work with.

Thanks also to my fabulous friends, Sue Cox, Pat Fletcher and Rosie de Courcy.

And last but not least, thanks to all my lovely loyal readers.

God bless,
KC xx

'We know what we are,
But know not what we may be'

William Shakespeare

PROLOGUE

From what I can recall, my early childhood was a happy one. I lived with me mum, Molly, dad, Eric, and younger sister, Vivian, in the East End of London. Whitechapel, to be precise.

My dad worked long hours down at the docks and it was Mum's job to cook, clean and look after me and Viv. Like most East End families, we didn't have much dough. But compared to those that lived in the slums, we were reasonably well off. We had a two-bedroom house all to ourselves and a hot meal on the table every evening.

Vivvy wasn't just my sister; she was my best mate too. When we weren't at school, we'd be outside playing from dawn to dusk. Marbles, rounders, release, conker fights and even cricket with the boys. It was warmer running around the streets than it was indoors at times.

Once every summer, Mum and Dad would take us to Southend for the day. We'd collect shells, fish for crabs and go paddling in the sea before eating a handsome fish-and-chip supper.

Hop-picking in Kent was another annual family outing. Aunt Edna, me mum's sister, would come with us too.

A *funny lady*, she would sing all the way there and all the way home. Viv and I loved Aunt Edna dearly.

But in life, things can change in an instant. That's certainly what happened to me. One minute I was this carefree teenager, the next I had to batten down the hatches as life as I'd known it smacked me in the chops over and over again.

Anyway, enough of me waffling on. Not for the faint hearted this, so put on your seatbelts and prepare for a rollercoaster.

My name is Queenie and this is my story.

PART ONE

'One might as well be hung for a sheep as a lamb'
Proverb

CHAPTER ONE

Summer 1939

Eric Wade chucked the newspaper to one side. 'It's gonna happen, Molly, I'm telling you. Now Hitler's invaded Poland, we're bound to get involved. Expect an announcement soon, my love. We're going to war.'

Molly squeezed her husband's hand. Eric was thirty-four, a medium height, broad-shouldered man who currently had the weight of the world on his shoulders. His own father had been killed in action during the Great War and Eric was petrified of being called up as he feared the same would happen to him.

'I was talking to Mr Ricketts yesterday and he said if the worst happens, it'll be the younger lads they call up, Eric. The ones without families. Try not to worry too much, lovey.'

Eric stood up. He wasn't a big boozer any more, but the thought of going to war was enough to turn any man to drink. 'I'm off to the pub. I'll see you later, love.'

Molly walked into the lounge to see her two daughters glued to the window. 'Queenie, Viv, come away from there.

You don't want the new neighbours to think we're a family of nosy parkers, do you?'

Viv obeyed her mother's orders while Queenie stayed put. She couldn't take her eyes off the boy she presumed was the youngest son. He was tall with a mop of wavy jet-black hair. At twelve, Queenie had boy mates but was yet to have a proper boyfriend. She decided there and then that when she was old enough she wanted a boyfriend just like this one. She'd never seen anyone so handsome before, but he was far too old for her she feared.

'Queenie, I won't tell you again. Move.'

Queenie reluctantly did so and was lunged at by her mother. Molly spat on her handkerchief and wiped the remains of her daughter's breakfast off her face. 'If you're going over the road to ask the new neighbours if they'd like a cup of tea, you need to look your best,' smiled Molly.

Queenie grabbed Viv's hand. 'Come on. Let's go meet them.'

The previous tenant of the house had been Nutty Nora. She'd died in hospital recently and wouldn't be sorely missed. She used to wake half the street up by dancing and singing in the middle of the night. Many a time, Queenie's dad had got up and led the senile old woman back inside her house, only for her to reappear in the street ten minutes later.

Queenie approached the woman who was standing on the doorstep. The two lads had disappeared. 'Hello. We live opposite you at number thirty-one. My mum sent us over to ask if you'd like a cup of tea?'

The woman was of medium build, smartly dressed and had beautiful thick wavy black hair that shone in the sunlight. She smiled. A kind smile that lit up the whole of her face. 'Patrick, Daniel,' she shouted in an Irish accent.

The two lads reappeared, and Queenie felt herself blush. The younger one was even more handsome up close. He had piercing bright green eyes, full lips and a cheeky grin.

'These lovely young ladies live over the road and have asked would we like a cup of tea.'

'Does the Pope pray?' the older lad chuckled.

Not knowing what that meant, Queenie and Viv glanced at one another.

The woman held out her right hand. 'I'm Mary. Mary O'Leary, and these two ragamuffins are my sons, Patrick and Daniel. We would absolutely love a cup of tea,' Mary smiled. 'And please do thank your mum.'

'OK. We'll be back soon,' said Queenie.

Daniel gently grabbed Queenie's arm. 'Not until you tell us your names, you won't. My mum's always told me and my brother we aren't to accept things off strangers.'

Realizing her sister was unusually lost for words, Viv stepped in. 'I'm Vivian and this is my sister, Queenie.'

Daniel winked. 'A pleasure to meet you both. Three sugars each for me and Patrick and two for Mum. Oh and don't forget the biscuits.'

Mary chuckled and playfully punched her youngest on the arm. 'You take no notice of this one, girls. He's a terrible wind-up merchant. I've got sugar and biscuits.'

When Daniel grinned at her, Queenie felt her insides flutter, a feeling she'd never experienced before.

Viv linked arms with her sister and led her back to their house. 'Why did ya act all weird?'

'I didn't.'

'Yes, you did. You stood there like a stuffed dummy.'

'You're talking rubbish.'

Vivian might only be nine, but she was astute for her age. 'Queenie and Daniel sitting in a tree, k-i-s-s-i-n-g,' giggled Viv.

'Shut your big mouth, else Mum will hear ya,' ordered Queenie.

'Are they nice people? Would they like tea?' asked Molly.

'They're very nice, Mum,' Viv replied. 'Oh, and Queenie fancies Daniel.'

'No. I don't,' Queenie glared at her sister, face turning a shade of beetroot. 'I'm going to lie down; I got a headache. You can take the tea over by yourself.'

'Whatever's a matter with her?' asked Molly, as her eldest flew up the stairs.

Vivian shrugged. 'Search me, Mum.'

The following morning, having recovered from the previous day's embarrassment, Queenie happily tucked into her breakfast. Kippers soaked in vinegar with a thick slice of bread was her favourite. 'You look nice, Mum. You going out somewhere?'

At thirty-one, Molly was plumper than she'd been when she'd married Eric. A five-foot-three brunette, she had a kind smile, big brown eyes and was wearing a floral dress. 'I'm popping down the Lane with Mabel. You two need new school shoes.' Mabel Brown lived next door. Queenie and Viv often played with her daughters, Aggie and Nelly.

'You're quiet, Dad. You OK?' asked Queenie.

'No. I'm not OK. It's only a matter of time now before Chamberlain sends in the troops. I couldn't sleep a wink last night.'

'Don't worry the girls please, Eric. Put that newspaper down and eat your kippers. They're getting cold,' ordered Molly.

Queenie and Viv glanced at one another. Both were thinking the same thing. What had happened to their once jolly dad? Lately, all he did was go on about the war and it was tiresome, to say the least.

Queenie was sitting on a kerb outside Derek Lewis's house swapping cigarette cards when Derek's mum bellowed, 'Kids, get in 'ere. The Prime Minister is about to make an announcement.'

Even though the small front room was packed with people, you could have heard a pin drop. 'I am speaking to you from the cabinet room at 10 Downing Street,' boomed Neville Chamberlain's voice. The radio was turned up to full volume.

Queenie squeezed her sister's hand. Had her dad been right all along about a war, she wondered? The Prime Minister's voice certainly sounded serious.

'This morning the British Ambassador in Berlin handed the German government a final note stating that unless we heard from them by eleven o'clock that they were prepared at once to withdraw their troops from Poland, a state of war would exist between us,' explained the Prime Minister. 'I have to tell you now that no such undertaking has been received, and that consequently this country is at war with Germany.'

'Flipping hell! Hitler's coming to get us. We're doomed,' cried Derek Lewis.

Derek's mum smacked him around the head. 'Shut it you, ya bleedin' bock.'

Confused and not really knowing what to do next, Queenie took Viv's hand and set off home.

The atmosphere walking a few streets from Derek's house to their own was strange. Everyone seemed to be outside their houses having a chinwag, but there was none of the usual hoots of laughter or happy faces, just solemn expressions and looks of concern.

'We ain't all gonna die, are we, Queenie?'

Queenie put a protective arm around her nine-year-old sister's shoulders. Everybody said how alike she and Vivian were. They ate well but were both skinny as rakes. They had the same mousy brown hair too that their mum made them wear shoulder length as she said it was too fine and looked straggly if they grew it any longer. 'Don't you worry,' Mum had told them. 'Dad'll look after us. We're gonna be fine.'

Nobody was at home, so Queenie and Viv sat on the kerb outside rather than sit inside alone. They had no idea where their dad was, but their mum would most certainly have got wind of the news down the Lane and was probably rushing home to them at this minute.

'Are your ma and da not in?' shouted a voice. It was Daniel O'Leary.

'No. But they'll be back soon,' Queenie managed to reply.

'Ma said come in for a cup of tea. You can wait for your ma and da with us.'

Queenie leaned towards Viv. 'You show me up and say I fancy him, I'll never speak to you again.'

Within twenty minutes of sitting inside Mrs O'Leary's house, Queenie had temporarily forgotten England was at war. Mary made them sweet tea to help with the shock and cut them each a slice of Irish apple cake, which was gorgeous. Then she told funny stories, mainly about her sons, to make them laugh. Daniel was eighteen, Patrick twenty-two, and Queenie could not stop smiling. The lads joined in with the fun too, telling stories about their

10

mother and the rest of their family back in County Cork.

'Have you not got a husband?' Vivian asked bluntly.

Queenie nudged her sister. 'You don't ask people such questions. Apologize to Mrs O'Leary at once.'

Mrs O'Leary waved her hand. 'It's fine, honestly. Yes, I do have a husband. Paddy. I kicked his useless backside out years ago, mind, the drunken old goat. Good for nothing, that man. Well, apart from giving me three gorgeous sons.'

'Our dad used to drink too much when Viv and me were little. My mum made him stop,' exclaimed Queenie.

'I don't ever remember Dad being drunk,' queried Viv.

'Neither do I. But that's what Mum told me. He was drunk when he registered your birth, Viv, that's why your name's spelt wrong.'

'What do you mean it's spelt wrong?'

Seeing the look of indignation on her sister's face, Queenie pretended she was joking and decided to change the subject. Their mum had nearly died giving birth to Viv, had been ill for ages afterwards. The spelling of her sister's name was meant to be Vivienne, but their dad had made a cock-up and registered it as Vivian, which was usually the man's version of the same name. 'Is your other son married, Mrs O'Leary?' enquired Queenie.

'Call me Mary. All my friends call me Mary. Seamus died, my love, back in Ireland. He would've been twenty now, God rest his soul.' She solemnly made the sign of the cross across her heart.

'I'm so sorry,' Queenie mumbled.

'Me too,' added Viv. She craned her neck. 'Aunt Edna's just turned up at ours, Queenie.'

'We better go now. Thank you so much for the tea and cake, Mary. It was very kind of you.'

Mary O'Leary smiled. 'You're very welcome, girls. The

11

boys go to work all week, so if you're ever bored, you're always welcome to pop in. That's if it's OK with your mum, of course.'

'Bye, girls,' said Patrick. 'And don't you be worrying about no war. Daniel and I will look out for you.'

'Too right we will,' Daniel added with a wink, and Queenie felt herself blush again.

Aunt Edna was the only other relation Queenie and Viv had that they knew of. A big lady with an even bigger singing voice, Aunt Edna had short dark curly hair and was the life and soul of any party. She loved to sing and could play the piano without even looking at the keys.

At thirty-five, Aunt Edna was four years older than their mum. She'd had her heart broken by a cheating fiancé in her younger years and had been single ever since. She treated Queenie and Vivian more like daughters than nieces.

Edna put an arm around both girls and held them close to her ample bosoms. 'I brought you some sweeties. Where's your mum and dad? I take it you've heard the news?'

Molly Wade arrived home at that very minute and joined in the hug. 'It'll be OK. We'll all be OK. Where's your father?'

'Dunno, Mum. Will we have to go to school tomorrow?' asked Queenie.

'I don't know yet, love. It's all been such a shock; I can't think straight.'

'Will Hitler bomb us, Mum? Derek Lewis says we're all doomed,' said Viv.

'Take no notice of Derek Lewis,' replied Aunt Edna. 'His mother talks rubbish an' all.'

Molly was worried, extremely worried. The war was

obviously her main concern, but Eric was another. He'd rolled home drunk last night, for the first time in years. The girls were in bed and thankfully hadn't witnessed it, but Molly's guess was he was down the pub again now and she couldn't go back to those dark days. She'd given Eric an ultimatum when Vivvy was three months old. He either gave up the booze or she was leaving him and she and the girls were moving in with her sister.

The ultimatum had thankfully worked and ever since Eric had been a good, kind husband and father. Eric had endured a tough upbringing. After his father got killed in battle, his mother had gone on the game to make ends meet. She'd been found strangled in an alleyway when Eric was nineteen years old, a subject he found difficult to talk about even now.

'Eat your sweets, girls. I got you some cola bottles and Parma violets,' urged Aunt Edna.

When the girls went out into the back yard with their sweets, Edna made her sister a cup of tea. 'Awful news, ain't it, lovey? But we must try and be bright in front of the kids. I'm surprised Eric isn't 'ere. Did he say where he was going?'

Molly's eyes welled up. 'He came home drunk last night. Started on me like the old days. Thank God it was late and the kids were fast asleep.'

'You gotta nip that in the bud, Moll,' Edna advised, her face full of concern. Eric Wade was a decent enough man until he had a drink inside him. Alcohol did not agree with Eric one little bit. It turned him into a monster.

An hour later, Eric arrived home as sober as a judge.

'There you are! Where have you been? I was worried sick, Eric,' Molly gabbled.

Edna glanced at her brother-in-law to check the state he was in, before going out in the garden to join her nieces. She had male friends, lots of them, but would never trust another romantically after what David Futcher had done to her. Singing and playing the piano in pubs brought Edna far more happiness than men ever had.

Eric held his wife in his arms. 'I'm so sorry about yesterday. It won't happen again, Molly.'

'It had better not, Eric, because now war has been declared, I couldn't cope with you off the rails an' all. I don't know if I'm coming or going as it bloody well is.'

Eric put his arm around Molly's shoulders and led her into the back yard. 'Girls, Edna, I know today's news is shocking, but I want you to know we're all gonna be fine. I went to see my pal, Canning Town Keith, earlier and he reckons he can put a shelter up for us 'ere, in our own back yard. That'll keep us all safe, eh?'

Queenie and Viv ran over to their father and hugged him. 'Will Hitler not be able to get to us if we all sit in our shelter, Dad?' asked Viv.

'Nope. Hitler won't be able to get at us in there.'

'That means Aunt Edna will have to move in with us,' said Queenie. ''Cause if the bombs start going off, she lives more than ten minutes away.'

'I can run round 'ere in five bleedin' minutes,' lied Aunt Edna. 'Anyway, we've all gotta carry on with our normal lives. There'll be no food on our tables otherwise. Hitler don't frighten me, ya know. I'll be singing in the Prospect of Whitby tonight as usual. It'll take more than a short-arse, pasty-faced kraut to stop me doing what I wanna do!'

As Queenie and Viv giggled like mad, Molly and Eric couldn't help but laugh too. Edna didn't only have a wonderful singing voice and a way with words, she also had the knack of turning a dark day into a positive one. Edna's glass was always half full, never half empty. She truly was a ray of sunshine to be around.

And in the dark days of the war ahead their little family would need all the help they could get.

CHAPTER TWO

I wasn't that scared at first. I flatly refused to be evacuated like lots of my friends. My classroom soon emptied as children were sent to live in different parts of the country.

It was sad saying goodbye to Aggie and Nelly Brown. They went off to live with a distant relative in a rural part of Wales. Viv and I had tears in our eyes as we said our farewells. We had no idea if or when we would see them again. Derek Lewis was evacuated too. He was sent to live with an elderly aunt in the countryside.

Some of the lads, including Joe Brown, Aggie and Nelly's brother, and Jim and Tim Lewis, Derek's brothers, volunteered rather than waiting to be conscripted. I thought they were ever so brave to volunteer. Mabel Brown was in pieces as she waved goodbye to her only son.

With the help of his pal, Dad built us an Anderson shelter. It took up most of the back yard, but the neighbours were impressed. Lots came to view it and a few followed suit. Viv and I spent hours in that shelter mucking about with our gas masks, eating sweets, playing games and planning our futures. Viv wanted to become a midwife when she left school and I wanted to work in a posh shop that sold fashionable women's clothes.

Christmas came and went without any drama, then in January 1940 the rationing started. Bacon, butter and sugar were the first items to become scarce. I was used to having three sugars in my tea, so I cut down to one and a half. I wanted to do my bit. I had to really.

By the summer of 1940, our neighbours in the East End were referring to the Second World War as the 'Phoney War' because nothing was happening. Lots of my friends who'd been evacuated began to return to the area, including Aggie and Nelly Brown. The laughter returned to our close-knit community and myself, Viv and our pals started to venture further afield again. We'd go over the marshes or Victoria Park. On hot summer days I loved going to Vicky Park. They had a lido there, so I always came home feeling nice and clean. It was better than washing in the sink or our tin bath at home. That took ages to fill with water, so mum would take me and Viv to the public baths once a week so we could scrub ourselves properly clean with soap and a flannel.

All good things must come to an end so they say, and that was certainly the case on 7 September 1940. That was the day the Blitz started. I will never forget the sound of that first bomb going off.

'Mum. Mum, you upstairs?' I squealed, as the house literally shook and the cup of tea I'd just made flew off the kitchen hob, scalding my legs. There was no reply and I knew my dad and Viv were out. Petrified, I crawled on all fours inside the larder and shut the door. 'Help! I think the house is falling down,' I screamed, as I heard something else smash. I honestly thought I was going to die

there and then. I even wet my knickers I'm ashamed to admit. Mum returned minutes later. She'd popped to the shops. The bomb had landed only two streets away from us. Too close for comfort.

Within an hour, Mum, Dad, myself and Vivvy were huddled together in our shelter in the back yard, but I didn't feel at all safe in there. We could hear screams, smell smoke drifting through the air. I couldn't help worrying about Aunt Edna. Was she OK? Had she made it to her nearest shelter? Then another bomb dropped and all but ruptured my eardrums. I was terrified at that point, so was Viv. My sister and I huddled together, crying.

I had no sleep that night. Not even when the bombing stopped. First thing the following morning Mum, myself and Vivvy walked round to Aunt Edna's. The devastation we saw on the way was gut-wrenching. A whole row of houses a couple of streets away from ours had been completely wiped out. My classmate Roger lived in one of those houses and I was relieved he and his family were all right. They'd made it to a shelter in time. Mr and Mrs King weren't so lucky though. They'd had a shelter erected in their back garden the same as ours and the bomb had ripped right through it, killing them both. I shuddered. That could so easily have been us.

Aunt Edna was indoors and thankfully OK. She looked shaken though, especially when Mum told her about Mr and Mrs King being blown up in their Anderson shelter. 'You must go to a proper shelter if the bombing starts again. Promise me,' Aunt Edna said holding me and Viv tightly. We both made her a promise. No way was I sitting in our shelter again – not when bombs were being dropped, anyway.

That night the bombing started again. It was terrifying, watching the sky lit up with fire as Mum, Dad, Viv and I ran to the nearest shelter with our neighbours. The shelter was busy, but we found Aunt Edna because we heard her singing 'Down at the Old Bull and Bush'.

People huddled together to keep warm and most, including me and Viv, joined in with Aunt Edna's repertoire. 'Maybe It's Because I'm a Londoner', 'Show Me the Way to Go Home,' 'My Old Man's a Dustman' and 'Leaning on a Lamp-post' were just some of the many songs we sang. It seemed to lighten the mood, taking our minds off what was happening outside. I suddenly felt brave. The complete opposite to how I'd felt the previous day. Instead of wetting my drawers like a coward, I comforted some of the other kids who looked scared. I even gave them the rest of my sweets and reassured them us East Enders were strong enough to fight off Adolf bloody Hitler.

The following day, Aggie and Nelly Brown left the area to return to their aunt in the countryside. After we'd waved them goodbye for a second time, Mum informed me and Viv that the next day we too would be leaving the East End. I begged Mum to come with us, but she said she couldn't; the offer wasn't extended to her.

I went to see Mrs O'Leary to tell her the news. I always called her Mary to her face, but would refer to her by her surname when mentioning her to other people. My mum had taught me that. Most of the neighbours I would refer to as mister and missus, or if they were close friends of my mum and dad I'd call them aunt or uncle.

Mrs O'Leary hugged me when I told her the news. 'It's for the best, Queenie. My heart would break if anything happened to you. At least you'll be safe.'

'But the only time I've ever been parted from Mum and Dad is when I've stayed round Aunt Edna's. I don't want to live with strangers,' I wept.

'You won't be alone. You'll have Vivian with you. Make sure you tell them that the two of you won't be separated.'

I nodded. 'I'm going to miss you, Mary. Say goodbye to Patrick and Daniel for me, won't you?' Daniel had a girlfriend now. A stunning blonde called Lucy. I hoped that one day when I was older I would look like Lucy.

I spent a good hour with Mrs O'Leary before saying a final goodbye.

'Don't forget, you can write to me every day if you wish. Not that you'll have time – I'm sure you'll be having too much fun for that. Never forget, I'm always here if you need me though. If the people aren't nice to you, Queenie, you must tell your mum. Or if you don't want to worry your mum, you can tell me. The boys'll be down there like a shot if you're being mistreated, let me fecking tell you.'

I giggled and gave Mrs O'Leary one final hug. She was always saying feck this and feck that, and the way she said it never failed to make me laugh. 'Bye, Mary. I'll write to you soon.'

The following day Viv and I said a tearful goodbye to Mum, Dad and Aunt Edna at the train station. We had our cases with us and were quickly ushered aboard a carriage with loads of kids we didn't know.

As the train pulled away, I waved and waved until my parents and aunt were out of sight. Dad was positive he would soon be called up and I wondered if I'd ever see him again. With bombs dropping night after night, I couldn't help but fear I'd never see any of them again.

Little did I know, Hitler's bombs weren't the real danger.

Queenie

Six Months Later

March 1941

'Queenie, Viv. There's some letters arrived for you.'

Queenie ran excitedly down the stairs. She loved receiving letters. 'Thank you, Betty.'

'Give me a shout once you've read them and I'll cook your breakfast,' smiled rosy-cheeked Betty.

Queenie handed Viv her two letters. She knew by the handwriting who they were from. One was from Aunt Edna, the other, Nelly Brown.

Ripping open the one addressed to both of them, Queenie read it out loud:

'Dear Queenie and Viv, I'm so pleased you're enjoying your time more in the countryside, now the weather is warming up a bit. Spring will be here soon and I'm sure you'll love watching the flowers bloom and seeing all the baby animals being born.

'Ivan sounds nice. I'm glad he's taken the two of you under his wing and you are earning extra pocket money. It's good of Ivan to drive you to the shops too to save you walking all those miles. Does he have children himself?

'Things are very much the same here, but please do not worry, as we're all OK. We get to the shelter early now as we know the bombs will be dropped at some point during the night. Big Fat Flo lost her house last Monday. That whole row is now a pile of rubble. Thankfully, nobody was hurt. They were all down the shelter.

'Re your question about Aggie Brown not writing to you, Queenie. I had a word with her mum and Mabel said she's not much of a letter writer and has made friends with some girls her own age where she is staying. It is

very rude of Aggie not to reply to yours though, I must say. The ignorant little cow!

'Please thank Mr and Mrs Briggs again from me for looking after you and feeding you so well. I bet I won't recognize the pair of you when I see you, what with all that country air and wonderful grub you're eating.*

'Dad and Aunt Edna both send their love, girls. Keep your chins up. You're both doing brilliantly and I'm so very proud of you. Love always, Mum.'

Viv smiled. 'Can I look at the letter now?' Both girls' biggest fear was that one day their mother wouldn't write back to them because she was dead.

Queenie handed the letter to Viv and winced. She had woken up with a bad belly ache and it seemed to be getting worse. 'Viv, do me a favour once you've read your letters: go down for breakfast and tell Betty I'm not feeling hungry this morning.'

When her sister left the room, Queenie read her letters from Aunt Edna and Mrs O'Leary, then curled up in a foetal position and held her aching stomach. She'd eaten the same as Viv yesterday, so it couldn't be food poisoning. Perhaps she had caught a bug? But she hadn't really been out anywhere.

Wishing she was at home so her mum could look after her, Queenie quickly reminded herself how lucky she and Viv had been. From the moment they'd met Betty and John Briggs, the couple had been extremely kind to them.

It had felt odd spending her fourteenth birthday and then Christmas with the Briggs, especially when Betty and John's sons had turned up on Christmas Day with their wives and kids. Both Queenie and Viv had felt they didn't belong there that day, but they'd put on brave faces and pretended to be jolly before excusing themselves and going to bed early.

The bedroom they shared was nice, bigger than their bedroom at home. It had pretty patterned curtains and oak furniture. They even had a proper wardrobe in which to hang up the small amount of clothes they'd brought with them. Their mum sent them money in the post to buy anything new they needed. Viv's feet had recently got too big for her shoes, so Mrs Briggs had taken them to a shop to buy some new ones.

Mr and Mrs Briggs were generous too. The farm was ever so cold and muddy in the winter, so they'd brought her and Viv Wellington boots and trousers. Queenie had never worn trousers at home, her mum said only boys wore them, and it felt weird at first. They were far more practical though, for roaming across the fields on the farm.

Feeling something trickle down her legs, Queenie leapt out of bed and was mortified to see blood, not only on her skin and clothes but on Mrs Briggs' white flannelette sheet.

Surely she wasn't dying? And how was she going to tell Mrs Briggs that she'd ruined her lovely white sheet? She lifted up the sheet and was horrified to see the blood had seeped through to the mattress too.

Queenie burst into tears. What was she going to do?

Betty Briggs had been ever so nice about her situation. She'd sat her down, wiped away her tears and told her not to worry at all about the sheet or mattress. She'd then explained about the birds and the bees and given Queenie something that looked like bandages to stem the blood flow.

Later that evening, Queenie lay in bed not only feeling very stupid, but also thoroughly annoyed with her mother. Why had her mum never explained that her body would change at some point in her teenage years?

'You still got a tummy ache, Queen?' asked Viv.

'No. The tablets Betty gave me worked far better than those awful-tasting Epsom Salts we're forced to take at home.' Queenie propped herself up on her elbow. 'I felt so humiliated today, Viv. I honestly thought I might be dying, that something had burst in my stomach. Why didn't Mum tell us about this, eh? Mrs O'Leary would have, I know she would. It'll happen to you too, you'll start bleeding in a year or so. It means you're ready to make babies.'

Eleven-year-old Vivian shuddered at the prospect. 'Not sure I want to have babies or be a midwife after all,' she said, wrinkling her nose in disgust.

When Vivian finally fell asleep, Queenie read Mrs O'Leary's letter once more. Because they were Irish, Patrick and Daniel wouldn't be called up to join the British Army. Ireland had decided to remain neutral in the war. Currently, the O'Learys were living back in Ireland, driven out of London by the Blitz. They still had the house opposite hers, but wouldn't return until the bombing stopped.

Queenie chuckled inwardly as she read one particular paragraph over and over again.

Daniel and that blonde tart have split up, Queenie. I'm fecking glad. Never liked the silly girl in the first place. She was all over him like a rash whenever he brought her round mine. I knew it wouldn't last. Good riddance to Lucy.

Queenie folded the letter up and put it in her bedside drawer. She never read Mrs O'Leary's letters to Viv. It didn't seem right. Mary was her friend, not her sister's.

24

Smiling, Queenie shut her eyes. She'd got over her embarrassment of earlier and Mrs Briggs had promised not to tell her husband or anybody else. Thinking about Daniel, Queenie drifted off to sleep with a smile on her face.

CHAPTER THREE

Two Months Later

May 1941

'What does Mum say?' asked Viv. 'Read it out loud,' she demanded.

Queenie's eyes skimmed over the letter. 'You can read it yourself. There's been no more bombs. That's over two weeks since they stopped. We still can't go home though,' sighed Queenie. It had been fun watching the spring lambs born and the little piglets, but overall, living on a farm was boring. It was so different to the East End, where the houses were close together and you only had to open your front door to bump into your friends. There was literally nothing to do here. And it was so quiet Queenie felt as though she needed to speak in a whisper.

'How d'ya feel today? The weather's glorious. Fancy going for a walk somewhere where we ain't been before?' asked Queenie.

'I still don't feel too clever. I don't mind sitting outside, but I'm not up to walking far. Why don't you go and find

Ivan, see if he'll take you into town? You can spend that money Mrs O'Leary sent us, and while you're there you can get me some magazines and a good book.' Mrs Briggs had been giving them lessons at home and it was she who suggested that they start reading books. Viv was currently reading *Oliver Twist* by Charles Dickens and loving it.

'It wasn't Mrs O'Leary who sent us the money, it was Daniel and Patrick – I told you that.' Queenie had been stunned when a ten-pound note fell out of Mrs O'Leary's latest letter. She'd never had so much money in her little purse before. 'Do you want me to bring you a cup of tea before I go out?'

'No. I'm fine, thanks. Mrs Briggs will bring me some breakfast up soon. I want to finish my book anyway. I need to know what happens to poor Oliver.'

Queenie put her purse in the pocket of her blue-and-white striped dress. 'Bye then. I'll see you later.'

Ivan Tumbleweed was a simple, thick-set, dark-haired thirty-year-old local man. He lived down the road from the farm in his caravan on some land his deceased father had left for him. His mum had abandoned him when he was young and taken his two older sisters with her. None of them had ever contacted him again, which at times grated on Ivan.

Seeing Queenie, Ivan drove towards her in his tractor. He liked young Queenie a lot and was sure she liked him too – why else would she spend so much time with him?

'Good morning, Miss Queenie. It's a beautiful day, isn't it?' Ivan greeted her in his thick country accent.

'Yes. It's lovely. Are you finishing at lunchtime as it's Saturday?'

'I sure am, Miss Queenie.' Ivan couldn't help but notice that since arriving at the farm, Queenie had turned from a girl into a woman. She had titties now, not big ones, but they were noticeable, especially when she ran. She obviously didn't wear a bra because he'd seen them bouncing up and down.

'If you aren't busy this afternoon, would you be kind enough to take me into town? Viv's still in bed with mumps and I need to get her a couple of bits. I also need some things for myself.'

Ivan smiled broadly. The farm was his life, that's why he had such big muscles. His only other interest was the pub. Every night he'd go to his local for five or six pints. 'That would be my pleasure. I will finish 'ere at twelve. You can help me with my jobs if you want?' He'd given Queenie lessons in driving the tractor yesterday and liked the feel of her body next to his.

'I don't want to get my frock dirty and I haven't had any breakfast yet. I'll meet you at twelve.'

'Miss Queenie, I think you're forgetting something,' grinned Ivan.

Queenie stood on tiptoes and pecked Ivan on his unshaven cheek. Ivan always reeked of sweat and wore the same clothes. He actually reminded her of home as he smelled like Stinkhouse Bridge. But he seemed pleasant and harmless, and she didn't want to hurt the poor sod's feelings, so she waited until he was out of sight before wiping her mouth with her hand.

The journey to the nearest town took about twenty minutes. Ivan drove a green truck and Queenie loved going out in it. Her father had never had a car, so being driven somewhere seemed ever so exciting and grown-up. 'Have you got a girlfriend, Ivan?' asked Queenie, politely trying to make conversation.

Ivan grinned. She obviously fancied him. She'd asked him only a couple of months ago if he had children and he'd told her he didn't because he was yet to get married. 'No, Miss Queenie. Not many women round 'ere to choose from, so I thought I'd bide my time until the right one came along,' he winked.

Queenie smiled politely. Ivan was simple, that much was obvious. 'Do you need anything in town?'

'No. I shall just be your bag carrier. That's what gentlemen do, Miss Queenie. They open doors for a lady and carry her bags.'

'Ahh. You're a sweet man, Ivan. I hope one day you meet a nice girlfriend.'

Even more positive that Queenie fancied him, Ivan grinned like a Cheshire cat. He'd never had a girlfriend in his life. It was about time his luck changed.

Queenie bought herself and Viv a new summer dress each, then spent ages choosing a book for her sister. She finally decided on *The Railway Children* by Edith Nesbit. Hoping now the bombing had stopped, they'd soon be going home, Queenie bought some thank you gifts for the Briggs: a pipe for John and a pair of slippers for Betty. She then decided to buy Ivan a small gift too. He'd been ever so kind running herself and Viv into town. Without him they'd never have got there, because John was always working and Betty didn't drive.

Lastly, Queenie bought herself and her sister a pair of comfortable sandals. They only had wellies and shoes to wear, which were far too warm now the weather was hot.

'I think I'm done now, Ivan. Oh, wait a minute, Viv asked for some magazines.'

'That's fine. I'll sit 'ere a minute with the bags while you buy your magazines.'

'Thank you. I won't be long.'

Ivan smiled. His Miss Queenie could take as long as she wanted.

Ivan opened the passenger side of the truck. 'There you go, Miss Queenie.'

Having kept Ivan's present separate to all the others, Queenie waited until he was seated before handing it to him. 'I bought you a gift. Open it.' The lady in the shop had kindly wrapped the dart flights in tissue paper for her.

Ivan could not believe his luck. No woman had ever bought him a present before, not even his own mother. 'I loves them. I needed a new set too. One of mine is split. How did you know I play darts?'

'Because I remember you telling me you play in the pub.'

'This is the nicest thing anybody has ever done for me, Miss Queenie. I will treasure them,' beamed Ivan.

'It's just a little thank you for driving me and Viv into town all the time, that's all. I reckon we'll be going back to the East End soon. I got a letter from my mum earlier. There's been no bombs dropped for over a fortnight now.'

Ivan grabbed Queenie's hand. 'I don't want you to go, Miss Queenie. Why don't you stay 'ere with me?'

Thinking Ivan was joking, Queenie laughed and snatched her hand away. 'As if! I honestly cannot wait to get home, see my family and friends. I've missed them all so much.'

Ivan's eyes clouded over. Why was she laughing at him and saying these things? He didn't like that. Not one little bit.

*

'Where you going, Ivan? Isn't the Briggs' farm straight on?'

'Yes. But I thought you might like to see where I live.'

'Erm, I would another time. But I think I should be getting back now. I need to see if my sister's OK,' said Queenie, beginning to feel the first stirrings of unease. When he carried on driving away from the Briggs' farm, she became more insistent: 'Please take me back now, I just want to go home.'

'It won't take long. I thought you liked me, Queenie. But it seems you're like all the others. You laugh at me and can't wait to get away from me. Just like my mum and sisters.'

It struck her that Ivan had been unusually quiet on the way home, as if he was sulking. There was a difference in his tone, too, and in the way he'd used her name, whereas in the past he'd always addressed her as 'Miss Queenie'. 'I do like you, Ivan. You're my friend. But please take me back to the farm now. Viv and me will both visit you when Viv's feeling better. I promise,' Queenie replied.

'No point turning back. We're 'ere now.'

They'd come to the end of the dirt track and in front of them was a grubby caravan, standing in a field with no houses or buildings in sight.

'Can you please take me home?' repeated Queenie, her heart thumping against her chest.

Ivan leaned in, giving her a whiff of his vile breath. 'You can't be a prick-tease like you been to me, Queenie, then laugh at me and say you can't wait to get back to the East End. It ain't right.'

Realizing he was deadly serious, Queenie opened the truck door and made a run for it. Ivan was soon catching up with her though. She could hear him cursing and his footsteps nearing. Queenie had never felt so terrified in her life. Suddenly paralysed through fear, she hid behind a tree and held her breath. Tears were streaming down her face. How could this be happening to her?

Unfortunately for Queenie, Ivan tripped as he ran past the tree and spotted her. All Queenie could do was burst into tears. She couldn't run any more, couldn't even move. 'I'm sorry, Ivan, if you think I led you on,' she managed to stammer. 'Please don't hurt me. I thought you were my friend.'

Ivan smiled, showing his dirty uneven teeth. He grabbed Queenie, threw her to the ground, undid the zip of his trousers and released his stinking penis. He then put his hand up Queenie's dress and ripped her knickers off with one hand. 'What about earlier? Kissing me and buying me a present. What is a man supposed to think, eh, Queenie?' Ivan's voice was husky now, his penis fully erect as he rammed it inside the girl of his dreams. 'And you wear no bra. You bounce towards me so I can see your little titties, I know you do. What you is, is a prick-tease. You can't treat me like that, then pretend you don't want me. I know you wanna be fucked.'

Queenie lay still, sobbing her heart out. She'd never felt pain like it. Fearing once Ivan was done with her, he might actually kill her, she shut her eyes and said a silent prayer. None of her family was religious, but Mrs O'Leary was. She'd told Queenie she prayed with rosary beads. How Queenie wished she had some of those now.

As Ivan tried to kiss her, Queenie retched. His breath was awful, as though he'd never cleaned his teeth in his life. 'I love you, Miss Queenie,' he groaned.

All of a sudden, he began making loud, weird noises. Queenie didn't have a clue what was happening; she could only hope her prayers had been answered and he was dying. Unfortunately, he wasn't.

Ivan rolled off her, zipped up his flies and smiled. 'You mustn't say nothing to the Briggs about this. They won't believe you anyway. John trusts me; I been working for him for years. I give you a lift back now. Your shopping is in the truck.'

As the monster led her towards his truck, Queenie was too scared to make a run for it. His grip on her arm was too tight and if she made him angry he might violate her again or even kill her. Instead, her whole body trembling, she focused her thoughts on seeing her family again.

The journey seemed to last for ever, with Queenie sitting rigid in the passenger seat, sensing his eyes on her. She knew she would never be able to tell the Briggs about this, or even Vivvy – it was far too disgusting to tell anybody. Besides, Ivan was right: it was her word against his, and Betty and John were bound to believe him over her, given that he'd worked for them so long. Betty obviously thought the world of Ivan. She fed him every day and talked about him as if he were part of the family.

As Queenie went to open the truck door and run to the safety of the farmhouse, Ivan grabbed her arm. 'No. I will open the door for you and I will bring your shopping to the front door. You won't say anything, will you?'

The engine was still running, so Queenie knew she had to say the right thing. If she didn't, she was petrified he might drive off with her. 'I won't say anything, I promise.'

Ivan smiled and stroked Queenie's cheek. 'Good. Our little secret. You're very beautiful, Miss Queenie. I will always love you, you know.'

Somehow, Queenie managed to force a smile. 'Will you get my shopping out for me, please?'

'Of course. Miss Queenie's wish is my command,' grinned Ivan. 'Hopefully, I see you tomorrow, yeah?'

'Yeah,' Queenie mumbled, before bolting to the Briggs' front door.

'Hello, Queenie. You all right? You look ever so pale,' said Betty. 'And you're shaking – look at your hands.'

'I'm not well. Got my thingy again and those awful pains in my stomach. Ivan's bringing my shopping in. I must go straight to bed. The pain is far worse than last time. That's why I'm shaking.'

'Oh dearie me. Poor you. I'll bring you up some painkillers and a cup of tea in a minute.'

Hearing Ivan's thick country accent greeting Betty behind her, Queenie flew up the stairs as fast as her legs would carry her. She never wanted to lay eyes on that monstrous pervert ever again. She needed to get away from here and back to the East End where she'd be safe.

CHAPTER FOUR

'Queenie, please, tell me what's wrong,' pleaded Viv. 'I know something is. You've not been right since you went to the shops with Ivan. Did something happen while you were out with him?'

'No. Don't be stupid,' spat Queenie. 'I've told you fifty bloody times what's wrong. I still got bad stomach pains and I've caught your mumps.'

'But your face isn't swollen like mine was, and you said you'd already had mumps and couldn't catch them again,' said Viv, clearly unconvinced. Apart from using the bathroom, Queenie had not left the bedroom for four whole days now, not even to eat. Viv knew Betty was worried about her too. 'Why don't you let Betty call the doctor in like she offered to? You might need some proper medicine, Queenie.'

'I don't need a doctor, OK? Please just stop going on at me, Viv. Go and have your breakfast and when Betty asks you, tell her I've started to feel a bit better, but I'm still tired. Got that?'

Shocked at her sister shouting at her, Vivian did as she was told.

When Viv left the bedroom, Queenie breathed a sigh of relief. It was so hard trying to act normal. She couldn't sleep or eat, her nerves were in tatters. Thankfully, the Briggs had a proper bath inside the farmhouse which she had loved when she'd first moved here. She'd thought of it as a luxury. Now she just saw it as a way to scrub his rancid smell off her, but no matter how much she scrubbed herself, she could still smell that awful reek of stale sweat and rancid breath. It had obviously left an imprint on her brain, just like he had. The vile, disgusting pervert.

Queenie shut her eyes. She'd written a letter to Mrs O'Leary, begging for help. She'd kept it short and sweet, telling her that something had happened and she would explain when she got home. In the meantime she asked Mary not to say anything to her family.

Viv had posted the letter on Sunday and Queenie knew by the other letters she'd written and received that Mary should have received it by now. Thank God the O'Learys were back in Whitechapel, because if they'd still been in Ireland, Queenie wouldn't have known who to turn to. Aunt Edna would have been the only other option, but Queenie couldn't tell her what had happened. She would die of shame if her parents ever found out. It was all too shameful for words. She wasn't even sure she could tell Mary, but knew she ought to tell someone. Say she'd caught something off the dirty unwashed nonce? She'd caught nits at school twice in the past because some of the other kids were so unclean. None of those kids were as dirty as *him* – the monster!

The tap at the door startled Queenie. 'OK to come in, Queenie? I've made you some breakfast and tea.'

'Yes. Come in, Betty.'

'Vivian informs me you're feeling a bit better. I'm so

pleased. I've done you two boiled eggs, toast, and put a sausage on the side. I know how you like our sausages, but don't worry if you can't finish it all. Just eat what you can.'

'I will. Thank you.'

Betty put the tray on Queenie's lap. 'We've all been worried about you, duck. John insisted I send for a doctor, but I told him you were adamant you didn't need one. Ivan sends his love too. He's left you a present downstairs. I'll bring it up later. Oh, and he said to tell Miss Queenie the dart flights you bought him brought him luck. He won last night,' smiled Betty.

Feeling the bile rise in her throat, Queenie put her hand over her mouth. 'Take the tray. Gonna be sick.'

Hearing the girl run from the room, retching, Betty made her mind up. Like it or not, Queenie was going to see a doctor.

A couple of days later, Queenie was lying on her bed reading *Oliver Twist* when Betty called up the stairs: 'Queenie, you have a telegram.'

Queenie dashed down to collect it. It must be from Mary. It had to be.

Thanking a rather bemused-looking Betty and the man who'd delivered it, Queenie ran back up the stairs before ripping it open. For the first time since her horrendous ordeal, she managed a smile.

'Who's it from Queenie? Mum?' asked Viv.

'No. It's from Mrs O'Leary. We're going home tomorrow, Viv, but you mustn't say anything to the Briggs. I will do the talking just before we leave, OK?'

Viv was stunned. 'What! How come? I thought Mum said we weren't allowed home yet?'

'We're going to surprise Mum. There's been no more bombs, so we'll be fine.'

'But we should tell Betty as soon as possible. Her and John have been ever so kind to us. It's rude to wait until just before we leave to tell them. And what about Ivan? He's been kind to us too. He even let me drive his tractor yesterday.'

'You what! When?'

'Yesterday afternoon, while you were sleeping.'

Queenie grabbed her sister by the shoulders. 'You say nothing and you go nowhere near Ivan again, d'ya hear me?'

'But why?'

'Because I bloody said so. He was looking at me funny that day I went shopping alone with him and he said some odd things. I don't trust him, Viv. Not as far as I can throw him.'

'Is that why you've been acting strange?'

'I've been ill, Viv. You know I have. You heard what the doctor said. There's a bug been going round the village.'

'Yeah, but you've still been acting weird.'

'I'm bored, that's all. Bored out of my brains. I can't wait to get home, see Mum, Dad, Aunt Edna, Mary and all our friends.'

'Neither can I.'

'Well, start packing your bits then and not a word to anyone. OK?'

'OK.'

Betty Briggs was stunned the following morning when Queenie announced at 11.45 a.m. that she and Viv were being picked up at noon and would be returning to London. 'I'm so upset you didn't tell me beforehand, girls. I would've cooked you a lovely farewell dinner last night had I known. I take it that's why you received a telegram?'

'Yes, Betty, and I'm sorry I never told you beforehand, but one of our family is really sick, and we didn't want any fuss,' lied Queenie. 'Thank you so, so much for taking Viv and me into your home and looking after us. This is for you, and I would like you to give this to John. It's just a little thank you gift, something to remember us by.'

Betty's eyes filled with tears. Since her sons had left home the farmhouse had felt very empty and it had been lovely having the girls around. She'd spent hours teaching them maths and English, and had given them numerous cooking and baking lessons. 'You must say goodbye to John and give him his present yourself. He's out the back. I'll call him. Ivan will want to say goodbye to you too.'

Queenie felt the colour drain from her face. 'No, please don't call them. We really don't want any fuss. It's our Aunt Edna. She's dying you see.'

Viv looked at her sister in astonishment. Their mum had always taught them never to tell such wicked lies in case they came true.

At that very moment, John walked through the back door. 'Any chance of a cuppa, love? I'm parched.'

Tears rolled down Betty's cheeks as she told her husband the girls were going home at short notice because a family member was seriously ill.

'Why didn't you tell us yesterday? Betty said you had a telegram, so we guessed it must be important. We would've loved to have given you a proper send-off,' John said, in his thick country drawl.

Queenie looked at her shoes. 'Viv and I were too upset to want any fuss. We're very close to Aunt Edna. She's the only aunt we have.' It was nearly noon now and she hoped Patrick wouldn't be long. Mary had said Patrick would pick them up in his car.

Betty opened her present and cried even more. 'They're beautiful slippers, girls. They'll keep my feet lovely and warm in the winter months and whenever I wear them, I will think of you.'

'Ahh, bless ya. You shouldn't have,' John said, as he put the new pipe to his mouth. 'It's been a pleasure having you stay with us and I know my Betty will miss your company. She always wanted a daughter,' winked John.

Betty hugged Queenie and Viv close to her chest. 'Please write to us. I would hate to lose touch with you.'

'As soon as we are settled at home, I'll write to you,' said Viv. She felt awkward and rude that they were leaving at such short notice. As for Queenie's lies about Aunt Edna, she'd be having strong words with her later.

Queenie was uncomfortable about lying to the Briggs and leaving them this way, so it came as a huge relief when their farewells were interrupted by the sound of a car horn outside. 'That's our lift home. Thank you so much for having us. We will never forget you.'

'Hang on. I'll bring your cases out,' said John. 'I must call Ivan too. He will want to say goodbye to you both.'

When John opened the back door and yelled 'Ivan', Queenie knew she had to get out of the house. 'I'll let Patrick know we're ready,' she mumbled, bolting for the front door.

She made it no further than the doorstep before colliding with Patrick, who was just about to knock. 'You all right, darling?' he asked, giving her a hug.

'I just wanna sit in the car. I've had a bug.' Queenie's legs were like jelly at the thought of seeing Ivan again.

John brought the cases out and Queenie froze as she heard Ivan's voice.

'Get out the car, Queenie. Don't be so rude,' hissed Viv.

Queenie couldn't move. Her legs were temporarily paralysed. She opened the car window instead. The monster was standing there, between Betty and John. 'Thank you for all you have done for us, Betty and John. We won't forget you.' Queenie could hear the fear in her voice.

Ivan approached the car. 'Bye, Miss Queenie. I'm going to miss you,' he grinned, showing his rotting teeth. 'And you, Viv.'

Queenie managed to swallow the bile that entered her mouth. 'Yeah, bye.'

Patrick watched the scene with interest. His mother had told him to. He earned his living by being an illegal bookie and would bet his car on Ivan being a problem. The geezer looked like a nonce. He started the engine. 'Ready, girls?'

'Yes,' Queenie said, putting her hands under her legs, so Viv wouldn't see them trembling. But Patrick didn't miss a thing.

'Bye Betty, bye John, bye Ivan,' Viv smiled. 'I'll write to you very soon, Betty. I promise.'

'Bye, girls,' said Betty and John in unison.

As the car pulled away, the last thing Queenie heard was the monster shouting, 'Bye, Miss Queenie.'

Pretending she was tired, Queenie closed her eyes on the journey home. She was so relieved to have got away from the farmhouse, yet was dreading seeing family and friends in case they guessed something was wrong with her.

Patrick and Viv were chatting away happily. Queenie's ears pricked up when she heard Daniel had a new girlfriend. But she wasn't that bothered. Not now. She could never imagine herself wanting a lad to touch her again, even Daniel.

Knowing she had to pull herself together, Queenie yawned

and pretended to wake up as they neared home. The sight that greeted her eyes as they entered London was shocking and dismal. Houses, buildings, shops, pubs, all reduced to piles of rubble. 'Jesus wept!' Queenie mumbled.

'Oh my God, Queenie! Thank God Mum sent us away,' said Viv.

Patrick looked in the interior mirror to size up Queenie's reaction.

Queenie flinched. She would rather have been blown up by a bomb than being forced to endure what she had.

Molly Wade was elated yet stunned when she walked into her home to see her two daughters sitting on the sofa. 'Oh, my babies! What you doing 'ere?' she squealed with delight.

Viv cried and hugged her mother for dear life. 'It's so good to see you, Mum. We missed you so much.'

'We couldn't stay there no longer. Betty and John were lovely to us, but we were so bored. There's nothing to do there. Both of us have been ill recently too. Viv had mumps, I caught a bug and we just wanted to be 'ere, with you,' explained Queenie.

Queenie felt her eyes well up as her mother hugged her. She wished she was still the same carefree girl who'd hugged her mum goodbye eight months ago. 'Is Dad at work?'

'Sit down, girls. I'll make us a cuppa. There's lots I have to tell you.'

Molly Wade reappeared with a tray of tea and biscuits, sat in between her two daughters on the sofa and held their hands. 'How did you get home by the way?'

'Patrick O'Leary picked us up in his car. We wanted to surprise you,' said Queenie.

'Ahh, that was nice of him. I'm not sure it's safe for you to stay here though. More bombs could be dropped at any time.'

'We don't care,' snapped Queenie. 'No way are we being sent away again.'

'Is Dad OK, Mum?' asked Viv.

'Erm, yes. I didn't want to worry you two, but Dad got called up not long after you left. He was in North Africa, last I heard. He's OK though.'

'When will he come home?' asked Viv.

'I don't know, lovey. But fingers crossed it won't be too long.'

'We got a shock when we saw the state of the area. When did the row of shops where the butcher's is get blown up?' asked Queenie.

'Around Christmas time. Lots of people you know have lost their lives too. Joe Brown was killed in action, so was Tim Lewis. Your school friend Linda Ruttle perished with the rest of her family when a bomb fell, Viv.'

Tears pricked Vivian's eyes. 'I don't think Nelly knows her brother is dead. She never mentioned it in her letters.'

'Mabel isn't going to tell the girls until they come home. She wants to be there to comfort them. She's been in a terrible state has Mabel, bless her. There's other families you know that have been wiped out, but let's not talk about that today. Let's celebrate you being home. Shall we go and surprise, Aunt Edna?' smiled Molly.

'Not yet. I want to know who has died first. You should have told us by letter,' snapped Queenie. 'I need to visit Mrs O'Leary too. We have her to thank for getting us away from that hellhole of a farmhouse. If it wasn't for Mary, we'd still be stuck there.'

'It wasn't that bad, Queenie. I know it was boring, but at least the people were nice,' Viv replied.

'I thought you were happy there,' Molly said dismally.

'I wasn't. But then, I begged you not to send me away in the first place, didn't I?' Queenie reminded her mother. 'It's just a shame you didn't bloody listen.'

CHAPTER FIVE

*I tried to put what had happened to the back of my mind,
but it was nigh on impossible. The nights were the worst.
That monster would appear in my dreams, lunging towards
me, and I would wake up terrified.*

*I went back to school and did my best to act normal.
But the East End had changed beyond recognition and I
was no longer that happy carefree girl I'd once been. I was
irritable, snappy, bitter and downright rude at times, especially to Mum. Though I knew what had happened wasn't
her fault, I couldn't help but blame her for sending me away.*

*Both Mum and Aunt Edna had heart-to-hearts with me,
tried to get me to open up, but I couldn't. I blamed my
period, how I thought I was dying at the time, and had
ruined Betty's lovely mattress. 'I've never felt so embarrassed in my life,' I told them.*

*I told the same story to Mrs O'Leary. I could tell she
knew there was more to it, but I couldn't bring myself to
tell her the truth. I felt far too ashamed to tell anybody.
I never felt clean any more, not even after a trip to the
public baths. I felt dirty, like a tramp.*

Then I heard the news my dad had been shot in the leg, was in the army hospital, and would be returning home once he was well enough to travel.

I looked forward to Dad's homecoming. It helped to take my mind off things. Viv and I made him a big banner welcoming him home. Mum and Aunt Edna baked cakes and made sandwiches, but Dad never showed. He arrived home the following morning, paralytic, and after that things went from bad to worse.

Things got to the point where I no longer had a father as far as I was concerned. Instead, there was a stranger living in our house. A nasty, evil, wicked bully who I totally despised.

It was no wonder I began to spend more and more time at Mrs O'Leary's. Her house was the only place I felt safe and loved.

The war was changing everything.

Three Months Later

Summer 1941

'Queenie, wake up. I think Dad's hurting Mum again.'

Queenie was already wide awake 'Mum's told us not to get involved. Go back to sleep. The noises'll stop soon.'

Putting her arms around Viv's back to comfort her, Queenie lay deep in thought. She knew what was happening all right. The drunken stranger who was once her father was forcing her mum to have sex with him again.

Hearing their mum begging their dad to stop, Viv started to cry.

'It's OK. They're just trying to make us a little brother or sister,' Queenie lied. She knew that wasn't the case.

She'd seen the bruises on her mother's body, knew what was happening was no act of love.

As Queenie heard her father grunt and groan, she felt ill. The monster.

Finally all was quiet, but still Queenie couldn't sleep. She would speak to Aunt Edna later; ask if she and Viv could stay with her this weekend.

The next morning, Queenie was in a foul mood as she took her seat in the classroom. She'd lain awake most of the night, and felt groggy and ratty. She was also dreading breaking up for the summer holidays on Friday. These days she had little interest in playing outdoors amongst the rats and the rubble, she would rather be at school, or losing herself in a book. There was no quiet indoors any more, so perhaps she'd go over the park and read alone? Books were the only thing that would temporarily help her to forget. She was currently engrossed in Laura Ingalls Wilder's *Little House in the Big Woods*. It was a world away from London and the Blitz.

'Good morning.'

'Good morning, sir,' Queenie responded in unison with the other kids.

Mr Archer pointed a finger in the air and silently began counting heads. 'Thirteen,' he said out loud. 'OK, today I have a special assignment for you. For the handful of you who were not evacuees, I want you to write a story pretending you were. How would you feel leaving your parents? Your pets? Use your imagination. As for the thirteen of you who were evacuated and have since returned, I want to hear every detail about your experiences. Where did you stay? What was the area and family like? Describe them in detail. Did you make any new friends?'

An image of Ivan flashing through her mind, Queenie was mortified as her breakfast flew out of her mouth with such force, some landed on Kenneth Holmes's back.

Kenneth leapt up. 'Urgh, ya dirty moo.'

As other classmates held their noses in disgust and murmured noises and words of distaste, an embarrassed Queenie knew she had to get out of there.

Yelling 'Sorry', she ran from the classroom in tears.

Mary O'Leary was chatting to her hairdresser Rosemary when she saw Queenie running hell for leather on the other side of the road. 'Queenie! You all right?'

Stopping in her tracks, Queenie burst into tears. She couldn't stand it any longer, the shame was burning inside her and she felt as though she didn't want to live.

Excusing herself to Rosemary, Mary ran across the road. 'Whatever's wrong?'

'Everything. I can't go on, Mary. Just leave me. Leave me alone.'

Seeing Queenie was shaking, Mary gathered her firmly into her arms. 'You've not been yourself since you returned from the Briggs'. What happened there? You know you can trust me, Queenie.'

'Nothing. Nothing happened,' wept Queenie.

Remembering what Patrick had told her, Mary held Queenie's cheeks and looked her in the eyes. 'It's that Ivan, isn't it? What did he do to you, darling?'

'He—' Queenie sobbed.

'Did he touch you inappropriately? You must tell me, lovey. A trouble shared is a trouble halved.'

Queenie nodded furiously. 'Yes. He touched me.'

*

Once inside the O'Learys' house, a tot of brandy in her hand, and urged on by Mary, Queenie found it a relief to finally spill her guts. She explained what had happened with Ivan, how she'd tried to get away from him and how dirty and horrible she'd felt ever since.

The news didn't come as a shock to Mary. Patrick had reported back that Ivan was a weirdo and he reckoned he was the problem. However, Mary's heart broke as she made Queenie endless cups of sweet tea, held her in her arms and reassured her that none of this was her fault, she would help her through it.

'You won't tell anybody, will you? I don't want Daniel to know, or Patrick – or anyone. I'd feel too embarrassed. Oh, the shame of what he did to me Mary, please—'

Mary stroked Queenie's hair. 'Of course not, angel. But you did right telling me. I can help you. I know it doesn't feel like it at the moment, but in time, things will get better for you.'

'It doesn't feel like that.'

'I know, but you have to trust me. Now I need to ask you some questions. Important ones.'

Queenie managed a half-smile. Mrs O'Leary was so kind. She'd washed her, rinsed out her sick-stained top, given her a fresh one to wear while her own dried in the garden.

Not wanting to worry Queenie unnecessarily, Mary chose her words carefully. 'You know I got you those Kotex pads? Have you had to use any yet?'

'Erm, no. Why?'

Mary's heart lurched. Surely the poor girl wasn't pregnant? Hadn't she been through enough already? 'May the cat eat that dirty bastard and may the devil eat the cat,' she hissed.

*

Queenie was terrified when Mary insisted she must visit Dr Parrott the following day. 'If I'm pregnant by that monster, Mary, I'll kill myself.'

Mary held the child in her arms. 'No, you won't. You're stronger than that, my love. Having felt your tummy yesterday, I honestly don't think you're with child. But we need to get you checked out, and to make sure you haven't been infected with any diseases. Dr Parrott is from Cork, same as me; he can be trusted. He's a family friend and a very nice man. You let me do the talking, OK?'

'I haven't got to take my knickers off, have I?' Queenie asked fearfully.

'I'll be with you all the time, I promise. The doctor will examine your stomach and I've already got your wee sample in my handbag. He might want to ask a couple of questions, but I've pretended a young lad took advantage of you.'

'Thanks for not telling him what really happened.'

Mary smiled. 'Whatever you tell me is between us, OK?' That wasn't strictly true because last night she'd given the heads up to her sons regarding the awful experience Queenie had been through. She hadn't gone into too much detail but, as expected, Patrick and Daniel were absolutely livid.

'You leave that nonce to us, Mum. We'll sort it,' Patrick promised.

'Too fecking right,' Daniel added. 'Poor little Queenie.'

And Mrs O'Leary knew that at least Queenie would never have to come face to face with the pervert who'd ruined her ever again.

The trip to Dr Parrott's was scary for Queenie. Mary held her hand as he examined her stomach with his hands and a stethoscope. 'I'm pretty sure you aren't pregnant, young lady. But we'll do the urine test just to be on the safe side.'

Urging Queenie to sit up, Dr Parrott then asked her some embarrassing questions. 'Have you had any discharge or pain down below, Queenie? Anything unusual since you had sex?'

Wanting to scream out that she didn't have sex, she was raped, Queenie bit her tongue and turned to Mary. 'What does discharge mean?'

'A substance. The doctor means have you noticed anything unusual in your knickers?'

'Like what?'

'Like a green substance or brown? Or have you noticed any change in the colour of your urine? Does it hurt when you use the toilet?' asked the doctor.

Queenie blushed crimson. 'No. Nothing.'

Dr Parrott smiled. 'That's good news. If anything changes though and you do start noticing something different, you must come back to me. In the meantime, I'll do your urine test and will let Mary know when I have the results.'

Queenie breathed a sigh of relief as they left Dr Parrott's house. 'Mary, how can a doctor tell by your wee if you're pregnant?'

'They inject your urine into toads.'

'Toads! What, as in like a frog?'

'Yes. They import a special breed from abroad and keep them in tanks.'

Completely baffled, Queenie said no more.

The school holidays began and instead of going out exploring the bomb sites with Viv or playing silly games,

Queenie spent most of her time with Mrs O'Leary or Aunt Edna. She much preferred being at their homes to staying in her own. She no longer felt close to her mother. Her dad was making all their lives a misery and in Queenie's opinion Molly Wade should be putting her foot down.

On the Tuesday, Viv squealed with delight as their neighbours Aggie and Nelly Brown arrived home from evacuation. 'Come on, Queenie. Let's go and greet them.'

Pleased that Viv would now have Nelly to hang out with, Queenie told Viv to greet them with their mum. She hadn't forgiven Aggie for blanking the two letters she'd written to her. Who did she think she was? She was no friend of hers any longer, the ignorant cow. Queenie had only written the second letter because, when she'd received no reply to the first, she assumed it must have got lost in the post. Queenie cursed herself. 'What an idiot,' she muttered.

Peeping through a tiny gap in the curtain, Queenie saw their landlord approach her mum. He looked annoyed and started pointing towards the roof of the house.

Viv ran back inside the house. 'Aggie says hello. Where's mum's purse, Queen?'

'Dunno. What's the landlord saying?'

'Dunno. Probably wants money.' Viv ran back outside with the purse.

Since their dad's army wage had stopped, their mum had been forced to take two cleaning jobs, just so they could eat and keep a roof over their heads. It was she who was handing all her hard-earned wages over to the landlord while her father drank any wages he earned down the pub. Queenie didn't know if her dad even had a proper job. The docks had been bombed badly during the Blitz and with his shattered right leg, that he now dragged behind him, she was sure he wasn't working back there, though her mum swore he was.

A serious expression on her face, Molly walked back inside the house and asked both her daughters to sit down.

'What's up?' Queenie asked.

Molly sighed. 'There's no easy way to say this, girls. Our landlord has insisted on renting the upstairs of our house out. There'll be a new family moving in next Monday.'

'But he can't! What about our bedroom? Where we meant to sleep?' shrieked Viv.

'We'll have to bring your mattress down 'ere, love. We'll manage. I suppose we should think ourselves lucky to have a bloody roof over our heads. Many families round 'ere haven't, have they?'

Viv was distraught. 'But what about our clothes and things? Where will we put those?'

'We'll find somewhere to put them,' replied Molly. 'Let's just be grateful Hitler has stopped bombing us. Well, for now, at least.'

Queenie was furious. 'But why are we losing the upstairs of our house? I take it it's because we're way behind with the rent?'

'Well, yes,' admitted Molly. 'But nobody is to blame for that, Queenie. Who could have predicted the war and your father being shot?'

'No one. But seeing as Dad is working at the docks and you're also working, how come we can't afford to pay the rent?'

Molly looked sheepish. 'Your dad could no longer work at the docks because of his leg. I didn't tell you 'cause I didn't want to worry ya. He is working though. He's helping a friend out, but the money isn't great.'

'Well, it can't be that bad,' yelled Queenie. 'He seems to be earning enough to roll home pissed out of his head every night, don't he?'

Tears streamed down Viv's face. She loved sharing a bedroom with her sister. It was bad enough listening to her parents' arguments and baby-making as it was; now she and Queenie would have to sleep in the same room as them.

'Look, I know this isn't ideal. But you mustn't blame your father. He's going through a tough time. He saw some terrible things while he was away, has awful nightmares. He isn't coping with his injury either. He's in a lot of pain with his leg and says the alcohol helps him cope with it. We must all stand by him; help him through this difficult time.'

Queenie could barely believe her ears. She leapt off the sofa and paced up and down. 'And we had it easy while Dad was away, did we?' she bellowed. 'How do you think me and Viv felt, being sent away, then coming home to a long list of friends and neighbours who'd died? As for losing half our home, I blame you as much as him, Mum. Why didn't you put your foot down and demand Dad hands over the rent money to you? That's what Mrs O'Leary would've done. She would've kicked Dad's arse out and only allowed him back once he'd got himself sorted.'

'Well, I'm not Mrs O'Leary and you shouldn't be discussing our bloody business with that woman,' fumed Molly.

'Who said I was? Everyone knows what's really going on, including me and Viv. We're the ones who have to listen to Dad beat and rape you most nights. No wonder we're always tired at school, eh? And now you're expecting us to sleep in the same room as you and *him*.'

'Whatever are you going on about, you stupid girl? I'm married to the man. Ya can't get raped by your own husband. This is her, ain't it? That nosy cow across the road. She's the one putting ridiculous ideas in your head. You're even copying her foul language. Always effing and blinding, *she* is. Well, I'm not putting up with this any more, young lady. You've changed since you came back from Lincolnshire, got far too big for your boots. I forbid you to visit Mrs O'Leary any more. It's not normal, you spending so much time with a woman who is older than me. You should be out playing with your sister and friends of your own age.'

Eyes bulging with fury, Queenie let rip. 'Do you wanna know why I spend so much time with Mrs O'Leary? Well, I'll tell ya. She's more of a mother to me than you'll ever be. It was Mary who bought me my first bra and menstrual pads, and explained to me about the birds and bees. What did you do, eh? Let me lils bounce up and down like some slag and let me think I was dying—'

'Stop it!' Viv screamed, putting her hands over her ears. 'Please, both of you, just stop it,' she sobbed.

Queenie gave her younger sister a hug. 'Come on; let's go out and get some fresh air.'

Molly Wade put her head in her hands. She could feel Queenie slipping away from her and in her bones she knew it was too late to bring her back.

Aunt Edna welcomed her nieces with open arms. And she wasn't too shocked to learn the truth of what had been going on. She knew from past experience that Eric was an arsehole in drink and she knew Molly hadn't been herself of late. However, she was furious to hear that Queenie and Viv had been lying awake night after night, listening to Eric force himself upon her beloved sister. That wasn't on.

'And Mum's got bruises. Loads of 'em. She won't even get undressed in front of us down the public baths,' added Queenie. 'She insists on bathing on her own since I asked her about them.'

'You never told me that,' Viv exclaimed.

'Only because I didn't want to worry ya. I know Dad drags his right leg like a cripple now and I do feel sorry for him for getting shot. But he shouldn't take that out on Mum and us. He don't even call Mum by her name, he calls her 'Woman'. He ain't got no time for me an' Viv either, Aunt Edna. He's 'orrible to us. Really 'orrible.'

Aunt Edna sat between the two girls who were like daughters to her and put a comforting arm around their shoulders. 'Right, 'ere's what's going to happen. I'm gonna make you a sandwich and a cuppa, then I'm gonna visit your mum whilst youse stay 'ere. I shall pick up some bits for you, then tonight you can come to work with me, have a singalong. Walter in the Crown won't mind. How's that sound?'

Queenie hugged her wonderful aunt. 'Does that mean we can stay 'ere the night?'

'You can stay 'ere whenever you want, you know that.'

'Thanks, Auntie Edna,' said Viv.

Queenie smiled for the first time that day. 'Love you, Aunt Edna.'

Edna's eyes welled up. 'And I love you two more than you'll ever know. Right, off to see your muvver now. You leave her to me.'

The weeks that followed were good ones for Queenie, the best she'd had since returning home. Aunt Edna had worked her magic on her mother and she and Viv were temporarily living with her. She also got confirmation from Dr Parrott, via Mrs O'Leary, that she definitely wasn't pregnant. To say that was a massive relief for Queenie was an understatement. Mrs O'Leary reckoned it was the trauma of what had happened that had stopped her from having any more periods since, but said they would return in due course.

While living at her aunt's, Queenie did not return home once to visit her parents. Viv did and said it was ever so cramped downstairs. She also said the new family traipsed through their home whenever they needed to use the kitchen or the toilet in the back yard. Queenie was furious about that. Say the man walked in while she was washing or getting dressed? It wasn't even their home any more by the sounds of it. Queenie dreaded going back there.

It was on a Thursday afternoon that Queenie received the first bit of good news. 'I visited your mum this morning, Queenie. Things still aren't great at home with your dad, so I convinced Mum to allow you and Viv to stay with me for the rest of your holidays,' explained Aunt Edna.

As for the second bit of news Queenie received. It wasn't just good, it was absolutely mind-blowing.

CHAPTER SIX

*I looked at Viv in amazement. 'A telegram! But it can't
be for us. Who would send us a telegram?'*

*'It is for us. I was at Mum's when the man delivered
it. It's got both our names on the envelope. It's from Betty
and John,' Viv explained.*

*For obvious reasons, I wanted to try to forget about
my time in Lincolnshire, so I hadn't written to Betty and
John, not once. Viv kept in touch with them though and
always signed her letters from herself and me.*

*'Aren't you going to open it then?' asked Aunt Edna.
'It must be important if it's a telegram.'*

'You open it, Queenie,' urged Viv.

*'No.' I hated it when Viv read out the letters from the
Briggs. It made me feel ill, especially their last letter, that
ended with 'Ivan is here. He sends his regards to you both
and wants you to tell Miss Queenie those dart flights she
bought him are still bringing him luck'.*

*'Give us the bleedin' thing 'ere, I'll open it,' demanded
Aunt Edna. She ripped open the envelope. 'Oh dear. It
isn't good news, girls, I'm afraid. A murder has occurred*

58

in Lincolnshire and a policeman will be visiting soon to speak to you both.'

'What! Why?' I asked. 'We don't know nothing about no murder.'

'It's not Betty or John, is it?' said Viv, her complexion white.

'No. It's Ivan who worked for Betty and John. You were both friends with him apparently. I'm so sorry, girls. What a shock for you both. Come give me a hug, then I'll make you a cup of sweet tea.'

My heart was leaping for joy. I wanted to jump up and down in celebration, but obviously I couldn't. So I put on a shocked act and pretended to be upset like Viv, while secretly wishing Ivan had died in the most excruciating pain known to man.

Unable to contain my excitement, I ran round to Mrs O'Leary's house to tell her the news. 'Good,' Mary said, grabbing my face in her big hands. 'Now you can finally move on with your life, Queenie.'

'But why do the police want to talk to me and Viv?' I asked.

'You can guarantee you weren't the first young lady he did such a terrible thing to – once a nonce always a nonce. If I were you, I'd lie to the police and say he was worried about a few enemies in the village, but never mentioned any names to you. It's the O'Leary family rule, Queenie: always lie to the coppers, always stay true to your family. Never done us no harm. We look after our family and friends alike, Queenie.'

'OK. That's what I'll say then. Thanks, Mary. You're just like a mum to me.'

Mary smiled. 'And you are the daughter I never had. Time for you to shine now, my darling. Forget about the past and move on to the future. You can't let what happened to you ruin the rest of your life.'

My eyes filled with tears. 'I'm not sure I can move on.'

Mary gave my shoulders a shake. 'Oh yes you will. Have you ever wondered why I felt your pain so much?'

'Because you're so kind,' I replied.

She shook her head and hugged me to her chest. 'What happened to you, my dear child, also happened to me back in Cork. I was younger than you. Twelve at the time.'

I started to cry, feeling her pain as sharply as if it was my own. 'Mary, I'm so sorry.'

Mary gave my shoulders another shake. 'Being sorry or feeling sorry gets you nowhere, angel. My brothers dealt with the bastard that abused me. And now Ivan has got his comeuppance. You have to move on. I did, and I ended up with three strapping sons. God rest his soul, my Seamus died, but I still have my Patrick and Daniel. They are my world. You must never tell anyone what I have told you today though. Even my boys don't know the full story. There are some things sons shouldn't know about their mother.'

I looked at Mary in awe. She was the strongest woman I'd ever known. 'I will never say a word, I promise. And you are so right. Now Ivan is dead, I want handsome strapping sons just like yours.'

Mary smiled at me and squeezed my hand. 'That's my girl.'

Nine Months Later

Spring 1942

Queenie squeezed Viv's hand as they listened to the latest dismal news bulletin. The Germans were bombing England again; not London this time, but there'd been attacks on Exeter, York, Bath, Norwich and Canterbury.

'D'ya think they'll bomb us again?' Viv asked fearfully.

Queenie shrugged. 'Not much left to bomb round 'ere, is there?' she replied truthfully. The horror of the Blitz was still everywhere you looked. Houses, buildings and businesses had been reduced to piles of rubble and many men, women and children were hobbling around due to injuries they'd suffered. It had been reported that tens of thousands had lost their lives; Queenie could well believe it. Many people she'd known all her life had been killed in the bombings or while fighting overseas. St Mary Matfelon was no longer a church. That had been bombed beyond repair. As had Freddie the fishmonger's. Poor Freddie had died, was burned alive while chopping up eels. Flo, his wife, had dropped dead at his funeral. A broken heart caused her death, the vicar reckoned. Even our coalman's poor horse had been blown up. A bomb had dropped on his stable. Our coalman was devastated, as we all were. Trigger had been a wonderful horse, a big part of mine and Viv's childhood.

Queenie hugged Viv. 'No point worrying about it. What will be will be. No way am I being evacuated again though. I'm fifteen now, old enough to go to work and make my own decisions.'

Viv hugged her big sister. 'I don't wanna be sent away again either. I want to stay with you. If we're gonna die, I'd rather us die together. I wouldn't wanna live without ya.'

'Cheerful pair, ain't we?' Queenie grinned. 'And for the record, I wouldn't want to live without you either.'

Once Viv left for school, Queenie sat out in the back yard with her book. Their useless Anderson shelter had now

61

been dismantled and taken away, so there was room to sunbathe once again.

A gorgeous day in May, Queenie put her book down and closed her eyes. She always found it therapeutic when she could hear the birds singing. Life wasn't too bad at the moment. In fact, it had turned out to be a godsend they'd rented out half their house.

After spending the school holidays with Aunt Edna last summer, Queenie and Viv had returned home. It was awful. The living conditions were cramped and their father would roll home drunk every night, waking everybody up.

Queenie begged her mum to chuck her father out. So did Aunt Edna, but her mum wouldn't hear of it. 'Your father is a war hero and a cripple. I can't throw him out on the streets. Whatever would people think of me?' were her mum's exact words.

Then one night it all kicked off big style. Queenie witnessed her father trying to strangle her mother and couldn't help but retaliate. The iron poker was the nearest object, so Queenie picked it up and repeatedly whacked it as hard as she could against her dad's bad leg.

After that, Queenie, her mum and Viv all went to live with Aunt Edna. But then her dad gave up the drink again, and her mum moved back home on the understanding that if Dad fell off the wagon, she would leave him for good.

Queenie flatly refused to return home and told her mother in no uncertain terms that she and Viv would be staying at Aunt Edna's. Her mother called a truce. The girls could sleep at Aunt Edna's, provided they came home for their meals and told the neighbours they were only staying at Aunt Edna's because it was now too cramped at home.

The arrangement had worked out well. Queenie loved

sleeping at Aunt Edna's and still got to see her mum and Mrs O'Leary every day.

Queenie's bond with Mrs O'Leary had grown stronger than ever. Ivan's murder had never been mentioned by either of them since the police had visited her and Viv. She'd done the talking, explaining that she'd spent more time with Ivan than her younger sister, and had calmly told the police Ivan had disclosed to her that he had a few enemies in the village whom he was scared of, but had never given her a reason or any names. The police toddled off quite happily with that information and hadn't returned since.

Viv still kept in touch with Betty Briggs, but Queenie told her sister to keep the letters to herself now. She didn't need or want any reminders, was afraid the terrible nightmares might return. Since she'd been staying at Aunt Edna's, Queenie hadn't had a single nightmare, and she'd taken Mrs O'Leary's advice not to allow herself to think of Ivan. If he popped into her mind for any reason, she would immediately switch her thoughts to Daniel O'Leary. Daniel had recently split up with his girlfriend and Queenie couldn't help but hope that one day, when she was older, she would marry him. She'd never disclosed such thoughts to Mrs O'Leary, mind.

Queenie's reminiscing was ended by her mum calling her. 'I'm going to the shops. Wanna give me a hand? I hope the queues aren't as bad as yesterday,' sighed Molly. Meat, tea, jam, biscuits, breakfast cereals, cheese, eggs, lard, milk, canned and dried fruit had all been added to the ration list. The queues were ever so long as women stood patiently, ration books in hand, desperate to get their hands on much-needed items.

'Yeah. I'll come with you,' smiled Queenie. Since her

mum had shown some backbone and left her father, then refused to return home until he gave up the drink, they were on much better terms. She still loathed her father though. Without a drink, he was the most miserable man in Britain. With a drink inside him, he was just a stranger.

The following morning, Queenie headed over to Mrs O'Leary's with her best frock, shoes and underwear in her hands. She'd only left school last week and was desperate to bag herself a decent job before all the good ones went. Aggie Brown already had a job, in the Trebor factory. That wasn't for Queenie; she would hate being cooped up inside a factory all day long. Encouraged by Mary, she had her heart set on working in a posh clothes shop.

'I've run you a bath, darling,' Mary smiled. 'I'll put the kettle on too. How you feeling? Not nervous, I hope.'

Queenie couldn't believe her luck when Patrick and Daniel had recently had a proper indoors bathroom fitted. Mary was forever running her baths, which was a dream come true for Queenie. 'I feel OK. I think I'd be more nervous if you weren't coming with me though.'

'I still think you're going to the wrong area, Queenie. If I were you, I'd try locally. You won't like all that travelling.'

'But the wages'll be more in the West End, Mary, and the clothes nicer. Please let's go there. I've never properly been to the West End before. I'd love to see where the posh people shop and live.'

Mary rolled her eyes. 'It's your call. But I bet you won't like the posh people or their fecking posh shops.'

Queenie laughed loudly. 'You're so funny. Thanks for running my bath. I'll get ready.'

*

The West End was a real eye-opener for Queenie. In the first shop where she asked whether there were any vacancies, not only did the woman look at her as though she was something awful she'd stepped in, the prices were exorbitant. One of the outfits Queenie looked at probably cost more than what her home was worth.

Each shop Queenie ventured into, she could tell she and Mary were looked down upon. In one, they were even followed by a man, who Mary said thought they were thieves.

'Told you they were all stuck-up feckers round 'ere, didn't I?' Mary reminded Queenie.

'You wasn't wrong. They all speak with plums in their mouths an' all. Did you see the way that last woman looked me up and down? I don't look that poor, do I?'

'You look grand. Take no fecking notice of them, darling. I was too busy looking at her teeth. Size of 'em. She could eat an apple through a letterbox with those.'

Queenie laughed. 'Oooh, look, Mary. This one's a nice shop, not as poncy as the others, and there's a vacancy note in the window, saying apply within.'

'Shall I start talking this time?' asked Mary. She could tell the reaction Queenie had got so far was taking a toll on the girl's confidence. She'd stammered her words in the last shop, the poor ha'porth.

Queenie smiled. Mary had the gift of the gab. 'Yes, please.'

Mary marched straight up to the young woman behind the till. 'Hello. Are you the manager? My niece has come about the vacancy in the window.'

'Oh, yes. That only went in the window this morning. No. I'm not the manager. I'll call her for you,' the girl smiled.

When the girl walked away, Mary nudged Queenie. 'She seems nice. Not as stuck-up as those others.'

'Yes. I think I'd get on OK with her. She doesn't look much older than me.'

The manager appeared and the look of distaste on her face was clear when she heard Mary's Irish accent as she introduced Queenie.

'The vacancy has already been taken, I'm afraid,' snapped the posh tall dark-haired woman.

'It can't have been,' replied Mary. 'The girl who works for you said it had only gone in the window this morning.'

'Erm, yes. But the job went first thing.'

'Why's the card still in the fecking window then?' Mary retaliated.

The look on the posh manager's face was one of horror. Queenie wanted to laugh, but instead joined in. 'Yeah, the card shouldn't be in the bloody window then.'

'Get out. Now!'

'Come on, Queenie,' said Mary. 'Got a face that'd sour milk, that one. You wouldn't want to work for her would you, darling? May she be afflicted with itching without the benefit of scratching.'

'I should coco. She's got a face like a smacked arse, an' all,' Queenie replied loudly, noticing the girl that worked there was smiling behind the manager's back.

Once outside the shop, Queenie rolled up. 'You were right, Mary. It ain't for me up 'ere.'

'Told you. 'Ere, look at this sign. That says it all about the people round here, sweetheart.'

The sign was on the door of a pub. *NO DOGS, NO BLACKS, NO IRISH*, it read.

'But wouldn't they let you in?' Queenie asked, astonished. Mary was such a smart lady.

'Nope. These posh feckers think all us Irish are thieves or tinkers. Come on, sweetheart. The boys insisted I treat you to a posh lunch. They're paying, of course. How d'ya fancy a nice juicy steak?'

'Really! You sure? I don't wanna take liberties.'

'You'll be doing nothing of the kind. The boys can afford it, trust me,' Mary winked.

The restaurant was owned by a friend of Patrick and Daniel's, and after Mary introduced herself as the lads' mother, saying Patrick had recommended they eat there, Queenie was amazed when the owner swiftly appeared, took them to the best table, then insisted they order whatever they wanted as the food and drinks were on the house.

'No, love. We're not liberty-takers,' said Mary.

The owner was a blond, good-looking man in his late thirties, Queenie reckoned. He was immaculately dressed and unlike her father, who always smelled of cigarette smoke, booze and sweat, the owner smelled gorgeous. He smiled at Mary. 'Your sons have done me many favours, Mrs O'Leary. Two top men you've raised, so well done you. No arguing. This is my treat. I recommend the fillet of steak. Melts in your mouth,' he smiled. 'Take your time looking at the menu and call a waiter when you're ready to order.'

Queenie studied the menu. The poshest place she'd ever eaten before was Alice's Cafe in Mile End. She didn't even understand what most of the food was. There were no eels, no pie and mash or faggots on the menu.

'Speak of the devil and two will appear,' chuckled Mary.

Queenie was gobsmacked as Daniel and Patrick sauntered towards them, immaculately dressed in expensive suits, shirts, ties and polished leather shoes.

'How's our two favourite girls doing?' grinned Daniel.

Mary beamed with pride as the manager came dashing over, shaking her sons' hands and making a big fuss of them. 'You didn't say you were having lunch with us,' Mary said to Patrick.

'We're not. We've got a meeting in Soho in an hour. I was hoping I might catch you though. I've seen a beautiful piece of jewellery I want you to take a look at. The shop's only a five-minute walk away. Have you ordered food yet?'

'No.'

'Well, come with me now. Daniel and I will treat you if you like it.'

Mary squeezed Queenie's hand. 'See how good to me these sons of mine are? I won't be long. Daniel will stay here with you.'

Daniel sat in his mother's seat and picked up the menu. 'The food's lovely in here. What you having?'

'I'm not sure,' blushed Queenie. 'I've never really eaten in a proper restaurant before.'

'First time for everything,' winked Daniel, before explaining to Queenie in plain Irish what each dish was.

'I think I'll have the steak, but not bloody.'

'You need to ask for it to be well done. I'll order it for you.'

'Thanks. Can I ask you something, Daniel?'

'Of course.'

'I hope you don't think I'm being nosy, but the price of the food is so expensive in here. More than the weekly rent on our house. If you can afford all this, why would you choose to live in Whitechapel?'

'Truthfully, I only live among those I can trust. You East Enders look after each other like the Irish do. Community spirit is important and Mum's happy in Whitechapel. People treat us like one of their own. Sod living in some poncey area where people look down their noses at us. I'd be clumping someone every other day if I lived around this neck of the woods,' chuckled Daniel.

'I'm so pleased you moved opposite. Your mum is like a second mum to me.'

'And you're like a little sister to me and Patrick. Never forget that.' Daniel leaned closer to Queenie. 'Any problems you ever have, you go to Mum. You can tell her anything, then if need be, me and Patrick will sort it for you.'

Queenie looked into Daniel's eyes and in that split second, she knew who had killed Ivan Tumbleweed.

'What do Daniel and Patrick actually do for a living?' Queenie asked. She had no intention of mentioning to Mary the conversation she'd had with Daniel. But in a way it had made her feel good, powerful in fact. If she hadn't opened up to Mary, that nonce would still be alive. He didn't deserve to be. It was a good thing he was dead and unable to do what he'd done to her to any other poor girl.

'My boys have their fingers in many pies, Queenie. I don't ask too much 'cause I would only worry. If they ever need an alibi, I'm there for them though. I encouraged them to make something of their lives. Law-abiding citizens like us get nowhere. I urged them to take risks, now they're reaping the rewards,' winked Mary.

'They look so smart, always.'

'Yes. I drummed it into 'em at an early age that appearance is extremely important. First impressions count massively. I had 'em strutting around in suits at thirteen. Not at school, obviously. But as soon as they got home, they'd change into their suits before going out and doing odd jobs. They got in with a couple of villains, did bits and bobs for them. Their reputations have just grown from there. People know they can be trusted. They're good men. Daniel can be a handful when he loses his temper. He's calmed down a bit of late, mind. Patrick keeps an eye on him.'

'Did you ever want a daughter, Mary?'

'Daughters are a worry. Sons are a joy, if you raise 'em right. From an early age, I used to make up bedtime stories for the boys. I told 'em that one day they'd be kings with enough money to buy whatever they wanted. We were piss poor at the time, but they never forgot those stories. I believe children need moulding at an early age into what you want them to be.'

Queenie smiled. It was nice to hear Mary open up about her sons. 'I would love to one day have sons like yours. Not sure I will though. After what happened, the thought of a man touching me fills me with panic.' That wasn't strictly true as Queenie often fantasized about Daniel touching her. She could hardly tell Mary that though.

Mary leaned across the table and squeezed both of Queenie's hands. 'I know exactly how you feel. At your age, I felt the same. But you mustn't let what happened stop you from becoming a mother, darling. Holding your own baby in your arms is one of the greatest feelings in the world. Children are a gift from God and I just know you'd make a fantastic mum. I hate sex, have never enjoyed it. I got married because I wanted babies. You will do the same. I will make damn sure of it.'

Later that evening, Queenie lay in bed deep in thought.

Even though she hadn't got a job, today had been amazing. The food in that restaurant was out of this world, the whole experience of being inside there was too. As for the steak, it was to die for. That conversation with Daniel had opened her eyes too. It's not what you know in life that counts, it's who you know.

Thinking of Mary, Queenie smiled. Not only was Mary funny, she was the kindest person she'd ever met. She'd thought it weird when Mary excused herself from the table between courses. Five minutes later, she returned with a posh bag. Inside the bag was the nicest frock Queenie had ever laid eyes on. Long, plain, emerald green, but so classy.

'I love it, Mary. You'll look beautiful in that.'

Mary had laughed. 'It's at least two sizes too small for me, darling. It's for you. Obviously, you will need some new shoes to match. We'll get those when we leave 'ere. Then we need to sort out your hair. I have a friend who's a hairdresser. I know your mum cuts it for you, but you're too old for those basin cuts now. I want you to look your best next time we go job hunting. Believe me, together we will nail this. Tomorrow, I shall give you a make-up lesson too. I know your mother doesn't wear make-up, but you should, Queenie. You are a beautiful girl and once I have finished with you, the world will be your oyster.'

Still smiling, Queenie closed her eyes. This was the best day of her life, by miles. Mary O'Leary was not only her closest friend, she was her hero and her inspiration to forget about the past and focus on building a better future for herself.

CHAPTER SEVEN

Eight Months Later

Winter 1943

'How do I look, Mary? Will I like it? Does the colour suit me?' gabbled Queenie. She'd been desperate to look as pretty and sophisticated as her new work friend, hence her taking the plunge to dye her hair blonde. Daniel liked blondes too. His current girlfriend Bridie was a blonde bombshell. She looked like the actress Jean Harlow. Queenie was sixteen now and so hoped once Daniel's latest relationship ended, he would ask her out. He'd been paying her a lot of compliments lately. Surely that was a good sign?

'You look beautiful. Blonde really suits you. Show her the mirror, Rosemary,' urged Mary.

'You look gorgeous, darling,' added Rosemary.

'Oh my God! I look so different, but I love it! It really does suit me, doesn't it?'

'That was never in doubt. A pretty face like yours could get away with any colour,' smiled Mary.

Queenie paid Rosemary, then left her house with a massive smile on her face. Not only had Mrs O'Leary taught her about fashion and how to choose things that would suit her, the job she loved so much had taught her a hell of a lot too.

Finding the job in Joseph Cohen's shop, which sold high-end ladies' fashion, had been a complete fluke. Queenie had been running an errand for her mum one day when she'd spotted the 'Assistant Wanted' card in the window. The shop was situated at the Bethnal Green end of Roman Road. Queenie had bowled inside, remembered Mary's advice, and sold herself to the owner. She'd started work there the following Monday and had been in her element ever since. It truly was her dream job.

'The boys are going to pop down to the pub to celebrate my birthday with us later. I hope that's OK?' Mary rolled her eyes. 'They'll insist on seeing us home, mark my words. They're not used to me going to pubs, so they get very protective.'

'Ahh, I think that's really nice, Mary. Sons should be protective of their mum. Of course it's OK. The more the merrier,' Queenie beamed, her stomach doing somersaults.

Mary took her ration book out of her handbag. 'I need to get some sugar. We're nearly out of it. You can walk on if you like, show your mum your pretty new look.'

'Mum won't like it. When I told her I was thinking of going blonde she nearly had a cardiac,' chuckled Queenie. 'I'll wait for you.'

The queue was long, but when the shop owner spotted Mary getting in line he called out, 'Mrs O'Leary. You come to the front dear.' All heads turned as Queenie walked to the front with Mary.

The shop owner put the sugar in Mrs O'Leary's bag, then refused payment. 'Give my regards to Patrick and Daniel, Mrs O'Leary. You take care of yourself.'

When Queenie and Mary walked out of the shop, both burst out laughing. 'Did you see the look on Freda Smart's face? If looks could kill,' Queenie chuckled.

'That's the third time that's happened in the past week, Queenie. My boys have certainly made a name for themselves, and I couldn't be more proud of 'em,' beamed Mary.

The Albion in Bethnal Green was where Aunt Edna now sang on a Friday night and when Queenie arrived with Mary, the pub was already heaving. 'What would you like to drink, Mary?'

'Just a lemonade will be fine. I'm not much of a boozer. My Paddy was enough to turn an alcoholic off the hard stuff,' laughed Mary.

'You must have a proper drink. It's your birthday. I'll have a proper drink too.'

'Just a small Guinness then. Your aunt's waving at us. I think she's saved us a table.'

'You sit down, Mary. I'll bring the drinks over.'

Aunt Edna liked Mrs O'Leary and greeted her warmly. 'Happy birthday, Mary.' Edna handed her a card and a small gift.

'Oh you shouldn't have. You are silly.'

'You're my Queenie's inspiration. She adores you and I for one am so pleased she has you in her life,' beamed Edna.

Mary's eyes welled up. She knew Queenie's mum disliked her, so Edna's approval touched her deeply. 'Thanks, Edna. That truly means a lot.'

Queenie returned with the drinks, which included a pint

of bitter for her aunt. When Aunt Edna was singing and playing the piano, she drank pints like they were going out of style. Not once had Queenie ever seen her drunk though. Unlike her father, Aunt Edna was a happy drinker, not a monster.

Mary took her coat off and Queenie gushed over the present she'd bought her. Green was very popular at present and the pretty frilly blouse she'd purchased from Cohen's not only suited Mary, it was the same colour as her piercing green eyes.

'I love it, Queenie. But you should never have spent all that money on me. You are naughty.'

Queenie squeezed Mary's hand. 'You're worth every penny. I don't know how I would've coped without your support and advice. You know, after what happened in Lincolnshire.'

Mary locked eyes with Queenie. 'You're a survivor, like me, sweetheart.'

Queenie smiled. Only Mary truly understood her. Both victims of rape, their bond was unique.

The evening was brilliant. Aunt Edna sang all her classics – 'When Father Painted the Parlour', 'Knees Up Mother Brown', 'Sunny Side of the Street', 'The Lambeth Walk', I've Got a Lovely Bunch of Coconuts', 'My Old Man's a Dustman' – then she called Queenie up.

Thanks to her aunt, Mary and her new job, Queenie now had much more confidence. She calmly took the mike, announced it was Mary's birthday, sang 'Happy Birthday' and the whole pub joined in with her. 'I would also like to sing my favourite song for my dear friend. Listen to the words, Mary. They were written for you.'

Queenie sang 'You Are My Sunshine' beautifully. Mary

watched her with pride, tears streaming down her cheeks. Queenie was such a different person from that scared young girl who'd been raped. She was her own person now. A beautiful, confident, young lady with hopefully a wonderful, happy life ahead of her.

Patrick and Daniel arrived at the Albion just after ten. Both looked immaculate, as always. There was no sign of Bridie, Daniel's girlfriend, and that pleased Queenie too.

It took the lads a while to reach their table as lots of men wanted to greet them. Their importance and aura stood out a mile.

As Patrick greeted his mother, Queenie's heart leapt at the way Daniel looked at her. She'd made a special effort tonight, was wearing her new classy black frock from Cohen's. 'Bloody hell, Queenie! I didn't recognize you at first. You look, erm, beautiful. Blonde hair suits you,' Daniel grinned, not taking his eyes off her.

'Thank you,' Queenie replied meekly. She felt her cheeks burning up. He'd never looked at her like that before. She couldn't believe her luck. Ever since their conversation in the West End, she'd thought about Daniel constantly. He was her knight in shining armour. She was sure of that.

Clocking the way her youngest was looking at Queenie, Mary piped up: 'Don't you be getting designs on our Queenie, son. You're a dirty dog when it comes to women. Queenie can do far better than lumping up with a fly-by-night like you.'

The butterflies in Queenie's stomach were fluttering enormously. If Mary had noticed it too, it could only mean one thing. Finally, she'd caught Daniel's eye. He actually fancied her.

*

Queenie was in her own little bubble for the rest of the evening. She caught Daniel looking discreetly at her a few times and she felt ever so adult when he bought her a drink and she asked him for a gin and tonic. That's what Doreen, her work friend, drank. Queenie guessed it must be pretty cool as Doreen knew all the latest fashions and trends. She didn't particularly like the taste but found it took the edge off her nerves. Daniel's intense gaze was making her feel all jittery.

Daniel had his posh new car outside, a black Ford Coupé super deluxe. Queenie felt like a queen as he escorted her to the car with Aunt Edna and Mary. Others leaving the pub were looking at them and the car in awe. 'There's no need to drop us at Aunt Edna's. I need to pop in Mum's to pick something up. We can walk from there. It's only a few streets away,' Queenie explained.

'Pick up what you need, then I'll drop you home,' replied Daniel, turning to Queenie so that she got the full force of his charm. His green eyes sparkled like the Irish sea and Queenie could barely breathe. 'A lady doesn't make her own way home eh, Mum?' Mary nodded approvingly beside her. 'You and your aunt will be escorted home in style.'

Queenie and Edna both hugged Mary when they got out the car. 'Don't forget, it's my birthday on Wednesday. You're more than welcome to join us,' Edna told Mary.

Knowing that Molly would be attending, Mary made up an excuse. She didn't want to make things awkward.

Queenie ran indoors and picked up her old umbrella. Her new one had broken yesterday; such was the strength of the wind.

The short journey to Aunt Edna's only took a couple of minutes by car. 'Thank you ever so much for the lift and the drinks, Daniel,' Aunt Edna said, as she got out the car.

'Yes. Thanks, Daniel,' added Queenie.

As her aunt turned her back, Daniel grabbed Queenie's arm. 'You seriously do look beautiful tonight. But Mum's right: you can do so much better than me. There's nothing I'd like more than to take you to bed right now, Queenie, but there are some girls you bed and others you marry and one day, Queenie Wade . . .' Daniel pulled her small hand to his mouth and kissed it gently, 'one day, Queenie. Hopefully you will be mine.'

Queenie's heart exploded into a thousand pieces but no words would come out of her mouth. She was shocked, in an over-the-moon way. Daniel O'Leary would be hers, even if she had to wait until the end of the decade to have him.

Hearing her aunt calling, Queenie scrambled out of the car. 'Goodnight, Daniel.'

The following Wednesday, Queenie rushed home to her aunt's with a spring in her step. She'd been on cloud nine ever since Friday night. Even though she hadn't seen Daniel in the meantime, she had barely eaten or slept for mooning over him. She didn't feel tired, however, or hungry, just so happy.

'Happy Birthday, Aunt Edna.' Queenie gave her aunt a big hug. 'I didn't want to wake you this morning as I heard you come in really late.'

'Oh, I had a right result last night with the cards. Wiped the floor with all the men. He weren't happy, that Billy Timpson. Had the right hump,' chuckled Edna.

Queenie smiled. When she wasn't singing, Aunt Edna was gambling. Every Saturday daytime she'd run to and from the local illegal bookie, and more often than not she'd win. Lots of locals called her 'Lucky Edna' and the men were always asking her for tips. 'I didn't know what to get you, but I'm sure you're gonna like this,' Queenie said, handing her aunt her present. It was her very own tankard with EDNA'S PINT engraved on the front.

Edna rolled up. 'I bleedin' well love it, Queenie! No bastard'll be nicking my drink any more. You're a star, my girl. So thoughtful.'

'What's for dinner?'

'The last of the lamb stew from yesterday. Dumplings are fresh though.'

'Lovely. I'll eat that, then get ready. Mum'll be round at eight.'

'Smashing. Big Al starts singing at nine, so we'll get round there a bit beforehand. So kind of 'em to throw me a party. They didn't have to.' Edna sang in the Albion two nights a week and also on a Sunday lunchtime. The landlord and his wife were a lovely couple and Edna had been chuffed to bits when they told her they were celebrating her birthday with a party. Thirty-nine, she was today. Yet still felt twenty-one at heart.

'Everyone loves you, Aunt Edna. Well, apart from the men you play cards with and the bookies,' laughed Queenie.

'They don't call me Lucky Edna for nothing, ya know.'

Little did Edna know as she uttered those words, she'd used all her luck up.

'You look nice, Mum,' said Queenie. Her mother never made an effort as a rule, but tonight she was wearing a floral dress under her brown winter coat. She'd also applied a bit of blusher and lipstick, which was unusual.

'Thanks, love. Happy birthday, Edna,' Molly said,

handing her sister a card, some chocolate and sweets. 'Sorry I couldn't afford anything more.'

'Don't be so daft, Moll. You know what a sweet tooth I've got. I wouldn't be this bleedin' size otherwise,' laughed Edna.

'You look lovely, Aunt Edna,' Queenie said genuinely. Even though her aunt was a big lady, she had a beautiful face and smile. Queenie couldn't imagine her thin and was sure it wouldn't suit her.

'Is it still OK if I sleep 'ere tonight, Edna?' asked Molly. 'Vivvy's staying round at Mary Moggins, and me and Eric had a big barney last night. Berlin was bombed the day before, weren't it? Eric's adamant I shouldn't come out tonight. He fears reprisals. Ya know what he's like.'

'Not drinking again, is he?' asked Edna.

'No. He's even got himself a better job in a factory. But he's obsessed with the war and listening to the bleedin' radio. That and newspapers. He has no other interests these days.'

'You stay 'ere with us, Mum,' smiled Queenie. 'My boss at work was talking about reprisals today too. But as Aunt Edna says, we just have to carry on our lives as normal.'

'Too right we bleedin' will. Sod Hitler and his not so merry men. Us East Enders ain't frightened of no bastard. Right, we ready?' grinned Edna. 'It's party time!'

Queenie was jovially chatting to her mum and aunt about work when there was a blackout. Seconds later, the sirens sounded.

'Gawd stone the crows!' gasped Edna.

'Run,' yelled Molly.

Queenie could not see properly, but was aware of the

panic around her. Everywhere she turned, people were running for their lives.

Bethnal Green tube station was the nearest shelter and as Molly grabbed her daughter's hand, she heard that formidable noise. The whirring, buzzing, the sounds of bombs dropping from the sky. 'Run, Queenie. Run!' shrieked Molly.

There was shouting, screaming, children sobbing, dogs barking as Queenie ran through the dark streets in the same direction as everyone else. It was mayhem and she could not help but feel scared. Not for herself, mind; she was far more worried about Viv, Mary, Patrick and Daniel. Were they running towards a shelter too? she wondered.

'We've lost Edna. Where is she?' Molly panted. She wasn't used to running, was completely out of breath.

Queenie let go of her mother's hand and tried to turn around. It was impossible though. They were nearing the entrance of the station and the crowds were surging towards them. Not all were panicking, but the women with children were.

As Queenie and Molly got lifted off their feet by the stampeding crowd behind, they found themselves inside the station and almost tumbled down the steps. 'Aunt Edna. Aunt Edna,' Queenie bellowed. Her voice could not be heard though. There were far too many other voices also shouting for their loved ones.

Recognizing someone she knew, Molly turned around and grabbed him. 'You seen Edna, my sister?'

'No, Molly. You seen my mum? I got separated from her. She's seventy-four, for Christ's sake.'

Guessing that, because of her size, Edna couldn't run as fast as most, Queenie had her eyes glued to the hordes of people trampling down the slippery steps. The lighting inside the station was dismal and the atmosphere claustrophobic as it began to fill.

'Aunt Edna! Aunt Edna!' Queenie yelled, frantically waving her arms in the air. Relief flooded through her as she spotted Edna among the crowd being herded like cattle down the steps.

All of a sudden, Queenie heard a commotion behind her. She turned to see a scuffle, and as she turned back, she saw a woman fall down the last few steps with a child in her arms. An elderly man then fell on top of her and mayhem followed.

Queenie screamed as people, including her aunt, tumbled like dominoes on top of each other. 'Aunt Edna,' she cried. 'Aunt Edna.'

'Do something, someone. Stop the crowds coming,' shrieked Molly.

But there was nothing anybody could do. The crowds just kept coming, then falling. Queenie sobbed. People were squashed, many dying in front of her very eyes, and Aunt Edna was at the bottom of the pile.

Overcome by the horror of knowing her sister was one of the fallen, Molly Wade fainted.

'Mum,' Queenie screamed. 'Mum, wake up!'

Queenie stood inside the station, one of the many who had loved ones missing. Her mum was in a terrible state. She couldn't stop trembling, neither could she speak.

Apparently, a single off-duty police officer had halted the chaos. He'd heard all the screaming and shouting and had stopped anybody else from entering the station.

There were lots of rumours flying around. A man behind Queenie was telling everyone that it wasn't bombs being dropped by the Germans that had caused the chaos. It was the new anti-aircraft rockets being launched for our own protection and the government were to blame as they should have pre-warned us what was going on.

Another rumour said the stampede was caused by a pickpocket, but Queenie didn't care what started it. All she could think about was her aunt. She could only hope and pray that Aunt Edna's size might have saved her life.

After the many injured were taken away, bodies were pulled from the scene. Tears flowed freely. There was a dead woman, still holding her dead baby in her arms. So many looked dead, lots of them children. It was awful. Heartbreaking. It was Aunt Edna's birthday too, thought Queenie.

As the bodies were taken outside by the men, Queenie felt sick. 'Talk to me, Mum. Please,' urged Queenie.

But Molly couldn't talk. She was too traumatized.

As a gap to the left of the stairs opened up, a policeman urged the women and children to form an orderly queue and leave the station. As she filed past the lifeless bodies, Queenie glanced to the right but couldn't spot Aunt Edna. One of the first to fall, she was too near the bottom of the heap to be visible.

Once outside the station, Queenie gulped in the fresh air, then watched in horror as each body that was brought out had a bucket of cold water thrown over it, to see if it would trigger any signs of life. One man sat up, but the majority just lay there lifeless, the cold water dripping off them.

'Take Mum down to St John's church, Queenie,' urged Mrs Simpson. 'That's where the bodies are being taken for identification. You don't wanna be watching this, love. I'll come down there with you.'

Mrs Simpson lived not far from her mum in Whitechapel.

Grateful to see a familiar face, Queenie held one of her mum's arms, Mrs Simpson held the other and they led Molly away from the chaotic scenes. 'My Aunt Edna, I saw her fall. She's near the bottom,' Queenie blurted out.

'Oh no, Queenie. I'm so sorry,' replied Mrs Simpson.

'I'm hoping, 'cause she's fat, it might have saved her,' Queenie explained, her lip trembling.

Mrs Simpson doubted anyone near the bottom of the pile could have survived. But there was no point in saying that. All she could do was be there for Molly and young Queenie. 'Miracles do happen. All we can do is pray. I'll stay with you until we find out what's happened to your aunt.'

'Thanks, Mrs Simpson.'

The bodies were brought into the church by the men who'd been told by the police to help out. Adults were carried by two men, children were carried by one.

Having lost track of time, Queenie had no idea how long she'd been at the church. She felt numb. Her mum still hadn't said a word. It was as though she'd been struck dumb.

Queenie waited and waited, praying for a miracle, then she saw four men walking towards her, obviously struggling to carry the body. Instinct told Queenie that was her aunt. She ran towards them. 'That's my aunt. Is she alive? Please tell me she is.'

'I'm afraid not, darling,' said one of the men. 'None of 'em survived near the bottom of the pile. Tragic.'

When her aunt's body was dumped on the floor of the church alongside many others, Queenie knelt beside her and held her hand. She looked a bit bruised, but she wasn't flattened or anything. She just looked like she was sleeping.

'Wake up, Aunt Edna. Please wake up. It's your birthday,' Queenie wept.

Aunt Edna lay lifeless. She would've loved to have woken up, such was her zest for life, but she couldn't. The life she'd loved so much had been crushed out of her.

Queenie sat on the church steps. There were ten or so kids playing in the rubble, playing tag, screaming with excitement. Oblivious to the death and destruction going on around them. That had been her not so long ago. Mucking around in the streets with Viv and her mates without a care in the world.

Queenie steeled herself. She would miss Aunt Edna dreadfully, but knew she had to be brave. Mum and Vivvy would need her strength to get through this.

'I miss my Seamus every day, but I refuse to mourn him. I only allow myself to remember the good times. Shedding tears for the dead doesn't bring them back, Queenie. So save your tears for the fecking living,' Mrs O'Leary had said to her only yesterday.

Queenie stood up. Mrs O'Leary was right. She'd run out of tears anyway, had none left to cry.

PART TWO

'From the end spring new beginnings'
Pliny the Elder

CHAPTER EIGHT

When you think of the dead at war, you think of boys in the trenches or in the fields, not of my Aunt Edna who died needlessly. There were no bombs dropped that night. The blackout, sirens, weird whirring noises were all part of new anti-aircraft rockets, supposedly being launched for our own protection by the government. I was furious. Why hadn't anyone informed us of what was going on? As if us East Enders hadn't been through enough already.

There was a total media blackout of the truth. No mention in the newspapers or on radio stations. Twenty-seven men, eighty-four women and sixty-two children was the final death toll, the youngest being a five-month-old baby. We only learned the actual death toll via neighbours, nurses and local bobbies. I heard rumours that those in authority had tried to bribe young children, offering five-pound notes to them if they'd keep their trap shut. My aunt's body had been taken from that church and chucked on the back of a lorry like a bag of bloody coal. I couldn't forgive our government and neither would I be able to forget.

Mrs O'Leary helped me clear out Aunt Edna's home and it was Mary who found just over two hundred quid stuffed in an envelope under the mattress. That enabled me to give my aunt the send-off she deserved. I chose a smart coffin and abided by my aunt's wishes. Even though I'd have loved to have chosen a nice headstone and been able to visit her grave, Aunt Edna had a terrible phobia of creepy crawlies, especially worms, and she'd told me and Mum numerous times that, if she were to die during the war, her wish was to be cremated.

I took Mary's advice and never told anyone else about the small fortune we'd found. 'I'll keep it safe at mine for you, Queenie. Don't be giving your mum the money if she's not thinking straight. Your father's bound to get his mucky hands on it if you do,' warned Mary.

I knew Mary was right. I guessed it must be gambling winnings and I knew Aunt Edna wouldn't want my father to waste it. She'd hated him. So I decided whenever Mum needed anything, I would give her the money in dribs and drabs and pretend it was wages I'd saved. I paid housekeeping money now anyway, to help out with the rent and bills.

Aunt Edna's funeral was very sad, yet it showed her popularity. Hundreds of people turned up – so many that most of them couldn't find room inside the church. Mum and Viv were in bits, but I managed to hold it together and read a eulogy. My aunt had been so good to me. It was the least I could do for her.

I hated sleeping back at home. My nightmares returned. They weren't about that monster Ivan any more though. They were about the stampede, people getting crushed. I could see Aunt Edna clearly in my dreams, reaching out to me, a look of panic on her face, and me desperately trying to reach her.

I wasn't the only one having bad dreams. Both Mum and Dad would wake Viv and me up, screaming and shouting. It truly was the house of bloody nightmares. Horrible.

Then finally some good news. The family upstairs were moving out. I urged Mum to tell the landlord we could afford to rent the whole house again, now I was working and Dad had a job in a factory that paid a steady wage. The landlord agreed, providing a deposit was paid up front in case we fell behind with the rent again. I paid the deposit out of Aunt Edna's money. I was elated to have my old bedroom back. So was Viv.

But, as usual in my world, good news was accompanied by bad. That same day I found out the landlord had agreed, I ran over to Mrs O'Leary to tell her the good news and collect some of Edna's cash.

Mary opened the door holding her rosary beads, her eyes red. 'Whatever's wrong?' I asked.

Mary led me into what she called her best room. 'It's Daniel. He's only gone and got his new bird, Bridie, in the family way. I warned him to be careful. Now he's lumbered himself for life. He don't love her. I know he don't. He's been seeing another girl behind poor Bridie's back.'

My heart sank. I fell backwards onto the sofa. I'd so wanted to marry Daniel, have his children. I was gobsmacked. Dreaming of a future with Daniel was all that had kept me going through the bad times, even though I knew he dated other girls.

Mary squeezed my hand, as always knowing more than I realized. 'You've had a lucky escape, darling, trust me. He'll not make a good husband.'

A month later, Daniel and Bridie got married. I feigned illness. No way could I watch the man I loved marry another. My future was over. Why was life so bloody cruel to me?

Nine Months Later

New Year's Eve 1943

'Oh come on, Queenie. It's New Year's Eve, for goodness' sake. You have to come to the pub with us,' urged eighteen-year-old Doreen Laine.

'Doreen's right, Queenie. Even I'm going and I rarely go to pubs. My dad said he'll pick me up, so he can drop you off home too. You won't have to walk all that way,' added Eliza, the boss's daughter.

Doreen smirked. 'There'll be lots of handsome men there and I can show you the one I've got my eye on. Please come. It'll be fun and you never know, you might meet the man of your dreams. I won't leave you again if that's what you're worried about. I promise.'

The only time Queenie had been out with Doreen was on her birthday. They'd got chatting to two strapping American servicemen. Doreen got sloshed, disappeared with one and the other insisted on walking Queenie home. On the way, he tried it on. He dragged Queenie down an alleyway, stuck his tongue down her throat and grabbed her tits. Petrified, Queenie had kneed him where it hurt the most and run for her life. She'd vowed there and then never to go out with Doreen again.

'Please come, Queenie,' urged Eliza. 'It won't be the same without you.'

Queenie rolled her eyes. Pubs reminded her of Aunt Edna, which was why she disliked going to them. She knew her aunt would want her to go out and enjoy herself though. 'OK. You've twisted my arm. But I haven't a clue what to wear.'

On the journey home, Queenie couldn't help but feel excited about her spur-of-the-moment decision. She had recently turned seventeen and this would be the first New Year's Eve she'd celebrated in a pub with friends. Watching Daniel O'Leary walk around with his new wife by his side hurt Queenie more than she could ever admit, but she was determined to show everyone in Whitechapel that she was getting on with her life as if nothing had happened.

Queenie opened her bag and ran her fingers over the pretty navy and white polka-dot dress. It was lovely material and by far the nicest thing she'd ever treated herself to. It was also only the second item she'd purchased for herself from the shop where she worked. Mr Cohen had been ever so kind, allowing her to buy the dress at cost price. Most of their customers were wealthy Jewish women and Queenie now knew why Mr Cohen lived in a posh house in North London and drove a Pontiac Streamliner. The mark-up on his dresses was immense.

Thinking about Doreen's words, Queenie hoped there would be plenty of handsome men to choose from this evening. She'd been asked out on a few dates, but none of those men had met the criteria she was looking for. Only five foot three herself, she was determined any potential suitor must be tall, like Daniel. She didn't want short kids. She also didn't want girls; she wanted big strapping sons who would grow up to protect her, like Daniel and Patrick. Daniel had a child now, a daughter. Queenie was glad it wasn't a boy. She'd have been even more jealous had it been. Mary kept urging her to go out with the girls, find the man of her dreams.

Picturing Clark Gable, her favourite actor, Queenie smiled. Tall, dark and handsome, that's the type of man she wanted. He had to be kind too, and a good provider. And having seen what alcohol did to her father, she would be steering well clear of drunks.

'What you all dressed up for? Where you going?' exclaimed fourteen-year-old Vivian.

'To a pub, with Doreen and Eliza from work. Do I look all right?'

Vivian studied her older sister. They used to look very much alike, everybody said so. Slim, petite, with the same mousy-brown hair, worn shoulder length. But Queenie had dyed her hair blonde now and she had breasts. She looked so pretty in her beautiful dress that had a tight bodice, Vivian could not help but feel a bit envious. 'But what if Dad comes home drunk and starts on Mum? What am I meant to do if I'm alone and you're out?'

Queenie squeezed her sister's hand. Their father had fallen off the wagon in spectacular fashion over Christmas. 'I'll be home not long after midnight. Just sit with Mum, and if Dad gets home before me, come up here and put the radio on like we usually do.'

Vivian scowled as her sister hugged her goodbye. Once upon a time, she and Queenie were inseparable and spent all their spare time together. Now Queenie was all grown-up, had a new life and friends. Vivian didn't like that, not one little bit.

Doreen was waiting at the station when Queenie arrived. 'Oh Queenie, you look amazing in that frock, but why the pale lipstick? Here, put some of mine on. Bright red gets you noticed.'

Queenie allowed her friend to apply the lipstick. Doreen Laine was five foot six and with her high heels on, looked like a giant in comparison to herself. She had short blonde hair and an aura about her – until she opened her red lips and started swearing like a trooper. Men seemed to adore her though. Doreen turned the heads of males even when she was working.

When Joseph turned up in his posh car with Eliza in the front, Queenie felt very grown-up as her boss dropped them off at the Beehive. Joseph stuffed some money in Eliza's hand, warned them all not to get drunk, but insisted the drinks were on him this evening.

On entering the pub, Queenie clocked a group of lads looking their way. She couldn't help but wonder if it was because they were an odd-looking set of friends. Doreen was the stunner. She was the average one, and poor Eliza bordered on ugly with her squat, plump body topped by a mass of fuzzy hair.

The atmosphere in the pub was one of jubilance. The East End had been through so much since the war had begun, but all that bastard Hitler had achieved was to make an already tight-knit community even stronger. The war might not be won yet, but everybody believed that England would defeat the Germans at all costs.

'What shall we have to drink?' Eliza asked, waving a ten-shilling note in the air.

'Gin and tonic for me, please,' Doreen shouted. The pub was ever so noisy.

'I'll have the same,' Queenie smiled. She'd rarely drunk alcohol in the past, would actually prefer lemonade, but didn't want to come across as immature in front of Doreen.

When a few American servicemen strutted over and began chatting to the girls, Queenie nervously sipped her drink. Two of them were extremely handsome, and tall, but Mrs O'Leary had warned her not to have anything to do with them. 'Lily Turner's eldest daughter and Clara Miller's niece both got in the family way with American servicemen. You steer well clear, Queenie. They only want one thing, and most of them probably have girlfriends and wives back home,' were Mary's exact words. Queenie had reassured her friend there was no way she'd have anything to do with them after having been dragged into an alley by one.

'Let's make our way over to the piano. That's where the bloke I like usually stands.' Doreen craned her neck. 'I can't see him in 'ere at the moment though.'

'What's his name? This mystery man of yours,' enquired Eliza.

'I don't know. I've only been in here twice before, with that Roger I dumped. He's ever so good looking and always surrounded by fluttering females. You wait until you hear him sing. He's got a lovely voice. I do hope he turns up. I'm assuming it's his local.'

'Let's get this party started, shall we?' bellowed the jolly-looking male pianist. There were whoops of delight as 'Bye Bye Blackbird' kicked off the evening's entertainment. Queenie smiled. Aunt Edna sometimes used to start with 'Bye Bye Blackbird'. Mary was always telling her to look out for signs. Perhaps this was one?

By 10 p.m., Queenie had already decided that this was the best night out she'd ever had. As much as she loved her mum, sister and Mary, it was wonderful to be able to temporarily forget about her shitty home-life and enjoy being a teenager with girls of a similar age.

'That bloke's looking at you again, Queenie. I bet he comes over in a minute,' nudged Doreen. The pianist was taking a well-earned break, so they could hear themselves speak at last.

'He's got a kind face, Queenie. Nice eyes too,' added Eliza.

Queenie turned her back on the lad in question. Dressed in a shirt, braces and checked cap, he reminded Queenie of one of the barrow boys off the market. 'He's not my type. I'm not interested.'

'How can you say that without even talking to him?' Eliza chuckled. She didn't get any attention from blokes, but that didn't bother her. Her parents expected her to marry a nice Jewish lad and had a list of possible suitors for her to meet next year.

'He's coming over,' Doreen lied.

Queenie glanced around, then playfully punched her pal on the arm. 'You fibber,' she laughed. In her stunning red frock with lipstick to match, Doreen was getting plenty of male attention. 'Why didn't you like that chap who bought us a drink? I thought he was cheeky-looking,' Queenie asked.

'Not my cup of tea, and he's a coalman. Imagine a man coming home every night covered in soot from head to foot. Sod that. I'd lock him out the bastard house,' Doreen laughed. She came from an extremely rough family in Poplar, but like Queenie, was determined to better herself. She spoke nicely when working at the shop serving all those respectable Jewish women. Well, apart from that time she'd stubbed her toe in front of Mrs Rosenthal and a 'fuck' had accidentally flown out of her gob.

'I'll get us another drink. I'm having a lemonade now. What do you two want?' asked Eliza.

'Gin and tonic again for me, please,' replied Doreen.

Queenie didn't reply. She was fixated on a man in a smart suit who had obviously only just arrived, as people were greeting him and shaking his hand. His hair was black and he had a twinkle in his eyes. He was very handsome and at least six foot tall, but most importantly, he reminded her of Daniel.

'Who you gawping at?' Doreen asked, before turning around. She gripped Queenie's arm. 'Oh my God! The man. That's him. Look, the one standing next to that chap in the trilby. He's wearing a dark suit.'

Queenie's heart sank. 'What! Is that the one you fancy?'

Doreen beamed from ear to ear. 'Yes. I didn't think he was going to turn up. I must pop to the ladies to powder my nose. Hold my drink for me.'

When Doreen shot off, Queenie stared at the man again. She wouldn't stand a cat in hell's chance of snaring him if Doreen had designs on him, that was for sure.

'I think you should have a soft drink now, Doreen, like Queenie and me. You're looking rather tipsy and my dad will be ever so angry if you're sick in his car,' Eliza warned as the evening wore on.

Doreen flung her arm in the air. She felt heady with excitement since her mystery man had arrived and was trying to pluck up the courage to talk to him. 'I'm not drunk and I promise I won't be sick. I'll have another gin. Honest, I'm fine.'

Queenie thought the pianist was fantastic. He played and sang along to all the songs she'd sung over and over again with her aunt. He also called others up to sing. A middle-aged lady had given a brilliant rendition of Gracie Field's 'Sally', and an elderly gentleman had sung 'The

Lambeth Walk' in spectacular fashion. He'd even done a little dance to it with his walking stick.

'Can I have my old mucker, Albie, up 'ere to give us a song,' bellowed the pianist. Queenie held her breath as Albie brushed past her. So that was his name solved.

'I'm Gonna Sit Right Down and Write Myself a Letter' was Albie's song choice and Doreen was right about his voice. There was a silky tone to it and he sang the song beautifully, effortlessly.

Doreen arrived back from the bar. 'Told you, didn't I? Wasn't he just born to sing? I think I'm in love.'

'His name's Albie,' Eliza informed Doreen.

'I must talk to him. I have to find out if he's single,' Doreen replied. She didn't usually get nervous around men, but Albie made her heart beat wildly.

After receiving a rapturous round of applause, the pianist played another song, then counted down from twenty, shouted 'Happy New Year' before handing the mike back to Albie, who sang 'Auld Lang Syne'. Everybody grouped together while singing along. Queenie even held the hand of the lad in the cap and braces who'd been eyeing her up all evening. He introduced himself as Terry afterwards, and Queenie was even less impressed when she realized he was also a coalman and the hair poking out from under his hat was ginger. She certainly didn't want ginger children. They'd get picked on at school like Sally Sharp in her class. So when he asked her out, she politely declined.

'We'd better stand outside soon. My dad won't want to come in looking for us,' said Eliza. She wasn't a regular pub-goer, but had felt comfortable in the Beehive because there were some fellow Jewish people. She'd even recognized a couple of ladies who came into the shop.

'Just let me talk to Albie first. I have to,' Doreen insisted, grabbing Queenie's arm.

'He's talking to some men. You can't just bowl over there and interrupt the conversation,' Queenie warned. Doreen was more than tipsy now. She was unsteady on her feet in those high heels of hers.

Queenie didn't have much choice in the matter when Doreen literally dragged her over to where Albie was standing. 'Excuse me. I'm sorry for butting in, but I just wanted to tell you what a bloody good singer you are,' Doreen slurred.

Queenie blushed. This was awfully embarrassing. But she could not take her eyes off Albie's. They were the most powerful green she had ever seen. Striking. He truly did resemble Daniel in many ways, apart from being a bit skinny. Daniel was very stocky in comparison.

'Why thank you, ma'am,' Albie grinned. 'I'm singing from nine until eleven in here next Friday, if you fancy hearing more of my dulcet tones,' he chuckled.

'And you have beautiful eyes,' Doreen gushed.

At that point, Queenie cringed. She was determined to let Albie know she wasn't drunk too. 'Come on, Doreen. We must go now. Joseph will be waiting for us.'

'Joseph's my boss, not my boyfriend. What's your name?' Doreen hiccupped. She wanted to find out his surname.

'Albie. Albie Butler.'

'I'm Doreen Laine and this is my friend, Queenie Wade. We work in Cohen's ladies' fashion shop in the Roman Road. Have you got a girlfriend or wife? Only we sell lovely dresses if you have.'

'Nope. I'm still up for grabs.' Even the men standing with Albie were laughing now. They were used to their pal getting lots of female attention, but this one was so forward and inebriated, she was extra funny.

Eliza appeared by Queenie's side. 'My father is outside. We really have to leave now.'

'Bye, ladies. It's been a pleasure talking to you,' Albie smiled.

'We are so sorry to have interrupted your conversation, gentlemen,' Queenie replied politely.

Albie winked at her. 'No problem. I'll hopefully see you next weekend.'

Queenie grabbed Doreen by the arm. Eliza grabbed her friend's other arm, so she wouldn't stumble.

On the journey home, Queenie felt a warm glow inside. She'd had the most amazing evening.

She glanced at her sleeping friend. Surely by being so drunk and cringe-worthy, Doreen had blown any chance she might have had with Albie? Men didn't like lushes, they liked ladies, her mum had always drummed into her.

Albie had winked at *her*, not Doreen. He'd also said to *her*, 'I'll hopefully see you next weekend.'

The following day, Queenie couldn't wait to tell someone her news. Her mum had been in a world of her own since Aunt Edna's death, Viv was too young, so Queenie got dressed and dashed over to Mrs O'Leary's.

'Well, well, well, a certain young lady looks radiant today. Tell me all about him,' laughed Mary.

'How did you know I was going to tell you about a man?'

'Because I'm clever. Come on, spill the beans.'

Queenie couldn't keep the smile off her face as she gabbled the whole story of her wonderful night out. 'And you know you told me to look out for signs from Aunt Edna. The first song the pianist sang was "Bye Bye

Blackbird". Aunt Edna often started her sessions with that song too. D'ya reckon it was a sign?'

'Without a doubt. That's your aunt's way of showing her approval that you're finally out enjoying yourself. Not before time too, might I add. We can't change the past, Queenie, but we can certainly strive for a better future.'

'I know Aunt Edna would approve of Albie's voice. He sings so well, Mary.'

'How old is Albie, would you say?'

'Older than me. About the same age as Daniel, I'd guess. He actually reminds me a bit of Daniel. He has black hair and bright green eyes too.'

'Sweet Jesus! Let's hope he treats his women better than my Daniel. A roving eye, my son has, that's for sure.' Mary craned her neck. 'Speak of the Devil. He's just pulled up outside. I'll put the kettle on.'

Usually, Queenie would avoid visiting Mary when Daniel and Bridie came by, or excuse herself and quickly leave if they turned up unexpectedly. It was time she grew up though, so she smiled as Daniel and Bridie walked in with the baby. 'Happy New Year to you all.'

Daniel bent down and kissed Queenie on the cheek. 'Happy New Year.'

Queenie stood up and looked inside the baby's pram. Emily, they'd called the child, and she looked nothing like Daniel. She was fair like Bridie. 'Ahh, she's gorgeous. She's got so big since I last saw her.'

'That's probably 'cause you usually do a runner as soon as we arrive,' winked Daniel.

Queenie felt herself blush. 'No. I don't. It's just I had to be somewhere the last time you visited,' she lied.

'What about the time before that then?' Daniel goaded playfully.

'Stop teasing my dear friend,' Mary chuckled, putting the tea tray on the table. 'Our Queenie went out with the girls from work last night and has met a potential suitor, haven't you, darling?'

Queenie felt embarrassed. 'Erm, I wouldn't go that far just yet, Mary. Let's wait and see if he asks me out first.'

'Well, he'd be silly not to. He won't be asking that lush of a friend of yours out now, that's for sure,' Mary grinned. 'Men don't like drunken women, do they, Daniel?'

'No. That's why I married Bridie,' Daniel replied, slinging a casual arm around his wife's shoulders. 'So who's this geezer then, Queenie? Where did you meet him?'

'None of your bloody business.' Mary winked at Queenie. 'You tell him nothing, sweetheart. The nosy toerag.'

Queenie drank her tea and then said her goodbyes.

Daniel saw Queenie out. 'Who is he then, this bloke?'

'Nobody you'd know.'

'If he's worth knowing I will.'

'My love life has nothing to do with you, Daniel.'

Daniel grabbed Queenie's arm and teasingly stared her in the eyes. 'I still care about you, ya know.'

Queenie snatched her arm away. 'Go back inside to your wife and child. They're your responsibility, not me.'

CHAPTER NINE

Queenie went back to work on the Monday with a spring in her step. She'd thought a lot about Albie over the weekend, but had thought even more about Daniel. It broke her heart to see him play happy families with a woman he clearly didn't love, but it was definitely time to move on.

Her mum had warned her not to get too carried away. 'You barely know anything about the man, love. Wait and see if he asks you out on a date first. I rushed into things with your father and look where that got me.'

Doreen was very sheepish on her arrival. 'Whatever did I do and say? It's all a bit blurry. I wish you'd stopped me drinking gin.'

'I tried to,' laughed Eliza.

'You weren't that bad, mate, honest,' Queenie lied. 'Albie and his mates liked you, they thought you were funny, didn't they, Eliza?'

Eliza nodded.

'Do you remember Albie inviting us to go back there next Friday to watch him sing?' asked Queenie.

'Yes. But I'm not going. I feel far too embarrassed.'

Queenie's heart sank. Apart from Daniel, she'd thought of nothing else but seeing Albie again. 'Oh don't be so daft, Dor. Half the bloody pub were paralytic. It was New Year's Eve, for Christ's sake.'

'Why you so keen to go back there? You got your eye on someone an' all?'

Feeling herself blush, Queenie gabbled her words. 'There were lots of handsome men and I had such a great time, I just want to go there again. Never going to meet a man if I don't go out, am I?'

Doreen raised her eyebrows. 'I've been telling you that for ages.'

Over the next month, unbeknown to Doreen, Queenie made up with Aggie Brown, her next-door neighbour. The reason being, she needed someone to drag up the Beehive on a Friday night. A plain girl with freckles and a nose slightly too big for her face, Aggie had developed an enormous crush on Terry, the lad in the cap and braces who'd asked Queenie out on New Year's Eve.

Queenie found out a bit more about Albie. He was twenty-four and even though he was always surrounded by females, he didn't seem to be courting anyone in particular. He definitely liked blondes though. Queenie would study him to see who he was singing to or eyeing up. He always spoke to herself and Aggie. Albie was a very polite and an extremely popular chap. Queenie could not help but feel frustrated though. She was getting nowhere fast.

Because she worked Saturdays, Tuesday was Queenie's day off and when she arrived at work on the Wednesday, she was in for an unwelcome surprise.

'Guess where we're going on Friday to celebrate Eliza's birthday?' Doreen grinned.

'No idea,' Queenie replied.

'The Beehive! Eliza said her dad will drop us off home again. I'm gonna treat myself to a new outfit and a new hairstyle. I'm determined to make a good impression on Albie Butler this time.'

Queenie had that feeling of dread in the pit of her stomach. The thought of Doreen impressing Albie was bad enough, but say someone put their foot in it and asked where Aggie was? How the hell was she meant to explain that one?'

'What's the matter? You don't look too happy. I thought you'd be pleased we were going back there. It was Eliza's idea actually, not mine. But I'm determined to get my man this time. It's weeks since Albie saw me pissed and time is a healer, so they say,' Doreen chuckled.

'I am happy. It's just I promised my friend Aggie I'd go out with her this weekend and I don't want to let her down. We only made up recently.'

'Bring Aggie with you, Queenie,' Eliza smiled. 'There's plenty of room in Dad's car. The more the merrier.'

The evening before her dreaded night out, Queenie sat in front of the fire with her mum.

'What's up, love? You're not yourself tonight,' Molly remarked.

Needing to unburden herself, Queenie blurted everything out. 'I just feel like I'm wasting my time, Mum. I can't compete with the likes of Doreen. You should see her new hairstyle and outfit. She's even bought one of those posh cigarette holders, and she's painted a black line in pen down the back of her stockings. She looks like a bloody film star.'

Molly put her knitting down. 'Now, now, I'm not having any more of this defeatist talk. You're a beautiful young woman, Queenie, with your whole life ahead of you, and if Albie Butler is too blind to see it, then that's his bleedin' loss. As for your mate Doreen, beauty's only skin deep. She has a mouth like a sewer and drinks like your father, by the sounds of it. If Albie chooses her, then he was never the man for you in the first place.'

Queenie was about to reply when her father staggered through the door and collapsed in a heap on the threadbare armchair. 'Where's my dinner, woman?' he slurred.

When her mum dashed into the kitchen like a skivvy, Queenie took herself upstairs.

An hour later, Queenie and Viv lay in silence as they listened to the horrid noises coming from their parents' bedroom. Their father was grunting like the pig he was.

Viv propped herself up on her elbow. 'I'm not sure I want to get married, Queenie.'

Queenie stroked her sister's face. 'I know what you mean, but when we get married it'll be different. We'll choose good men, not a bad one like Mum did.'

'But we'll still be forced to have sex with them, won't we? I don't think I'm going to like sex. It sounds awful.'

'I know it does. But hopefully with a good man it won't be so bad. We have to do it if we want to have babies.'

Vivian breathed deeply. The noises had stopped now. 'Night, Queenie.'

'Night, Vivvy. Sleep tight and don't let those bed bugs bite.'

Arriving home the following evening, Vivian was peeved to see her sister all done up to the nines again.

'You look all dirty and sweaty, Viv. What you been up to?' asked Queenie, as she carefully applied her eye-liner.

'Playing rounders with Mary Moggins and Nelly Brown.

You're not going out again, are you?' Vivian snapped.

Queenie swung around and held her sister's dirty hands. 'I'm seventeen now, Viv. I'm too old to be playing rounders and hopscotch. You've got Mary and Nelly to play with, haven't you? I know you've got a cob on because I've started going out on a Friday night. But I'm just at a different stage of my life than you. It doesn't mean I love you any less. You'll always be my number one best friend. Just think, in a year or so, you'll be working and as soon as you look old enough, we can go to the pub together.'

'Really? What, on our own? Without Doreen? I don't mind Aggie so much.'

Queenie smiled. It was only natural Vivvy was a bit jealous. She'd probably be the same, if the boot was on the other foot. 'Yes, really. Without Doreen. Never forget, blood is thicker than water, Sis.'

It was Queenie's idea that she and Aggie get to the pub early, so they could get all their hellos to the regulars out of the way before Eliza and Doreen arrived.

Bagging their usual table, Aggie Brown was beyond herself with excitement when Terry Marney kept looking over and smiling, then approached her and offered to buy herself and Queenie a drink.

'I told you he kept staring at you last week,' Queenie said, genuinely pleased for Aggie. 'I bet he asks you on a date before the evening is over.'

Eliza and Doreen turned up just after eight. Queenie stood up, hugged both and introduced them to Aggie. 'Aggie comes here quite often, so knows a lot of people in here. She's been introducing me to some.'

'Ooh, do you know Albie Butler?' asked Doreen.

'Yes. He's a nice chap. His fiancée is lovely too. He's singing in here tonight,' Aggie replied, repeating word for word what Queenie had told her to say.

'Albie's engaged?' Doreen exclaimed.

'As far as I know, yes. To Suzanne,' Aggie replied.

Queenie wanted to laugh at the look of shock on Doreen's face, but obviously couldn't, so instead insisted she get the first drink. In Queenie's eyes, this was payback. Doreen should never have left her alone with that Yank who'd tried to take advantage of her. It wasn't a total lie that she and Aggie could get caught out on, as Dennis the pianist had told them only last Friday that Albie had been engaged to a lass called Suzanne and they'd broken up when Albie had gone away at the start of the Blitz.

'Hello, treacle. Let me get these drinks,' said a dark-haired man in a smart suit. He had a big scar across his cheek and looked a bit of a villain. 'I want you to introduce me to your blonde mate. What's her name?'

'Doreen. Doreen Laine. Four gin and tonics then, please, and can you make one a double?'

The man winked. 'My pleasure. I'm Jimmy, by the way. Jimmy Foster. She single, is she, your mate Doreen?'

Queenie forced a smile. She'd seen the way men's heads turned when Doreen entered the pub and she was desperate for Albie not to look at her in that way. 'Yes. Doreen's single. Help me carry the drinks over and I'll introduce you.'

Queenie handed Doreen the double. 'Doreen, meet Jimmy,' she grinned.

The rest of the evening was a success. Doreen was tipsy and seemed to be rather taken by the charming Jimmy

Foster. Albie did look at Doreen a few times, but she was too engrossed with Jimmy to notice.

Queenie politely declined the offer of a lift home. Terry had finally asked Aggie on a date and Queenie wasn't going to be the only girl left on the shelf. Even Eliza was courting now. She was sweet on a Jewish lad called Alan.

Queenie waved goodbye to Eliza and Doreen and watched intently as Albie sang his last song of the evening: 'For Me and My Gal'. She'd drunk more gin than usual, was feeling brave. If Albie wasn't interested in her, it was best she knew so she could move on and find another man with the right credentials. Life at home wasn't getting any easier.

'Where you going?' asked Aggie.

'To speak to Albie. I'll be back in a minute.'

Albie was talking to a man, but Queenie marched over and tapped him on the shoulder nevertheless. It was shit or bust time. 'I'm sorry to interrupt you, but could I have a quick word alone with you, Albie?'

'Of course, lovey. It's Queenie, isn't it? I always remember your name as my dear departed nan was a Queenie too,' Albie smiled, leading her over to a quiet corner of the pub.

Queenie took a deep breath and looked up into the dazzling green eyes of the man who towered over her. 'I'm not going to beat around the bush, Albie. I like you. You seem a nice man and I was wondering if you'd like to accompany me to the dance that's being held in the church hall in Stepney next Saturday evening?'

For once in his life, Albie Butler was at a loss for words. He'd been aware that Queenie was sweet on him, like many other women were. But never had one been so bullish as to march up to him and ask him on a date before. That took guts. It was always the gentleman's duty to ask the lady.

Albie studied Queenie. Her blonde mate was far more his usual type. But there was something endearing about Queenie and he could hardly say no to her face, could he? 'It would be my pleasure to accompany you to the dance next Saturday.'

CHAPTER TEN

Queenie could barely contain her excitement, waiting for the following Saturday to arrive. It had been difficult to keep a lid on it at work, but thankfully she'd had Mary to confide in of an evening. This would be her first proper date and she felt ready to start courting. Daniel had annoyed her on New Year's Day. It was cruel of him to show such interest in her when he was married with a child. It was definitely time to forget all about Daniel O'Leary.

'Look at you! You look a picture, sweetheart. You truly do,' gushed Molly. The smart black dress and red pillbox hat she'd bought at cost price from Cohen's looked so classy. As did her stiletto shoes.

Vivian could not help but feel envious. Queenie was all grown up now and Viv was dying to see what Albie was like. 'Why isn't Albie coming here then? Is it because he's ugly?'

'No,' Queenie snapped. 'Because of Dad. No way do I want Albie bumping into our father.'

'Where you meeting him then?' Vivian enquired.

'Not telling you, because if I do you'll follow me. Please don't let her follow me, will you, Mum.'

'You get off and have a wonderful time, love. Viv's staying here with me,' Molly smiled. She was so excited for Queenie, what with this being her first proper date.

Queenie picked up her handbag. 'Bye then. I won't be too late.'

Albie Butler owned two suits, one black, one grey, which he'd alternate every time he went out of an evening. Tonight he was wearing the black one, with a white shirt, black shoes and striped tie.

Lighting up a Woodbine, Albie leaned against the outside of the Blind Beggar pub. It had been Queenie's idea to meet here, but he'd never felt less enthusiastic about going out on a date. Queenie seemed a nice enough girl, but he'd been very tempted to blow her out when his mates had informed him they were going to a party up the Commercial Road tonight. His conscience had got the better of him though. Deep down he had a good heart and would hate the thought of the girl hanging around waiting for him like a lemon, especially if she'd spent ages getting ready.

Glancing at a smart woman in stiletto shoes and a pillbox hat walking towards him, Albie looked at his watch. Queenie was ten minutes late. He'd give her another twenty minutes, then go out with his mates.

'Hello. Sorry I'm a bit late.'

Albie dropped his cigarette in shock. The smart woman walking towards him in her heels with the pillbox hat on was Queenie.

The live band was fabulous. Queenie had never jived properly before, but Albie soon taught her how to as the band played Glenn Miller songs. Everybody was up and dancing. If the war had taught East Enders anything, it was to grab life with both hands and enjoy every minute while they could.

'I've had a lovely evening, Queenie. Thank you for inviting me,' said Albie Butler, as they walked down the Mile End Road.

To say Albie was pleasantly surprised by how well this particular date had gone would be putting it mildly. Not only had Queenie turned up looking a million dollars, she was very articulate and bright for a seventeen-year-old. His mother was always telling him he chose the wrong kind of girls and he had a feeling that she would really like Queenie. His mother hadn't liked his ex-fiancée one little bit. She'd said she was 'shallow'.

'Do you fancy going on another date in the week, Queenie? Any evening suits me.'

Queenie smiled. 'Yes. I would like that very much.'

'This is my road. I'll be fine from here. Thank you for a lovely evening, Albie.'

'I must walk you to your door, Queenie.'

'No,' Queenie snapped. 'It's my dad. Long story, but I'll explain more when I see you Tuesday.'

Albie bent down and kissed Queenie on her right cheek. 'See you at seven on Tuesday outside the Blind Beggar then.'

'Bye, Albie,' Queenie grinned.

Queenie's smile soon vanished as she approached her house and thanked God that Albie wasn't there to hear the shouting coming from inside. As she opened the front door, Viv was sitting on the stairs, white as a ghost and shaking.

'Thank God you're home,' Vivvy cried. 'Dad's accusing Mum of having an affair with an American serviceman.'

Queenie burst into the front room. 'Get off her, you bastard,' she bellowed. Her father had her mother pinned to the floor and was prodding her with the poker they used to stoke the fire.

Eric Wade turned his head towards his eldest. 'Get upstairs, you. Now,' he slurred.

Queenie picked up the lump of cast iron they used as a doorstop. 'I said, get off Mum,' she hissed.

'No, Queenie, no,' Molly pleaded, tears streaming down her cheeks. 'Please, sweetheart, put that down. Do it for me.'

Standing behind her sister, Vivian gingerly grabbed the doorstep. 'Do as Mum says, Queen.'

Queenie let go of the object. If she got sent to jail for murder, there'd be nobody to look after her mum and Viv.

Eric went sprawling as he tried to stand up, then managed the simple task on his second attempt. He had rarely laid a hand on his daughters in the past, but furious, he slapped Queenie hard around the face.

'No. Eric, nooo!' cried Molly.

'Leave Queenie alone,' Vivian shrieked.

'Get to bed, the pair of ya, and don't you ever speak to me like that again. I'm your father. I put the food on the table in this house. Show some bloody respect.'

Molly stood up and forced a smile. 'Do as your dad says, girls. Go on, go to bed. It's late.'

Tears of pure anger streamed down Queenie's face as she bolted up the stairs. She would never forget her first proper date. But now she would remember it for all the wrong reasons.

The following morning the atmosphere was fraught, to

say the least. With rations at an all-time low, Sunday was the only day the family all sat down together to tuck into a cooked breakfast, but this morning neither Queenie or Viv was hungry.

'You have to leave him, Mum,' Queenie insisted. The bastard was still in bed and he had left more than a hand mark across her face. He'd caught her with the big aluminium ring he wore, which had left a very noticeable bruise on her cheekbone. She couldn't tell the girls in work the truth tomorrow, she'd have to pretend she'd fallen down the stairs or something. Just like her mum always did.

'And where we going to go, now Edna's gone? How we meant to pay rent and put food on the table without your dad?' Molly replied in a low voice.

'He's getting up,' Vivian hissed.

Eric Wade came down the stairs with a heavy heart. The previous evening was patchy, but he could clearly remember slapping Queenie. The war hadn't helped his anger issues. He'd seen some awful things while serving his country. Men had their heads and limbs blown off while in close proximity to him. Then he'd taken a bullet and the limp he'd been left with made him feel far less of a man than the one he was before. Eric knew he was lucky to be alive, but it didn't seem that way at times. The war haunted him. And sometimes when he closed his eyes at night he wished that he were dead.

Tuesday arrived and after bolting down her dinner, Queenie darted upstairs to get ready. She didn't have a lot of nice clothes. Few women did since they'd lowered the rationing coupons. She tried on her grey utility frock and was surprised at how much nicer it looked with her blonde hair, bright red lipstick, thick black mascara and stockings with the black pen drawn line up the back. Utility clothing was labelled CC41 and been introduced by the government during the war. Queenie smiled. Mrs O'Leary had kindly slipped her a couple of extra ration coupons earlier that Patrick and Daniel were getting hold of. She'd use those at the weekend to buy a more glamorous outfit.

Queenie smiled at her reflection. Working in the shop and meeting Doreen had taught her a lot about fashion. So had reading *Woman's Own*, *Everywoman* and *Star Weekly*. Those were the three magazines herself, Doreen and Eliza read. They would each buy a copy, then swap them over once read. Apparently Hitler hated women looking glamorous. He didn't want them wearing make-up or perfume back in Germany. That's why the magazines urged all women in England to do themselves up to the nines. Not only did it make you feel better, by doing so you were also getting one over on that bastard Hitler.

Vivian sat on the bed. She couldn't wait to leave school herself, get a posh job and wear nice clothes and make-up. 'You look nice. Where is Albie taking you?'

'Thanks,' Queenie smiled. 'I don't know where he's taking me yet.'

'When will we get to meet him?'

'Soon, hopefully. That's if all goes well, of course.'

It was Albie's idea they go to a pub for their second date so they could get to know one another a bit better. 'We can hardly rabbit all the way through a film, can we?' he chuckled.

Queenie had seen enough of Albie to guess he only

owned two suits. Tonight he was wearing the grey one and as usual looked clean and smart. Not as suave as Daniel, but Daniel only wore the best clobber and had a style of his own, as did Patrick.

Albie's choice of pub was the Hoop and Grapes in Aldgate. As he sauntered inside, lots of people made a fuss of him, shaking his hand and slapping him on the back. Queenie was impressed by this. Was Albie a bit of a force to be reckoned with, like Daniel, she wondered?

'Hello, me old china. Who's this lovely lady? I'll get these,' said the man behind the bar.

'Thanks, Micky. This is Queenie. She'll have a gin and tonic and I'll have a pint of stout please, mate.'

Micky winked at Queenie. 'Punching above his weight with you, is our Albie.'

Albie chuckled and put a protective arm around Queenie's shoulders. 'Take no notice, my dear. He's only jealous.'

Albie led Queenie over to a table in the corner. 'It's quiet 'ere and we won't be pestered.'

'You seem well known in here. Is this your local?'

'No. I used to sing in 'ere on a Sunday lunchtime. Micky's a good pal of mine. He sings too. Everyone calls him Micky One Ear. If you look at his left ear, he lost half of it. Was bitten off by a dog I believe, but Micky likes people to think he lost it in a fight,' laughed Albie. 'He's not long taken over as landlord. Gonna give me my Sunday lunchtimes back soon.'

'Do you have a day job too?'

'Nah. My old mum's disabled, bless her. She's only got one leg. Me and my brother Bert take it in turns to look after her. He works daytimes and I work the nights. I don't just sing, I've got other money coming in. I'm me

118

own person, me. Prefer earning a few bob for meself than making some other git rich,' Albie grinned. 'What about you? Tell me more about your job.'

Queenie told Albie all about life working at Cohen's shop and how much she enjoyed her job. He had just gone up in her estimation if anything. Not many men would look after their disabled mother. That alone showed what a good heart he had. His brother must be a decent man too. 'I take it you live with your mum then?'

'Yeah. And my brother. We got a house in Whitechapel.'

'Whitechapel!' Queenie was shocked. She'd never seen Albie around before. 'Whereabouts?'

Queenie's heart sank a little when Albie reeled off his address. That was the street her mum had once forbidden herself and Viv to play in. The church on the corner had been bombed during the Blitz and it had since become a haven for prostitutes to work from.

'Tell me more about your family, Queenie,' Albie smiled.

Queenie spoke fondly about her mum and sister, then finally mentioned her father. She didn't go into too much detail, just told Albie he would stagger home drunk often. Thankfully, the hand mark on her face had now vanished and the bruise she'd managed to cover up with face powder.

'What's your dad's name?'

'Eric. Eric Wade. Do you know him?' Queenie asked, praying that Albie didn't.

'I don't know him personally, but I know of him,' Albie said truthfully. Eric Wade had a reputation all right, as a violent, drunken shitbag who terrorized the brasses. People talked in the East End and he hadn't heard a good word about the man.

Queenie could feel her cheeks reddening. She didn't know the half of what they said about her dad, but she could imagine. She stuttered out an excuse. 'He got shot and was medically discharged from the army last year. Since he's been home, things have got worse. I keep urging my mum to leave him, but she won't. She says we won't manage on our own, but I know we'd be happier, even if we were poorer,' Queenie explained.

Albie leaned across the table and squeezed Queenie's hands. His own father had run off with another woman when he and his brother were young, so he'd had it tough too. 'The war's had a strange effect on a lot of men who came home battered and bruised,' he said kindly.

'Did you get called up?' Queenie asked.

'Erm, no. I wanted to fight, of course. But I'm Mum's carer. She'd never manage alone. Fancy another drink, love?'

Queenie smiled. 'Yes, please.'

The rest of the evening went smoothly. Conversation flowed easily with Albie and Queenie liked the fact he was popular and witty. He made her laugh out loud. He didn't give her butterflies like Daniel, but now Daniel was married with a child, Queenie had to move on. She couldn't wait to be a mum, have sons of her own.

'Did you have a nice evening, Queenie?' Albie asked, as they reached the corner of her street.

Queenie squeezed his arm. 'Yes, thanks. I really enjoyed myself.'

'Good. You coming down the Beehive on Friday?'

'Erm, yes. That's if you want me to?'

Albie tilted Queenie's chin and stared into her eyes. 'Of course I do. You're my girl now, ain't ya?'

CHAPTER ELEVEN

So, that's how I became Albie Butler's girl. And once I had my claws in him, I had no intention of letting him go.

We soon fell into an easy routine. I would proudly watch my man sing in the Beehive on a Friday and the Hoop and Grapes of a Sunday, and Albie would take me out twice in the week and on a Saturday night.

I met his mum, Ida. She was a large lady in a wheelchair who stank of piss. But she was nice enough, had a lovely kind face, and I kind of felt sorry for her. It was my idea that on my day off in the week, Albie and I take his mum out. We'd wheel her down Roman Road market and treat her to pie and mash. Ida loved going out and made no secret she thought I was the greatest thing since sliced bread. She was forever singing my praises to Albie.

After we'd been courting for around four months, I plucked up the courage to invite Albie round to meet my family. My dad was on his best behaviour, which I found weird, but he knew of Albie and was keen to meet him properly. As for my mum and Viv, they'd been pestering me to bring him home for months.

My mum liked Albie on sight, thought he was charming.

My dad got on exceptionally well with him too. But Vivvy played up. She spent the whole time Albie was there with a face like a smacked arse and when she wasn't asking stupid questions, she was being downright rude. In the end my dad sent her to bed and apologized to Albie. 'Younger sister syndrome. The green-eyed monster,' he explained.

Albie just laughed Viv's antics off, but I was furious and confronted her the next day. 'Don't like him,' was the only explanation I got before my sister stomped off. I didn't bother arguing with her after that. Mum hit the nail on the head when she said, 'Her nose has been put out of joint.'

Mrs O'Leary liked Albie too. 'He's handsome and he's kind, Queenie. I could sense that the moment he walked in. He'll never lay a hand on you, believe me, and I'm a good judge of character,' said Mary, clasping her rosary beads. 'I know you had your heart set on our Daniel, but you let that boy go now, Queenie.'

Like any couple, Albie and I had our ups and downs. One night he put his hand on my right breast and I responded by slapping him around the face and not speaking to him for the best part of a week.

Mary had told me, 'Make Albie wait until he marries you, love. Get that ring on your finger first, otherwise my boys will be after him.'

'But what's it like, Mary? You know, properly – not what happened to me before. If I marry Albie, I'll need to know what to do.'

'Lie back and think of Ireland – or England in your case – darlin'. Sex is only enjoyable for men. No pleasure for us women. But it provides us with the biggest gift of all: children. Where would I be without my two boys?

You're a beautiful young woman, Queenie, and this is your time to shine. Don't be worrying about that Doreen. As I've told you before, lushes are only good for one thing to men. Sex. Albie's taken with you. You'd have handsome children with him, let me tell ya. I'd snap him up if I were you, providing he treats you right, of course.'

So that was that. The end of my sex education – and I was still none the wiser. There were so many questions I wanted to ask, but I couldn't.

Nobody was more surprised than me when Terry Marney got down on one knee and proposed to Aggie Brown on her birthday. We were in the Beehive at the time. Aggie squealed with delight, threw her arms around Terry's neck and shrieked, 'Yes!'

I was genuinely pleased for Aggie. Terry was a decent, hard-working lad and he and Aggie were very well suited. I couldn't help feeling just a tad jealous at the same time though. She had told me only the previous week that they'd already discussed how many children they wanted. Albie and I had never discussed anything of the sort and the one time I had tried to broach the subject, Albie had laughed it off, treated it as a joke.

I still hadn't got around to telling Doreen and Eliza I was dating Albie. I had planned to, a few months earlier, when Doreen was loved up with Jimmy Foster.

All weekend I had rehearsed what I was going to say, ready to blurt out on the Monday morning that Albie had asked me on a date. But when I got into work that day, Doreen was bawling her eyes out with Eliza consoling her. 'Whatever's wrong?' I asked.

'It's Jimmy. He's married,' Doreen sobbed.

'Oh no,' I mumbled. At thirty, Jimmy was a lot older than Doreen and he'd been a bit unreliable. A couple of

*times, he hadn't turned up for a date and had come up
with some cock-and-bull excuse. I had wondered did he
have a girlfriend, but I was stunned he was married. 'How
did you find out?' I enquired.*

*'It doesn't matter, does it? I lost my virginity to him. I
feel such a fool,' Doreen wept.*

*Seeing as I was the one who'd introduced Jimmy to
Doreen and brought him over to our table, I could hardly
then admit I was dating Albie Butler, the bloke Doreen'd
had designs on in the first place.*

*So I kept schtum, said sod all. But secrets always have
a way of worming their way out into the open, don't they?*

Queenie was showing the latest stock to Mrs Ackerman,
an extremely wealthy Jewish lady who tended to buy in
bulk, when she heard a familiar voice behind her asking
the price of something.

Queenie froze. It was Trappy Linda, who worked behind
the bar in the Beehive. Desperate not to be recognized,
Queenie quietly suggested Mrs Ackerman try on the items
she'd already chosen. The changing room was out the back.

'No, thank you. I'd much rather try everything on
together,' Mrs Ackerman snapped.

'Queenie!'

Cringing and blushing, Queenie had no alternative but
to turn around. 'Hello, Linda.'

Linda grinned. 'Albie said you worked in a shop, but I
didn't know you worked in a posh one like this. Well
expensive this clobber, ain't it? Any chance of a discount
for Albie's favourite barmaid?' Linda chuckled.

Feeling her face flush, Queenie glanced towards Doreen
and Eliza. Both were looking her way. She glared at Linda,
a warning look. 'I know you're *Alfie's* favourite barmaid,'

Queenie said in a loud voice. 'But I'm afraid I can't give you a discount. My boss will kill me,' she added, smiling nervously at Eliza and Doreen.

'Oh right. Never mind. Best I go down the market to treat myself to something new. I couldn't afford a pair of bleedin' drawers in this gaff,' Linda laughed.

Mrs Ackerman looked around in horror. 'Charming,' she mumbled.

'Bye, Linda. I've got work to do. See you soon,' Queenie gabbled.

'You not down the Beehive tonight?'

'Erm, no. I don't think so.'

'Oh well. I'll tell loverboy I saw you. Bye, Queenie.'

As usual, Mrs Ackerman tried on about twenty outfits and while Queenie was assisting her, she tried to get her story straight. She knew it would be easier to come clean, but while Doreen was still in pieces over finding out Jimmy Foster was married, she could not bring herself to rub salt in her friend's wounds.

'Eliza, Mrs Ackerman would like to purchase these items,' Queenie smiled as she came out the back with an armful of clothes. Because of the amount she bought, Eliza always gave Mrs Ackerman a decent discount.

Expecting a barrage of questions, Queenie was surprised when she approached Doreen and her friend sparked up a conversation about a film she wanted to see at the pictures.

The rest of the day went slowly and Queenie was shocked that neither Doreen nor Eliza had pulled her on what Trappy Linda had said. They must have heard something, surely? Linda's gob was bigger than Hitler's. 'I'm off now, girls. Have a lovely weekend and I'll see you Monday,' Queenie said jovially.

Doreen smiled falsely. 'Bye, mate. Have a good un. Don't do anything I wouldn't do.'

'See you Monday, Queenie,' Eliza waved.

When the door closed behind Queenie, Doreen turned to Eliza. 'Two-faced bitch. I'm going down that Beehive tonight and I shall have great pleasure watching that lying cow squirm. I knew she was up to something, I knew she was seeing someone. No wonder she fixed me up with that bastard Jimmy. She was after Albie herself, that's why. I'll never forgive her for this, Eliza. Not ever.'

Doreen was very rough and ready, but had a heart of gold and Eliza was extremely fond of her. Queenie, on the other hand, was a bit of a dark horse. 'I'll come to the Beehive with you tonight. My dad will pick us up and drop us off. I honestly think there is some mix-up though. Albie and Queenie don't work for me as a couple. No disrespect to Queenie, Dor, but Albie could have his pick of all eligible women. Why would he pick Queenie?'

'Because she's a conniving cow who'll stop at nothing to get what she wants. I told you, every time she went to the bar, my drinks tasted stronger. She wanted me to get drunk and show myself up; I'd put money on it.'

'Oh, I don't think she'd stoop that low, Doreen.'

'Really? Well, let's find out how low she's stooped when we surprise her in the Beehive later, shall we?'

Sitting at her usual table with Aggie and Terry, Queenie smiled as Albie sang 'Me and My Girl'. He always looked at her while singing that song and she loved everybody in the pub knowing she was his girl.

Five minutes later, Doreen and Eliza walked in and Queenie wanted the floor to open up and swallow her.

'What am I gonna do, Aggie? As far as Albie knows my work friends know about our relationship.'

'Well, you can't exactly ignore 'em. Go over and, oops, they're coming over 'ere.'

'Good evening, Queenie. I thought you were staying in this evening,' Doreen smirked.

'Erm, I was. Then Aggie twisted my arm to go out, didn't you, Aggs?'

'Yes. I invited Queenie out with me and Terry.'

'Ahh, that's nice,' Doreen's tone was full of sarcasm and Queenie could tell she knew.

'Go and snatch those two chairs, Eliza. You don't mind us sitting with you, do you, Queenie?' Doreen grinned.

'No. Course not.'

'Shuffle up then.'

'I'll get us a drink,' said Eliza. She felt awkward and kind of wished she hadn't offered to accompany Doreen now.

'Just a single for me. Don't get me a double like some people do,' Doreen shouted out.

Feeling the bad vibes, Terry Marney couldn't wait to get away from the table. 'I'm going to have a chat with Mick the Fish. You coming to say hello to him, Aggie?'

'No. I'll stay with Queenie.'

Doreen sipped her drink while watching Albie try to catch Queenie's eye. She was livid. She had truly thought of Queenie as one of her best friends.

Knowing the game was up, Queenie took a deep breath. 'There's something I need to tell you, Doreen. I wanted to tell you before now, but when you found out Jimmy was married, I didn't know how to.'

'Cut the bullshit, Queenie. I heard every word your loudmouth mate said in the shop earlier. Alfie, my arse. I hate fucking liars. My mum reckons they're worse than thieves. You are a conniving, nasty little bitch and I do hope you have the decency to jack in your job as I never want to lay eyes on you again.'

Queenie was stunned. 'It's not my fault that Albie preferred me to you, is it? Perhaps if you hadn't acted like a drunken tramp on New Year's Eve, throwing yourself at him, things might have been different for you. That's why I never told you. I knew you'd be jealous. As for my job, I ain't going nowhere. You leave the shop.'

Eliza was horrified. People were looking. 'Come on, Doreen. Let's go.'

'You evil little cow,' Doreen shrieked, chucking her drink in Queenie's face.

Spotting the fracas, Albie appeared by Queenie's side. 'What's going on? You OK, my love?'

'Yes, I'm fine thanks, Albie.'

'Come on, Doreen. Let's go,' Eliza urged, grabbing her friend by the arm. Her dad would be furious if he heard about this. He liked Doreen, but didn't approve of his daughter socializing with her outside of work. He said she was a common shiksa with a drink inside her.

Doreen stood up. 'Albie Butler. The man who sells bootleg booze for a living. Oh yes, I've done my homework on you too, asked around. Good luck to the pair of you. You deserve one another.'

CHAPTER TWELVE

The following week was an awful one for Queenie. The atmosphere at work was toxic. Doreen wouldn't speak to her at all and Queenie could tell Eliza was on Doreen's side.

On her day off, Queenie went to visit Ida, and spotted her drunken father going inside the bombed church with a dirty old brass. She was shocked to her core. Queenie debated whether to march in there and catch him in the act, but decided not to. Hopefully he'd leave her mum alone tonight if he'd sown his oats elsewhere, the dirty disgusting bastard.

On the Friday, Queenie couldn't face work, so took a day off sick. Albie's attitude had started to annoy her and she'd stomped off in a huff last night on their date. She needed to speak to Mrs O'Leary, get some advice.

'What's up, darling? Why you not at work? You mustn't let that Doreen get to you,' yawned Mary. She couldn't stop sleeping just lately, was forever tired. Patrick wanted her to see a doctor, but Mary wasn't keen on being prodded and pulled about. She insisted she felt OK in herself.

Kimberley Chambers

'It's not just Doreen. It's everything. I had a row with Albie last night. He'll never discuss marriage or kids, treats both subjects as a joke. I know he was engaged to that other girl, so why won't he propose to me? I wanna settle down and have a family while I'm young, Mary. I'm not sure Albie's taking our relationship as seriously as I am. He's too laid back.'

'Give him an ultimatum. Tell him you're keen to get married and start a family and if he doesn't feel the same, then perhaps you should call it a day. Talk to his mum as well. You know she's very fond of you. She might give him the kick up the arse he needs to put a ring on your finger.'

'But what if he says he isn't ready to settle down?'

'Tell him it's over. That'll give him food for thought. You're beautiful inside and out, Queenie. Albie'll do no better than you, and if he can't see that, best you finish with him and court a man who appreciates you more.'

'Do you think I'm being a bit rash? I mean, we haven't been together that long, have we? I just hate my dad so much, I need to get out of there. I want a home of my own.'

'Then you gotta take the bull by the horns, darling. Have it out with Albie once and for all. Life's too short to be wasting your time on a man who is not willing to commit.'

Queenie smiled. 'Yes. You're right. I'll have it out with him tonight. Thanks, Mary. I dunno what I'd do without you at times.'

Queenie took a special effort to get ready that evening. She put on her classy black frock, knowing that was Albie's favourite. Mary did her make-up and she finished

130

it off with bright red lipstick. The price of cosmetics had gone through the roof during the war, but luckily Patrick and Daniel could get hold of them on the cheap. She and Mary got theirs for nothing.

Hearing a wolf whistle, Queenie turned around. It was Daniel. He was alone. 'Looking good, Queenie. Where you off to?'

'She's going to the Beehive to give her bloke an ultimatum, aren't you, darling?' replied Mary.

Queenie felt embarrassed. She didn't want Daniel knowing her business.

'Why. What's he done?' Daniel's green eyes flashed with curiosity.

'Nothing. We had words last night, that's all,' Queenie snapped.

'I'm out on the ale tonight. I might pop in the Beehive later, check this bloke of yours out. Someone has to make sure he's good enough for ya.'

'No. I'll be fine, honest.' The last person Queenie wanted turning up there was Daniel.

'You sticking your oar in ain't gonna help. You stick to your usual haunts,' ordered Mary.

Queenie felt butterflies in her stomach. Daniel was giving her his intense gaze that always made her feel funny. She stood up. 'I'll be off now, Mary. Aggie's expecting me to knock for her.'

'OK, love. Pop over in the morning; let me know how you got on. Good luck.'

As Mary went into the kitchen, Daniel saw Queenie out. He took her hand, 'Queenie, don't go there tonight. Come out with me. By the sounds of it, this geezer doesn't deserve you.'

Queenie shook him off, 'You have no right to say who

I can and can't be with, Daniel O'Leary. You're a married man.' Her eyes welled up as she looked up at him.

'I'm just looking out for you, Queen, don't be getting upset now, darling.' He touched her face.

'Daniel – want a cuppa?' Mary hollered from inside. 'Where are you, boy?'

Queenie stepped away. 'Let me live my life,' she hissed.

'I'm sorry.'

Without a backwards glance, Queenie ran from the only man she'd ever truly love.

Albie was surprised to see Queenie walk in with Terry and Aggie later that evening. He'd had a feeling she wouldn't turn up tonight. He walked straight over to her and put his hand gently on her back. 'You OK, Queen? Can I get you a drink?'

'No, thanks. Terry's getting them.'

'I'm glad you came,' smiled Albie.

Queenie smiled back. 'Me too. But we need to talk, after you've finished work. I have some stuff I need to get off my chest.'

Albie nodded. 'Fine.'

Queenie sat in her usual seat, then halfway through the evening, did what Mary had urged her to do a while back. She walked up to Albie and asked if she could sing a song.

'Erm, yeah, of course.' Albie handed Queenie the mike as she whispered to the pianist her song choice. Queenie then blew everyone away with a fantastic rendition of 'You Are My Sunshine'.

'Wow! I didn't know you could sing like that,' Albie said, as Queenie handed him the mike back.

'You never asked me, did ya?'

'Hello, Queenie. How you doing? You got a brilliant voice,' gushed Freddie Angel. He'd been a year above Queenie at school and had always had a soft spot for her.

'Freddie! Come and sit down with us. I haven't seen you for ages. Where you been hiding?'

'I was away doing my police training. I'm a copper now, look,' Freddie said, proudly showing Queenie his badge.

'Good for you. I always remember you saying you wanted to be a policeman when you were a little boy.'

Queenie continued chatting to Freddie, glancing at Albie, hoping he was jealous. He didn't seem to be, was singing along happily without a care in the world.

'I've got to go now, Queenie. I'm on duty early tomorrow. It's been wonderful seeing you. You look so glamorous now – not that you looked bad at school,' gabbled Freddie. 'Erm, would you do me the honour of coming on a date with me in the week? We can go for a meal, to the pictures, wherever you want.'

Queenie glanced at Albie. He was still taking no notice, annoyingly. 'I'm actually seeing someone at the moment, Freddie. But it's not going too well, between you and me. If I end it, have you got a contact number or address?'

Freddie scribbled down a number. 'You can call me at work. If I'm not there, just leave a message and I'll get back to you,' beamed Freddie.

Queenie liked Freddie, but not in a romantic way. He wasn't bad looking, had a cheeky face, but no way did Queenie want to date a copper. The O'Learys would be horrified for a start. However, Freddie might come in handy in her quest to snare Albie.

Freddie kissed Queenie on the cheek. 'Bye then, Queenie. I hope to hear from you soon.'

'Bye, Freddie.'

Aggie moved nearer to Queenie. Terry was up at the bar, chatting. 'Did Freddie ask you out?'

'Yeah. He didn't realize I was courting.'

'You got another admirer an' all.'

'Who?'

'Daniel O'Leary. He came in about ten minutes ago. He's standing at the bar and is yet to take his eyes off you.'

Shocked, Queenie looked around and Daniel grinned. She sighed. Her stomach was doing somersaults again.

Daniel strutted over. 'That weren't him, the geezer who just left, was it?'

'No.'

'Good. 'Cause you're not bringing the filth back to our street. Where is he then?'

'He's the singer.'

Daniel studied Albie for a few seconds, then turned back to Queenie. 'Did you pick him 'cause he looks a bit like me?' he chuckled.

Queenie felt flustered. 'No. Don't flatter yourself. I picked him 'cause he's a nice man.'

'Didn't sound like it earlier when you were talking to Mum.'

Queenie rolled her eyes. 'What you doing 'ere, Daniel?'

'I need to talk to you in private. Come outside with me.'

Queenie noticed Albie looking as she followed Daniel outside the pub. 'What's this about, Daniel? You're clearly very drunk.'

'It's about you and me. I like you a lot and I know you feel the same.'

'You're married with a baby.'

'Yeah, but I don't love her. I hate the thought of you being with a bloke, settling down. I've got money, plenty of it, and I can give you kids. As many as you want. So how about it? I can set you up in a lovely little drum somewhere. Not round 'ere obviously. How about Essex?'

Queenie was stunned, her legs like jelly and her heart soaring. 'What, you're going to leave Bridie?'

'Well, no. I would if I could, but I can't, can I? Mother would go apeshit and I've got a nipper.'

'Are you asking me to be your mistress then? Your dirty little secret?'

'Nah. You'd be far more than that. I think a lot of you, Queenie.'

Queenie was devastated. She had dreamed of this moment and yet again he'd let her down.

'I'd never lower myself to be some man's bit on the side and I could never betray your mum in such a way. How dare you even ask me such a thing!'

Daniel shrugged. 'Suit yourself, but see him in there, he's one of life's losers. I could give you the life of Riley. Think about it.'

Queenie was about to reply when Albie came outside. 'Everything all right, Queenie?'

Queenie glared at Daniel, 'Yes. This is Daniel, Mary's son. He's just leaving.'

Queenie's mind was all over the place for the rest of the evening. She couldn't concentrate on chatting to Aggie, or watching Albie sing. She'd told Aggie that Daniel had wanted to speak to her about his mum. No way would she tell anybody what he'd said, especially Mary. Mary would go bloody ballistic. What front he had to expect her to settle for a life as his mistress. Who the hell did Daniel O'Leary think he was? That was the first time she'd ever seen him drunk and she'd hated his cockiness.

If he'd told her he would divorce Bridie, things might have been different. But even then, she could never break Mary's heart. It truly was time to forget about Daniel for good. An arrogant womanizer like her father, that's what he was, Queenie tried convincing herself. But she was hurt more than she could have ever imagined. The knot deep down in her stomach wouldn't go.

By the time the pub emptied and Queenie sat with Albie at a table in the corner, she wasn't in the best of moods. Albie smiled. 'I'm sorry if I upset you last night. I'm not quite sure what I did wrong though.'

'Whenever I mention marriage or kids you seem to think it's some big joke, Albie,' Queenie replied, before pouring her heart out.

Albie listened in earnest. 'We can't rush into things, love. We've only been together a matter of months. Of course I'm serious about you and Mum adores you too.'

Queenie sighed. 'Aggie and Terry had only been together a matter of months, but he proposed to her. I want to settle down, have children while I'm young.'

'I want to settle down too and have kids. One day. I'm different to Terry. I've never rushed into things.'

'But you were engaged to Suzanne,' Queenie argued.

'Yeah, I was young, foolish. That's why I'm more wary now.'

'We're getting nowhere are we, Albie? It seems we want different things in life, so it's best we call it a day, I think.'

Albie leaned across the table and held Queenie's hands. 'Don't say that, Queen. We get on smashing and we do want the same things. I just feel we should get to know one another better before signing up for any serious shit.'

Queenie snatched her hands away and stood up. 'I'm

sorry, Albie. My mind's made up. I wish you well for the future.'

Albie Butler was stunned as Queenie stomped out of the pub.

Queenie contacted Freddie, but decided to be fairly straight with him. She was using him, therefore didn't want to build his hopes up. He deserved better.

'I'm so pleased you rang me, Queenie,' Freddie grinned, as he kissed her on the cheek outside the Blind Beggar.

'This isn't exactly a date, Freddie. I have broken up with my ex, but it's too soon for me to jump straight into another relationship. I do hope that's OK with you?'

'Of course. Where would you like to go? There's a good film on at the cinema.'

'I so enjoyed our chat the other night, I thought we might go to a pub. The Hoop and Grapes have a woman on the piano tonight. Let's go there.'

Micky One Ear looked at Queenie with a bemused expression on his face. 'All right, sweetheart? No Albie tonight?'

Queenie had known Albie wouldn't be in the Hoop and Grapes this evening – he was singing at a wedding reception – but she was certain she could rely on Micky One Ear to inform him that she'd been in there with another man. 'No. We've split up. This is Freddie. We went to school together.'

'Oh, right,' replied Micky. He was shocked Albie hadn't told him. He'd been in on Sunday, singing.

Freddie felt a bit of a fool. 'No wonder you wanted to bring me 'ere, Queen. You hoping to make your ex jealous, or what?'

'No,' Queenie lied. 'I just like watching the woman sing

and play piano. She reminds me of Aunt Edna.'

Queenie had a nice time catching up with Freddie, but as they said goodnight, she knew she wouldn't bother going out with him again. He really liked her, she could tell, so to string him along was wrong.

Albie Butler missed Queenie and his mother was on his case too. 'That poor girl has an awful home life with that father of hers. You'll have a struggle finding a better woman than Queenie, let me tell ya. She knocks spots of all your exes, especially that up-her-arse Suzanne you proposed to,' ranted Ida Butler. 'None of your other girlfriends have ever given me the time of day, apart from Queenie. She's got a heart of gold and will make a wonderful wife and mother. She's caring, considerate and reliable.'

'But what's the rush to get hitched, Mum?' argued Albie. 'We've not even been together six months.'

Albie wasn't sure what was making him have cold feet about it all, but something in his waters felt wrong.

Ida shrugged. 'Up to you, boy, but you'll regret it if you lose her and she finds someone else. My health ain't great. I won't make old bones. There's nothing more I'd like than to see you settled down with a nice girl. You're not a teenager any more, Albie, you're knocking on a bit, truth be told. Besides, I know you're missing Queenie, 'cause you wouldn't have been moping around indoors all week if you weren't.'

'I'm twenty-four, Mum, not forty! But I get your drift. I'm off to work now.'

Albie thought about his mother's words as he walked towards the Hoop and Grapes. It was nine days now since Queenie had ended their courtship and he hadn't been his usual jolly self since. He'd hated it when Aggie and Terry

138

had turned up in the Beehive on Friday night without Queenie. It just wasn't the same.

'Morning. You all right, stranger?' asked Micky One Ear.

'Not really. Pour us a pint, Mick. I ain't been in 'cause I split up with Queenie.'

Micky plonked the pint on the bar. 'Yeah, I know. I hate to break it to you, but she was in 'ere on Thursday night.'

'Was she! Who with?'

'Some bloke she went to school with.'

Having just taken a large gulp, Albie spat his beer out all over the bar.

Queenie sat in Mrs O'Leary's by the window. She knew if Albie hadn't been in the Hoop and Grapes beforehand, he would definitely hear about her being in there with Freddie today.

Mary reckoned she was psychic and swore blind Albie would turn up today, begging forgiveness. Queenie wasn't so sure, but was feeling excited nevertheless.

'My Daniel ain't happy with Bridie you know, Queen. He turned up yesterday half-cut and poured his heart out to me. Gave him what for, I did. I said he should've thought of that before getting her in the family way. I don't like seeing him unhappy, but he's made his bleedin' bed, love. He has to lie in that now.'

'Yeah. You're right,' replied Queenie. She hadn't seen Daniel since the night he'd turned up in the Beehive and for once she had no desire to. 'Gawd, stone the crows!' Queenie craned her neck. 'It's Albie. I'm sure it's him.'

Mary rushed to the window. 'Yep. That's Albie all right. What did I tell ya!'

Queenie felt her tummy doing somersaults as she

watched Albie knock at her front door and her mum point at Mary's house. She hadn't even told her mum or Viv they'd split up. Aggie had kept schtum for her too.

'Right, sit in the armchair, pretend you're reading the paper. Act like you're not that bothered,' Mary advised, as she went to open the front door.

'Hello, Mary,' smiled Albie. 'Molly said Queenie is 'ere. I need to speak to her.'

'Come in, love. Queenie, Albie's here, wants to speak to you.'

Queenie looked up from the newspaper. She could smell the alcohol fumes. Dutch courage, she imagined. 'Oh, hello, Albie. What do I owe this pleasure?' she asked, sounding far calmer than she felt.

'I miss you, Queenie. We need to talk.'

'I need to change the beds upstairs. I'll leave you two to it,' said Mary.

'Are you drunk?' Queenie asked.

'A bit. I heard about you being out with another bloke. Who was he?'

'Just a lad I went to school with. He's a good friend.'

'Look, I know you're unhappy living at home and Mum would love you to move in with us. Why don't ya?'

'Living in sin! I think not.'

'No. I don't mean us sleeping together. You could have my bed and I'll sleep on the sofa.'

'No, Albie. You know how people talk. I'm not ruining my good reputation for you or anybody else.'

Albie ran his fingers through his thick dark hair. 'Marry me then.'

'What!'

'I said, let's get married.'

'Get down on one knee and ask me properly then.'

Albie did as asked. 'Queenie Wade, will you marry me?'
Queenie grinned. She'd played the perfect game and
won. She couldn't quite believe it had been that easy. It
was time to forget Daniel O'Leary once and for all. 'Yes,
Albie Butler. I will.'

PART THREE

'From this day forward, you shall not walk alone. My heart will be your shelter and my arms will be your home'

Anon

CHAPTER THIRTEEN

'*I now pronounce you man and wife. You may kiss the bride.*'

Barely five months had passed since Albie's half-hearted proposal and as he lifted my veil, I felt a mixture of joy and fear. I might've got my man, but that night I would be sharing his bed with him at his mother's house and the thought terrified me.

I looked beautiful, I knew that. My wedding dress was pure satin, with big puffy sleeves and hand-sewn lace. It had belonged to the daughter of one of the wealthy ladies who shopped at Cohen's. The daughter's fiancé had unfortunately been killed serving our country in the Middle East, so I'd been offered the dress on the cheap. Mum hadn't wanted me to wear it, in case it brought me bad luck too, but I wasn't one to look a gift horse in the mouth. I'd paid for my lovely dress out of Aunt Edna's money, knowing full well she would approve.

After the confetti was thrown and the photos taken, I grabbed hold of Mrs O'Leary. My blood running cold. Sheer panic setting in. 'Will Albie know that I'm not a virgin?' I whispered. 'Will he be able to tell?'

'No. Paddy never knew. Everything'll be fine. Stop worrying.'

'I'm so nervous. The thought of sharing a bed with Albie scares me,' I admitted.

Mary put her hands on my shoulders. 'Now, you listen to me. You're one of the strongest women I've ever met. I'm not going to lie to you, Queenie, I never enjoyed sex. However, I'd be lost without my boys. Albie's a handsome man, so just lie back and think of those handsome sons you want him to give you.'

'Why didn't Daniel come today?' I blurted out. Patrick had come with Mary.

With a sigh, Mary took my hands in hers and squeezed them so tightly it began to hurt a little. 'Probably the same reason why you cried off at his wedding, sweetheart. I'm not stupid. You need to forget all about Daniel now, Queenie Butler. You're married to Albie and he's a good man. He'll not break your heart.'

I forced a smile. 'Thank you, Mary. For everything.'

'Your dad looked sober when he gave you away. That's one good thing, eh?'

I rolled my eyes. I hadn't wanted Dad to give me away, but Mum had insisted. 'He promised me he wouldn't get drunk today, but I put money on it he shows me up when we get back to the pub.'

Mary's face suddenly drained of colour. She clutched the top of her head.

'Mary, what's wrong?' I cried, frightened to see her so clearly in pain.

'Me head. I can't see straight.'

As Mary fell to the ground, I started to scream. 'Help. Mary's collapsed. Somebody do something. Quick . . .'

*

146

Instead of enjoying her reception in the Hoop and Grapes, Queenie was sitting in a corridor of the London Hospital still in her full wedding regalia, hoping and praying for some positive news.

Queenie was devastated. Mary wasn't just her friend, she was her mentor, understood her more than anybody else in the whole wide world. Life without her was unthinkable.

'Darling, you must come to your own wedding reception. I know you're worried about Mary, but you can't leave Albie there with all the guests on his own,' urged her mother. 'Patrick's here and Daniel will be here soon. You can pop back later or in the morning. This is your big day.'

Queenie looked at her mother in disgust. 'If you think I'm going to a pub to celebrate while my beautiful friend is lying in 'ere, possibly at death's door, you got another think coming.' Queenie stood up as Patrick returned. His face looked grave. 'Any more news?'

'Yeah. They reckon it's an aneurysm. I can't believe it. I know she'd been a bit tired lately, but she was fine yesterday. Buzzing with excitement about your wedding. They've gotta operate to relieve the pressure on her brain.'

Tears streamed down Queenie's face as she hugged poor Patrick. She felt that same horrid gut-wrenching feeling she'd had when Aunt Edna died and she could only stand by, helpless.

Mum went off to the reception to inform the guests that Mary's condition was deemed critical, therefore Queenie wouldn't be able to attend.

Albie was understanding. He even popped up the hospital with some sandwiches, but neither Patrick nor

Queenie were hungry. 'You go back to the reception and entertain the guests, Albie. I have to stay 'ere. I'm sorry.'

'I understand, darling. I know how close you are to Mary. I do wish her well. Will you be coming back to Mum's later? D'ya want me to pop back for you?'

'I honestly can't be making any plans. I'll shoot back to my mum's soon and get changed, then come straight back here.'

Albie kissed his beautiful bride on the cheek. 'OK, my love. Well, if I don't see you later tonight, I'll come and find you tomorrow.' This wasn't exactly how Albie had planned his wedding day, but it wasn't Queenie's fault. It was just one of those things.

Not long after Albie left, Daniel turned up looking flustered. 'I heard Mum fainted. Where is she?'

When Patrick explained the true horror of the situation, Daniel was shell-shocked. 'Sweet Jesus, no. Not Mum. Fucking hell.'

Queenie felt ridiculous wearing her wedding dress in front of Daniel. 'I'll pop home. While I'm there, I'll nip in your mum's and pick up her rosary beads. She'll want them when she wakes up, I know she will.'

'Did you end up getting married?' Daniel looked at Queenie and couldn't hide the hope in his eyes. Now wasn't the time, but he couldn't help himself.

'Erm, yes. Your mum became ill after the service. I won't be long.'

The next few days were a blur for Queenie. Mary woke up, but couldn't speak properly or move her limbs. To see her dear friend like that tore Queenie apart.

The doctors and nurses were kind, but could give no guarantee that Mary would ever return to her previous self. They said only time would tell if the damage her brain had suffered would be temporary or permanent. They also said that Mary was lucky to be alive as many don't survive such trauma.

Struggling to get her head around what was happening, Queenie visited Albie and her mum, but couldn't face staying with either. Sleeping at Mary's house made her feel close to her lovely friend. She'd cook for Patrick and Daniel, make sure they had at least one good meal inside them a day. Daniel didn't leave her side. Mary always fussed over feeding her boys; therefore Queenie knew she'd approve of her helping out.

One person who didn't approve was her mother. 'It's wrong, you sleeping at that house with two grown men, Queenie. People will talk. Albie's been very patient with you. You even left the poor man on his wedding night. I know you're upset about Mary, but you need to put your own husband first. Your father ain't happy, let me tell you. He saw you and Daniel entering that house alone late last night and he said Daniel had his hand on your back.'

'Dad's a fine one to talk,' hissed Queenie.

'And what is that supposed to mean?'

'Nothing,' lied Queenie. 'Daniel's married and Patrick has recently got engaged, in case you'd forgotten. They're also Mary's sons. Nobody else understands how I feel, only them and vice versa. So sod what the gossip-mongers say or think. I couldn't give a shit.'

Queenie felt herself becoming closer to Daniel than she'd ever been. She saw a vulnerable side to him she'd never witnessed before. She knew from stories Mary had told her that Daniel had a vicious temper, but he was like a little boy lost now Mary was seriously ill. He opened up about his marriage to Bridie and admitted he'd never loved her. Queenie couldn't help but feel she'd married the wrong man, but it was too late for regrets. Like Daniel, she'd made her bed, so would now have to lie in it.

As the days passed, Mary's condition began to improve. She still couldn't walk, but had started to move one hand and try to talk again. She was hard to understand, but Queenie quickly learned what she was saying. Sometimes Queenie would turn up to see her clutching her rosary beads, tears running down her cheeks. 'No crying now, Mary. You're going to make a full recovery and I'm going to help you,' Queenie would tell her, meaning every word.

One morning when Queenie was at the hospital, Albie turned up unexpectedly. 'Queen, it's been nearly a week now since we got married and I've barely seen you. Mum's asking questions, so is Aunt Liz who you haven't even met properly yet. What's going on, love?'

Queenie's eyes welled up. 'I'm so sorry; I've been a crap wife. I was just so worried about Mary, I needed space. I'll come home tonight, I promise. Mary's sort of on the mend now. Thank God.'

Albie breathed a sigh of relief. He'd heard whispers. People were talking, speculating on why his wife wasn't coming home and he hadn't fancied confronting those O'Leary brothers. Albie hated the sight of blood, especially his own. 'I'll get Mum to prepare us a nice bit of grub. What time can I expect you?'

Queenie forced a smile. She was still dreading sharing a bed with him, but knew she couldn't put it off any longer. 'Seven, Albie. I'll be home by seven, and thanks for being so understanding.'

Albie kissed her on the forehead. 'See you later.'

*

150

Later that afternoon, Daniel pulled Queenie to one side. 'I spoke to the doctor earlier and they reckon Mum could come home as early as next week. Please don't take this the wrong way, Queenie, as I would never disrespect you. You're like a daughter to Mum. But you were saying the other day how unhappy you are in your job with those girls giving you gyp. So how d'ya fancy helping to care for Mum? Patrick and me will pay you more than you're currently on. No way will Mum want a stranger looking after her, and I know how close you two are. You can help with her rehabilitation more than anyone else I know.'

Patrick walked over, catching the back end of the conversation.

'Oh, I'd love to, but how can I take money off you two? Mary's like family to me. That would be wrong.'

'Don't be daft. We're hardly skint, Queenie. It would be such a weight off mine and Daniel's shoulders if you could help out, and you need the money. Name your price. Obviously, I know you can only be with Mum during the daytime as you have your own life. You can do the same hours you work at the shop. What do you say?'

Queenie had once loved working at Cohen's, but not any more. She still got on well with the customers, but not Doreen or Eliza. She'd even offered an olive branch which had been rebuffed. 'Will I still get a day off in the week and Sundays off?'

'Yeah. You can't do everything, so we'll be bringing someone else in to help out too.'

'OK, I'll do it. I'll hand in my notice at Cohen's tomorrow.'

'Thanks, Queenie. You're a diamond,' grinned Daniel.

'She sure is. Mum'll be chuffed when we tell her. I'm just gonna have a quick word with the doctor.'

When Patrick dashed off, Daniel squeezed Queenie's hand. 'This little arrangement means we get to see more of one another too.'

About to reply, Queenie was horrified as she clocked Bridie walking towards them, minus the baby. She snatched her hand away from Daniel's. 'Hello, Bridie. How are you?' she asked.

'Missing this one like mad,' Bridie replied, linking arms with Daniel while looking up at him adoringly. 'How's your mum today?' she asked him.

'So, so.'

'I'm gonna shoot off now Bridie's here, Daniel. I need to pick up a few things from the shops and visit my own mum.'

'Don't rush off on my account. Daniel adores you,' smiled Bridie. 'He always says you're like his little sister.'

Queenie forced a smile back, while experiencing that horrible gut-wrenching feeling in her stomach. 'I have so much to do. Honestly. I've hardly seen my husband since I got married. Bye, Bridie. Bye, Daniel. Tell your mum and Patrick I said goodbye as well.'

As Queenie reached the exit, she stared dismally at the torrential rain. 'Damn,' she mumbled, realizing she'd left her brolly inside the hospital. She'd have to go back for it. It was teeming down.

Queenie made her way back through the corridors and as she turned the corner to where she'd left her umbrella, she was shocked to the core. Bridie had her arms around Daniel's neck. He had his hands on her buttocks and they were kissing passionately. She couldn't believe it. Daniel had convinced her there was no passion in his marriage, swore he was only with Bridie because they had a child

152

together. What a load of old cock and bull that was. They looked like love's young dream.

'Erm, sorry to disturb you two lovebirds, but I forgot my brolly,' Queenie said, trying to keep the sarcasm out of her tone.

'Don't mind us. I have missed him, though. Be glad to snuggle up to him again tonight,' smiled Bridie. 'Emily's missed him too,' she added. 'My mum has her at present. We're going to pick her up on the way home.'

Queenie glanced at Daniel. He looked terribly embarrassed, and so he should after pouring out all his marriage woes to her.

Queenie grabbed her umbrella and forced another smile. 'Bye again. Tell Mary I'll see her tomorrow, Daniel.'

As Queenie walked off, Daniel told Bridie he'd be back in a minute. He chased after Queenie and once out of sight of Bridie, he grabbed her arm. 'That's not what it looked like, sweetheart. I swear it's not.'

Queenie stared into his dazzling eyes and for once they didn't have the usual effect on her. 'I am going home to my husband now, Daniel. I will always love you as a brother, as you love me as a sister. But I can't listen to your bullshit any more. I want to make a go of my marriage and I suggest you do the same.'

'Queenie,' Daniel shouted as she walked away.

Queenie didn't turn around. It was time for her to be a proper wife to Albie.

The lamb stew wasn't a patch on her mother's and Queenie struggled to eat it. She had things on her mind, some of them silly. What would she do when she wanted a wee in the middle of the night as she often did? Ida's toilet was out in the back yard like her mum's. Weeing in a bucket in front of Viv was one thing, but she could hardly do that in front of Albie. It wasn't exactly ladylike, was it?

'You not that hungry, love?' asked Ida.

'No. I'm ever so sorry. I've not eaten much all week, worrying about Mary.'

'Bless ya. Well, I'm glad your friend is now on the mend,' smiled Ida.

'Seeing as you missed our reception, why don't I take you down to the pub for a couple, Queen?' Albie hadn't had sex for Christ knows how long and was hoping a couple of drinks might ease Queenie's nerves. He couldn't wait to take his wife in his arms later and make love to her for the first time. But she seemed edgy. Albie guessed it must be because she was a virgin, bless her.

Queenie smiled. 'Yes. I'd like that.'

Queenie drank four gins in quick succession, which calmed her nerves somewhat.

Albie knocked back the last of his pint. 'Shall we go home now? Have an early night, darlin'?'

'Erm, yes. But do you mind if I go upstairs first, so I can get changed into my nightdress. I've never got undressed in front of a man before.'

'Of course.' Albie put an arm around Queenie. 'Please don't be scared. I'm a gentle man.'

Queenie said a quick goodnight to Ida then ran up the stairs. She put on her floral nightdress, then took the wet flannel and Wright's Coal Tar soap out of her bag. She rubbed the soap on the flannel, then rubbed the flannel under her armpits and around her noonie. She'd thankfully had a nice soak in the bath at Mary's this morning. There was only a tin bath at Albie's.

When Albie entered the bedroom, Queenie ordered him to get undressed with the light off. He sidled into bed next to her and began kissing her passionately. She was used to his kisses, but was shocked by how hairy his back was. It was like stroking a monkey.

'You OK?' whispered Albie. 'Why don't you take your nightie off?'

Queenie felt silly as she awkwardly tried to wriggle out of her nightdress under the sheet and blankets. Her first job tomorrow would be to wash the bedding. It stank of male sweat.

Queenie took Mary's advice and lay there thinking of the sons she hoped to have as Albie sucked her left tit. Surely this wasn't normal? Only babies did this, didn't they?

By the time Albie's middle finger made contact with her vagina, Queenie was so tense, she just wanted it over with. 'I'm sorry, Albie, but what with this being my first time, I'm nervous. Just put your thingy inside me. I'll be fine with that.'

Having popped quite a few cherries in his past, Albie Butler was slightly bemused. Most women loved a bit of foreplay, but he wasn't about to disagree with his wife. He eased his penis inside her.

Queenie gasped, through pain, not pleasure. Less than a minute or two later, Albie groaned, then his penis shrank and thankfully popped out of her.

'I didn't hurt you too much, did I?' Albie asked worriedly.

'No. I'm fine.' Queenie breathed a sigh of relief. At least it was all over quickly.

CHAPTER FOURTEEN

VE Day

May 1945

'Land of Hope and Glory, Mother of the free,
How shall we extol thee, who are born of thee?
Wider still and wider shall thy bounds be set;
God, who made thee mighty,
Make thee mightier yet,
God, who made thee mighty,
Make thee mightier yet.'

Queenie had goosebumps as the song came to an end and 'God Save the Queen' was then sung. The atmosphere was electrifying. Winston Churchill's announcement that the Germans had surrendered officially spelled the end of World War Two, in Europe at least.

As Queenie made her way through the masses celebrating victory in Europe, she was hugged by neighbours, strangers and flag-waving children. Motorists were beeping their horns, cyclists ringing their bells, the Union Jack flag hung proudly from the windows of homes and businesses. People were dancing amongst the rubble, relief, pride and jubilation in their voices and expressions. There were tears too; sadness for the many who'd lost their lives. A lone tear ran down Queenie's cheek as she thought of Aunt Edna. Edna hated the Germans, she would've loved today and no doubt would have ended up the life and soul of the party.

'So sorry I'm late, Dolores. I've never seen anything like it out there. The streets are mobbed,' Queenie explained. Dolores was the pretty Irish girl who was Mrs O'Leary's live-in carer. She was only eighteen, and Queenie liked her very much, but knew Mary much preferred it when she took over.

'No worries. Mary's eaten and is having a little nap. I shall be off out now. I might not be English, but I shall celebrate with the neighbours nevertheless,' giggled Dolores.

Mary had never fully recovered. She was paralysed down her right-hand side. It was such a shame, everything moved on her left side, her arm, leg, facial expressions, mouth. But on her right, everything was still.

A proud woman, Mary hated going out these days. She loathed having to use a wheelchair and couldn't stand people's looks of pity. She hadn't lost her sense of humour though. She might talk a lot slower, but what came out of her mouth was still as funny as ever.

'There you are! I thought you were never coming,' Mary said.

'It's mayhem out there. Good mayhem, mind. I thought you were asleep.'

Unable to get upstairs any more, Mary's bed was downstairs in her best room. She sat herself up, clutching her precious rosary beads in one hand. 'Pretended to be asleep. She don't stop talking. Verbal diarrhoea, the girl's got.'

Queenie chuckled. 'Don't be so cruel. Dolores thinks the world of you.'

'Not me. My Daniel. Always flirting with him. I might be partly a vegetable, but I ain't fecking stupid. He's coming over later. You watch her fluttering her eyelashes at him. Dirty little hussy.'

Queenie's heart sank. She hadn't seen Daniel for months and had no wish to. 'Right, let's get you glammed up, Mary. No way are you sitting in 'ere today. We'll go outside and enjoy the street party. Where's your make-up?'

'In the top drawer. Take more than a bit of make-up to make me look glam, Queenie.'

'Now, now. None of that talk. We're celebrating victory today. It's all about our heroes and you're my hero.'

'Albie coming?'

'Yes. I told him in no uncertain terms that we're not celebrating with the riff-raff. He's wheeling his mum round in a bit.'

'Great. At least I won't look out of place sat next to her.'

Queenie burst out laughing. 'Stop it! Behave your bloody self, ya naughty woman.'

As always, Albie obeyed his wife's orders with a smile on his face. He certainly hadn't married a wallflower. Queenie ruled the roost. She was a bloody good wife, mind. Since moving in with him, Queenie had turned their dreary home into a small palace. It was spotlessly clean, with lots of feminine touches, and every night she'd rustle up a decent meal for the whole family. She even washed his mum on a daily basis, so she didn't stink. Plus she worked in the daytime too. A feisty little grafter was Queenie.

'What a day to be alive eh, son?' Ida shouted. It was hard to make herself heard above the jubilant crowds that had filled the streets.

'Sure is,' Albie grinned. The war was over, Queenie was four months pregnant. He couldn't wait to be a dad and his mum couldn't wait to be a nan. Life was grand.

'Hello, Queenie. Long time no see. What an atmosphere, eh? Will go on for days the celebrating, I bet,' grinned Freddie Angel.

'Look at you, all smart in your uniform. I thought they'd have given you the day off.'

'Nah. Someone has to be on duty. Bound to be those who can't hold their beer and get out of hand.'

'Oh yeah, like my dad.' She was long past the days when she'd cover up for him out of shame. 'You picked him up lately, Freddie?' Her father's behaviour had gone from bad to worse. He could no longer hold down a job and drank morning, noon and night. Queenie had lost patience with her mum. Her dad paid nothing towards the bills or rent, yet still the silly woman wouldn't kick him out. The pair of them wouldn't even have a roof over their head if Queenie wasn't giving her mother rent money out of Aunt Edna's cash, and she couldn't be doing that for much longer as she needed to buy things for her baby.

Freddie looked sheepish. 'A colleague of mine arrested your dad a week or so ago, but let's not talk about it today. I'll tell you next time I see ya.'

'No. Tell me now. You won't spoil my day. I already know what a horrible waste of space he is.'

Freddie sighed. 'He attacked a brass, put her in hospital. She's OK, the girl, nothing life-threatening. We charged your dad though, so he'll have to go to court.'

Queenie was disgusted, but not shocked. Viv hated being at home these days, so spent most of her spare time with herself and Albie. 'I hope he gets banged up, the filthy pig.'

Freddie raised his eyebrows. 'So how's married life? You're looking well.'

Queenie's marriage was by no means perfect. Albie's brother Bert was the main breadwinner at home, not Albie. It was Bert who paid the rent while she and Albie scraped together to pay the bills. But Albie was a gentle man. He never forced sex on her and she'd made it quite clear she didn't want him fiddling with her breasts or noonie, which he'd accepted. She patted her stomach. 'I'm pregnant.'

Having had his heart set on marrying Queenie himself, Freddie couldn't help but feel slightly melancholy. 'That's great news. I'm really chuffed for you. Albie's a lucky man. I gotta go now, Queen. I'm being summoned. I'll catch you later. Enjoy your day.'

'Your face, Mum! Where is the bastard? I'll kill him.' One side of her mother's face was black and blue. Her eye was swollen too, like a bloody golf ball. Queenie was furious. It was by far the worst injury she'd seen inflicted upon her mother.

'I know you're not going to believe me, love, but I fell down the stairs last night. Your father wasn't even in at the time,' Molly replied truthfully.

'Too right I don't believe you. Why you always covering up for that shitbag, eh? You're worth so much more. If only you could see it.'

Molly's eyes welled up. She hadn't stopped thinking about Edna since Churchill's announcement. 'Let's not argue today please, love. I do wish your aunt was celebrating with us.'

'Yeah. Me too. Listen, Mum, I can't afford to keep giving you a huge chunk of my wages to pay your rent any more, we need stuff for the baby soon and Albie needs me to help out with the bills. Dad's gonna have to get off his drunken arse and get another job.' No way would Aunt Edna want her to continue to pay her mum's rent if that bastard was knocking her about like that.

'OK, love. I understand.'

Spotting her sister, Queenie ran over to her. 'Was you at home when Dad attacked Mum?'

'No. Mum swears he didn't do it. She was in bed when I come in from yours last night and Dad came in after me. There was no arguing. Dad crashed out on the sofa.'

'Oh believe me. He did it, Viv. I hate him. I wish he were dead.'

People pulled furniture out of their houses so they could hold a street party. Queenie had made corned beef and tinned ham sandwiches and everyone was bringing out plates of something or another. The beer was flowing freely amongst the men and most of the women were sticking to gin, vodka or soft drinks.

Albie put a comforting arm around his wife's shoulders. 'Chin up. Worrying ain't gonna do the baby any good, treacle.'

Queenie patted her stomach. She'd started to show now, loved having a little person growing inside her. She smiled at Albie. 'You're right. Gotta look after our boy, haven't I?'

'I dunno what you're gonna do if it's a bleedin' girl,' Albie laughed.

'It's not. It's definitely a boy. Bridget did the all-important ring test yesterday.' Bridget was her new rough and ready next-door-neighbour. She had no teeth, five kids by different men and another on the way. She supported herself by selling her body of an evening, but Queenie didn't judge her. Bridget had a heart of gold deep down.

'What's the ring test?'

'A ring on a piece of string. I used my wedding ring and Bridget hung it over my naked belly. If it swings in a circular motion, that means you're gonna have a girl. But if it swings side to side, that tells ya you're having a boy. Three times we did the test and three times it swung side to side like a pendulum. Bridget said she could feel the power holding the string. Gonna be a right little bruiser, I reckon. She says the test is never wrong. She's predicted all her own kids' sexes.'

Albie rolled his eyes. 'You women and your old wives' tales.'

'You won't be saying that when I give birth to our son, Albie Butler. Speaking of which, now the war is over, I think you should get yourself a proper job. We'll never get our own home otherwise and I don't want our kids being raised in your mum's street.'

Albie looked at his wife in dismay. He was a fly-by-night who'd always got by. A proper job did not appeal to him one bit. Why did she have to spoil his day? Today of all days.

Queenie was consoling Mabel Brown, who'd lost her only son during the war, when she heard a voice from behind her. 'Queenie, where's the Guinness? Mary wants one.'

Queenie swung around. It was Bridie, Daniel's wife. 'Hi, Bridie. How are you?'

'Good thanks. Congratulations on your pregnancy. Mary's ever so excited about it.'

'Thanks. Where's your little un?'

'Daniel's cleaning her up in Mary's. She dropped a drink all down herself. She'll be having a little brother or sister soon.'

'Sorry. I didn't quite catch that.'

'I said I'm pregnant again.'

As Daniel appeared with his daughter in his arms, Queenie excused herself to get Mary's drink. All that bullshit he'd fed her about not wanting more kids with Bridie and not loving her, when would she ever learn when it came to Daniel O'Leary?

Albie ruffled Vivian's hair. She spent an awful lot of time with him and Queenie now, too much time if he were honest. But Albie didn't moan. The poor little mite had a shit home life with that father of hers. 'Gonna get your favourite brother-in-law a beer, Titch?'

Vivian frowned. 'Stop calling me Titch. I'm not a kid any more. I'm nearly as tall as Queenie.'

'I know you are. Only messing, Titch,' Albie winked. 'So you gonna get me a beer or what?'

'You can get your own sodding beer.'

Albie laughed as Vivian stomped off. He was relieved she seemed to have gotten over her schoolgirl crush on him. She'd made a pass at him on the evening of his wedding reception, tried to snog him outside. He'd laughed it off, but had never told his wife. Queenie would go ballistic.

Queenie kissed Mary on the cheek. The poor woman was tired and wanted to go indoors with Patrick. Daniel and Bridie hadn't stayed long. She hadn't even spoken to Daniel and he'd made no effort to speak to her. She sensed he wanted to avoid her just as much as she did him, but she could feel his eyes on her without even looking. 'I'll pop in and see you before I go home, Mary.'

'Queenie,' yelled Albie. 'You remember meeting Aunt Liz, don't you?'

A tiny woman with short blonde hair and a mouth like a foghorn, nobody would forget meeting Aunt Liz in a hurry. She was Ida's sister. Chalk and cheese, they were.

Liz patted the chair next to her. 'Come sit 'ere, me darlin' and 'ave a Guinness. Good for the baby, a bit of iron.'

Having not had an alcoholic drink all day, Queenie sat down and gratefully sipped the Guinness. Albie was bladdered, most people were.

'What a day, eh girl? Bollocks to that bastard, Hitler. You'll never beat the English,' cackled Liz.

'It's been great,' grinned Queenie. 'So many outsiders see us East Enders as common trash. But our community is the best. Solid as a rock. I'd like to see all these posh farts cope like we did during the Blitz.' Queenie craned her neck. She hadn't seen her father all day, but here he was, staggering along with another bloke, arms around each other's shoulders, beers in hand. There was no point in confronting him about her mother's injuries while he was that inebriated.

'So how's our Albie treating you? Good, I hope. Never thought I would see him married off with a little un on the way. Don't get me wrong, he's got a good heart has Albie. But he's always been a bleedin' spiv. He'll make an all right father though, I reckon. Loving, ya know.'

'What do you mean exactly? Albie was engaged before he met me to Suzanne. He told me about her.'

'Oh, her. Yeah, she was never Albie's type, that one. She was a bit posh, not one of our own. Didn't come from the East End. I think she was bowled over by his voice, like most women are,' laughed Liz.

'What d'ya mean, he's a spiv?'

'Well, he's not exactly a spiv – most of them have money and Albie's usually skint. He's more what I'd call a ducker and diver. Never had a bleedin' proper job in his life. Bert's always been the grafter out the two. Albie's the charmer.'

'He's going to have to change now we've got a child on the way,' Queenie replied shirtily. 'I've told him he'll have to get a proper job.'

'You'll be bleedin' lucky,' Liz guffawed. 'Albie'll never be a grafter, love. He hid in my loft every time there was a knock on my door during the Blitz. You should've seen the look of panic on his face when he got his call-up papers. Round mine like a rocket he was, refused to leave. Probably the best thing for the other soldiers though. Last bloke you'd wanna be in the trenches with is Albie.'

'Albie told me he couldn't join up 'cause he had to care for his mum.'

Liz tilted her head back and roared with laughter. 'Ida was living on her own in Whitechapel during the Blitz. Bert went off and did his national service while Albie hid at my drum.'

Queenie was bemused. 'How did Ida manage on her own with one leg?'

'She had two bleedin' legs back then. Ida only lost her leg the Christmas before last. It went gangrene through diabetes.'

Queenie felt the colour drain from her face. Ida must have lost her leg only a matter of weeks before she'd first met Albie. As for a grown man climbing into his aunt's loft to get out of fighting for his country, that made her blood boil.

'You all right, love? Don't be upset what I say about Albie. I'm allowed to rip the piss out of him 'cause I'm his aunt. He's got a good soul ya know. You could've chosen a far worse husband.'

It took an effort to restrain herself from walking over to her husband, who was currently larging it in front of the neighbours, crooning song after song, and punch him in the side of his cowardly, lying head. Instead, Queenie somehow managed to compose herself. 'Yes. I'm fine, thanks. I just need to pop in Mrs O'Leary's to check on her. I won't be long.'

Queenie was raging as she sipped her tea. Daniel was a liar. Albie was a liar. Her father was a liar. That monster who'd raped her was a liar. Were all men liars? she pondered, putting a protective hand on her bump.

'Right, I'm gonna make a move now, ladies. I'll see you tomorrow, Mum,' said Patrick. He'd moved out since Dolores had moved into Daniel's old room, had his own bachelor pad, a flat. Not for much longer though, as his wedding was all booked for August and his beautiful wife would then move in with him.

'Bye, Patrick,' Queenie said.

'What's up? I can tell by your face you ain't happy,' Mary said, as soon as the front door banged shut.

Queenie paced up and down the lounge, explaining in detail the conversation she'd had with Aunt Liz. 'I'm furious, Mary,' she ranted. 'What type of man have I married? A coward, that's what.'

Mary patted the bed. 'Calm down, sweetheart. Come sit next to me.'

Queenie sighed deeply as she did so. 'Say my sons turn out like him?'

Mary rubbed Queenie's hand. 'They won't. Trust me. My Paddy was a coward also. That's why I raised my boys. I didn't allow Paddy any say in their upbringing. You gotta do the same. I'll help you. A son will always look up to his mother. All men are liars, Queenie. Well, most I've met are. I did meet one nice lad before I met Paddy, mind.'

'What happened?'

'He was too normal for me, Queenie. I liked a bit of excitement back then. Had I married him, I'd have been loved, but bored rigid. He ended up joining the Garda an' all.'

'The Garda?'

'The Irish police. Now, you listen to me and you listen carefully—'

The conversation was cut short by someone hammering their fist against the front door. 'Queenie! Queenie, you in there?'

Recognizing Freddie Angel's voice, Queenie flung open the door. 'What's up?'

'Come quickly. It's your dad. He's inside with your mum and sister and it's all kicking off. I clocked him dragging Vivvy in by her hair.'

As Queenie weaved her way in between masses of her inebriated neighbours and friends, she spotted Albie dancing with Aunt Liz. She put her hand through the letterbox and reached for the key that hung on a piece of string. She could hear her sister screaming.

'I'm coming in with ya. I'll nick him,' said Freddie.

'No. You stay 'ere. Whenever you nick him, all you do is let him go,' Queenie snapped, as she slammed the front door in Freddie's face. 'Viv, Mum,' she bellowed.

'Queenie, help us,' shrieked Viv.

Queenie ran up the stairs. Her mum was lying in the doorway of her bedroom, in obvious pain, clutching her stomach. Her father was leaning against the wall, a bottle of Scotch in one hand and holding her little sister's hair in the other. His face was covered in blood, so were his clothes. 'You bastard! Let her go,' screamed Queenie.

Eric laughed loudly, blood dripping from his mouth, thanks to the teeth that'd been kicked out. 'Ere she is, the other wrong un. You think I'm frightened of those O'Leary lads, d'ya? Fought through a fucking war me, saw all sorts. I ain't frightened of no bastard. Neither did I beat your mother up last night. But I have today, and I'll clump her again if I don't find out who the snitch is.'

Queenie was perplexed. 'What the hell you going on about?' Her father had his elbow around Viv's neck now. Not tight, but she could see how frightened her little sister was.

Molly managed to sit up. Eric had booted her so hard, she was sure her ribs were broken. She might have put up with the odd slap over the years and Eric's demands for sex on tap, but never had he threatened the girls in such a terrifying way. Queenie was right. She had to sling him out. 'The O'Leary brothers beat up your dad and he's blaming us. Daniel accused him of beating me up last night and he didn't, Queenie. I swear I fell down the stairs.'

Queenie was stunned. Mrs O'Leary must have told the boys. 'Let Viv go now, ya nutter. It was me who told the O'Learys you beat Mum up. Not Mum or Viv.'

Eric let go of his youngest and drunkenly lunged at Queenie. 'You don't even fucking live 'ere any more. You got no right sticking your trunk in, causing trouble. You've always been a trouble maker, you.'

Queenie booted her father in his gammy leg, then felt

relief as he fell to the floor. 'Get out and don't ever come back. You're a drunk and a bully!' Queenie felt her baby kicking her belly and a strength rose up in her that she'd had no idea she possessed. 'We never want to see you again. And believe me, you so much as lay a finger on Mum or Viv, I'll have you fucking murdered.'

'Queenie, don't make matters worse,' Molly pleaded. Eric was becoming more and more irate.

'You treacherous little mare,' Eric roared, picking up the whisky bottle and unsteadily rising to his feet.

Spotting her dad stumble right at the top of the stairs, in a split second Queenie saw an opportunity to end her mother and sister's suffering once and for all. She pushed the bastard with all her might.

'No!' Molly screamed. 'Queenie, what have you done?' she cried, as Eric tumbled backwards, landing with a thud at the bottom of the stairs.

Vivian was frozen to the spot, hand over mouth. 'He's not dead, is he?' Her father was crumpled in an awkward position at the bottom of the stairs. His neck looked all twisted and he wasn't moving.

Queenie ran past the man who'd made all their lives such a misery, without even glancing at him. She yanked open the front door. 'Come in, Freddie,' she said calmly. 'I'm not gonna lie. Mum can barely move 'cause Dad kicked her so hard in the gut. He tried to strangle Viv, then he lifted his whisky bottle and I thought he was gonna smash me over the head with it. So I pushed him down the stairs.'

Molly hugged Vivian close to her aching ribs. Both were petrified. 'Oh, Queenie. You can't go to prison. You're pregnant. This is all my fault. I should've been stronger. I know I should. I'm so sorry.'

169

'I can't lose you, Queenie. You're not only my sister, you're my best friend,' cried Viv.

Freddie bent down and checked Eric's pulse. He could see his neck was broken, so it was no surprise he couldn't feel a pulse. A serious expression on his face, Freddie ordered Molly and Viv down the stairs. 'Right, 'ere's what we're going to do. I shall call for help, but you're not to say Queenie pushed Eric. You tell my superior that Eric was drunk and tumbled down the stairs while the rest of you were in the bedroom, OK?'

'OK. Yes,' replied Molly, her voice jittery.

Freddie swung around and placed his hands on Queenie's shoulders. 'Ya know what you've gotta say, don't ya, Queen? My job's on the line 'ere if you cock this up. Nobody will disbelieve you if you stick to the story. Everyone down the station knows what your dad is. Or was, should I say. Keep calm. Don't panic. I don't wanna see you face trial or go to prison. You don't bloody deserve it.'

'I won't mess up. Thanks, Freddie. I'll never forget this act of kindness.'

As Freddie put his hand on the latch, he swung around. 'And not a word to anyone. Not even family.'

'Of course not,' Molly replied.

'I would never say anything,' Viv added.

Queenie glanced at her dead father. She felt no remorse or sadness whatsoever. Not for the first time, the O'Learys had come up trumps on her behalf. If they hadn't beaten her father up today, the bastard would still be alive.

CHAPTER FIFTEEN

I *was indoors washing Ida's arse when my waters broke. She had a habit of crapping herself just lately and if I didn't clean her up, the whole house would reek of shit.*

'Baby's on its way,' Ida exclaimed gleefully.

I flew into a panic. Ida could no longer hop on one leg. She was too fat now. So I stumbled outside and banged on Bridget's front door. Luckily she was in. 'Me waters have broke,' I gabbled. 'Go call the midwife.'

As I went back indoors, I felt the first bad contraction. The pain was awful, indescribable. I sank to my haunches, trying to breathe.

My birthing kit had been delivered the previous month, so I grabbed that and crawled up the stairs on all fours. I'd left the front door open so the midwife could let herself in.

As I lay on the bed, I had another contraction, one so vicious it took my breath away. I wanted to push, my whole body was telling me to push, but I didn't want my son to arrive before the midwife got there.

'Queenie! Where are you? I bumped into Bridget,' a voice shouted. It was Albie.

'I'm upstairs, but don't you come up. If you wanna make yourself useful, go get my mum for me,' I bellowed. Albie still didn't have a proper job, but he was bringing home a bit more dosh thanks to his ducking and diving. Not enough to get us our own place though, and I'd grown sick of living with his brother and mother. I was desperate for a home I could call my own.

It seemed ages before the midwife arrived, but was probably only fifteen minutes or so. She was a lovely Irish lass who lived with the nuns at the convent; Maria was her name. 'Now let's have a look at you, Queenie. I doubt baby is ready to come out just yet,' Maria smiled.

'I think he is,' I told her. I could see she was baffled by my insistence I was having a boy, but I didn't care. I knew in my heart what was growing inside me.

My mum and Viv turned up at the same time. Our bond had grown stronger since the death of my dad, but we never spoke about what happened that evening. Dad had broken his neck as he'd fallen down the stairs and the authorities had swallowed that it was an accident.

As the contractions became more regular, Mum wiped my sweaty brow with a cold flannel, while Vivvy clenched my hand for support. I had never felt pain like it.

'Everything all right up there? Do you need anything?' Albie called up the stairs.

'Yes. For you to shut up. Go down the bastard pub,' I shouted, while digging my nails into Vivian's hand.

'He's only trying to help, love. Don't be too hard on him,' my mum said.

'I can see the head,' Maria exclaimed.

Time stood still as I continued to push when ordered to. There were times I felt like giving up, my body had no strength left in it to bloody push.

Finally, the midwife said, 'The head's out, Queenie. Now one more push, brave lady. I know you're tired, but you need to push with all your might.'

I shut my eyes and temporarily forgot the excruciating pain as I gave one almighty push.

'You did it, Queenie! Well done, darlin',' my mum gushed.

'Is he OK?' I was on the verge of panic, until I heard a cry, a shrill cry.

'Well, well, you were right all along, Queenie,' the midwife smiled. 'You have a son – and what a big boy he is! No wonder you had trouble pushing him out. He's got a full head of hair an' all.'

As my son was placed in my arms, my heart just melted. Lots of babies I'd seen were ugly, but not mine. He had a mop of wavy almost black hair, with some curls stuck to his forehead. He was the most stunning baby I'd ever seen in my life and as his fist clenched around my little finger, I knew I was born to be a mother.

'Oh, Queenie. Ain't he 'andsome,' my mum sobbed.

'He's so big, Queenie. I can't believe I'm an aunt. What you gonna call him?' asked Vivian.

I kissed my boy on his forehead. For all Albie's faults, Mrs O'Leary had been right about one thing. He created beautiful babies. 'I'm not sure. I want to get to know him first, so I can choose a name that truly suits him. Let's just call him Baby Blue until I decide.' I'd been that convinced I was having a boy, every item of clothing I'd bought was blue.

Later that evening, Albie cried when he held his son in his arms for the first time. 'He's a belter, Queenie. Bleedin' size of him. I don't think I've ever seen such a big newborn with so much hair. He definitely takes after his old dad with that colour barnet.'

Baby Blue had weighed in at nine pounds two ounces. I was pleased he was a big baby, hoped it was a sign he'd grow up to be big and strong. Maria said he was the heaviest she'd delivered all year and seeing we were now in autumn, I doubted that would be beaten.

Albie rocked our baby in his arms, gazing at him in wonder. 'I dunno how my dad walked out on me and Bert without a backward glance. I could never do that to this little fella. What we gonna call him, Queen? I quite like Michael or Daniel.'

No way are we calling him Daniel, I thought, but I didn't say that out loud. I'd actually spent ages after I'd politely asked my mother and sister to leave, just staring at my wonderful creation, debating what I should call him. Then it came to me. There used to be one customer who shopped in Cohen's that stood out from all the rest. He was tall, dark, well-dressed and good looking. He spent tons of cash at the shop. Bought the same outfits each time in a small and larger size, which always struck me as odd.

Joseph was adamant he was a villain who had a wife and a mistress. Doreen used to salivate over him, but even though we'd pried, we couldn't find out anything other than his Christian name. He was a mystery man.

'You gonna let him sleep in his cot?' Albie asked as he handed me back my son.

Credit where it's due. All our neighbours' babies slept in drawers. I had no idea where Albie had got a brand-new cot from; I very much doubted he'd paid for it, but I was grateful for it anyway. 'Yes. He'll sleep in his cot. But you sleep downstairs. I'm sore, tired and I need to feed him now.'

'OK, *love. Just give me a shout if you need anything,*' Albie said, *kissing me and our son on the forehead.*

I waited until Albie had gone downstairs before tiptoeing out of bed with my boy in my arms. I pulled open the curtains. Albie had an old sheet up over the window when I'd first moved in, but I soon made him get rid of that. 'See that star, boy, that big star in the sky,' I said. 'Well, one day, that star's gonna be you, Vinny.'

My son clenched his fat hand around my little finger and I beamed with pride. It was a bond only a mother could understand. 'Vinny Butler, my little superstar in the making.'

Three Years Later

Autumn 1948

'For as much as it has pleased Almighty God to take out of this world the soul of Ida Florence Butler, we therefore commit her body to the ground, earth to earth, ashes to ashes, dust to dust, looking for that . . .'

'Why they putting Nan in the mud, Mum?' enquired Vinny in a loud voice.

'Shush, love,' Queenie said, pulling her beloved boy closer to her side.

'But won't Nan get eaten by worms?' Vinny asked in an even louder voice, interrupting the committal once more.

When Roy, his youngest son, started crying, Albie glared at Queenie and gestured to her to take the boys away from the graveside. The little swines had played up throughout the actual funeral service too. It had been Queenie's idea to bring them here. Albie had insisted the boys were too young and would be better left with a neighbour, but as usual his advice had fallen on deaf ears.

'Nanny always stink of poo-poo,' Vinny announced, as he was led away.

'Sorry about that,' Albie said to the vicar and his brother. Bert squeezed his fiancée's hand and said nothing. He couldn't abide Albie's eldest boy. A spoiled little brat who in Bert's eyes needed a good hiding. The lad had far too much to say for himself as well. Children should be seen and not heard.

Albie threw some mud on top of his mother's coffin. She'd had no quality of life in the end, was housebound and doubly incontinent. 'Rest in peace now, Mum,' Albie wept as he walked away.

'What happens when you die, Mum?' Vinny enquired, as his father walked towards them.

'Shush now, love. No more talk about Nanny Ida. Talk about Nanny Molly instead.' Vinny had recently turned three and was an inquisitive little monkey. He was very bright for his age and Queenie patted herself on the back for that. She spoke to him as though he were an adult and he responded in a mature manner. She hated all that silly baby talk.

'Don't bring the boys to the pub, Queenie. Let one of the neighbours keep an eye on 'em if you wanna come. Roy's tired, Vinny's got the devil in him and I just wanna relax, have a few beers and raise a glass to my mum.'

'The boys are coming to the pub with us, Albie. You know I don't like the neighbours looking after 'em.'

Albie said no more. Instead he walked off with Bert.

Ida's wake was held in the Hoop and Grapes. Micky One Ear laid on a selection of sandwiches and Bert and Albie put some money behind the bar.

Queenie sat down with her mum, Viv and the boys. Viv was nineteen now and worked in the local greengrocer's for Sid Barnes, a family friend.

'Want me to hold Roy? Your arms must be aching,' Viv offered.

Queenie handed over her youngest. Roy was one and had also been a whopper as a baby. Eight pounds twelve ounces. His hair was black like Vinny's and his eyes had recently turned green. Vinny's eyes were a piercing green now, just like Albie's, and Queenie hoped Roy's would end up the same colour. They were striking-looking kids, her boys. Everybody said so.

'Nice send-off, wasn't it?' Molly said to Queenie.

'Yeah. Went as well as these things do. At least Ida's at peace now. She wasn't happy towards the end, found her incontinence humiliating. I'll miss her, but I won't miss clearing up her shit. It was the right time for her to go.'

'You told Queen about Marjorie?' Viv asked her mother.

'Marjorie's moving out, Queen. She's going to live in Dagenham with her sister,' Molly explained. Marjorie was the war widow who rented the upstairs of Molly's house.

'Oh no. What you gonna do?'

'I'm going to see if I can get an extra cleaning job and Vivvy's gonna get some bar work of an evening. Hopefully we'll manage. If we don't, we'll have to rent the upstairs out to someone else.'

'Perhaps me and Albie can rent it,' Queenie replied excitedly. She still looked after Mrs O'Leary and would love to live opposite her again. Mary adored her boys, Vinny especially. 'Bert's getting married soon, so he'll be moving out. Albie won't be able to single-handedly afford the rent on our house, and I don't wanna live in that street for a moment longer than I have to. There's a rat infestation next door at present. The boys would love living at yours.'

'Oh, Queen. That'd be brilliant,' beamed Viv.

'I'd love you to move back in. But what about Albie? He might not want to live with his in-laws.'

'Well I've had to live with his family, haven't I? What's the difference? It won't be for ever, will it? Bit of luck, it might make Albie get his arse into gear and get himself a proper job.'

'Well, if you're sure,' Molly grinned. 'I don't really want Viv doing bar work, she works hard enough as it is.'

'And so do you, Mum. Wait there, I'll talk to Albie now.'

Albie was about to give a small speech and toast to his mum when Queenie dropped the bombshell. 'Jesus wept! My mum ain't even cold yet, Queenie. Give it a rest, will ya! How can you ask me something like that, today of all days?'

'Because we live in a shithole where brasses sell themselves on the corner and next door's overrun with rats, Albie. I've done my bit caring for your mum, now it's your turn to help my family out. I thought that's what marriage was all about, give and take.'

'We'll talk about it tomorrow, OK,' hissed Albie.

Queenie was relieved when her mum and sister got up to leave. Albie's Aunt Liz had plonked herself at the table, telling funny stories of Albie as a child. Queenie had silently prayed she wouldn't mention him hiding in her loft, and thankfully she hadn't. Apart from Mrs O'Leary, Queenie had never told anyone. 'Bye then, Mum. I'll speak to Albie tomorrow about you know what. Then I'll pop round and see you after your cleaning jobs. Bye Viv.'

'Nice lady, your mum. Shame for her what happened to your dad. Imagine fighting in the war, then losing your life in a tragic accident like that. Life's so bleedin' unfair at times. Look how poor Ida suffered. She was a beautiful woman years ago, ya know. Could have had her pick of men. I knew Charlie Butler was a womanizing bastard the moment she first brought him home. I clocked him looking me up and down on more than one occasion. Ida just got on with it when he walked out on her and the boys, bless her. She was never the same after losing her leg though. Sapped her personality, that did,' explained Aunt Liz.

'What did he look like, Charlie Butler? Albie doesn't really remember him.'

'Look at Albie and that's Charlie. Albie's a dead ringer for his father. Same mop of black hair, piercing green eyes. Bert looks more like Ida, poor sod,' Liz chuckled.

'Did Charlie work?' Queenie enquired.

'Yeah. Always had money, did Charlie. Nobody was sure what he actually did, mind.' Liz tapped the side of her nose. 'Rumour had it he was a bit of a villain.'

'Really!'

'Yeah. I heard through the grapevine he worked for the Italians. They ran all the race tracks, were into horses – amongst other stuff.'

Albie craned his neck to check on his sons and couldn't believe his eyes. 'No. Surely not,' he muttered, as he darted past his wife.

Vinny had always been jealous of Roy from the day his brother was born, but to see him holding a cushion over his little brother's face made Albie's blood run cold. 'What the hell d'ya think you're doing?' Albie grabbed Vinny by the arm and smacked him hard on his backside. He then picked up Roy and comforted him. The poor little sod was fighting for breath.

Remembering his mum had always told him if anyone kicked or hit him, he had to kick or hit them harder, Vinny booted his father in the leg before running over to his mum.

Queenie scooped Vinny up in her arms and walked over to Albie. 'Whatever's going on?'

'Whatever's going on! I'll tell you what's going on, shall I?' Albie pointed at Vinny. 'That little bleeder just tried to suffocate his own brother with a cushion. Look how red Roy's face is. He's still coughing and spluttering now. Caught him bastard-well red-handed, I did. Another minute and this poor little sod would've been a goner.'

Queenie was horrified. She knew Vinny was jealous of Roy, had often caught him pinching or tormenting him. But never had he tried anything like this. She put Vinny on the floor and wagged a finger in his face. 'What did you do to Roy, eh?'

Vinny shook his head. 'Wasn't me, Mum.'

Queenie slapped Vinny repeatedly on his hands. 'Don't you ever lie to me or let me catch you doing anything like that again. Do you hear me? What you did is fucking wrong. You're a bad, bad boy.'

Albie rubbed Roy's back. His breathing had thankfully returned to normal now. 'This is your fault for spoiling him like you do,' he told Queenie. 'You'll be the ruination of that boy. I've told you that 'til I'm blue in the face, and this is the fucking outcome.'

'Give me Roy 'ere,' Queenie ordered.

'No. You take that little bastard home. I'll bring Roy home in a bit. Don't you ever leave him on his own with Roy again, Queenie. I mean it. Not normal behaviour that, love. Not normal at all.'

Later that evening, Queenie lay in bed studying her two sons while they slept. She wasn't a bad mother as Albie had insinuated. Her boys were her life. She'd walk over hot coals for them if she had to.

Life hadn't been a bed of roses since the war ended. There was still rationing for food, clothes and toiletries, amongst other stuff. And although the O'Learys sent round packages here and there, luxuries were hard to come by. Queenie had gone without herself to buy Vinny his first proper suit to wear today. Albie had said it was a waste of money and vouchers as their son was sprouting up faster than Jack and the Beanstalk, but Queenie had wanted her eldest to look smart for his grandmother's funeral. It was what she called respect. Aunt Edna's money was long gone now.

Vinny opened his eyes. Even at his young age, he knew he'd done something bad and was in big trouble. 'Do you hate me, Mum?'

Queenie had always thought of Vinny as her perfect son. Until today. Nevertheless, she still held him close to her chest. He often slept in the bed next to her. Roy slept in Vinny's old cot nearby and now his mother was dead, Albie was sleeping downstairs. 'I could never hate you, Vinny. But what you did today was very wrong. Promise me you'll never do anything like that again to your brother. Brothers are meant to stick together, have one another's backs.'

Vinny didn't have a clue what his mother was talking about but could sense by her and his dad's reaction earlier that he was in the doghouse and must never put a pillow over Roy's face again. 'Sorry, Mum. I be a good boy from now on. Promise.'

CHAPTER SIXTEEN

'Once upon a time in the middle of the jungle, a lioness gave birth to a cub.'

'Yeah,' Vinny giggled. 'I bet I know his name.'

'No, you don't,' Queenie winked, knowing full well Vinny had memorized her special bedtime stories word for word. Roy was asleep and was too young to understand them anyway.

'This was Queenie the lioness's second cub. Not quite as special as her first cub, as first cubs are always the most important. But Roy was Vinny's little brother and it was Vinny's duty to protect him from all the other nasty creatures in the jungle.'

'Like dogs and cats, Mummy?'

'No. Like spiders and snakes. Vinny was the older cub you see, the one destined to become king of the jungle, so he needed his brother to help him become king.'

'But why?' Vinny asked, putting his thumb in his mouth.

Queenie tapped Vinny's thumb. 'Only babies suck their thumbs and you're a big boy now like Vinny the lion, aren't you?'

Vinny patted his chest. 'Yeah, I'm a big boy. Does Vinny turn out to be king of the jungle like that other story you tell me, Mum?'

'Only if he takes care of his younger cub, Roy. He needs Roy to help to protect him, see.'

A bit perplexed, Vinny was about to ask another question when there was a knock on the front door.

Scooping her eldest in her arms, Queenie was surprised to see Patrick O'Leary standing on her doorstep. Never had he visited her at this address before, she always saw him round his mum's. His expression looked grave. 'Whatever's wrong? It's not your mum, is it?' panicked Queenie.

Patrick sighed. 'Can I come in?'

'Bed now, Vinny,' ordered Queenie.

'Not tired.'

'Do as I say. Now!'

Knowing he was still in his mother's bad books for trying to suffocate Roy, Vinny did as he was told for once.

'Sit down, Patrick. D'ya want a cup of tea?'

'You got anything stronger, Queenie? I've had the day from hell.'

Queenie opened a bottle of Albie's bootleg brandy.

Patrick downed the brandy in one, topped it up and told Queenie to pour herself one. 'You're gonna need it, sweetheart.'

Queenie could feel her heart beating rapidly. 'Mary's not dead, is she?'

Patrick took a deep breath. 'No. But she doesn't have long, Queenie. Mum has a tumour on the brain, hence all those headaches. We only found out on Wednesday, but Mum didn't want you to know straight away. She knew you had Ida's funeral to contend with first.'

'Oh my God. Oh no. There must be some hope for her, surely?' Tears streamed down Queenie's face. Life without Mary seemed unimaginable.

'You haven't heard the rest of it yet. Dolores.' He shook his head. 'Mum told me ages ago she thought the girl was pregnant as her gut was growing by the day. Did she mention it to you?'

'Yeah. But only the once. I mean, I'd clocked Dolores had put on a bit of timber when we changed shifts – she was wearing baggier clothes.'

Patrick sank another brandy and put his fingers through his dark hair. 'The baby's Daniel's. Bridie found out, kicked Daniel out, so now he's fecked off with Dolores and I haven't even had the chance to tell him Mum's dying yet.'

Queenie took deep breaths to try to control her emotions. 'How long has your mum got left, Patrick?'

'Weeks. Six at the most. She's going to get worse, Queenie, be in a lot of pain. Now Dolores is out of the picture, there's no way you can take care of Mum alone. You've got your own family, responsibilities. I'm going to find her the best local hospice that I can. That way, we can visit her regularly and she can be given any pain relief she might need. I could strangle Daniel with my bare hands, I honestly could. He's never failed to disappoint my mother, not even on her death bed.'

Patrick found Mary the most wonderful hospice. It was a big house in Finsbury Park and there were only three other patients there.

Queenie visited her friend every day, sometimes with the boys, but as Mary began deteriorating rapidly, she went alone. It was awful to see her once vibrant friend wasting away in front of her eyes. She'd also become a bit confused and forgetful.

Queenie always visited in the daytime and the boys loyally visited every evening without fail. When Patrick finally tracked down his brother, Daniel had been devastated to learn his mother was dying. Patrick said he'd broken down in tears. Tears of guilt, Queenie surmised. But Queenie knew how much Mary loved both her sons. No matter what they did, she would stand by them.

One day when Queenie arrived at the hospice, Mary was sitting up and seemed in better spirits. Queenie kissed her.

'How are you today, Mary? You're looking much brighter than yesterday.'

'Better. Bridie visited me last night with the grandchildren.'

'Oh, how lovely,' Queenie smiled. Bridie had two children with Daniel, a girl and a boy. 'Was Daniel here too?'

'No. Patrick told him to stay away. Patrick drove Bridie here, so I could say goodbye to the children.'

Tears pricked Queenie's eyes as she held Mary's bony hand. 'You're not going anywhere yet, my lovely friend.'

'Bridie is moving back to Ireland with the children. She's asked Daniel for a divorce. Good luck to her, is what I say. She deserves better than that boy. I hope she meets a decent man one day. Pass me my handbag, Queenie.'

Queenie did as asked. Mary could still only move one side of her body and her speech was slower than ever.

Mary handed Queenie an envelope and her rosary beads in their velvet pouch. 'There's money in the envelope. Fifty pounds. Treat yourself and the boys to something nice and save the rest for a rainy day. As for the beads, you know how much they mean to me, which is why I want you to have them. I want you to think of me every time you hold them. I haven't got long left now, Queenie, but I don't want you to be sad when I go. I want you to remember all the good times, all the fun and laughter we shared.'

Tears streamed down Queenie's face. 'Oh, Mary. I don't want you to leave me. I love you so much, like a mum.'

'And I love you like a daughter. You enriched my life, Queenie, far more than you'll ever know. But I'm ready to go now. God will take good care of me and heal me when I get to heaven, and believe me, I will always look down on you with pride. Don't forget what you need to do in raising your boys like lions. Look at my two. I used to love the days when I'd get called to the front of the queue in the shops. That'll be you one day, Queenie. You'll make a fine mother. You're already doing a good job. Now, is there anything you want to ask me?'

'Did you ask Patrick and Daniel to beat my father up on the day he died?'

'Of course not, love, but I told them how upset you were and that someone should give your father a taste of his own medicine.'

'Thank you. And what about Ivan?'

'I think you already know the answer to that question, Queenie. Now is there anything you want to tell me?'

'No. Only that I love you so very much.'

'Fine. Now don't you live in the past. The future is far more important to think about. I'm getting tired now, love. Will you bring Vinny to see me tomorrow? I want to say goodbye to him.'

Queenie couldn't control her tears. This seemed all so final. She handed Mary the envelope back. 'I'll take the beads and treasure them, but I can't take your money.

Patrick's given me some cash so I can afford to pay my bills while visiting you. I'm not skint, honestly.'

'Nope. You take it. My boys are cake-o, they don't fecking need it. I can't wait to see my Seamus again. Knowing I'll be buried with him gives me great comfort. Oh, another thing. My funeral will take place in Ireland, but I don't want you to travel all that way, dear. It'll be too upsetting for you, I know it will. You can put some flowers in a vase at home and light a candle for me on that day. No more tears now. Be strong, my special friend.'

The following day when Queenie took Vinny to the hospice, Mrs O'Leary looked so frail and ill, she could barely open her eyes. Queenie pulled a nurse to one side. 'What's happened? Mary was fine yesterday, sitting up and talking to me.'

'She's nearing the end now I'm afraid, Queenie. Quite often patients will perk up just before they are ready to pass.'

'How long's she got, d'ya reckon?' Mary had only been at the hospice three days.

'Days or even hours. I'd say your goodbyes now if I were you.'

Queenie sat down next to Mary's bed and held her hand. She knew Mary was aware she was there as when she spoke, Mary slightly squeezed her hand. 'I've brought Vinny with me, Mary.'

'Is she dead?' asked Vinny in a loud voice.

Queenie clipped her son around the ear. 'No. Now I'm gonna lift you up and you're going to kiss Auntie Mary on the cheek. I want you to say goodbye to her and tell her you love her.'

'You sure she ain't dead? She looks dead.'

'Do as I say,' Queenie hissed, lifting her son up.

Vinny turned up his nose and closed his eyes. 'Bye, Auntie Mary. Love you.'

'Queenie,' Mary's voice was no more than a whisper, so Queenie leaned closer. She could tell Mary was near the end. The death rattle was clear to hear in her throat.

'What is it, Mary?'

'You ever need anything or are in trouble, promise me you'll go to my boys.'

'I promise you, Mary. I will.'

As Mary went back to sleep, Queenie kissed her on the forehead, then left. She had a strong feeling this would be the last time she'd ever see her dear friend.

'You sure she weren't dead?' Vinny asked yet again.

This time Queenie walloped him hard on his backside. 'You ask that question once more, I'll give you such a fucking fourpenny one when I get you home, you won't sit down for a month. As to referring to Mary as "she", show some respect, boy. *She* is the cat's mother. That lady who you've just said goodbye to is Auntie Mary. Got that?'

'Yes, Mum. Auntie Mary ain't dead.'

Later that evening, there was a knock on the door. Queenie feared the worst, yet was shocked to see Dolores standing there.

'It's Mary, Queenie. She hasn't got long now. Daniel asked me to give you this, said you're to take a taxi up there.'

Queenie was inwardly furious he'd sent his trollop to her front step. But she took the ten-pound note and asked Albie to look after the boys.

When Queenie arrived, Patrick and Daniel were both at their mother's bedside, looking like broken men.

'I thought you might want a few minutes alone with Mum, Queenie,' Daniel said.

'Thank you. Yes, I would.'

The rattling in Mary's throat was loud. Queenie sat down and held Mary's hand. 'I'm not sure you can hear me, Mary, but I just want to thank you for everything you've done for me. You've made me into the strong woman I am today and I will always continue to use your values for the rest of my life. I love you so much and you'll always be in my heart. I don't know what I'm going to do without you though. But I promised you I would be strong, so I will be.'

Queenie was stunned as Mary's eyes flickered open, then quickly shut again. 'Nurse, nurse. Mary just opened her eyes, I swear she did.'

The nurse checked Mary's pulse. 'Mary's gone, my love. I'm so sorry.'

Patrick and Daniel came back into the room. Both put their arms around Queenie and as she sobbed her heart out, so did they.

What a woman Mary O'Leary was. And now she was gone for good.

CHAPTER SEVENTEEN

'Can you give me some money, Albie? I need a new outfit to wear at your brother's wedding. It's been ages since I treated myself to anything nice. I'm gonna get Linda the dressmaker to run up a little suit for Roy too. She did such a good job with Vinny's.' It was over a fortnight since Mary had died and even though it was difficult, Queenie was trying her hardest to carry on as normal. The day of Mary's funeral, Queenie hadn't stopped crying. But it was time to move on now for the sake of her boys. She'd also promised Mary she'd be strong and had no intention of breaking her promise.

Albie took his wallet out of his pocket and handed Queenie three pound notes. 'Roy's only bleedin' one, can't even walk properly yet. A waste of money if you ask me, getting him a suit made. Hardly likely to get any wear out of it, is he?'

'Three measly bleedin' quid! That's not enough! I'm going to Cohen's to get my outfit. Joseph's running the shop now, by all accounts. I bumped into one of our old customers the other day. I'm sure he'll give me some kind of a discount as I never had no falling out with him, but you can't even buy a decent hat and pair of stockings in there with what you've given me.' No way was Queenie using the money Mary had given her. She wasn't working now, so it was Albie's duty as a man to support his wife.

Albie felt embarrassed. Queenie had a habit of making him feel like he was some kind of loser. 'That's all the spare money I've got until later, love. A lot of the publicans owe me dosh for spirits I dropped off to 'em last week. I'll chase 'em up today, get 'em to weigh me out.'

'Well, best you do, Albie. Because if I haven't got a decent outfit to wear for Bert's wedding, then I ain't bleedin' well coming.'

Albie perched himself on the bar stool in the Hoop and Grapes. 'Large brandy please, mate.'

'On the house,' Micky One Ear said, as he plonked the drink down in front of his pal. 'Bad day?'

'You could say that. Been a bad year, if I'm honest, Mick. What with losing me mum and stuff. Now I got to sort out new living arrangements as Bert moves out straight after his wedding. Queenie wants us to move in with her mum and sister, but that ain't gonna work. The sister's round ours all the bleedin' time as it is. On top of all that, Queenie's been on my bloody case this morning for some posh new outfit she wants to buy. I got about ten geezers who owe me money for fags and booze, but only two have coughed up this morning. The rest have told me to come back later in the week. I dread going home tonight if I ain't got enough dosh to give the old woman.'

At forty-six years old, Micky One Ear was a lot wiser and older than Albie. Most of the locals knew that Albie had shirked his duties to fight for his country, but nobody really disliked him because of it. Albie was a joker, a true character, but had never been able to fight his way out of a paper bag. 'I'll lend you whatever dosh you need to buy Queenie her outfit. On one condition though.'

'What?'

'That you come out on the piss with me this afternoon. My treat. My Sheila's given me the rest of the day off.'

Albie Butler grinned. 'You're on.'

'Stop fighting and sit up straight,' Queenie ordered Vinny. He was sulking because she'd walloped him and given him a good telling off earlier. Time and time again she'd told him never to touch a dead rat and this morning she'd caught him red-handed. He was pulling the insides out of one he'd found with his bare bloody hands. There were lots of stray cats hanging around lately and Queenie guessed one of them had caught the thing before Vinny had found it and decided to give it an autopsy. She'd had to boil a kettle and scrub the dirty little sod's hands with a brush and Coal Tar soap until they'd almost bled.

'Feel sick, Mum,' Vinny announced.

Queenie placed her hand on her son's forehead. He didn't seem to have a temperature, but it was common knowledge that rats carried terrible diseases. 'We're getting off next stop. You'll be fine once you get some fresh air. And if you ain't, I'm blaming your bleedin' father.'

Albie was thoroughly enjoying his unexpected jaunt with Micky One Ear. They'd lined their stomachs in Manze's with pie, mash and eels, and were currently in the Lord Palmerston in Hewlett Road. Every boozer they'd been in, Micky had been greeted warmly by the guvnor and their first drink had been on the house. Micky had also recommended the bootleg booze Albie got his hands on via Paddy Adams, and Albie had promised to pop back tomorrow with a sample of everything he sold.

'You knock any booze over West Ham, Canning Town way, Albie?' asked Micky.

'No, mate. I'm always a bit wary of punting it off me own patch in case I tread on some bastard's toes. I can't be bringing trouble to the door now I got a wife and kiddies.'

'I got a lot of contacts in Canning Town and West Ham. When we leave 'ere, I'll take you down there, see if we can drum up some more business for ya. Let me do the talking and don't worry about treading on anyone's toes. I'll check whose supplying 'em first. The whisky, brandy and rum you get hold of is far better than all the other bootleg versions round 'ere. You should expand a bit, Albie. I'll help ya. I'll expect an extra discount off me own, mind,' Micky winked.

Queenie had been surprised when Aggie had moved to Bow earlier in the year. She'd also been a tad jealous as Terry Marney was turning out to be a wonderful husband. He'd actually bought Aggie a home, not just bloody rented it. 'D'ya feel all right now, Vinny?' Queenie enquired.

'Wanna wee-wee.'

'You can go when we get there, and don't you dare upset Little Terry today. You made him cry the last time we visited.'

Vinny didn't like Little Terry. Recalling what had happened the last time he'd visited, Vinny allowed himself a wry smile.

'Oh my giddy aunt! I don't believe it! Albie Butler! Even more 'andsome than I remember. Look at you!

All grown up. I can still see you in your little shorts holding your mam's hand as she dragged you off to school. You hated school, ya never wanted to go when you were a nipper,' chuckled Cilla Watkins, the barmaid in the British Lion.

Albie felt like a teenager all over again as he locked eyes with Cilla. He remembered her birthday was the day after his, which made her thirty-seven now as she was eight years older than him. By God, she was still as buxom and beautiful as ever. Her thick long chestnut hair glistened and her smile was as cheeky as always. 'Well I never! You're the last person I expected to bump into today. How long's it been since I've seen you, Cilla? You haven't changed a bit, darlin'.'

'I take it you two know one another,' joked Micky One Ear.

Albie and Cilla locked eyes once more. Both smiled. Cilla had been Albie's boyhood crush and his first ever sexual experience. How could he ever forget her?

In nearby Bow, Queenie was being shown around Aggie's palace of a home. She wasn't a nasty person, and she was pleased for Aggie, but the work Terry had done inside the home and the sweat he'd grafted to attain it in the first place just enlightened Queenie to what a failure she'd married. And to think Terry had first tried to chat her up in the Beehive that New Year's Eve and she'd mocked him to Doreen for being a coalman. Turned out he wasn't just a coalman after all. He also grafted all hours with his father, who was a rag and bone man.

'This is our bedroom now, Queenie. Remember how tatty it was when you last saw it? Terry wallpapered this himself an' all,' Aggie gushed.

The wallpaper was green with yellow flowers on it and there were green curtains at the window to match. 'It looks beautiful, Aggie. Ever so posh,' Queenie said, genuinely bowled over.

'Thank you. Right, let's have a cuppa and some cake now. Come on, Little Terry, downstairs we go,' Aggie said, in a silly childlike voice.

'Getting big, ain't he? And look how handsome he is now,' Queenie lied, playfully pinching Little Terry's cheek. That was the one area she had the upper hand on. Terry Marney might be a grafter and good at decorating, but by God did he produce ugly kids. Aggie was currently pregnant again and Queenie couldn't help feeling sorry for her if it popped out looking like the last one. Ginger, with a wonky eye, Little Terry looked a poor little ha'porth in his glasses with a patch over one eye. He was the same age as Vinny, but was tiny in comparison.

Aggie put the kettle on and cut up the Lazy Daisy cake her mum had brought round the previous day.

'Bored, Mum,' Little Vinny complained.

'Eat your cake, then you can ask Auntie Aggie if you can play in her garden.' Queenie had brought her sons up to address their elders the way she'd been raised. Close neighbours and friends were to be called aunt and uncle, other adults were addressed as mister or missus.

'Cake,' Roy giggled, pointing at the plate.

'Getting big now, ain't he, Queen. Gonna be tall like Vinny I reckon,' Aggie said.

'Yeah. He is. I want Vinny to wear him out before we leave. He's too big to be in that pram now, but he's heavy for me to carry all the way 'ere. He wants to walk wherever we go lately, but it takes for ever and he tires quickly.'

'Finish. Can I play in the garden, Aunt Aggie?' Vinny asked.

'Please! You forgot to say please,' Queenie corrected her son.

'Please, Aunt Aggie.'

'Of course you can.'

'Little Terry, come,' Vinny said, pointing at the boy who wouldn't make eye contact with him.

Little Terry shook his head and clung to his mum like a limpet. Last time he'd played in the garden with Vinny, he'd been force-fed a live worm which had made him sick.

'Take Roy with you, Vinny. Little Terry's not been well, so he'll stay in the warm with me,' lied Aggie. Vinny was a boisterous child and she knew her son was scared of him. She also knew Vinny had made him eat a worm, had been fuming at the time and was ready to march around Queenie's the following day to tell her what a nasty, spiteful bastard her eldest son was. It had been Terry who'd advised her not to. 'Boys will be boys, love. I remember me and my pals daring one another to put worms in our mouths. You can't be over-protective with Little Tel. Once he starts school, he's gonna have to learn how to stick up for himself,' Terry had insisted.

Aggie had said nothing. She didn't trust Vinny as far as she could throw him. Neither did she like the child. There was something about Vinny Butler only a mother could love.

Cilla Watkins slipped Albie a piece of paper. 'I've written me shifts down and my home address. Be lovely to have a proper catch-up with you in the future. My husband works away. Don't be a stranger,' Cilla winked.

Well aware that Cilla was coming on to him, Albie felt flattered yet awkward. 'Erm, thanks. It's been lovely seeing you, it really has. See you again soon hopefully,' Albie said, before bolting out the pub door.

Micky One Ear slapped his pal on the back. 'You're well in there, mate,' he chuckled. 'Pretty lady an' all. So what's the story? You and Cilla got history?'

'Nah, nothing like that. I had a crush on Cilla as a lad and during my early teenage years. She lived with her mum, opposite mine.'

'Well, I think boot might be on the other foot now. She was certainly sending out signals. You gonna see her again?'

'Is the guvnor interested in me booze?'

'Yeah. Alf said to drop some samples in. Reckons the cheap spirits he's been offered on the black market are shit.'

'I'll probably see Cilla when I pop back with the samples then. I'd like to have a good catch-up over old times with her.'

'By the look on Cilla's boat-race, she wants more than a chat about old times. Once a stud, always a stud, Butler,' laughed Micky.

'Shut up,' Albie chortled. 'I'm a happily married man and I certainly wouldn't be getting on the wrong side of my Queenie. I like me bollocks intact, thanks.'

Queenie put two bowls of leftover beef stew on the table and two doorstop slices of bread. 'Don't waste that now, boys. Eat it all up. You want to grow big and strong, don'tcha?'

'I'm a big boy now,' Vinny replied.

Roy dived straight in, unfortunately missing his mouth

198

with the spoon. 'Dadda,' he said, hearing the front door open and close.

It wasn't Albie. It was Viv.

'All right, Queen? Got you another bag of goodies 'ere. Tomatoes and apples are a bit rotten, but I'm sure you'll still make use of 'em. The rest of it looks OK.'

'Ooh, lovely.' Vivian working for Sid at the greengrocer's certainly had its perks; he often allowed Viv to bring home fruit and veg that was no longer deemed fit for sale. With certain food still being rationed and hungry mouths to feed, Queenie would find use for even the most rotten fruit and veg. 'You staying for tea? I bought some sprats. Albie can have the rest of the stew.'

'Yes, please,' Vivian beamed, her face flushed.

'Come on, out with it. What you looking so happy about?'

'You know me only too well,' Viv laughed. 'There's this bloke who comes in the grocer's quite a lot to get fruit and veg for his mum. He's ever so handsome, Queen, and often treats me to a cheeky grin as he leaves. He's funny too, got the gift of the gab. Sid knows him, I think, 'cause he usually serves him, but today Sid had popped out, so there was only me and Simple Brian there. Anyway, as I was serving him, he started asking questions. He asked how old I was and if I had a boyfriend. Then as he left, he turned back, winked at me and said, "I'll see you again very soon, treacle," in a seductive voice.'

Alarm bells instantly rang in Queenie's head. She had and always would be protective of her younger sister. Vivvy was nineteen now, but had never had a proper boyfriend. She was smart, pretty and fussy, and was yet to have her head turned by the lads she'd met at dances.

Vivvy loved films and would spend every weekend watching at least one at the cinema. She would often rattle on about romance in a certain movie, but never in the real world. So Queenie was slightly taken aback.

'Say something then. D'ya think he likes me? He must do surely, otherwise why ask those questions?'

It was weird hearing Viv gush over a lad for the first time ever. Queenie didn't want to piss on her sister's parade, but felt she must say something. 'He sounds really nice, Viv, but a bit of a flash Harry. Be careful, that's the only advice I can give you. Don't build your hopes up too much until he asks you out, eh? Don't you know anything about him?'

'Only that he shops for his mum and his first name's Bill.'

'Well, my advice would be to ask Sid—'

The conversation ended abruptly as Albie arrived home. 'All right, Queen,' Albie said, ruffling his sons' hair to greet them. 'Oh, hello, Viv,' Albie muttered. Her pushbike wasn't outside, so he'd hoped she wasn't here for once.

'Did you get me my money?' Queenie asked, unwrapping the sprats.

Having hopefully drummed up lots of new custom and got Queenie the money for her posh outfit, Albie wanted this moment to be between just the two of them. He was also hoping it might lead to a night of passion. It had been ages since he and Queenie had even slept in the same bed, let alone had sex. Seeing Cilla again had made him feel amorous and he was desperate to hold his wife in his arms tonight. 'Yes. We'll talk later, love. I'm starving. You got me some sprats I see, bless ya.'

'The sprats are for me and Viv, Albie. I've saved you the last of the beef stew.'

'But I've had that two days running already,' Albie said dismally.

'So have the boys, but they're not bloody complaining, are they?' Queenie spun around. 'I knew it! Could tell by your voice. You're sloshed, ain't ya?'

'No. I've only had a few. Oh, d'ya know what, stick your beef stew up your harris. I'm going for a lie-down, on *my* bed.'

'Charming! Sod ya then. The boys can have seconds.'

When Albie stomped up the stairs, Vivian carried on talking about Bill. Unbeknown to Queenie, the real reason she'd never had a boyfriend up until now was frankly because she'd never quite gotten over her crush on Albie. She knew that was wrong, but couldn't help the way she felt or what she dreamed about. Many a time in her dreams, Albie had taken her in his arms and made passionate love to her. Well, up until about six weeks ago anyway. That was around the time Bill had started to come in the greengrocer's and she was thankfully now dreaming about him instead. 'How long did it take Albie to ask you out, Queen?' Viv enquired.

'Oh, I can't remember. A couple of months or so, I think. How old is this Bill, would you say? And what does he look like?'

'He's got blond hair, but not too light, and I reckon he's about five foot ten. He's definitely older than me, about twenty-three I'd say,' Vivian said, a vacant expression on her face.

Queenie plonked a plate of sprats, the vinegar bottle and a slice of bread in front of her little sister. 'If he asks you out, make sure he picks you up from here. I want to meet him before you go gallivanting off into the night, OK?'

Albie dug into his pocket for the piece of paper Cilla had given him. He'd been an early starter when it came to women, had lusted after Cilla from around the age of ten. Her bedroom window faced his and he was sure when he reached his teenage years, she knew he was watching her as she got undressed.

It was a bitterly cold New Year's Eve when Albie's dreams had finally come true. Cilla had split up with her current boyfriend over Christmas and he knew she drank in the Carpenter's Arms. So he dragged a pal there. He was fourteen at the time, but looked a lot older.

Cilla was tipsy, with a group of pals, and kept making eyes at him. It seemed only natural Albie would offer to walk her home, seeing as she lived opposite him. Albie remembered feeling all grown-up when Cilla held his arm as they walked down the High Road. Then she started telling him how handsome he was and how she wished she were nine years younger.

Albie made some joke about him being a man not a boy, and that's when she kissed him. It wasn't just a peck, Cilla stuck her tongue right down the back of his throat, so Albie did what any horny fourteen-year-old virgin would have done. He led her down the alleyway next to Macca's hardware shop and shagged her up against the wall. A minute, he lasted inside her – if that.

Albie had hoped it would be the start of something wonderful, but it wasn't to be. Cilla apologized for leading him astray a couple of days later and begged him not to tell anyone what had happened.

Albie's reminiscing was ended by the sound of Vivvy leaving his house. Seeing Cilla earlier had reminded him of the person he once was. He marched down the stairs.

'All right, grumpy? Want your stew now?' asked Queenie.
'No. We need to talk.'

'Can't it wait until tomorrow? I need to put the boys
to bed and tell 'em a story.'

'No. It bastard well can't. I'm sick of feeling like a spare
part round 'ere. I've even been kicked out me own bed
by my three-year-old son. It ain't bloody right. Vinny's
old enough now to sleep in my mum's old room with
Roy. I know you wanna move, Queen, but we're not
moving into your mum's house. We get no alone time as
it is. When was the last time you bothered to come and
watch me sing? Or we went out on our own? I'm your
bloody husband. Don't you think I have needs too?'

'Needs! What about my bleedin' needs? D'ya wanna
know where I've been today?' she spat. 'I'll tell you anyway,
shall I? Remember my mate Aggie Brown, d'ya? She
married Terry Marney,' Queenie added sarcastically. She'd
been bridesmaid at Aggie and Terry's wedding and Albie
had sung at their reception. 'Well, I went to visit Aggie
today in that house Terry bought for them in that lovely
quiet cul-de-sac. Terry is what you call a real man, Albie.
He's done that house up like a bastard palace. They even
have a toilet indoors.' Queenie shook her head in despair.
'And you wonder why I ain't all over you like a rash! Try
getting yourself a proper job like Terry and providing for
your family. Until then, I would rather sleep with my
sons.'

Albie took a tenner out of his wallet, screwed it up and
slung it at Queenie. 'There's the money for your outfit,
but I wouldn't even both to come to Bert's wedding if I
were you. It's obvious you regret marrying me. I am what
I am, Queenie. I'll always earn a pound note, but if your

expectations are higher, I suggest you move on. Find yourself your very own Terry Marney. I'm off out again now. You might not want me in your bed, but there are plenty of women that do.'

Queenie was horrified as her husband walked away from her. Surely he hadn't meant what he'd just said? Albie might not be perfect, but she didn't want to lose him. A divorce was unthinkable. When she'd said her vows, she'd meant them, for better or for worse. Not only that, she wanted more sons. Two wasn't enough. 'Albie, don't go. I know I get on your nerves at times. But I only moan at you 'cause I want a better life for our sons than we had.'

'Don't you think I want a better life for our boys too? We don't starve, Queenie. Our sons are well fed and clothed. You knew I didn't have a proper job when you married me. Yet you still walked down the bloody aisle. Now all you do is put me down all the time. You make me feel useless, and I'm not. Even my opinion counts for nothing. I've told you time and time again that we're not moving in with your mum and sister. Yet you're still adamant we are. You don't show me any love or affection. Sick of it I am.'

As Albie went to put his coat on, Queenie flung her arms around his waist. 'I'm sorry. I do love you. I'm just no good at expressing my emotions. My dad is to blame. I know he is. I still have nightmares, flashbacks of how he treated my mum.'

Albie was somewhat taken aback. He couldn't remember the last time Queenie had apologized to him, or told him she loved him. He immediately softened. When he'd said his wedding vows he'd meant them too. 'Your dad's dead now, sweetheart, and your mum's OK. You need to forget about the past and concentrate on your future. Our future. I would never harm a hair on your head, you know that.'

'I do. I saved you some sprats, ya know. Why don't you fry those while I tell the boys a story to send 'em to sleep? Me and you can sleep in your mum's room tonight, if you like? Then tomorrow, I'll move the boys in there.'

Albie held Queenie close to his chest. 'That's my girl.'

PART FOUR

'Men are what their mothers made them'
Ralph Waldo Emerson

CHAPTER EIGHTEEN

Six Years Later

'Once upon a time in the East End of London there were three brothers. But they weren't like other boys, they were special boys. Very special indeed.'

'Does Vinny become king, Mum?'

'Listen carefully and you'll find out,' I smiled. Vinny was getting a bit old for the jungle stories now, so I was making up new ones.

'Are their names Vinny, Roy and Michael, Mum?' asked Roy.

'Yep,' I told him. 'Vinny's the oldest, Roy the middle son and Michael the youngest. But they're very close. They knock around together and watch one another's backs. That's why they're destined to become very successful in life, 'cause if brothers stick together, they become a force to be reckoned with.'

'Do they become rich, Mum?' asked Vinny.

'Yeah. But only because they work hard and work together. They don't take no crap off anybody either. If a lad punches them, they punch him back twice as hard.

209

They never hit girls though, 'cause that's wrong, ain't it?'

'Yeah, 'cause girls are weak,' said Vinny.

'Not all girls are weak,' I laughed. 'Mummy was a little girl once and she don't take no crap off anyone, does she?'

'How do they become rich?' asked Roy.

'They look out for good opportunities and when they're older they wear the finest suits and polished shoes. Always remember appearance means everything. First impressions do count and if you wanna be someone in life, you gotta look and act the part, haven't you?'

'Will they be rich enough to buy themselves a bike each?' enquired Michael.

I chuckled. 'They'll be that rich they can buy themselves anything they want. Flash cars, even a castle out in Essex.'

'I wanna be king of the castle, Mum,' Vinny smiled.

I stroked my eldest's cheek. 'You will be king of the castle as long as you do as your mum says. Right, go to sleep now. Lights out.'

'But you ain't told us the rest of the story,' complained Roy.

'I'll tell you the next part tomorrow.'

'Night, Mum.'

I kissed my three little princes and shut their bedroom door. One day they would be kings, in some way, shape or form. I would make damn sure of that.

Spring 1954

'Sing to me, Daddy,' ordered young Michael Butler.

Albie picked up his youngest son and sang 'When Father Papered the Parlour'. Michael was a bright kid for four and truly was Albie's little ray of sunshine. He loved all his sons equally, of course, but had a special bond with Michael as he was thankfully a 'Daddy's boy'. The other two doted on Queenie, Vinny especially.

Queenie chuckled as she had a quick dust around the front room. She was fastidious about housework, even more since she'd moved into her own home. Rented, two bedroomed, in a nice street with pleasant neighbours. It was only a few streets away from her mum's. 'What you up to today, Albie? You staying local?'

'Yes, love. I did all my deliveries yesterday, so was just gonna have a game of cards and a couple of pints in the Grave Maurice. Why? You off out?'

'Yeah. I'm gonna kill two birds with one stone. I'm going shopping down the Roman with Viv. I'm determined to confront her over Bill. Then I'll pop round Aggie's to have it out with her. I can't abide liars, Albie, you know that.'

Albie put Michel down and gave his wife a hug. 'People are strange, Queen. Me and the boys love ya though.'

'Yuck,' sneered eight-year-old Vinny, as he burst into the front room and caught his parents cuddling. It was a rare sight.

'You ain't making more babies, are ya?' giggled six-year-old Roy.

'Don't be so silly,' Queenie replied, pushing Albie away. 'Michael, you can come with me today. We're going down the Roman with Auntie Viv.' Queenie wagged her finger at both Vinny and Roy's faces. 'You two behave yourselves. No winding up the neighbours or stealing anything from down the bleedin' market. Your dad will give you some money to spend and as I've told you 'til I'm blue in the face, we don't steal off of our own. OK?'

Hands in his trouser pockets, Michael ran over to his

brothers. 'Don't wanna go out with you. Wanna play out with Vinny and Roy. I'm a big boy now, Mum.'

Having heard through the grapevine his eldest two were little sods, Albie shook his head. 'No, Michael. You go out with your mum, boy.'

Vinny stared his father in the eyes. 'Nah. We'll look after him. Won't we, Roy? Brothers look out for one another.'

Queenie beamed with pride. Her bedtime stories had obviously worked a treat. 'Michael starts school soon, Albie. He'll be well looked after by his brothers. Now who fancies an egg and bacon breakfast?'

'Me.'

'Me.'

'And me,' Michael shrieked.

Queenie squeezed Albie's arm. There weren't many families that could afford a fry-up on a Saturday morning as well as a Sunday, but they bloody well could. Life was grand and Queenie could not wait to let Albie into a little secret later. But first of all, she wanted to tell Viv.

Queenie bought Albie a couple of shirts, new underpants, a skirt for herself and the boys a couple of pairs of shorts each. The fifty quid Mary had left her was long gone. But she'd spent it wisely, mainly on her sons and her home. She still thought about Mary every single day but kept her thoughts to herself. Nobody would understand, apart from Daniel and Patrick and she hadn't seen them for ages. She'd heard they were doing well though, which was good.

Viv bought herself a couple of dresses, then suggested they stop for a bit of pie and mash.

'I was thinking we'd pop in the pub for a couple of drinks. Aggie only lives five minutes from here and I could do with a bit of Dutch courage to confront her,' Queenie fibbed. She was determined to get Viv to open up and was hoping a couple of drinks might loosen her tongue. 'We can get pie and mash after we've been to Aggie's.'

'We can't go to a pub alone, Queen! Not on a Saturday lunchtime. It will be full of men. We'll look like two hussies on the pull! What would Albie say?'

'Oh don't talk so daft. Times are changing, Viv. The men round 'ere would never have got through the Blitz without us women. We were the bloody strong ones. No man will bleedin' well look down on us. I'll give 'em what for if they do.' Queenie grabbed her sister's arm. 'Come on.'

In the Grave Maurice, Albie Butler wasn't having the best of days. Usually, he'd win one or two games of cards, but today, his luck was well and truly poxed. He sipped his pint of bitter. 'My last game this one, lads. Queenie's out shopping and I promised her I'd keep an eye on the boys. Michael's out street-raking with Vinny and Roy today. I dread to think what they're teaching him,' Albie chuckled, rolling his eyes.

'He's a handful, your Vinny, ain't he, Albie? Did you hear what happened at his school?' asked Ronny Tobyn.

'No.'

'Beat seven bells out of the Big Bri Higgins' boy. Apparently, Higgins' boy is a bit of a bully, but your lad gave him what for. Ended up at the London with a broken jaw and nose. Never told his father what happened either. Said he'd fallen down the stairs.'

Albie felt his blood run cold. Big Brian Higgins was an ex-amateur boxer who now weighed about twenty stone. The man had a loud voice, a violent temper and Albie liked to steer well clear of him. He wasn't a very nice person at all, especially when inebriated. 'I doubt my Vinny had anything to do with his son's injuries, mate. Vinny ain't come home bloodied or duffed up. Queenie would've told me. Who told you it was Vinny?'

'My grandson. He witnessed the fight along with a few others. None of 'em will grass, so don't worry. They all want to be Vinny's best pal now, don't they?' laughed Ronny.

Albie forced a chuckle, but was secretly crapping himself. If this was true and he got a hiding from Big Bri, then it was all Queenie's fault. She'd filled his sons' heads with shit from the day the poor little sods were born.

Queenie knew exactly why Viv had dumped Joey Jenner, the nice blacksmith she'd courted for around six months. She also knew why Viv was so uncomfortable sitting in this pub. It was because of that tosser who was currently banged up, but due out of prison soon. 'Why you sat facing the corner and afraid to turn around, Viv?' Queenie was fuming that her sister had not been truthful with her. She'd had her suspicions for a while, but had only found out for sure the other day when she'd popped round her mum's, secretly searched Vivian's room and found the letters from Bill Harris stuffed under Viv's mattress.

Bill Harris was the bloke Viv had fallen for six years ago when he'd walked into the greengrocer's where she worked. They'd started courting and when Queenie had met him, she'd hated him on sight. Bill was handsome, walked with a swagger, yet was one cocky bastard.

Queenie had ordered Albie to do his homework on Bill and it turned out he'd already spent time in prison for petty crime. She informed Viv of this, but Viv flew at her like a banshee, insisting she was jealous and Bill had already told her about his past and was a changed man.

It turned out Bill hadn't changed his ways. Not only did he mess Vivvy about something chronic, by arranging dates, then ending up out on the lash with his mates instead, he then got arrested again for being a getaway driver on an armed robbery. Four years he'd been sentenced to, and Queenie was well pleased. Viv was distraught at first, but started going out with her friends and meeting men at dances again.

'Can we go now please, Queen?' Viv mumbled. The Needle Gun was Bill's local; he'd brought her in here many times and wouldn't be happy if he heard she'd been in here today.

Queenie could not help the sneer on her face. She leaned forward. 'Didn't we once promise, after everything that happened in our shitty childhood, we would always be truthful with one another? I ain't bastard-well stupid, Viv. I know Bill Harris is due out soon and I know that's why you dumped poor Joey. I also know you've been visiting the bastard.'

Vivian's stare was steely as she locked eyes with her sister. 'Don't be lecturing me, Queenie. Joey was a nice man, but I never loved him. Bill makes my heart flutter every time I see him. People in glass houses should never throw stones. Your marriage is hardly perfect, is it? Yes, you have the handsome sons you craved for. But I know you don't really love Albie. When Bill is released, I shall marry him whether you and Mum like it or not. I bet you wished you'd have married Daniel O'Leary when you had the chance.'

'You cheeky mare!' Queenie said, determined not to rise to the bait despite the mention of Daniel's name.

'Nothing wrong with my marriage. Albie and I rub along quite well together I'll have you know.'

'Only 'cause he's earning a few bob now. You had no time for him at all before he upped his game. Your sons and yourself are the only people you bloody well love.'

Queenie was hurt. She and Viv rarely rowed. 'How can you say that? I've always been there for Mum and you, watching your backs. That's why I'm worried about you. How's he going to support you, Viv? By pulling off more robberies? You don't want to be lumbered with a man who's in and out of prison all his life. You'll be struggling to make ends meet and raising your kids alone.'

'Bill's changed. He's promised me he's going straight from now on, and I believe him. This is my life, Queen, and I'm old enough now to make my own decisions. Can't you be happy for me, just this once?'

Vinny and Roy often took their little brother out, but usually they stayed within the local vicinity. Seeing as their mum was out today, the boys decided to take Michael on an adventure to educate him on what they got up to on the quiet.

Firstly, they hung around the market and earned a few bob doing odd jobs for the stallholders. Then they took Michael down to Stinkhouse bridge before heading to Hackney Marshes where the gypsies kept their horses. Vinny enticed them with the carrots they'd blagged from the market, then bravely jumped on the back of one.

'Can I 'ave a go?' Michael squealed, excitedly jumping up and down.

'Oi, ya little feckers. What ya think you're doing?'

Seeing one of the gypsy men waving a walking stick

and heading their way, Vinny slid off the horse and yelled, 'Run for it.'

Aggie Marney felt ever so awkward as she opened her front door to Queenie and Viv standing on her freshly scrubbed doorstep. Terry was out, working hard as usual, so she was home alone with Little Terry and her two daughters, preparing dinner. 'Oh, hello. This is a nice surprise,' she lied.

'You gonna invite us in then?' Queenie asked.

'Erm, yes, of course. I'll put the kettle on.'

'Two sugars in mine and one an' a half in Viv's,' Queenie replied abruptly.

'Look, Auntie Queenie and Vivvy have come to visit us,' Aggie said in a silly childlike voice.

Queenie stared at the three children and politely smiled. Not a looker among them, the poor little mites. As for the boy, he was a complete no-hoper, him.

'So, to what do I owe this unexpected visit?' Aggie smiled, as she handed Queenie and Viv their cups of tea.

Not one to beat about the bush, Queenie decided to get straight to the point. 'I'd like to know why you keep your distance from me these days, Aggie. I have always classed you as a good friend. I heard you had a party for Terry and was very hurt that you never invited Albie and me. If it wasn't for me introducing you, you would probably never even have met Terry. As far as I'm concerned, I've never said or done anything to upset you.' She took a long sip of her tea, then concluded haughtily, 'So would you be kind enough to enlighten me, please.'

Aggie wanted the ground to open up and swallow her. It was Terry who'd insisted she mustn't invite Queenie and Albie to his party as he didn't want their children there.

'I'm sorry, Queen. It's Little Terry. He's petrified of your Vinny for some reason. That's why I haven't invited you round recently and didn't invite you to Tel's birthday bash. I got to put my own son first. But I do still want to be your friend. You are always welcome to visit. Just maybe don't bring the boys with you for a bit. They're so boisterous in comparison to Little Terry and the girls. I do hope you understand, Queen. I would hate us to fall out over this.'

Viv squeezed her sister's arm, urging her not to blow a fuse. Aggie had explained the situation politely.

Queenie's lips pursed. 'What exactly are you trying to say? That there's something wrong with my boys? Cause the only wrong un I see 'ere is you. The so-called friend who blanked my letters throughout the Blitz.' Seeing her friend's lip tremble, Queenie's fuse blew. 'Fuck you, Aggie. I dislike you immensely and never want to see you or your notright kids again.' As Queenie made her exit with Viv in tow, she thought of Mrs O'Leary. Mary had never liked Aggie much either.

'Wait there,' Vinny ordered his brothers when they reached the corner of their road. For as long as he could remember, Mrs Beard had been a bit of an obsession with him. When he was little he'd been scared of her. She looked like a witch with her unkempt long black hair and missing teeth. And her name suited her perfectly; reason being, she had thick black hairs sprouting out of her chin. She also had loads of black cats as pets. All the kids were certain she was a real witch and they'd hang around outside her house to torment her. Not for long though. Mrs Beard hated children and within seconds of clocking any close to her property, she'd come flying out of her front door with a broom, shouting abuse and shooing them away.

Vinny got on all fours to check the coast was clear, then crawled back around the corner. 'Right, I'll go inside her front garden and tie the string to next door's fence. You tie it this end, Roy, and you be lookout, Michael.'

Roy suddenly had a bad feeling about this. He didn't like Mrs Beard. She was scary. But his mum always insisted they must respect their elders and Mrs Beard was very old now. 'It's raining, Vin. Let's just go home. Mum'll be back soon with our pie and mash, and if she catches us 'ere, we'll be in big trouble.'

'Shut it, Nancy Boy,' Vinny hissed. 'We've been saying for ages we gonna do this. She's bound to land on her broomstick and fly off. How else we gonna find out if she's a real witch?'

When his brother crawled around the corner, Roy rather reluctantly tied a knot in the string. His belly was rumbling now. He was starving.

Vinny tied his string in a double knot, checked the coast was clear, then crawled back around the corner. 'Right, cross the road now and start being as noisy as we can. We don't wanna stand right outside her house.'

The deranged old woman flew out of her front door, broom in hand, with a face like thunder. 'Get away from my house, you little buggers,' she yelled.

Seconds later, Mrs Beard fell flat on her face. But instead of flying off on her broomstick, she landed on top of it and stopped moving.

'Shit,' Roy mumbled. He could see blood mixed with the rain on the pavement.

Michael's lip began trembling. 'Can we go home now?' he asked, tugging Vinny's arm.

As curtains began to twitch and neighbours started to appear, Vinny acted quickly. He ran into Mrs Beard's garden and cut the string from both sides of the fence with his penknife, then hid it in his pockets.

'Oi! What you doing?' shouted a neighbour.

Always a quick thinker, Vinny held up one of Mrs Beard's pets. 'Just checking the cat was all right, mister. I thought Mrs Beard had squashed it.'

As people began surrounding Mrs Beard, Vinny ran over to his brothers, who were standing there like two stuffed dummies. He put an arm round their shoulders. 'Let's go home. We say nothing, OK?'

Both in shock, Roy and Michael nodded silently. 'Is she dead?' Roy asked, his eyes welling up.

'I don't know – and don't be bloody well crying,' Vinny hissed. 'Not our fault she didn't fly, is it?'

Albie was snoozing in his favourite armchair, as he often did after a Saturday session down the boozer, when he was awoken by a barrage of knocking on his front door.

Bleary-eyed, Albie shuffled to the door, thinking it would be either Queenie or his sons. Both were late home and he was starving, hadn't eaten since breakfast. It was neither his wife nor sons, it was Micky One Ear. 'You OK to talk?' Micky asked.

'Yeah. Just waiting for Queenie to come home. Why? What's wrong?'

'I had to warn you. Don't go near West Ham, Canning Town, Upton Park or East Ham next week, Alb. A little firm, or big firm should I say, turned up a bit heavy-handed in the pubs you supply last night. Rumour has it, it's the Turners out of Poplar, and you don't wanna mess with them. They're not gentlemen you can reason with like Harry Mitchell and his mob. The Turners are fucking feral. Anyway, they're taking over your patch, mate. No one has been in my boozer yet, so let's just hope they stick to their own. They're offering pub protection as well as the spirits in a joint venture, and apparently the spirits ain't too bad. On sort of a par with yours. The Turners are Irish, so might even be getting the goods from your pal Paddy, like you do.'

Albie's face turned ashen. He wasn't sure who he was more scared of. The Turners, or Queenie when she found out there'd be no more decent money coming in.

Being teatime, the pie and mash shop was heaving. 'I got something important to tell you an' all,' Queenie added.

'Ooh, what?' asked Viv.

'Tell you on the way home. Too many eyes and ears in 'ere,' Queenie replied.

'Well? What news you got?' Viv asked, the moment they stepped out of Kelly's.

'Don't have a go at me for not telling you sooner. I didn't want to tempt fate this time.'

'You're pregnant again!'

Queenie smiled broadly. 'Yep! About four an' 'alf months, I reckon. Albie don't know yet, nor the boys. I wanted to leave it as long as I could, just in case. I ain't even told Mum. I'm beginning to show now though, I wanted you to be the first to know.'

Viv put her bags down and gave her big sister a hug. 'Thrilled for you, Queen. I truly am.'

Nobody could tell Queenie why she'd lost her last baby, not even the midwives or nuns at the convent. One of the elderly nuns had even told her, 'It was God's work. But you're not to let this put you off having more children.'

As for Albie, he was a man, he didn't understand. 'I know it's sad, Queen. But the baby weren't even formed properly yet. As soon as you feel up to it, we can try for another,' he'd said.

Vinny was the only one to show any emotion. She'd already had the ring test done by Bridget and had told the boys, only a week before losing the baby, they would be welcoming a baby brother into their lives soon. Roy and Michael hadn't said much, but Vinny had insisted on sleeping in her bed with her that night. He'd only been six at the time, bless him. But he'd hugged her and they'd shed tears for their loss together.

As Queenie continued the conversation, discussing possible baby names, little did she know she was going home to absolute mayhem.

CHAPTER NINETEEN

'Everything all right?' Queenie asked. There were half a dozen neighbours standing outside Mrs Beard's house and Mr Sharples had a bucket and broom and was scrubbing the old girl's path.

'Ask your bleedin' sons,' spouted Loudmouth Lena, who lived next door to Mrs Beard.

'I beg your pardon!' Queenie snapped.

'You bloody heard.'

Mr Sharples stopped scrubbing. He liked the Butler family, would often chat to the boys and have a pint with Albie. 'Let's not jump to conclusions, eh? Mrs Beard is eighty-four. Chances are she just tripped. The police will get to the bottom of it, I'm sure.'

'Police!' Queenie shrieked. 'Oh don't be ridiculous, since when did we bring in the police around here!'

'Yes, the police,' hissed Loudmouth Lena. 'I found the evidence and gave it to 'em. They're probably at your house now.'

Shopping bags in hand, Queenie and Viv ran the short distance. The bicycle outside the house confirmed the police were in fact present.

'Thank gawd you're home,' Albie said, as his wife burst through the door.

'Hello, Queenie,' smiled Freddie Angel.

Queenie felt flustered as she took off her plastic rain bonnet. Freddie was married himself now with a child, but Queenie would always have a soft spot for him after what he'd done for her.

'Hello, Freddie. What's happened?' asked Viv. She would never forget Freddie helping them out the night Queenie pushed their dad down the stairs either.

Vinny held out the palms of his hands. 'We didn't do nuffink, Mum. I swear. We been out all day. We just walked round the corner mucking around and Mrs Beard ran out the door, like she always does, shouting at us.'

'Vinny's telling the truth, Mum,' Roy insisted.

'Yeah. Didn't do nuffink,' Michael shouted. He had nearly shat himself when their local bobby turned up. He would hate to be sent to prison.

'My boys don't lie, Freddie. I haven't raised them that way. If they say they didn't do anything, then that's the truth.'

'Mrs Beard's in quite a bad way, Queenie, so I do have to investigate what happened. She's definitely broken her nose, wrist and lost some teeth.'

'Never had no teeth anyway,' Vinny remarked.

Queenie clipped her eldest around the head. 'Don't be so bloody rude, you.'

PC Angel produced some string from his pocket. 'A neighbour found this tied to Mrs Beard's fence. She said she saw Vinny go into the garden to retrieve the rest.'

'No I didn't. I only went into the garden to check the cat was all right. I thought she'd fell on it.'

'The boys are gonna have to empty their pockets I'm afraid, Queenie.'

'Do as the policeman says,' Albie ordered.

Vinny wasn't daft. The first thing he'd done was hide his penknife and string in a bush. 'See none of us have got nuffink, but sweets. We're innocent. Loads of kids round 'ere tie string to fences so people fall over. It could be any of 'em.'

PC Angel wagged his finger at all three boys. 'Tying string to people's fences is a very dangerous and stupid thing to do, lads. Mrs Beard could've died. She might still die. You see anyone doing that again, you need to tell me, OK?'

Vinny nodded. 'We will,' he lied.

'I'll be off now then. Thanks for your time.'

'No problem,' Queenie replied. 'How's that beautiful little girl of yours doing, Freddie? I saw her sitting outside Mr Singh's shop last week in her pram. Looked a picture, she did, with her lemon knitted bonnet on.'

Freddie smiled. 'Thanks, Queenie. My little cherub, she is. Light of my life.'

Queenie said goodbye and shut the front door. She would wait until the morning until telling Albie and the boys she was pregnant again.

'Did you hear how Mrs Beard is?' asked Michael, the second his mother returned from the shop the following day.

Seeing Vinny slyly poke his brother in the back, Queenie's suspicions were confirmed. She decided to scare the life out the deceitful little sods. 'She died.'

'What! When?' Roy asked.

'Last night. The police'll probably come round here

again later. They got to get to the bottom of this now. It's a murder charge.'

'But whoever did it wouldn't have meant to murder her, Mum,' Vinny pointed out.

'Doesn't matter. The string caused her death, so the police will find the boys who did it and lock them up. They'll search the street for the rest of the string and probably find the culprit's fingerprints all over it.'

Watching the colour drain from her sons' faces infuriated Queenie. She didn't mind them lying to the police, but not to her. She'd given birth to the little rascals, for Christ's sake.

When Michael started to weep, Queenie wagged her forefinger. 'It *was* you three, wasn't it?'

'We were only mucking about, Mum. We didn't mean to kill her. We thought she would land on her broomstick and fly off,' admitted Roy.

'Where's the string?' Queenie asked.

Vinny stared at his feet. 'In Auntie Kay's privets.' Auntie Kay wasn't the boy's real aunt, but they always referred to her as such out of respect. She was forever giving them sherbet lemons and humbugs, and the odd penny or two.

'Best you go and get the evidence then and make sure nobody bloody well sees you. Take your cricket ball with you and pretend you've lost it in the privets. Bring the string back 'ere and I'll get rid of it for you. But only on one condition.'

Roy's eyes bulged with fear. 'What?' He couldn't believe he was a murderer. It was a hard thing to take in.

'That you never bloody tie string outside anyone's door or lie to me again. You did the right thing lying to PC Angel, but you never lie to your mother. You wouldn't even be on this earth if it wasn't for me.'

'Sorry, Mum,' Vinny said.

'Me too, Mum,' sighed Roy.

'Sorry too,' Michael added.

'Go on. Off you trot – and don't get bleedin' caught.'

'Oi! What you little bleeders up to now?' bellowed Loudmouth Lena.

Having already found the string and shoved it inside his underpants, Vinny waved the cricket ball in the air. 'Just getting this back.'

'Go play down your own flipping end. We don't want the likes of you up our end of the street. Not after what happened to Mrs Beard. You're nothing but trouble.'

'You got the penknife?' Roy enquired.

'Yeah. Come on. Let's go.'

Not many of the neighbours owned a motor car, so when a green one the boys had never seen before passed them at a slow pace, all three stared inside.

'Nah,' Roy mumbled. 'It can't be.'

'Gawd stone the crows!' Vinny had heard about ghosts, but had never seen a real one before.

When the car stopped and Mrs Beard stepped out of it, Michael literally shit his pants. 'I scared, Vinny. What's happening?'

'She's come back to haunt us, that's what,' Vinny shivered. 'Run. As fast as you fucking can.'

Queenie was in the middle of stirring the mixture for her bread pudding when the boys burst in the door as white as chalk.

'Mrs Beard, Mum. We just see her ghost in a green car,' Vinny explained.

'Oh well. Perhaps she's come back to haunt ya. Only

got yourselves to blame, haven't you?' Seeing their horrified expressions, she gave them a wicked grin. 'Or perhaps I lied to you like you lied to me and Mrs Beard is actually still alive?'

Vinny shook his head in disbelief and relief. 'Thank gawd for that.'

'You're naughty, Mum,' Roy added.

'Not as naughty as youse. Now give me the evidence.'

Vinny took the string out of his pocket and handed it to his mother.

Queenie held the string over the kitchen sink. 'You say nothing to your father or anybody else. This is our little secret. I'm not even telling Auntie Viv.'

All three boys nodded. 'And in future, you respect your neighbours and elders, understand me? And if you think you might be in trouble, you come to me, whatever it is, got me? Not anybody else. You speak to me alone.'

When all three said 'Yes, Mum,' in unison, Queenie smiled, lit a match, burned the string and flushed it down the sink. She thought of Mrs O'Leary as she did so. Mary might not be here in person any more, but in spirit she was still helping her raise her boys. Queenie was sure of that.

CHAPTER TWENTY

Five Months Later

Autumn 1954

Queenie kicked her slippers off and put her throbbing feet in a bucket of water with Epsom salts. Her due date was nearing and this pregnancy hadn't been as easy as her others.

The sickness was horrible, the first time Queenie had suffered badly from it. It wasn't just in the mornings either. She'd felt so stupid when she'd vomited on the floor in the butcher's one afternoon recently.

Queenie had already decided that this would be her last child. She'd be twenty-eight this December and four boys was enough, especially seeing how tight money was now.

The boys were good, would chop up the wooden crates left by the market traders, flog it for firewood and give her the money. Queenie had already made her mind up, though, that once the baby was born and she felt up to it, she'd go back to work herself. A couple of little cleaning jobs would suit her. She could work those around the kids.

'Cooey. It's only me. I bought you round a nice crusty loaf and some boiled bacon,' shouted Molly, as she let herself into her daughter's house. She knew Queenie was struggling at present and had been helping out as much as she could.

'Hello, Mum.'

'You stay there. I'll make the sandwiches,' Molly ordered. Times had been hard since the war. She still had to rent the upstairs of her house out. Two young Irish nurses were currently renting it while she and Viv lived downstairs. She hated it when *he* came round though, that cocky shyster, Bill Harris. Vivvy could do so much better, but who was she to choose her daughters' husbands after the bastard she had married.

'You been out, love?' Molly asked as she reappeared with the sandwiches and a cuppa.

'No. Not lately, Mum. Not felt that well. My feet are bleedin' killing me.' Queenie had hardly any money in her purse, which was another reason she hadn't gone out, but would never admit such a thing to her mother, or Viv. They knew money was tight, but she was too proud to tell them how tight. She felt embarrassed by her husband's inability to provide.

'Not long to go now, darling.'

'Ooh,' Queenie winced, taking her feet out of the bucket. 'I gotta do a wee. Thought I was gonna wet me knickers then.'

As Queenie stood up, she did more than wet her knickers. Her waters broke and saturated the carpet.

Albie rolled off Cilla Watkins, lit up two Salem cigarettes and handed one to his lover. He always felt guilty afterwards, but never beforehand. Queenie had banished him from her bed for the past four months and what with his luck being poxed financially, Cilla had become a welcome distraction in his mundane life.

Cilla didn't feel any guilt whatsoever even though she knew Queenie was about to drop. She knew Albie didn't sleep with his wife any more, therefore Queenie only had herself to blame that he'd strayed, was Cilla's take on the matter. 'Fancy a cup of Rosy?'

'I wouldn't mind a tot of brandy, then I'd better make tracks, love. Gotta earn *some* money today. You around tomorrow evening, darlin'?'

'No. I'm out with the girls. Pop round Monday or Tuesday. I was gonna ask you, Albie. I could do with an extra few bar shifts. Do you reckon your mate Micky might need an extra pair of hands?' Having split up with her old man, Cilla was struggling to pay her rent.

'Leave it with me and I'll ask him, treacle,' Albie smiled as Cilla's pert buttocks walked away from him. After being sex-starved for years, he couldn't get enough of her.

Vinny, Roy and Michael were sitting at the bottom of the stairs, all in a state of eager anticipation to meet their new brother.

'I wonder what he'll be called?' Michael pondered.

'Johnny. I overhead Mum telling Auntie Viv. But don't say nothing 'cause I was earwigging,' Vinny grinned. He found out so much juicy gossip by listening in on his mum's conversations, especially about the neighbours.

'Johnny Butler. I like that,' Roy replied, as his mum screamed out in pain again. His nan and Auntie Viv were upstairs with her as well as the midwife, and he and his brothers had done their bit by taking clean towels, hot water, soap and even cups of tea upstairs.

After what seemed like an eternity to the boys, there was the shrill sound of a baby's cry.

'Yes!' Roy punched the air in delight.

'Can we see him now?' Michael leapt up and down, clapping his hands.

'No. Not until Mum says so,' Vinny replied, as protective as ever.

'I beg your pardon!' Queenie said. The midwife wasn't her usual one. Sister Cleary was a nun as well as a midwife.

'I said, you got yourself a beautiful bonny daughter, Mrs Butler,' explained Sister Cleary in her chirpy Irish accent.

'There must be some mistake. Have another look, ya know, down below,' Queenie ordered.

Molly and Viv glanced at one another. Because of Queenie's belief in the string test, both had knitted and bought everything in blue.

'Oh, there is no mistake, Mrs Butler. For sure you have a daughter. Here you are. You can take a look for yourself,' Sister Cleary smiled, handing Queenie her baby wrapped in a towel.

Queenie stared at her baby's genitals and could barely believe her eyes. She was furious with that lush Bridget. The boys had been so looking forward to having another brother. Plus, she'd told all the neighbours and everyone round the shops she was having another boy. Talk about make herself look a prat.

Molly touched her granddaughter's cheek. 'She's beautiful, Queenie. What a blessing to have a little girl after three boys. What you going to call her?'

'Well, not Johnny, obviously,' Queenie hissed, as Vivian also gushed over the child.

'Whatever's wrong with you, Mrs Butler?' snapped the midwife. 'You have a beautiful healthy daughter. I delivered a still-born last week and the poor mother was devastated. You already have three sons. To add a daughter to your lovely family is a blessing from God.'

Queenie stared at her unexpected blessing. She looked nothing like the boys had at birth. She had little hair and what she did have was the same colour as her own natural shade. A dull brown. Queenie burst into tears. 'I'm sorry. It's just I've had a terrible pregnancy this time round. I'm in shock, that's all.'

Molly patted her daughter's arm. 'We understand.'

'When can we see our little bruvver, Mum?' Michael shouted out.

'Hide that afterbirth and those dirty towels, then send the boys up,' Queenie ordered. She had no idea where Albie was, but guessed he'd be pleased. He'd always wanted a daughter.

The boys ran excitedly up the stairs. 'I'm the oldest, so can I hold him first?' Vinny gabbled.

'You can hold *her* first, Vinny. You haven't got a little brother. You've got a little sister,' Queenie explained.

Vinny turned his nose up. 'I don't like girls.'

'Neither do I,' Roy chimed in.

Michael was intrigued. 'Can I hold her first then, Mum? I like girls.'

'She's your little sister, boys. You will grow to love her,' Vivian smiled.

Queenie pursed her lips. 'Go an' see if you can find your father.'

Albie had never felt so guilty in his life as he ran towards home. He'd bumped into Mr Sharples who'd informed him Queenie had given birth. What type of man was he? Fornicating with Cilla at probably the exact same time his wife was in labour. If his dear old mum was looking down, she'd be so disappointed in him.

'All right, Molly? Are Queenie and the baby OK?' Albie panted.

'Both are fine, love. Queenie's a bit tired, mind. Vivvy's upstairs with her. Go on up and I'll bring you a cuppa.'

Albie ran up the stairs. He was sick of Viv being at his house all the time banging on about her lover-boy ex-jailbird. That's why he tended not to come home early any more. 'I wanna spend some time with Queenie and the baby alone please, Viv.'

Viv handed the child back to Queenie and blanked Albie. 'Call me if you need me, Queen,' she said.

'Let's have a look at him then,' Albie urged.

Queenie moved the shawl away from her daughter's face.

'He's bonny, ain't he? Hair's lighter than the other three. Can I hold him, love? Well done by the way.'

'Her, Albie. You can hold her.'

'Her!'

'Yes. You have a daughter.'

Tears welled up in Albie's eyes as he held the child in his arms. He loved the smell of newborns. 'She's a beauty, Queen. Look at her. Look at her little nose. I can't believe we got ourselves a daughter.'

'Me neither. I thought we might call her Brenda. It's quite a trendy name and I think it rather suits her. What do you think?' Queenie had toyed with calling the child Mary after her dear friend, but thought it might prove too upsetting for her. Mary's death was still too raw.

'Perfect!' Albie kissed his daughter on the forehead. 'Welcome to the world, Brenda Butler. Your daddy loves you very much.'

Queenie's eyes also welled up. It had been a strange day, full of emotion and she felt so sore and tired now. 'You're a big softie you are, Albie Butler.'

Albie squeezed his wife's hand. 'I know I'm not perfect, but I do love you, Queenie. Thank you for our beautiful daughter.'

Queenie tenderly rubbed Albie's arm. 'You ain't so bad yourself. That's why I married ya.'

An unusual tender moment between them, Albie felt the guilt surge through his veins. He wasn't a bad man, just lonely at times. He would end his relationship with Cilla. He must do the right thing.

CHAPTER TWENTY-ONE

Brenda Butler wasn't an easy baby. Unlike the boys who had all been fairly good sleepers, Brenda cried all night, then slept all day. She wouldn't breastfeed either, would only take milk from the bottle.

Queenie was shattered and, without Albie's help, she had no idea how she would have coped, getting up numerous times during the night. Even the boys were irritable.

Aware that her sons were huddled around the coal fire, whispering, Queenie eyed them with suspicion. They looked like butter wouldn't melt in their three-quarter strides, smart white shirts, thick woollen knee-length socks, grey tank tops and matching floppy hats, but she wasn't born yesterday. 'What you three looking so shifty about?'

'Nuffink, Mum,' all three protested with a look of fake innocence.

'Your porridge is ready. Get it down your neck and get yourself off to school.'

'What time we gotta be back for the fireworks tonight, Mum?' enquired Vinny.

'Why? Where you going?'

'My mate Paul is having his fireworks early 'cause it's his birthday and he's invited us round to watch 'em. Can we go, Mum, please?' Roy pleaded.

'I wanna see 'em too, Mum,' Michael added.

'You better not be lying to me because I will find out and you know how much I hate bloody liars,' Queenie warned.

'We're not, Mum. Honest,' Roy lied.

'OK then. But don't stuff your faces too much round Paul's, because I'm cooking jacket potatoes and Bill's bringing faggots and sausages for your tea.'

'We won't and I promise we'll be back by half seven,' vowed Vinny.

All three boys bolted down their porridge as fast as they could. They had a plan and couldn't wait to put it into action.

Having had a little flutter on a dog tip and won, Albie Butler whistled away happily as he strolled towards Stepney to collect his booze and baccy money. He'd won a fair bit since One-Eyed Harry had started giving him a bit of inside info. He daren't tell Queenie that, mind. She didn't like him gambling, said it was a mug's game.

Catching his reflection in the cafe window, Albie straightened his tie. His suits weren't made of the finest cloth and his shirts were off the market, but he still managed to look smart. Even his shoes were gleaming. His mum had always drummed the importance of polishing his shoes regularly into him.

Seeing Cilla Watkins' mum inside the cafe with another lady, Albie continued his journey thinking about Cilla. She'd been surprisingly calm when he'd ended their relationship, had even agreed it was for the best.

Albie sighed. He knew he'd done the right thing, but he did miss the intimacy. Cilla used to love to put his Hampton in her mouth and give it a good old suck. Queenie would have a fit at the thought of such a thing. His wife didn't even like relieving him with her hand and on the odd occasion she had, she'd turned her head away while manhandling his John Thomas as though she was changing gear in a car. It had bloody well hurt, which was why Albie chose to relieve himself in the bathroom these days.

Other than being sex-starved, things were pretty good at home. Brenda's arrival seemed to have brought himself and Queenie closer together. He had no problem getting up in the middle of the night to tend to his daughter's needs. Most men would run a mile at the thought of changing a shitty nappy, but he enjoyed feeling useful.

Albie bowled into the Horn of Plenty with a spring in his step. Every Friday he would meet Ernie in here and lay him on fifty pouches of tobacco and pick up the dosh from the previous week.

'The usual, Albie?' asked the barman.

'Yes please, Del,' Albie glanced around and felt as though he'd had a catapult hit him in the stomach. Surely not? It couldn't be, could it?

Realizing it was, the spring left Albie's step instantly, so much so, he couldn't move, was temporarily paralysed. 'What the—' he mumbled. He knew she'd been working for Micky; he'd got her the job. But what about poor Sheila? Canoodling like a pair of horny teenagers in public. Albie was sickened by the sight.

Cilla was the first to spot Albie. She nudged Micky, who quickly swung around on his barstool. 'Oh, shit!'

As Micky approached him, Albie wanted to run from

the pub, but his legs still would not move. Cilla Watkins
and Micky One Ear. How? Why? When did that happen?

His face ashen and etched with guilt, Micky tried to
explain. 'It ain't what you think, Albie. Honest. Me and
Sheila had a massive barney, she's sodded off to her mother's. I'm just letting me hair down with Cilla. You know
how it is. Me and her are just pals, mate.'

'Albie, I'm over 'ere. Everything all right?' shouted Ernie.

Albie waved and nodded. 'Be over in a minute, Ern.'
He had to pull himself together; otherwise the whole of
the East End would know. Gossip travelled faster than
the speed of light around his neck of the woods, especially
if it was juicy.

'Albie, talk to me, please,' begged Micky.

Albie glanced at Cilla. She couldn't even look him in
the eye. People were staring now, trying to work out what
was going on. 'Excuse me, Mick. But I'm 'ere to see Ernie.'

'Been reefing round that blonde tart for the past couple
of weeks. Seem 'em in 'ere a few times, I 'ave,' Ernie
informed Albie. 'Rumour 'as it, Sheila's left him,' he added.
'Gonna have your usual tipple with me, Albie?'

Desperate to get out the boozer, Albie shook his head.
There was no need to count Ernie's money; the old boy
always got it spot on. 'I can't today, mate. We got a family
firework thingy later and Queenie's ordered me to get me
arse home early. I'll see you next week. We'll have a drink
then.'

Albie left via the opposite door to where love's young
dream were sitting. Unsurprisingly, within thirty seconds
he felt his right arm being grabbed from behind. 'Please,
Albie. I don't wanna fall out with ya. I would never step
on your toes, you know that. But seeing as you and
Queenie are all good again and you got your baby

daughter, I honestly didn't think you'd be that bothered, mate.'

Unable to stop himself, Albie drew back his right fist and punched Micky so hard, he smacked his head against the wall and slumped to the pavement.

Cilla ran outside the pub and crouched and cradled her new beau in her arms. Micky had spent a small fortune on her in the past few weeks, was the meal ticket she'd always craved for a better life. 'What the hell do you think you're doing, Albie?'

'That's for Sheila,' Albie said, walking away.

Cilla chased after Albie and smacked him hard around the face. 'Talk about pot calling kettle black! That one's for Queenie.'

Queenie checked on Brenda. who was fast asleep, then decided on a catnap herself. She couldn't have dozed off for more than five minutes when a knock on the door awoke her.

'Hello, Mrs Higgins,' Queenie yawned. 'What can I do for you?'

'I thought I'd better tell you, I just come from Bethnal Green and saw your boys having a bit of a barney with some lads much older than them. I asked if they were OK and they said they was, but I didn't like the look of those other lads, Queen. Proper ruffians. If I were you, I'd send Albie or one of the men down there to check your boys are OK.'

Queenie was that tired she could barely think straight. 'Bethnal Green! But they're meant to be at a friend's house.'

'Well, they're not, love. They're sitting outside the station, with a guy.'

'What guy?'

'Not a man, a bleedin' stuffed guy – Guy Fawkes night, innit? They're asking passers-by to give 'em a penny for him.'

'Everything all right?' Viv asked, as she walked up the path with a bag full of fruit-and-veg leftovers from work.

Queenie was livid. Not only had her sons blatantly lied to her, they were begging, something she had always forbidden them to do, outside the station where poor Aunt Edna lost her life so tragically. 'How bleeding dare they?' Queenie spat. She grabbed her grey winter coat. 'Viv, keep eye on Brenda for me. I gotta go to Bethnal bastard Green.'

'We should get going in a minute, Vin. Mum'll kill us if we're late,' Roy warned his brother.

'Penny for the guy, please, mister,' Vinny said, as a suited man with an umbrella came out of the station.

When the gentleman threw half a crown on to the piece of cloth they had lying next to their deformed-looking guy, whose head was actually a football, Vinny disagreed. 'All the rich people are coming home from their posh jobs up town now. We gotta stay longer. Mum won't mind if we're a bit late.'

'Vinny, Roy,' Michael prodded his brothers to get their attention.

They'd had an altercation earlier with some older boys who'd turned up wheeling a guy in a pram and accused them of nicking their patch. When they'd insisted the Butlers take their guy elsewhere, Vinny had retorted, 'Make us,' before telling the older boys to 'fuck off'.

'Penny for the guy please, ma'am,' smiled Vinny.

The woman bent down. She was dressed in a fur coat, classy clothes, had a very posh voice and was obviously pissed as not only were the fumes of alcohol potent, she was also slurring her words. 'Look at you three. So handsome. I was unable to have children, but I would have given my right arm to have sons like you. What are your names and how old are you?'

'I'm Vinny and I've just turned nine. This is my brother Roy. He's nearly seven.' Vinny pointed at Michael. 'We call him little squirt but his real name's Michael and he'll be five next month. We're only sitting 'ere today because our dad's out of work and we want our mum to have a nice Christmas. Every penny we get, we will give to our mum.'

'Oh, how sweet!' the woman gushed, fumbling inside her handbag. 'What a credit you are to your mummy. You take this and make sure she has a wonderful Christmas.'

Vinny could not believe his eyes as the woman handed him a ten-pound note. Neither could Roy. Only Michael wasn't taking any notice. Reason being, he knew he and his brothers were in big trouble.

'Thank you, ma'am. That's so very kind of you,' Vinny beamed.

'My pleasure,' the woman said, before kissing all three boys on the head then staggering off down the road.

'What a fucking result!' Vinny said, staring at the note in his hand. He turned to Michael. 'Whaddya keep poking me for? You never even thanked the lady. You need to watch and learn.'

'They're back, Vinny. Them older boys. Look! They're over the road screwing us out.'

'Shit!' Roy said. He turned to Vinny. The older boys were at least eleven or twelve. 'What we gonna do?'

'Jump on the train.' Vinny pocketed the ten-pound note and urged Roy to put all the coins in his pocket. 'Right, when I say run in a minute, we run as fast as we can, OK?'

'What about our guy?' asked Michael.

Vinny turned to his youngest brother. 'Well that can't fucking run, can it? We leave it 'ere.'

'But his head is my football.' Michael reminded his brother.

'I'll buy you another one. Right, ready? One, two, three, run!'

Queenie hopped off the bus and ran across to the station. There was no sign of her sons. 'Excuse me, have you seen three young lads hanging around 'ere with a guy, as in Fawkes?' Queenie asked the paper seller.

'Yes, love. They ran into the station, chased by some other lads. They left their guy, if you wanna take it home to 'em. It's over there,' he pointed.

Queenie was even more furious as she laid eyes on the guy. It had Albie's cap on, the good one she'd bought him from the posh menswear shop opposite Cohen's. Not only that, it had her green cardigan on, a pair of Vinny's trousers and Albie's dealer boots!

Cursing her sons more than ever, Queenie ripped the trousers off the guy, took the cardigan off the bastard thing, then picked up the cap and boots. She would throttle those little toerags when she got home.

Queenie then started to worry. She prayed the lads chasing her brood didn't throttle them first. If anything bad happened to her babies, it would kill her.

Having spotted the two eldest Butler boys being beaten to a pulp by much older lads, the Kelly brothers had stopped their car, chased the other lads away and driven the battered and bruised pair home. They were worried about their brother Michael though, who'd disappeared during the fracas.

'Please don't tell our mum we were sitting outside the station asking for a penny for the guy. She'll kill us,' Vinny said, holding the side of his jaw that was throbbing. He'd held his own with a couple of those lads to a degree, had kicked one in the nuts and punched another hard in the gut. But it hadn't been enough to stop them taking the ten-pound note out of his pocket. They'd held him down, the bastards. Thankfully the Kelly brothers had pulled up before they got the chance to frisk Roy. Lots of the change they'd collected was scattered over the pavement, but hopefully they still had something left for their troubles.

The Kelly brothers were two of the most feared men in Whitechapel. They'd taken on Mary O'Leary's lads as youngsters and now Patrick and Daniel were carving out a decent future in the West End. They still took a cut, though, of course. But they looked after their own impeccably, were always helping out the good people, but took no nonsense from the wrong uns in the community. 'We're no grasses, Vinny lad. You tell your mum what you want. But a word of warning, if you were outside Bethnal Green station for hours, some nosy bastard is bound to have seen you and will snitch to your mother. Loose lips sink ships and there's plenty of loose lips round our neck of the woods. You might be better holding your hands up and coming clean,' warned Billy Kelly, feeling sorry for the lads. They'd taken a real kicking.

'I can't hold my hands up,' Roy snivelled. 'I think my arm's broke. It's killing me.'

Vivian Wade put her hand over her mouth. 'Gawd stone the crows! Whatever happened to 'em?' asked Vivian, as she clocked the state of her nephews.

'They got jumped by some older lads and we happened to drive past,' said Johnny Kelly. 'The boys'll explain to ya. They've not said much to me and Bill,' he fibbed.

'Is Queenie in?' asked Billy Kelly.

'No. She's out looking for 'em. Where's Michael?'

'He ran off. My arm hurts, Auntie Viv. I can't move it,' Roy said mournfully.

Regarding himself as an up-and-coming face, Bill Harris bolted towards the front door. He would love to get in with the Kelly brothers, although the Krays from Valence Road had started to make a big name for themselves too. 'Johnny, Bill, come in, chaps. What would you like to drink?'

'Nothing, thanks. We're gonna have a drive round; see if we can spot young Michael. We'll pop back though, definitely,' said Johnny.

'I'll come with you, if you like?' Bill Harris asked eagerly.

'Nah. You stay here, look after the boys and the ladies,' Johnny replied.

Bill Harris was elated as he sauntered back into the kitchen. He put his arms around Vivian's waist and held her tight.

'Stop it!' Viv giggled as Bill rubbed his groin against hers. They had done things, but not *that* yet. Viv did want to go the full way though, despite Queenie having forbidden her to. Bill Harris excited her like no man had ever done in the past, every time he held her close. 'I gotta see to the boys, Bill. Queenie'll go mad if she sees the blood on 'em. She'll have heart failure. I'm gonna clean 'em up. Why don't you have a wander, see if you can find Michael?'

Bill Harris was currently working for a local firm that got hold of hooky gear from the docks. It wasn't a bad little earner, but nothing on the level he could be on if he got in with the Kelly brothers. He kissed Viv on the forehead. If he became the hero of the hour this evening, the Kelly brothers were bound to look at him in a decent light. 'Yeah, you're right, treacle. I'm going to look for Michael right now.'

To arrive home to two battered sons and one missing was the last thing Albie Butler needed. His day had been bad enough as it was. He couldn't get the image of Micky and Cilla out of his mind. Did Cilla suck Micky's todger the way she sucked his? The thought of that made Albie sick with jealousy. He cursed himself for getting Cilla a job in the Hoop and Grapes. Sheila had been a wonderful wife to Micky, so supportive. She didn't deserve this shit and it was all his fault.

'The Kelly brothers are out looking for Michael and so is my Bill,' Viv informed Albie.

'Michael weren't hurt. The boys just picked on me and Roy, Dad,' Vinny said. 'They were a lot older than us,' he added. 'That's why we lost the fight.'

'What happened then? You must've said or done something to antagonize these lads?' Albie asked, staring directly at his eldest for answers.

'We didn't do nothing. Honest,' Roy winced, holding his poorly arm. He was in agony.

Queenie arrived home and left the evidence outside the front door. Viv explained that Michael had run off and Bill and the Kelly brothers were out looking for him.

'My poor baby,' Queenie said, her voice full of emotion. Michael wasn't as streetwise, he was only five and she hated the thought of him scared and out alone in the dark.

'I think Roy needs to go to the hospital, Queen. His arm looks broken to me,' suggested Albie.

Queenie turned to her eldest two. If they lied to her, they'd have more than a broken arm between them. 'What happened? And I want the truth.'

Vinny and Roy recited the same cock-and-bull story they'd told Aunt Viv and their father which was like a red rag to a bull as far as Queenie was concerned. She marched outside, gathered up the clothes she'd ripped off the guy and threw them at Vinny and Roy. 'Recognize these?'

Vinny and Roy glanced at one another. Neither said a word.

'Oi! That's my best cap,' Albie yelled.

Queenie walloped both boys hard around the head. 'What have I told you about lying to me, you deceitful little toerags. As for begging, what have I told you about begging, eh? Only paupers beg – and you're not fucking paupers. Your dear Aunt Edna died at that station and you got the cheek to sit outside and beg! The Kelly brothers never begged when they were your age. They worked hard, used to be barrow boys on the market. That's why people respect them so much these days. Nobody respects beggars.'

'But lots of other kids made guys too, Mum, and we only did it to earn some money to buy you nice Christmas presents,' said Vinny.

'I once knew a lad who dressed up as a guy himself. Got stabbed to death, he did. Some nutter came along and stuck a knife straight through him. Begging brings bad luck. Look what's happened to you today. I take it the bigger lads tried to thieve your money?'

Vinny bowed his head. 'Yeah. They took it.'

'Serves ya bleedin' right.'

'Mum, my arm, I think it's broken,' Roy moaned, yet again.

'Tough shit! You two need to go out and find your

brother. You lost him, you can bloody well find him. And you'll be going straight to bed when you get home. Naughty boys don't deserve fireworks.'

'Your feet aching? Want me to carry you?' Bill asked young Michael. He'd found him wandering along The Waste, hobbling.

'Yes, please. I'm gonna be in big trouble with me mum,' Michael informed Bill as he lifted him into his arms. Michael had lost one of his shoes when he'd legged it in Bethnal Green and was unable to find the bloody thing even though he'd gone back and searched high and low for it.

Bill grinned as the Kelly brothers pulled up beside him in their posh Daimler. 'Hop in,' ordered Johnny Kelly.

Bill didn't need asking twice. This was all working out rather well.

'He OK?' asked Johnny.

'Yeah. Worried his mum's gonna have a go at him as he lost a shoe, but other than that, he's fine.'

'They were my new shoes,' Michael said dismally.

'Never mind. I'll give your mum some money to get you a new pair. Then she won't have a go at you, will she?' said Johnny.

Queenie was that relieved to see her youngest home, she forgot her annoyance and hugged him tightly. 'Where did you go? I was ever so worried about you.'

'I ran off and hid 'cause they were big boys, Mum. Then I got lost walking home.'

'My poor little soldier. Where's your other shoe?'

Desperate to impress the Kellys, Bill Harris thrust a tenner at Queenie. 'He lost a shoe. Johnny was gonna buy him another pair, but I thought, seeing as I'm virtually family now, I'd step in.'

'But you're not family, are you? You haven't even proposed properly or bought our Vivvy a ring yet.'

When Queenie handed him the tenner back in front of the Kelly brothers, Bill felt a right mug. 'Thank you for the offer, but Albie and I are quite capable of buying our own children's shoes.'

'Bill found Michael and he's only trying to help, Queen,' Vivian said, linking arms with the man of her dreams.

'We'll leave you to it now. Have a good weekend,' said Johnny Kelly.

'Bye, gentlemen, and thanks for your help. It's very much appreciated,' Queenie said, as she waved the brothers off.

Bill Harris followed the brothers up the path. 'I hope you don't think I'm taking liberties, but if you need any men at all, would you keep me in mind, please? I'm a hard grafter and I know how to keep me mouth shut.'

'We'll keep you in mind if anything comes up,' lied Johnny. Bill Harris was a typical wideboy and lads like him always attracted trouble. He wouldn't trust him as far as he could throw him.

When Vinny and Roy returned, Albie took Roy up the London Hospital to check his arm wasn't broken.

Queenie put the jacket potatoes in the oven and went upstairs. Vinny was sitting alone on his bed. 'I'm really sorry, Mum, for lying to you. I swear it won't happen again.'

With his jet-black hair and striking green eyes, Vinny was so bloody handsome. All her boys were. But her firstborn would always hold that special place in her heart. 'Get your arse downstairs then. As soon as Roy gets home, we'll start the fireworks.'

Vinny grinned. 'Cheers, Mum.'

*

Bill Harris was in a foul mood. He'd brought round the fireworks, sausages, faggots and even found Queenie's youngest son, yet still she did nothing but dig him out. As for embarrassing him in front of the Kelly brothers, he found that one hard to forgive, which is why he'd devised a little plan. 'The bloke I work for is looking for fresh legs, Albie. Gets busy this time of year, coming up to Christmas. Want me to put a word in for you? The money's pretty good.'

Cooking the sausages, Queenie swung around just as Bill had known the nosy old cow would. Yes, he did let Viv down on odd occasions, when he ended up on benders with his pals. But he always made it up to her afterwards. As for properly proposing, he would do that when he was good and ready. He wasn't going to be pushed into stuff by her domineering sister. He had far more dosh than bleeding Albie did and he hadn't even been out of the clink that long. So what right did Queenie have to dictate to him? The soppy cow.

'Albie's looking for some extra work, aren't you, Albie? What exactly would he be doing?'

Albie said nothing. He'd only just returned from the hospital with Roy. His son's arm wasn't broken, but was badly sprained and he was now wearing a sling.

'Collecting money, that's all. My boss supplies people with some knocked-off gear from the docks, but he don't like to get involved himself, so employs geezers to collect his wonga. It's simple, with very little risk.'

'You can do that, can't you, Albie?' Queenie said, plonking a plate of sausages in front of her sons.

Albie was unsure. He didn't like Bill Harris very much. Unbeknown to Bill or Queenie, he'd spotted Bill all over birds in pubs a couple of times recently, but thankfully

Bill hadn't spotted him. Albie liked a quiet life, so wasn't about to spout his mouth off. Vivvy, he also owed nothing to, the way she'd spoken to him this past year or so. A match made in heaven. Let them both get on with it, was Albie's take on the matter. 'I'm not sure, Queen. Let me speak to Bill man-to-man, see what it actually entails first.'

'It's just you collecting some dosh and giving it to me. I'll then take it to the boss. You don't even have to meet him. It's very simple,' replied Bill.

'He'll take the job,' Queenie snapped. 'With Christmas coming up, we can do with some extra money for the boys' presents.'

'Thanks, Bill. That's really kind of you,' Vivian gushed.

Bill smirked. Queenie and Albie both needed to be taught a lesson. It would serve them bloody right for underestimating him.

CHAPTER TWENTY-TWO

As Christmas approached, with the extra money Albie was bringing home, Queenie decided to spruce their house up a bit.

The landlord wasn't at all interested when Queenie told him the wallpaper was peeling off, the paintwork was flaky and there was damp in the boys' room, but when she asked if it was OK if she decorated it herself, the sly old bastard could not have been more keen.

Green was the in colour at the moment, so that's what Queenie chose. She even had her dressmaker run her up some apple green curtains with some material she'd bought down the Roman Road.

'What you up to today, love?' Albie asked his wife.

'Taking Brenda to be weighed, then I'll do a bit more present shopping. I'm gonna get us some nicer decorations an' all. I want this to be the perfect Christmas,' Queenie smiled.

'Don't be spending no more on the boys, Queen. You've spent a fortune on 'em as it is.'

'That's only 'cause this is the first year I've ever been able to splash out. That new job of yours has been a godsend, Albie. It truly has.'

'I'm glad you're happy. I was reading in the paper the other day that televisions are on the rise since the Queen's Coronation. So I thought, after Christmas, we might get one. Ronny Tobyn rented one recently and says that's the way forward in case the bloody thing goes wrong.'

Queenie's eyes lit up. 'Oh Albie, that would be wonderful. I would have loved to have watched the Queen's Coronation rather than listened to it.'

'I'll sort it then.' Hearing his wife's favourite song 'I'll Be Seeing You' by Billie Holiday on the radio, Albie grabbed her round the waist with one arm and waltzed her around the front room. He still hadn't quite got over the shock that Micky and Cilla were a couple, but he'd hidden that well from Queenie. He hadn't even told her he was no longer singing in the Hoop and Grapes of a Sunday lunchtime. He must think up some excuse to tell her soon, mind. The grapevine was always in full throttle around the East End. 'I'd better be off now. I'll be back in time for tea.'

'Queenie!'

Recognizing the voice immediately, Queenie stopped pushing Brenda's pram and turned around. 'Eliza! Oh my God! Are those three beauties all yours?' Queenie had not seen Eliza since she'd walked out on her job in Cohen's.

'Yes. These are my three youngest. Four, I now have, and that's my lot. I wanted a girl and thankfully my little Simone popped out last,' Eliza chuckled. 'How you doing, Queenie? Dad said you pop in the shop from time to time. Is this your youngest? Ooh, she's gorgeous,' Eliza gushed, peering inside the pram.

'Yes. Brenda's my fourth and last too. I'm doing fine, thanks. But I must apologize for how I spoke to you that day I left the shop, Eliza. I didn't mean what I said, I swear to you.'

'Forget it. I'm not one to hold grudges and my dad always loves seeing you. So where are you living? Has Albie brought you your dream house yet?'

'We're still renting at present. But Albie has a wonderful job now, so we're saving up for a mortgage. What about you? And Doreen? Do you still keep in touch with her?'

'My husband is in the rag trade and doing very well. He owns a wholesaler's down the Commercial Road and supplies to many shops and market traders. We bought a house in Barnet, not far from where Mummy and Daddy live. As for Doreen, after kissing many frogs, she finally found her prince. He's a professional footballer, plays for Fulham. He recently whisked Doreen off to Paris and proposed!'

'Oh how lovely,' Queenie replied. She didn't begrudge Doreen happiness, even though they'd fallen out. Now Albie was earning good money, she would soon have a lovely home of her own. 'Please apologize to Doreen for the way I spoke to her when I left the shop too, Eliza, and congratulate her on her engagement.'

'I will. I promise.'

Queenie smiled. 'I'd better be going now or I'll be late. I'm taking madam here for a check-up at the baby clinic. It's been lovely seeing you again, Eliza.'

'You too, Queenie.'

Bill Harris hugged Hounslow Harry. They'd met in prison, been cell-mates, and Bill trusted Harry more than his own family. He was in his late fifties, had a bald head and an ex-boxer's nose, but was as sound as a pound.

'And what do I owe this pleasure?' asked Hounslow Harry.

'Got a little job for you, mate. A geezer I know is gonna be picking up a fair bit of dosh. I will tell you his route and exactly where to pounce. I thought we'd go fifty-fifty.'

Hounslow Harry chuckled. 'Seventy-thirty and you got yourself a deal. What's this geezer's name?'

'Albie Butler. You won't have heard of him. He's a nobody.'

'All right, Queen? How's it going?'

Queenie hadn't seen her old neighbour Bridget since she'd wrongly predicted her last string test. 'Christ! You got another on the way? Who's the father?'

'Don't ask. Wasn't planned. But hey ho, ya know me. No way was I gonna get rid. Another little bastard to add to me collection of little bastards,' chuckled Bridget.

Queenie pursed her lips. 'Don't bother with your ring and string test, eh. I bought all blue for this one, thanks to you.'

Bridget peered inside the pram. 'Oh well, got your first three right, didn't I? She's a beauty, ain't she? Look at her long eyelashes.'

'She's a little moo in the night. Keeps us all awake and she's a finicky eater. I wouldn't be without her, mind. Albie dotes on her he does.'

'Ooh, speaking of Albie, what happened with him and Micky One Ear? My mate saw the fight, said Albie all but knocked Micky spark out.'

'I beg your pardon!'

'The fight, outside the Horn of Plenty. Albie ain't singing

in the Hoop any more either. I popped in there last Sunday and a bloke called Max was singing.'

Queenie was that taken aback, she couldn't even reply.

'Up to your bedroom now, boys. I need to talk to your father,' Queenie said, as she heard Albie arrive home. She was furious he'd said nothing to her regarding Micky One Ear. As far as she was aware, the sneaky bastard was still singing in the Hoop and Grapes every Sunday.

'Albie, what's all this about you having a fight with Micky and now you're not singing in his pub?'

Put on the spot, Albie began digging a little hole for himself. 'I didn't want to tell you, love, 'cause I didn't want to worry ya.'

'So you thought you'd pretend you still sung in the pub! If there's anything I hate, Albie, it's bloody liars, ya know that. I also don't bleedin' well appreciate hearing what my husband's up to via the gossip-mongers. So what happened then?'

'Micky's having an affair with one of the girls who works behind the pump for him. His wife Sheila is such a nice lady, as you well know, Queenie. She don't deserve that. I see Micky out with his old tart. All over one another in the Horn of Plenty they were. That's why I clumped him one. I was sticking up for Sheila.'

Queenie walked towards Albie and put her arms around his waist. 'I think that's a very honourable thing to do, Albie. You're a good man deep down and I know I don't say this often, but I do love you, ya know.'

As Queenie locked lips with her honourable husband, little did she know she'd soon be hearing a rather different version of events.

*

The following morning, Queenie counted out the money Albie had given her. 'That's not enough, Albie. Not to pick up all three bikes.'

Albie sighed. He'd told Queenie that three pairs of boxing gloves were more than enough for the boys' main presents and they should be saving for a rainy day, but Queenie being Queenie had insisted they buy all three of their sons bicycles with his hard-earned dosh. 'I ain't got any more money, Queen. You've spent it all. You'll have to wait until tonight and pick the bikes up tomorrow, love,' Albie said, straightening his tie. His new job involved knocking on the doors of houses or poking his head in pubs to collect money for the man he only knew as 'The Boss'. Albie had been told to dress smart to look the part, so that's what he did. Any money he collected, Albie was given a 5 per cent cut of. Bill Harris was the man who he dealt with solely. Bill would divvy up what he was owed and pay him his cut at the end of the week. There were a few who couldn't pay up and Albie just reported those back to Bill. It wasn't particularly a dangerous job; he was only collecting money from hooky gear. But with Christmas a couple of days away, it had been busy. Too busy for Albie's liking, as he was collecting more money than he'd ever seen before. 'I'm off now, love. Got a busy day ahead. Christ knows how many buses I'll have to hop on.'

'You need to learn to drive, Albie. That'll make your job so much easier. Lamb stew with dumplings, I'm cooking tonight. That'll warm your cockles when you get home.'

Albie kissed his beloved on the forehead. 'Bye, treacle, and I'll have the rest of the money tonight so you can pick up those bikes and anything else you might need. I promise.'

*

'Look! Over the road, Viv. That must be Micky's fancy piece. Look! He has the cheek to 'ave his arm round her an' all. Talk about flaunt it in public. My Albie ain't a violent man. But I'm ever so proud of him for clumping Micky one, the dirty bastard.'

'No spring chicken, is she? Poor Sheila. She's a lovely woman.'

Queenie grabbed her sister's arm. 'Come on. Let's go and give 'em a piece of our mind. Bleedin' disgusting, if you ask me.'

Vivian allowed herself to be dragged across the other side of the Whitechapel Road and was the first to speak. She gestured her head towards Cilla. 'Poor Sheila. We were stunned when Albie told us. Gone down in our estimation, you have.'

Micky held up his hands in protest. He had loved his Sheila. She'd been his rock, but in the end they were more like best friends than Romeo and Juliet. Cilla however, had awoken a desire in him. She'd made the play for him and he'd fallen for her hook, line and sinker.

When Queenie began to berate her, Cilla thought it was high time she stuck up for herself. She pointed at Vivian first. 'You're a fine one to talk. Bill Harris – don't make me laugh. He's had more birds than a tom cat, love. He was draped all over some young Doris when I saw him in a pub the other night.'

'Liar!' Queenie shouted.

Cilla turned her attention to Queenie next. 'As for your wonderful husband, why don't you ask him the real reason why he's so jealous of me and Micky? Bet he don't tell you the truth, sweetheart.'

'Who you calling bleedin' sweetheart? Ya cheeky mare.'

As Micky and Cilla walked away arm in arm, Queenie

grabbed Vivvy's arm as she tried to chase after them. 'Leave it, love. They want us to react. Don't! They ain't bloody worth it.'

Vivian Wade was in shock. Queenie led her into the nearest pub and bought them both a port and brandy to clear their heads.

'Do you think that old slapper was telling the truth, Queen? About my Bill?'

Queenie shrugged. 'Men are deceitful creatures, can't keep it in their trousers. Remember what our dad was like? The dirty bastard. I'll be having it out with Albie as soon as he gets home later and if I have an inkling he's had his todger anywhere near that blonde bit, I shall kick him out. I will not be made a fool of.'

'Nor me. I've smelled women's perfume on Bill before ya know, Queen. I pulled him on it and he said it was a dear old auntie who'd hugged him. It weren't the type of perfume an old auntie would wear though. Neither was the red lipstick I spotted on the collar of his shirt.'

Queenie squeezed her sister's arm. 'You don't wanna be with a man who cheats on you, Viv. You're beautiful inside and out, could get any man you wanted. I wasn't going to tell you this, but I've heard rumours too, about Bill.'

'What rumours?' Viv snarled.

'Nothing major. But he has been spotted in pubs with his arm draped around other women. If I was you, I'd end your courtship while you still can. I mean, when he was in prison, you said he proposed to you. He's never mentioned it since. Not even bought you a bloody ring.'

Queenie was shocked when her younger sister burst into tears. 'Don't cry, sweetheart. These men ain't worth it. We've got one another, me and you. If we're both single by tomorrow, we'll get by.'

'But it's not that simple. I've done something stupid, Queen. Something you always told me not to do.'

'Oh no. You haven't, ya know, been doing *it* with him?'

Vivian nodded dismally. 'Yes. Since firework night. And to make matters worse, I think I might be pregnant.'

Albie Butler whistled. 'Show Me the Way to Go Home' as he made his way towards the Grave Maurice. Bill would be pleased with him. Everybody had surprisingly paid him in full today.

Tomorrow was Albie's first day off in over a fortnight, that's how busy they'd been in the lead-up to Christmas. He'd planned a game of cards and a Christmas Eve lunchtime drink with the lads down the pub.

There was little lighting in the alleyway, so Albie didn't see the stocky thick-set man at first. But as he neared him, Albie clocked he was wearing a dark balaclava. Sensing danger, Albie turned on his heels and ran back the way he'd come from.

Unfortunately for Albie, he was too slow though. Way too slow.

Queenie and Viv were indoors discussing her possible pregnancy. 'I cannot believe you've been so stupid after everything I said to you. Dropping your drawers before marriage isn't the done thing, ya silly girl. Whatever was you thinking? The least you could have done was make him wear a dunky.'

Viv was glad when there was a knock on the door. 'Queenie, it's Mr Sharples. He says it's urgent.'

Queenie ran to the door with Brenda in her arms. The boys were out. 'What's up, Mr Sharples?'

'It's your Albie, love. He's been attacked by the sounds of it, has gone up the hospital.'

'You what! Where? Is he OK?'

'I don't know, lovey. Best you pop up the London and see for yourself. I'm sure he'll be fine, mind. Strong as an ox, is your Albie.'

Ordering Viv to look after Brenda, Queenie slung on her coat and ran down the road.

Albie was in a bit of a daze and was gutted he'd been robbed. Temporarily putting what Cilla had said out of her mind, Queenie inspected his injuries. The poor soul looked as white as a sheet. 'Your jaw looks broken.'

'It might well be. That bastard didn't arf pull a punch, Queen. He knocked me out cold.'

'Did you get a good look at him?'

'No. He jumped me in the alleyway and had a balaclava on. I tried to get away from him, but he chased me and that was it. I don't remember much else. What am I gonna say to Bill? There was a lot of money in me bag today, Queen. I hope I still get me wages.'

'Well of course you'll still get paid. Not your fault what happened, Albie. I told you when you first started the job that you were asking for trouble carrying that silly bag around with ya.'

'Bill said I had to use it. Lots of people pay with loose change and on days like today, I could never have fitted it all in me pockets. Say Bill thinks I've pulled a fast one like?'

'Don't you be worrying about that cocky little shyster. You leave him to me.'

Bill Harris was up the bar in the Grave Maurice when he clocked Queenie storm in. He knew Hounslow Harry had the dosh as he'd rung the pub from a callbox like he'd told him to. 'Hello, Queenie. You haven't seen Albie, have ya? He was meant to meet me in 'ere over a bleedin' hour ago.'

'I need to talk to you in private,' Queenie snapped. Bill wasn't bad looking with his wavy blond hair, blue eyes and big grin. But his eyebrows met in the middle, just like her father's had. She never trusted a man whose eyebrows joined together. 'Albie's at the hospital. He's been done over by some bloke in a balaclava down the alleyway that leads to the post office.'

Bill feigned a look of surprise. 'You gotta be kidding me! Is he OK, like?'

'He's a bit concussed with a broken jaw. The money's gone. The geezer who attacked him ran off with it.'

'Nah. Nah. He can't be doing this to me, Queenie. The boss'll go bleedin' well apeshit, love.'

'Not Albie's fault he got mugged, is it? You got his wages?'

'No. I was going to give it to him out of what he'd collected today.'

'Well, best you drop it off to me first thing in the morning. I need to pay the balance of the boys' bikes.'

'I need to speak to the boss first. He seriously ain't gonna be happy, Queenie.'

'Well, speaking of not being happy, I've heard rumours you've been seen out with other women. Sisters talk and believe me, if you cheat on my Vivvy you'll have me to deal with. Understand?'

Bill smiled as Queenie stomped out the pub. Who did she think she was, Ma bloody Barker? He couldn't wait until tomorrow to ruin her Christmas completely. That would teach her to keep sticking her oar in where it wasn't wanted.

*

Albie had slight concussion and was kept in hospital overnight then allowed home the following morning. His jaw had a slight fracture. It hurt like bloody hell and so did his head where he'd smashed it against the pavement.

'I'll make you a cuppa and a fried egg sandwich, then I'm taking the boys round Mum's. That bastard better turn up with your wages, Albie. Don't fall asleep, will ya, in case you don't hear the door.' Queenie was yet to mention what Cilla had said, but didn't believe Albie would cheat on her. She would pull him on it, though, when the time was right.

'What happened to you then, Dad?' asked Roy.

'I already told you, your father got mugged. Now go and wash your hands and faces, you three. We're popping round Nanny's.'

'Did you hit the other bloke back?' Vinny enquired.

'Sink, now! And wash those ears an' all. You'll have carrots growing out of 'em otherwise.'

'Why ain't Nan spending Christmas with us this year?' Michael asked, as they neared his granny's house.

'Because Viv and Bill will probably turn up after dinner and Nanny don't like Bill.' Vivvy was having Christmas dinner around Bill's parents' and her mum had decided to spend it with her church friends.

'Why don't Nan like Bill?' asked Vinny.

'Because he's a bleedin' arsehole,' Queenie replied, staring at Mrs O'Leary's old house. Patrick and Daniel had sold it soon after Mary's death and that was the last time she'd seen the lads. She'd heard they were doing well, through the grapevine, so was pleased about that.

'Will Nan be all on her own?' Michael asked.

'No. She's spending it with the bible-punchers.'

'But you said Nan wasn't religious,' Roy reminded his mother.

'She's not religious. Now stop giving me the third degree. You're driving me bloody mad.' Queenie could not help but worry. She'd already paid for Vinny and Roy's bikes, but was still eight quid short for Michael's. No way could she give two boys a bike and not the other. It wasn't fair.

Queenie tapped on her mum's front door.

'Oh, you bought the boys with you. I thought you were just bringing Brenda,' said Molly.

'I thought you wanted to give the boys their presents.'

'Yeah, I do. Tell 'em to behave though,' Molly whispered. 'The vicar's popped in for tea and cake.'

'Hello, Vicar,' grinned Vinny, nudging Roy. They loved winding their nan up when the vicar was there.

'Why don't you play outside for a while, boys?' Molly suggested.

'Nah. We wanna talk to the vicar, Nan,' replied Roy.

'You boys should come to my Sunday school. You'd love it. There's lots of other girls and boys your ages,' smiled Reverend Christopher Clark.

'What d'ya do there then?' Vinny asked.

Molly glared at her grandsons as they asked Christopher more and more stupid questions. 'Let the vicar finish his tea in peace, lads. Outside you go,' she snapped.

'My mum reckons my nan ain't religious,' Vinny informed the man of the cloth. 'Mum calls Nan's friends bible-punchers. Are you a bible-puncher too, Vicar?'

Feeling her face flush beetroot red, Molly physically pushed her naughty grandsons out into the back yard.

'Nanny just said the f and b words, vicar,' Vinny shouted out. 'She called us "Little fucking bastards",' he lied.

How Queenie stopped herself from laughing out loud,

she did not know. Her poor mother's expression was priceless. So was the vicar's.

As soon as Queenie arrived home, she knew by Albie's expression that something was seriously wrong. 'Well? Did Bill turn up?'

'Yeah. But it ain't good news, love. The boss was apparently furious. I've been sacked.'

'Sacked! How can he blame you for what happened?'

Albie shrugged his shoulders dismally. 'I gotta pay back the money I lost an' all.'

'You gotta be kidding me! No way are you paying a penny back, Albie. Did Bill bring you your wages round?'

'No. I'm not getting paid 'cause of what happened.'

'For crying out loud, Albie! Well that's just bloody brilliant. Some Christmas this is gonna be. We haven't got a pot to piss in.'

After a sleepless night, Queenie did her best to plaster a smile on her face. She'd managed to get the boys' bikes. Kenneth who owned the bike shop had told her she could pay off the eight quid she owed a pound a week. The trouble was, she had no idea how she was going to pay it. What's more, they had no Christmas dinner. She hadn't had the money to pick the turkey up.

Albie had begged her to borrow some money off her mum or Viv, but Queenie was far too proud for that. Neither did she want that Bill Harris knowing her business. She'd have a few choice words for him later, that was for sure. That's if he had the guts to show his smarmy face.

'We're going out on our bikes now, Mum. What time d'ya want us back for dinner?' asked Vinny. All three of her sons were confident riders as they'd often ridden their friends' bikes. They'd been overjoyed with their boxing gloves and bikes. Their little faces had been a picture.

'Come back about three-ish. We've only got saveloys, potatoes and veg, I'm afraid. But we've got a cake I baked for afters, and custard.'

'Aww. I wanted turkey, Mum. We always have turkey,' complained Roy.

'Well, not this year we bleedin' don't. You wanna think yourself lucky, you three. I bet there ain't many boys who got boxing gloves and bikes. You don't know you're born sometimes.'

'Are we skint 'cause Dad got mugged?' enquired Vinny.

'No. We're skint because I spent all Dad's hard-earned cash on you three. Now sod off out for a while and leave me and your father in peace.'

Hearing the boys excitedly ride off down the road, Queenie picked up her screaming daughter and turned to her husband. 'Whatever we gonna do, Albie?'

'I don't know yet, love. But something's bound to crop up. It always does.'

'I got a bone to pick with you an' all. What's the story with you and that blonde bit Micky is besotted with? Only I bumped into 'em the day you got attacked and she sort of hinted that you and her had history.'

Albie felt his heart rate increase tenfold. 'I knew her when I was a lad, that's all. Cilla used to live opposite my mum.'

'And . . . ? Only if Micky's expression was anything to go by, there's more to you and Cilla than meets the eye.'

Albie could feel his cheeks burning up. 'If you must know, I had my first proper little fumble with her. I was only a lad at the time.'

'How old is she?'

'Oh, I can't remember offhand. I hadn't seen her for years. If I had to guess, I'd say she's about eight years my senior.'

'Did you have sex with her?'

'Goodness, no, Queenie. It was only a fumble,' Albie lied. 'And I was only about fourteen if I remember rightly.'

'Gawd stone the crows! The woman wants locking up. She's a danger to society, the dirty bleedin' mare. You wait until I see her again. She won't be looking down her nose at me next time, when she hears what I have to say.'

'Please, Queenie, no. If you see her and Micky again, just ignore 'em. That's what I shall do.'

Queenie pursed her lips. 'We shall see about that.'

'Right, you wait 'ere with Michael and the bikes, Roy,' ordered Vinny.

'What you gonna do, Vinny?' asked Michael.

'You'll see,' grinned Vinny. He knew his mum would kick his arse if he robbed off one of their own. But they didn't know many people in Canning Town so that's why they'd ridden here.

Vinny knocked at the first half a dozen doors and when they were answered, lied he was visiting his Auntie Mary and couldn't remember her new address. 'There's a Mary lives down the other end of the road, son. Number sixty-four. Is her surname Walton?'

'No. That ain't Auntie Mary. But thanks anyway, mister. I think I might have the wrong street.'

Spotting an elderly couple leaving a house further down, Vinny waited until they'd turned the corner before crossing the road. He knocked on the door. There was no answer. Checking nobody was watching him; Vinny put his hand through the letterbox. Bingo. He was sure he could smell cooking and the key was there.

Usually, men went to pubs of a lunchtime on their own, Vinny knew that, as his dad always did. But at Christmas, some of the women were allowed to go too. He remembered his mum and Auntie Viv going to the pub with his dad a couple of years ago, before his mum was pregnant with Brenda. His mum had left the turkey cooking and he'd looked after his brothers. They'd all come home a bit tiddly, even his nan.

Vinny expertly lifted the string off the hook and opened the front door. He was in and out within twelve seconds, with a partially cooked turkey under his arm.

Vinny felt elated as he charged down the road towards his brothers. His mum had brought them the best presents ever and now it was time to pay her back.

'Whatever's wrong?' Queenie asked, as she answered the door to Vivian, who was sobbing like a child.

'Bill has finished with me and it's all my fault. I accused him of seeing other women and he was ever so upset. He said if I don't trust him we should call it a day.'

Albie was sitting in his threadbare armchair listening to the radio. Bing Crosby's 'White Christmas' was playing, a song Albie had recently learned the words to so he could sing it himself. Queenie ushered her sister into the kitchen. 'Did you tell the bastard you might be pregnant?' she whispered.

'No. I got my period late last night. I wish I was pregnant now. I love him so much, Queen. I'll never find another man I love so much, I know I won't.'

'Yes. You will. Thank God you're not pregnant by him, that's all I can say. I know you're upset at the moment, Viv.

But believe me; you've had a very lucky escape. One day, you'll meet the man of your dreams. Trust me. You will.'

'Queenie!' Albie bellowed.

The boys were standing in the front room, Vinny holding a turkey in his hands. 'It's a bit cooked, Mum. Put the oven on. You'll know when it's done properly.'

'Where did you get it?' asked Queenie.

'I nicked it. But not from round 'ere 'cause you tell us never to steal from our own. We nicked it miles away, didn't we, Roy?'

'Yeah. We did, Mum. We rode our bikes 'til our bums were sore,' explained Roy.

'I'm starving, Mum,' announced Michael.

Queenie took the turkey out of her eldest son's hands. 'Where did it come from?' Albie wanted to know.

'An 'ouse,' Vinny replied.

'You can't cook it, Queen. The little buggers will never know right from wrong if you serve 'em that for dinner. They can't go breaking into people's homes, stealing. It's totally wrong, love.'

'It was me that nicked it, not Roy or Michael.' Vinny didn't want to get his brothers into trouble. 'It was all my idea too. 'Cause you bought us nice presents, Mum, I wanted to do something nice back.'

'By breaking into some poor sod's home and stealing their half-cooked turkey!' Albie couldn't believe what he was hearing.

Queenie glared at her husband. 'At least the boys showed initiative, Albie. Got off their arses and actually put food on the table. Perhaps now we're destitute again, you should take a leaf out of Vinny's book.'

Vinny grinned like a Cheshire cat. He loved making his mum happy. He also loved being the man of the house.

CHAPTER TWENTY-THREE

Nine Months Later

Autumn 1956

I knew something was wrong even before the doctor was sent for. Call it sisterly instinct or call me a witch, but I just knew.

Viv was in excruciating pain, but all she kept rambling on about was she couldn't have Dr Andrews looking up her crotch.

I was in need of a break, desperate for a wee and a fag, so when the doctor arrived, I excused myself for a few minutes.

Bill Harris was pacing up and down in the hallway. 'How is she? What's happening?'

'The baby's breech, hence the doctor being called. Viv's a fighter. She'll be fine,' I told him.

I went to the toilet. I'd been holding it that long, I sounded like a horse peeing. I then walked out into the garden and sparked up a cigarette. It'd been hours since I'd had one and the nicotine made me feel lightheaded.

I leaned against the fence and even though I'm not overly

religious, I held Mrs O'Leary's rosary beads in my hand and prayed for Viv and that baby. I was so angry when Viv got back together with Bill last New Year and even more livid when she got up the duff for real soon afterwards. After her pregnancy scare, Viv had obviously done it to trap Bill, but now I didn't care about any of that. I just wanted my sister and her baby to be OK.

Bill walked into the garden and handed me a brandy. 'You look shattered, Queenie. Drink that, it'll calm your nerves.'

'Thanks, but no thanks,' I said. I was shattered. Fourteen long bloody hours Viv had been in labour for, but I was far too proud to go back into the room smelling like a lush in front of Dr Andrews and the midwives.

'Shall I make you a cup of Rosy?' asked Bill.

'Nah. I'd better get back up there,' I said. I'd warmed to Bill a bit. He did the right thing and married Viv in a registry office in March before she properly showed. He'd also treated her exceptionally well during her pregnancy, rented them a nice house about a ten-minute walk from mine, and was very excited about becoming a father. Viv didn't care what sex the child was, but like myself, Bill craved a boy. He wanted to name the child Lenny after his beloved grandfather who'd recently died. His grandfather had by all accounts raised Bill.

'Oh, Jesus, Queen. What's happening?' Bill asked. The scream was shrill, awful in fact.

I ran up the stairs. After all those hours holding Vivvy's hand with her fingernails digging into mine, I'd missed the actual birth.

The child lay motionless as the umbilical cord was tied then cut. I could see it was a boy, a big boy, and he looked just perfect, but he wasn't making a sound. I silently prayed once again.

My heart was beating rapidly as Dr Andrews took charge. A handsome grey-haired man in his late forties, the whole of Whitechapel trusted Dr Andrews. He had helped deliver many babies and on the odd occasion Albie and I had been able to afford a doctor, he'd been brilliant with the boys.

'Why ain't he crying? Why ain't my baby crying?' Vivian sobbed. 'Please God make my baby live. Please God,' she screamed.

I said nothing, but couldn't help feel how odd it was that both Viv and I were turning to God when we'd always mocked religion.

Dr Andrews blew into the baby's windpipe. The midwives exchanged worried glances. I feared the worst. A minute had passed, perhaps two.

All of a sudden, the baby made a choking noise and then started to cry.

'He's alive. Thank you, God. Thank you,' sobbed Viv.

I'd honestly thought the baby was a goner. Relief fooded through my veins. 'It's a miracle, Viv. A miracle,' I whispered in awe.

The baby was placed in Viv's arms. His face was very red and his hair was blond like Bill's. 'Hello, Lenny. You didn't arf give us all a scare,' Viv smiled.

I couldn't stop smiling. 'He's perfect, Viv. Truly perfect.'

Three Years Later

Autumn 1959

'Lenny. No!' Vivian grabbed hold of her son's hand, just in time to stop him grabbing a handful of the birthday cake Queenie had spent ages making.

Relieved the cake was still in one piece, Queenie lifted her nephew up. 'Who's a little tinker, eh? That Lenny is, that's who,' she chuckled.

Lenny laughed so hard, he had an unfortunate accident and shit himself.

'Gawd stone the crows! Whatever 'ave you been feeding him, Viv? It smells like a rat crawled up his bleedin' arse and died.'

'Good job I bought a spare set of clothes round for him.' Vivian screwed her nose up. 'Come on, stinky bum. Bath for you.'

Vinny Butler pocketed his wages and trudged dejectedly down the market.

Roy caught up with his eldest brother. 'Whassa matter with you? You've had the hump all day.'

'Ripped me strides earlier, didn't I? I like these strides an' all. Caught 'em on a bastard nail. I doubt they can be repaired, look.'

Roy glanced at the square of material flapping loosely against Vinny's right knee. 'You should just wear your old clothes for work like I do, ya div.'

'Nothing divvy about wanting to look smart, Roy. You never know who you might bump into,' Vinny snapped. For the past couple of years himself and Roy had worked as barrow boys on Roman Road market. On Tuesdays and Thursdays they would ride to the Roman on their bikes to help pull the barrows out before school. On a Saturday they would walk there as they did odd jobs for stallholders until it was time to take the barrows back in. The job seemed OK at first, but now Vinny was getting older he couldn't help but feel it was a bit beneath him. The money wasn't great and he knew he had the brains to earn far more. Still, the dosh they earned helped their mum out, so until he found something better, he would stick with it.

Queenie handed her sister a cup of tea. Neither of their marriages had turned out to be idyllic, which was why they spent so much time in one another's company these days. 'Is Bill coming round tomorrow?'

Vivian shook her head sadly. Her son wasn't like other children. He was what one doctor had callously described as 'backward'. 'I told Bill you were having a bit of a shindy for Vinny's birthday, but you know what he's like, said he had to work.'

Queenie subtly changed the subject. When Lenny was born he'd looked and behaved just like any other baby. They'd had no inkling that anything was wrong with him until he was around a year old. The doctors reckoned Lenny being starved of oxygen at birth had led to him having some kind of brain damage. Queenie and Viv adored the boy. He was unique, funny, a real little character, and anyone who met him seemed to fall under his charm. Vinny, Roy and Michael worshipped Lenny too. They called him 'Champ' and vowed to always look out for him. Albie and Brenda also loved him dearly. Unfortunately, the only one who couldn't seem to accept Lenny was his own father. Bill Harris had very little time for his son and Queenie knew how much this hurt her sister. Lenny wasn't brain damaged, not to them. He was their wonderful special boy.

'I see Old Mother Taylor's eldest today. Didn't recognize him at first. Turned into a Teddy boy, but it don't bleedin' well suit him, Viv. His suit looked ten sizes too big. Probably trying to get a girlfriend. No chance with his spotty face and that frowsy mare of a mother. One look at her is enough to make any girl run a mile.'

Vivian chuckled. 'I saw him the other day, down The Waste. Got such a big nose an' all and he's as skinny as a rake. Poor bastard looks like he's fallen out the ugly tree and hit every branch on the way down.'

'You're so cruel,' Queenie laughed.

'You bleedin' started it,' Viv retorted.

So much had changed in the East End since the war. There were still a lot of bombsites and reminders of the Blitz, but overall things seemed to be on the up. Rationing was a thing of the past finally and most men were now working. Apart from Albie, that was. He'd lasted all of a week when Queenie had forced him to take a job as a builder.

Music and fashion had changed too. The Teddy boy culture had begun to creep into society in the early fifties and had since caught on with many of the youngsters. The lads wore draped jackets and drainpipe trousers that looked too short, as you could see their socks. Their hair was greased back in an enormous quiff and on their feet they'd wear crepe-soled shoes. Clumsy-looking things they were. Vinny and Roy called them 'Beetle Crushers'.

Teddy girls dressed slightly better. Especially the ones that wore tight pencil skirts and their hair in pretty plaits. Some wore rolled-up jeans, mind. Queenie hated seeing girls in jeans. Denim was so unfeminine; workmen's trousers, so her mum reckoned.

Music had changed a lot too. There was a weekly chart now and record shops seemed to be popping up everywhere. Rock and Roll was all the rage, a sound adopted by the Teddy boys and girls. Lenny loved music, especially Rock and Roll, so Queenie and Viv had taken a shine to it too.

'What you thinking about, Queen?'

'How times flies. I can't believe Vinny is fourteen tomorrow. I remember giving birth to my Baby Blue like it were yesterday. I hope he don't become one of these bleedin' Teddy boys when he leaves school.'

'Nah, course he won't. Your boys have too much class to follow silly fashions. I was thinking earlier, about Aunt Edna. I still miss her you know.'

As flashbacks of the Bethnal Green tube disaster entered Queenie's thoughts, she quickly blanked them out. Viv had no idea of the real horror Queenie and their mum had endured that evening, and she never would.

Queenie stood up. 'Right, I'm gonna wake Brenda and Lenny now and put me corned beef hash in the oven. The boys'll be home from work soon and Christ knows where Michael is. Probably out with that new friend of his, Kevin.'

'What you looking at?' Roy asked his brother.

'That Austin Healey sports car. It's ace! Look at it. The same car was parked outside the other day. Let's hang around a bit, see who owns it. I wanna know what business they're opening. We might be able to get a better job.'

'Vin, I'm starvin'. Can't we come back 'ere after dinner? Mum always has dinner ready for us at this time,' Roy said, glancing at the watch his mum had bought him for his birthday.

'You go on. Tell Mum I had to work later than you. I won't be long.'

The building in question had been dilapidated up until recently. The windows were blacked out, but Vinny spotted a tiny gap and peered inside. It was too dark to see properly, but he could make out an assortment of large objects.

Unbeknown to Vinny, he'd been spotted. The door of the property opened and a man stepped outside. 'All right, sonny. What you up to?'

Vinny was rather taken aback by the striking-looking bloke. He had jet black hair with a small quiff and green eyes as bright as his own. He had on drainpipe dark jeans, a white shirt, black winkle-picker shoes and a thin black tie. He looked like the singer Elvis Presley. 'Erm, all right. This gaff yours, is it? I weren't sizing it up to break into or nothing. I was just trying to work out what it was gonna be; only I'm after a job.'

Thinking what a good-looking lad Vinny was, the man smiled, showing a set of perfectly straight teeth. 'How old are you? Sixteen? Seventeen?'

Already five foot eight, Vinny towered over all the lads in his class. He knew he looked older and acted more mature than others his age. 'I'll be sixteen tomorrow,' he lied. 'So what business is it gonna be?'

'A launderette.'

Vinny couldn't help but feel disappointed. No way was he working in a launderette.

The man held out his right hand. 'Me name's Dave, but everyone calls me Macca. And you are . . . ?'

'Vinny.'

Macca smiled. A strong handshake, cheeky charm, good looks. Young Vinny had it all. 'Why don't you come in, have a beer for your birthday? I'll let you into a secret an' all. This ain't my business. I manage a club.'

Vinny grinned. 'Yeah. OK.'

Queenie opened the oven door once again. Patience had never been a virtue of hers. 'How long did Vinny say he was going to be, Roy?' she shouted.

'He didn't say, Mum.'

'Oh well. Dinner's gonna be dried up unless we eat it now. Vinny can eat his cold, same as your father. Everyone want beans?'

'Yes, please,' clapped Brenda. Baked beans were her favourite food.

'Don't give Lenny any beans. His arse is still on fire, Queen,' warned Vivian.

The corned beef hash went down a treat with all, apart from Brenda. She was still a finicky eater, a skinny little thing, and Queenie was always trying to feed her up.

Queenie told Viv to take the little uns in the front room, then pushed her plate to one side. 'You haven't said anything to Vinny, have you, boys? About tomorrow?'

'I ain't, Mum,' said Michael.

'Nor me,' Roy added.

Queenie smiled lovingly at her sons. They were good boys, always kept their word. Her unusual style of parenting had obviously paid off. They were loyal, family orientated, loving and generous. She'd never bothered telling Brenda her special bedtime stories. It was different for girls. She just read her ordinary ones. 'Did you invite some friends like I told you to?'

'Yeah. My mates Pete and Paul are coming,' Roy replied.

'And what about this mysterious friend of yours, Michael? I'm beginning to think Kevin is a figment of your imagination.'

Michael looked sheepish. 'Erm, I wanted to ask him, but I didn't. Kev's really ace, but I ain't sure you'll like him.'

'Why ever not? Come on, spit it out. Not a poofter, is he?'

Roy nudged his youngest brother. 'Just tell her, ya nutter.'

'You tell her,' mumbled Michael.

Roy sighed. 'Kev's black. Well, half-black. His dad comes from Jamaica, but he ain't ever seen him. Kev's mum's white and he's just like us. He even talks like us and he ain't that dark. Sort of half an' half.'

Queenie digested this information before answering. England had changed, especially London, the Blitz had seen to that. Lots of Caribbeans had fought side by side with the English during the war. Then they'd been invited over to help rebuild the country. Queenie could remember reading an article about the *Empire Windrush* ship arriving at Tilbury Docks; that must have been the late forties. Thinking about the signs that Mary had to face – *No Irish, no blacks, no dogs* – she said, 'Your friend Kevin is very welcome in this house, Michael. I trust your judgement and Roy's. Sod what the neighbours think. Who are they to judge us?'

Michael beamed from ear to ear. He couldn't wait to tell Kev. 'Cheers, Mum. You're the best.'

'I'd better make a move now. Thanks for showing me around and stuff. I hope it does well, your business. I'd ask for a job, but I know I ain't cut out to work in a laundry,' Vinny smiled.

Macca smiled back. 'I've got the perfect job for you. In my aunt's club. It's great money. Why don't you pop back tomorrow night and in the meantime I'll have a word with my aunt. I'm living upstairs in the flat so just press the buzzer outside. I'll be around anytime from after seven.'

'Really! What sort of club is it?'

'I'll explain all to you tomorrow. No point getting your hopes up until my aunt's OK'd it. She's gonna want to meet you first.'

'No probs.' Vinny felt a bit wobbly as he stood up. He

wasn't used to alcohol and had matched Macca beer for beer. Three he'd had and now felt light-headed.

Macca saw Vinny out, ran up the stairs and picked up the phone. 'Auntie, I've found us a great new recruit. You're gonna love him. So will our punters.'

CHAPTER TWENTY-FOUR

'Happy birthday to you
Happy birthday to you
Happy birthday, dear Vinny
Happy birthday to you.'

Vinny excitedly ripped open his gift. He might have the body
of a man, but was still a big kid when it came to presents.
'Oh wow! It's ace, Mum! I bloody love it. Thank you.'

'Don't he look smart, Albie?' Queenie crowed. It had
taken her months to save for the jacket. She'd put a few
bob in her savings tin every week.

'Very suave, son,' Albie replied.

The bomber jacket was a replica of the one James Dean
had worn in *Rebel Without a Cause*. Vinny was a James
Dean fan, had watched his films numerous times at the
cinema and had been gutted when Dean had got killed
in a car crash in 1955.

'You'll have to grow your hair now, have it waxed back
with a bit of a quiff,' Roy joked.

Vinny ran his right hand through his hair. He hadn't
had it cut for a while. 'Can I use your Brylcreem, Dad?'

'Yes, boy. Help yourself. It's in the bathroom cupboard.'

When Vinny returned a few minutes later with his hair greased back, both Roy and Michael rolled around laughing. 'You look like an iron,' Roy shrieked.

'Vinny is a poofer, Vinny is a poofter,' Michael chuckled.

'Stop it now. Don't be so nasty to your brother on his birthday. He looks nice,' said Queenie.

Vinny studied himself in the bathroom mirror. This was a similar style to Macca's. What did his brothers know? They were only kids. Macca wasn't. He was twenty-six, a proper man.

Albie Butler smiled as Brenda got on the sofa, stood on his knees and put her arms around his neck. His sons rarely showed him any affection. Vinny was a proper Mummy's boy and Roy wasn't far behind him. Michael was affectionate to both parents, and showed Albie more respect than the other two. But Brenda was his little favourite, the baby of the family. 'Daddy's going to get some seafood. Do you want anything?' Albie grinned, knowing full well what the answer would be.

'Winkles, winkles, winkles!' Brenda clapped her hands excitedly.

Chuckling, Albie lifted his daughter up in the air. If Brenda could live on winkle sandwiches and baked beans, she would. The fussy little thing turned her nose up at most of Queenie's dinners, which Albie found quite amusing as it annoyed his wife immensely.

'Why don't you take her down the Lane with you? I've got lots of food to prepare and could do without her under my feet,' Queenie said.

'I can't, love. I've got a bit of work to do before I pick up the seafood. Sorry.'

Queenie rolled her eyes. Albie's latest venture was flogging fresh meat and poultry in pubs. He gave her money every week, a pittance really. It didn't even cover the rent. If it wasn't for her cleaning jobs and Vinny and Roy chipping in with the bills, they'd freeze and starve. 'Be back 'ere by half two then and don't come home pissed,' Queenie snapped.

'Erm, I meant to tell you, I visited Aunt Liz yesterday. She's really not well, can barely breathe. Anyway, Bert and Ivy were there, so I invited 'em all round this afternoon.'

'You did what!'

'Queen, have a heart for Christ's sake. I know you were good to my mum and I'll never forget your kindness. But, Aunt Liz is seriously ill and she's never even seen this house. Neither has Bert.'

'And you want to know why? Bert married the most boring woman on earth and Aunt Liz can't keep her trap shut. You better warn her not to start telling her stories about you hiding in her loft during the war. Our sons think little enough of you as it is.'

Unusually for Albie, he saw red. 'I wonder why that is? It wouldn't be anything to do with you and your sister putting me down constantly, would it?'

'Oh don't be so touchy. Me and Viv only have a laugh. You ain't gonna bleedin' change now, are you? I've given up trying to push you to better yourself. You can only smack your head against a brick wall so many times. Never forget it was me who got you out the shit that time you were mugged, mind. If I hadn't have stood up to Bill Harris, you'd have had to pay all that money back.'

'Oh not that again! Whaddya want, a medal? I'm off now and if my family turn up, you and that witch of a

283

sister of yours better be nice to 'em. Since Lenny's been born, I've had to suffer those two being 'ere morning, noon and night. This is as much my house as yours. I pay the bloody rent every week.'

'No you don't. You pay towards the bloody rent. If it wasn't for me and *my* boys, we'd all be bloody homeless.'

'Well thanks very much,' a voice said shrilly. 'So sorry you've had to suffer me and my son.'

Albie swung around in horror. Vivian had her own key and had obviously heard every word. 'I didn't mean it like that, lovey. I adore Lenny as much as everyone else does, you know that.'

Queenie shook her head in despair. 'Just go out Albie, will ya.'

'We gonna see if Diane wants any help first?' Roy asked his brother. Every Sunday they would head down Petticoat Lane and earn a few bob. Diane owned the pet stall, sold cats, dogs and even small monkeys. She paid well and was always the lads' first port of call.

'Nah. We're not working today. I ain't spoiling this jacket. We're shopping instead,' Vinny replied.

'For what?'

'Drainpipe jeans.'

'But you've never worn jeans. Mum hates 'em.'

'I ain't a kid any more, Roy. I'm quite capable of choosing what I wear. I've decided, now I'm fourteen I'm leaving school, getting a proper job. Mum shouldn't have to work for that posh bitch, cleaning. She's shattered the days she has to graft and then she has to cook dinner and see to Brenda. It ain't fair.'

'Mum won't let you leave school until you're fifteen,' Roy warned.

Vinny grinned. He already had a plan should Macca's job offer come off. 'Best I get meself expelled then, eh bruv?'

'Surprise!' Queenie shrieked.

Vinny glanced at his mum, the cake and then around the front room. Apart from his dad's relations being there, there was no surprise. His mum had always baked a cake and invited people around for his birthday for as far back as he could remember. 'Thanks, Mum,' he grinned.

'Give Nanny a kiss then, and Auntie Liz and Aunt Ivy,' Queenie urged her sons. She then clocked what Vinny was wearing. 'Whatever you got on your legs?'

'Jeans. I treated meself. They go with my new jacket.'

'Workman's clothes,' Queenie hissed. 'In my day the O'Leary brothers, well they looked like real gentlemen. You don't see the Kelly brothers or the Krays wearing jeans, do you?'

'No, but—'

'No buts, Vinny,' Queenie interrupted. 'You're not wearing those bloody things when you come out with me. Even your father wouldn't be seen dead in them.'

'Told ya,' Roy grinned.

Vinny punched his brother on the arm. 'Shut it, you.' Little did his brother know, he'd only bought the jeans to try and impress Macca and land himself a job.

Lenny prodded Vinny in the leg. His speech was slower than other kids his age, but perfectly understandable. 'Music, Vinny, music.'

Vinny picked up his beloved nephew. 'Come on then, Champ. Let's put the records on.' Every couple of weeks Vinny would pop into a record shop and treat Lenny to a new tune. The boy was music mad.

When Lenny started dancing to Elvis's 'Heartbreak Hotel', Vinny caught his mum's eye and smiled. He'd never forgotten those bedtime stories she'd drummed into him as a child. She was a fantastic mum, had held their family together virtually single-handed. Now it was time for him to show his worth, get his mum a TV and a radiogram. Even his Aunt Viv had a TV.

Queenie walked over to her birthday boy and slipped her arm around his waist. Vinny towered above her now and she was glad he'd inherited Albie's height and not hers. 'Sorry what I said about your jeans. I'm an old fuddy-duddy, so take no notice of me. I know they're in fashion.'

Vinny kissed his mother on the forehead. 'I'm wearing 'em for a reason, trust me. Look at this place. It needs decorating and we need new furniture. I'm not a kid any more, Mum. You've done so much for me over the years, now it's my turn to do stuff for you.'

Queenie stroked his cheek. 'You're a good son, Vinny. I couldn't have wished for better.'

'Mum, meet Kevin. Kev, this is my mum and that's Auntie Viv,' Michael said proudly.

Queenie held out her right hand. Kevin was a caramel colour with afro hair. 'Hello. It's lovely to finally meet you, Kevin,' Queenie said slowly.

'Hello, Kevin. Do you live locally?' Viv asked, in an even slower tone.

Michael looked at his mum and aunt in horror. Why were they talking to Kevin as though he were a retard?

Creasing up laughing, Vinny nudged Roy. His mum and aunt were so old-fashioned. It was obvious they were talking in ridiculous tones in the hope Kevin would understand them.

'Would you like a cup of tea, Kevin? Do you like tea?' Queenie asked dumbly.

'Course he likes tea. Why wouldn't he like tea?' Michael spat.

Thankfully, Kevin saw the funny side. Growing up in London as a mixed-race lad hadn't been easy for him, but he'd learned taking it all in his stride was the best way to deal with life. 'Hello, Mama. Hello Auntie. I am honoured to be invited 'ere today inside your beautiful home,' Kevin said in a thick Jamaican drawl. Even though he'd never met his dad, Kevin knew other Jamaicans and had easily picked up the lingo. 'My people don't drink tea. It brings us out in spots. Big white spots.'

By this point, Vinny and Roy were bent double. Their mum and aunt's expressions were priceless.

Kevin winked at the two astonished women. 'I'm only winding you up, ladies. I'd love a cup of Rosy, please.'

Queenie and Viv blushed. Both felt stupid. Even Michael and Kevin were rolling about laughing now. 'You had us going there, Kevin, and we had you going,' Queenie guffawed, desperate to dig herself out of a hole.

'Yeah, righto, Mum,' Vinny chuckled.

'Believe that and you'll believe anything, Kev,' Roy added.

'I did warn you what they'd be like,' said Michael.

Thinking what a lovely boy he was, Queenie and Viv both gave Kevin a welcoming hug. Neither had ever had a black person in their homes before. Times were changing faster than they knew.

'He won't put that bleedin' monkey down. Sleeps with it and it has to be with him every moment of the day. Stinks, it does,' Vivian informed her sister. Zippy the Monkey was Lenny's favourite toy. They'd mislaid it once and he'd screamed the bloody house down all afternoon.

'Albie's a bleedin' liar,' Queenie whispered. 'He told me Aunt Liz was at death's door. She ain't stopped eating, drinking, smoking and talking. The greedy old cow ate all those whelks to herself. No other bastard got a look in.'

All of a sudden there was a commotion. Aunt Liz seemed to be choking. Her face reddened as she struggled to breathe. 'Do something then, Albie,' Queenie bellowed. Albie was currently singing 'You'll Never Know'.

Bert leapt up and began slapping Auntie Liz on the back. Seconds later a jellied eel catapulted out of her gob and hit Albie straight in the face.

Queenie and Viv held on to one another for support. They couldn't stop laughing.

The rest of the afternoon passed without incident. Aunt Liz, Bert and Ivy were the first to leave. Then Pete and Paul.

'Me and Kev are going out now, Mum,' Michael shouted.

'Thanks for inviting me round, Mrs B. I've had a lovely day. All the food was ace. I won't be needing no supper.'

Queenie smiled. Kevin was as polite as her own boys. 'You're welcome round 'ere anytime, lovey, and I mean that.'

Vinny glanced at the clock, then kissed his grandmother on the cheek. 'Thanks for my socks and pants. Bye, Nan. See you soon.'

'Where you going?' Roy asked Vinny. 'I'll come with you.'

'No. You can't.'

'Why not?'

Vinny tutted. ''Cause I said so.'

'What time will you be back?' Queenie asked.

'Dunno. I'm meeting a mate.'

Queenie peered out the window to see which direction her son walked in. It was unlike him to be secretive and as far as she was aware, he didn't have any close mates. The one good mate he'd had, had recently emigrated to Australia with his parents.

'Maybe he's meeting a girl?' suggested Viv.

Queenie doubted that. Neither Vinny nor Roy were yet to show any interest in girls. Michael was the little lothario. He had a different girlfriend every other week.

'Shall I follow him?' Roy suggested.

Queenie shook her head. 'Vinny's not a kid any more, therefore doesn't have to tell us his every move. If he wants some space, let him have it.'

'Vinny, meet my Auntie Marnie.'

Vinny held out his right hand. Auntie Marnie was tall and glamorous, probably in her late forties. Her hair was long, brunette, and she wore lots of diamanté jewellery and a real fur jacket. Vinny had never seen such high-heeled stilettos and he couldn't help but feel a bit nervous. She was a formidable-looking woman.

Auntie Marnie looked Vinny up and down. 'Walk towards the door, then turn around and walk back towards me,' she ordered.

Thinking what a croaky voice the woman had, Vinny did as she asked.

'Right, tell me a bit about yourself,' smiled Aunt Marnie.

Vinny rattled off a few lines about his life and family. He didn't mention his surname though, or his parents' names. He also mentioned that today was his sixteenth birthday and he wanted a decent job so he could help his mum out more.

'Sit down,' ordered Auntie Marnie. She sat next to Vinny and smiled. 'I run a club, but it's no ordinary club. I have a lot of important members who have high-profile jobs. Therefore, if you work for me, you say nothing to nobody about who you might meet or what you do. What goes on in my club, stays in my club. Get my drift?'

Not really understanding what the hell Auntie Marnie was talking about, Vinny nodded. 'I ain't no snitch. I'm an expert at keeping me trap shut.'

'Good. That's what I like to hear.' Aunt Marnie turned to her nephew. 'Bring Vinny down on Wednesday and show him the ropes.'

'What will I actually be doing?' Vinny enquired.

'Talking to people. I'm in the entertainment business. I'll give you a week's trial. If you cut the mustard, you'll then get paid four quid a shift. I will expect you to work at least four shifts a week, but if you want to work five or six you can. The only day we're shut is on a Sunday.'

Vinny could feel the adrenalin pumping through his body. He couldn't believe his luck. If he worked six shifts he'd bring home twenty-four quid a week. An absolute bloody fortune! 'Thanks ever so much. I won't let you down, I promise.'

Of course Vinny had no idea what he was actually signing up for at that point. No idea at all.

CHAPTER TWENTY-FIVE

'Is everything OK, Mrs Huntingdon-Brown? If so, I'll be off now.'

'Did you polish all the mirrors like I asked you to?' snapped the posh bitch who Queenie loathed so very much.

'Yes, Mrs Huntingdon-Brown.'

Pearl Huntingdon-Brown got off her fat arse to double-check for herself. 'This long one still has a smear on it, Queenie. Look,' she pointed. 'Do it again, please.'

Cursing under her breath, Queenie did as she was told. She had been working for the Huntingdon-Browns for almost two years now. Basil, the husband, was a jeweller, owned his own shop in Hatton Garden and was rarely at home. The daughter Clarissa was fifteen, an up-her-own-arse prat, just like her unbearable mother.

Queenie worked for the family three days a week, Monday, Wednesday and Friday. The journey to and from Finsbury Park was a cowson, but Queenie could not do without the five pound a week she earned. That paid towards the rent, the food, the coal and the gas. There was never any money left over at the end of the week.

Any money the boys gave her, Queenie bought the kids clothes with or saved for presents and Christmas.

'I'll be off then, Mrs Huntingdon-Brown. Would you like to check the mirror again before I go?' There had been no smear on it in the first place.

'No. That's OK. See you on Monday, bright and early. Your wages are on the kitchen counter.'

Queenie picked up her dosh, then left the huge Victorian property. She slammed the front door. 'Stuck-up bitch.'

Albie huffed, puffed, grunted, groaned, then rolled off Fishy Fanny. His latest bit on the side had an unfortunate nickname, but it wasn't what it seemed. Her name was actually Fanny and she sold fresh fish down by the docks.

An unselfish man, Albie put his middle finger inside Fanny's fanny and kept it there until she also came.

'Cheers, Albie. You better make a move soon in case Stan comes home early.'

Albie jumped out of Fanny's bed and quickly got dressed. Unlike his affair with Cilla, this was just a once a week booty call. It was the same for Fanny. She adored her elderly husband who ran their fish stall with her. Stan was sixty-two now, twenty years older than her and, according to Fanny, he couldn't raise a gallop any more.

Fanny got up, put on her dressing gown and kissed Albie on the cheek. 'Same time next week?'

Albie nodded. Fanny was buxom, plump, but no looker. Thanks to Queenie, this is what his life had come to though. He and Queenie had not had sex since she'd got pregnant with Brenda. He wasn't even allowed to sleep in her bed any more. He'd been relegated to the sofa. 'You take care, Fanny. See ya next Friday, girl.'

*

On the train home, all Queenie could think about was Vinny. He'd got himself expelled from school last week by smacking his teacher around the head, then the following day had miraculously found himself this so-called wonderful job which he was yet to get paid for.

Clumping Mr Edwards, his form teacher, had actually done Vinny's reputation the world of good. A thin, medium-height man with a massive bald patch and over-sized moustache, Mr Edwards was a bully to the lads he taught; he got off on clouting the boys and caning them. Queenie had received lots of congratulations from other mothers, praising her Vinny for giving him a taste of his own medicine. The police hadn't been called, thankfully. But Vinny had been expelled on the spot and had walked out of the school to a round of applause from his classmates.

Queenie got off the train at Whitechapel and trundled down the road. Viv no longer worked. For all Bill Harris's faults, he managed to financially support his wife and child. Viv looked after Brenda while Queenie was at work. Queenie would drop her daughter round Viv's on the way and she would spend the day playing and watching TV with Lenny. Both were addicted to *Pinky and Perky*.

'Queenie!'

Recognizing the voice, Queenie spun around. She hadn't seen him for a few months and it seemed unusual to see him out of uniform. 'Hello, Freddie. How are ya?'

'Not bad. I saw Mrs O'Leary's sons yesterday.'

Queenie felt her heartbeat quicken. 'Round 'ere?'

'No. Up town. They're doing well for themselves. They've bought a club. Fancy a coffee? I could do with your advice actually.'

Wanting to hear more about Daniel, Queenie smiled. 'Yeah. Why not.'

Marnie's club was in Soho. A dingy gaff in a basement. The inside was better than the outside. The bar was quite plush, the sofas leather, the background music jazz.

'A gentlemen's club with a difference', that's what Marnie called it. Membership only, it was full of rich men with one thing in common. They all liked young men. Vinny had been stunned at first, hadn't known places like this existed. Some of the men were married with kids and most had high-profile jobs. Vinny had spent yesterday evening in the company of a judge.

Vinny's job was to entertain the men and get them to spend big money. He didn't use his real name, he called himself Terry. The drinks were expensive and he was told, when offered a drink, to ask for champagne. The men would usually then order a bottle of the finest which lined Marnie's pockets.

'Excuse me, young Terry. One needs to use the bathroom.'

Vinny grimaced as the ugly old bastard stroked his face before struggling to get off the sofa. His name was Cecil; he had a mop of wild grey hair and lots of the same growing out of his nose. He looked like a mad scientist.

Seeing Vinny's perturbed expression, Macca walked over to him and sat by his side. 'Everything OK? You're doing really well, you know. My aunt's pleased. The punters love you.'

'I'm all right. It's fucking difficult talking to these nonces day after day though. Most of 'em are older than my dad.'

Macca squeezed Vinny's knee. 'I know how you feel, pal. I was the same at first. It's a shock to the system for sure. Just think of the dosh though. You've done five shifts this week, that's a score you'll be taking home. It's money for old rope when you think about it.'

Unlike his brothers, who had best mates at school, Vinny was one to keep himself to himself. The lads of his age were so immature in comparison; he couldn't be bothered with them. He'd had one good mate, but he'd now gone to live in Australia. That's why meeting Macca had been a godsend. Macca was older, cool, and far more on his level. He'd also given him the opportunity to give his mum something she truly deserved. Decent money, every week.

Macca slipped away as Cecil returned. Cecil put an arm around Vinny's shoulders. 'You truly are a beautiful boy, Terry. Shall I order us another bottle of champagne?'

Vinny nodded and smiled. 'Yes please. That would be lovely, Cecil.'

As the drunken buffoon made his way up the bar, Vinny glanced around at the other lads entertaining. He was one of ten working today. Not all of the clientele were there to chat up the likes of him. Some had lovers they would meet at the club. It was safe, Vinny supposed. No one was going to rat on them here.

There were also half a dozen private rooms at the back end of the club. Ten pound an hour Marnie charged to use those. What went on inside made Vinny feel nauseous, but he was told he didn't have to go inside the rooms with anybody. Apparently, it was up to the lads who worked there if they chose to, and they could keep any money a client paid them for extras for themselves. Vinny had no intention of ever setting foot in the rooms, no matter what he was offered. Just the thought of it made his stomach turn.

Clocking Macca looking his way, Vinny grinned. Macca actually ran the club for his aunt, which was handy for Vinny as he got a lift to work and a lift home. Glancing at his watch, Vinny forced a smile as his client returned with an ice-bucket. Only another five hours of listening to and talking bollocks and he'd be on his way home with more money in his pocket than he'd ever had in his life.

'So sorry I'm late, Viv. I bumped into Freddie Angel and he needed a shoulder to cry on. I could hardly say no after all he did for us. He ain't happy with that Shirley, ya know. Should never have married her.' Freddie hadn't had any more gossip regarding Daniel, but Queenie was glad Mary's boys were doing well for themselves nonetheless.

'That's OK. The kids have been as good as gold.' Vivian's voice was flat.

'What's the matter? You've been crying. I can tell.'

'It's Bill. He didn't come home until the early hours again this morning. Reckons he was working, but I don't believe him, Queen. I was sure I could smell another woman on him. He's having an affair, I know he is.'

'Well, did you confront him?' Queenie didn't have such worries with Albie. She doubted any other woman would want him.

'Yes. But he denied it, of course. He swore he was working and, in fairness, he did give me a load of money.'

'How much?'

'Forty quid. He told me to treat myself and take Lenny somewhere nice. He won't come with us though. I see the way he looks at Lenny. He don't love him. Neither does he understand him. Not like we do. Bill wanted a son like himself, a chip off the old block, and Lenny ain't ever gonna be that, is he?'

'No. But with our love and the guidance of Vinny, Roy and Michael, Lenny's gonna be just fine, Viv. My boys have got his back, you know that.'

Vivian's eyes filled with tears. 'I know. It just breaks my heart though that his own dad don't love him.'

Queenie held her youngest sister in her arms. 'Look, I'm not Bill's biggest fan, but chances are, he'll come round in time. He's very generous to you, Viv. I'd have a cardiac if Albie came home and shoved forty quid in my hands. Look at your beautiful home. You've got lovely carpets, curtains, ornaments. You've even got a TV and a radiogram. We had sod all as kids, remember that? I wish my home was as posh as yours. So my advice to you is stick by Bill for the time being. I've heard no rumours about him having an affair and until you have proof, do nothing.'

The conversation was ended by Lenny and Brenda running into the kitchen. 'Did you buy us our sweets, Auntie Queenie?' asked Lenny.

Every Friday when she got paid, Queenie would pop into the newsagents and bring home a selection of sweets for Lenny and Brenda. Today though, because of meeting Freddie, she'd forgotten all about it. 'I'm sorry, my loveys. I had to work late today and by the time I got off the shop was shut.'

Lenny put his hands on his hips. 'Well that ain't good enough, is it?'

Queenie chuckled and took some coins out of her purse. She handed some to Lenny. 'There you go. Mummy'll take you to the shop in the morning and you can pick your own sweets.'

'What about me?' squealed Brenda.

'You can come to the shop with me and choose whatever you want.'

Lenny and Brenda glanced at one another. Both shrugged, which Queenie found hilarious.

Macca handed Vinny another beer.

'Nah. I'm all right, thanks. I'd better be making a move now.'

'Drink it. One more won't hurt you. Anyway, I've got a proposition for you. A business one. Good money involved. Very good money.'

'Fire away then.'

'My aunt holds a party once a month round her gaff. Similar to what goes on at the club, but it's all women and no men.'

'And?'

'And a lot of these women are stone bollock rich and after a bit of fun with handsome young guys like us. They pay a lot of money, Vinny. Some have more money than sense.'

'Oh, I dunno. It don't really sound like my thing. I don't mind talking to 'em like I do the men. But I don't want 'em touching me.'

Macca chuckled. 'You've not even seen 'em yet. Some are quite attractive. I thought it was every young lad's dream to be taught by an older woman. Don't you like women?'

Vinny felt uncomfortable. 'Erm, no, not old women.'

'But you like young women, yeah?'

'I suppose so. But I ain't never really had a proper girlfriend. I've always been too busy grafting for that.'

'Well have a think about it. The party isn't for another fortnight and you could come away with over a hundred quid in your pocket, if you play your cards right.'

'More than a hundred quid!' Vinny quickly calculated what he could do for his mum with that type of money.

'I swear to you I ain't lying. No pressure. You don't have to do it if you don't want to. But Aunt Marnie thinks you'll be great and I'll be there with you, watching your back. We have to wear suits for that bash, so let me know say in a week's time and I'll get you a suit made. My aunt'll pay for that. Oh, and while I think of it.' Macca put his hand in his pocket and handed Vinny twenty pounds.

'What's that for?'

'That's what you earned on your trial week. You need to spend it on clobber though. Wearing the same outfit in the club every night isn't a good look. You don't want these men to think you are poor. Go shopping and spruce yourself up a bit.'

Vinny didn't know if he was coming or going all of a sudden. He was in a seedy world that he knew nothing about. He took a gulp of his beer. All of a sudden it tasted better. 'Do you do things at your aunt's parties, Macca?'

'Whaddya mean?'

'With the women? Do you have sex with 'em?'

Macca smiled. He could tell Vinny was inexperienced. 'Some of these sad old bitches pay twenty-five quid to give you a wank. You just lie there and get paid for it. Easy money, Vin. My dad was a bank robber. Twenty years he got for his last job. That's how I ended up being raised by Auntie Marnie. There's no risk of prison with what we do. We're just providing a service for desperados. It's the easiest and safest way to get rich, ever.'

Vinny grinned. Macca was right. The Kelly brothers had once been banged up for their part in an armed robbery and he didn't fancy prison life. 'OK. Tell your aunt I'll come to her party.'

*

Vinny arrived home with a spring in his step. He could not believe he had forty quid in his pocket. It was beyond his wildest dreams. 'All right? What's up?' he asked. His mum was having an argument with Michael.

'You need to have a word with your brother, Vinny. He's nothing like you and Roy. He's lazy, has your father's genes.'

'No, I'm not lazy. I'm only nine!'

Vinny sat on the edge of the threadbare sofa. If he did that job, the ladies' party, he would easily have enough dosh to buy his family a new sofa, he thought. 'What's this all about?'

'Brian has told Roy that Michael can have your old job bringing the barrows in and out. Only problem is, Michael can't be bothered to do it. He says he's too young and should be out playing with his mates. The cheek of him, Vinny.'

Vinny sat next to Michael and put an arm around his shoulders. 'Why don't you want the job, boy?'

''Cause me and Kev have started earning money. We're building go-karts and selling 'em to lads at school. I like building stuff, Vinny. I'm only small. Them barrows are big and hard to push. I don't wanna work on the markets.'

Vinny pulled out his wallet and handed his mum fifteen pounds.

Queenie was stunned. 'Fifteen! I thought you were joking when you said you were giving me a tenner?'

'Nah. I never joke about money, Mum. Michael doesn't need to work on the barrows just yet. Perhaps in a couple of years' time, but not now. Me and Roy were older and taller than him when we started that job and believe me, it is hard graft. Let Michael do what he wants for the time being. I'll be able to support us on my wages.'

'I can't take all your wages, boy. Take some back,' Queenie insisted.

'I've kept what I need for myself, Mum. That's what I can spare for you. Take it, please.'

Queenie was stunned and worried all at the same time. 'But how did you earn this type of money in a hotel, Vinny?'

Vinny grinned. 'Arabs. Rich Arabs. If you're polite to 'em, they don't arf bloody tip well, Mum.'

When Vinny left the room, Queenie stared at the money in shock. If true, it was wonderful if Vinny had landed a legitimate job that was paying him that much money. But she had her doubts. She knew her eldest better than anybody and he'd been acting very secretive and weird of late.

'Can I go out now, Mum?' Michael asked.

'Yes,' Queenie snapped. Her instincts were never far wrong. Something about that posh hotel job didn't ring true.

CHAPTER TWENTY-SIX

The queue was long in the greengrocer's, so Queenie took her place at the back. Fifteen minutes, she'd been standing there, when she heard Sid shout out, 'Violet, come to the front, sweetheart.'

Violet Kray's sons' Ronnie and Reggie had made a real name for themselves in the East End of late. They'd become even more notorious than the Kelly brothers.

A woman behind Queenie nudged her. 'Not bloody fair, is it? Her boys ain't nice, ya know. Charlie's OK, but those twins aren't the full shilling.'

Queenie ignored the woman. Mad Freda was her nickname; she was a well-known local gossip.

Craning her neck, Queenie stared in awe as Violet was treated like royalty, and given her groceries for free. She remembered the days Mary O'Leary would be ushered forwards. Oh how she missed her old friend and her sons. 'Give my regards to your boys, Violet,' Sid said loudly.

Other people in the queue wanted to speak to Violet and shake her hand as she tried to leave the shop. Violet looked a bit embarrassed, which Queenie found odd. She would love it if she were in Violet's shoes.

All of a sudden, Queenie's spirits were lifted. 'Queenie!' Sid shouted. 'I didn't see you there. You come to the front of the queue too. I won't mention no names, but your boy is a legend, clumping that teacher. That tyrant made my sons' lives hell.'

Aware that most of the queue were staring at her, Queenie marched to the front. 'Thank you, Sid. My eldest is a good boy. Takes no crap off anybody.'

Sid filled Queenie's bag up and then refused to take any money. 'This is on me. Give my love to Vivvy an' all, sweetheart.'

Queenie felt as proud as a peacock as she turned around to face the queue. The expressions on the majority of the old dragons' faces were priceless. She thanked Sid and thought of Mary. Queenie hoped she was looking down on this. She would have bloody loved it.

Vinny grinned as Macca held up a sequined blazer. His new best pal had offered to take him out shopping and so far they were having a right laugh. 'No way am I wearing that, mate. Not even in my coffin.'

Macca chuckled and put an arm around Vinny's shoulders. 'I'm only messing with you. Let's go for a nice meal. My treat. Then I'll take you to the shop afterwards where I buy all my clobber. You'll love it. Trust me.'

Vinny grinned at his mate. Macca was so cool. He truly was a dude.

Turning into her road, Queenie bumped into Freddie Angel in uniform. 'All right, Freddie,' she said calmly. 'I'm glad I've bumped into you again. You know when we were in Jack's cafe last Friday and I told you Jack's son seemed a bit strange. Well, I was right. He assaulted a young girl down our road on Monday. Put his hand up her skirt and touched her noonie.'

'Between me and you, Queen, that's not the first time the boy has done that. We've had a few complaints down at the station. But you must keep that information to yourself. I know I can trust you.'

Queenie smiled. 'Of course. So how's things with you? You sorted things with Shirley?'

'Yes, I have actually. Any chance we can chat at yours, Queenie? I've been walking up and down here for the past two hours hoping to bump into you. I knew you were out, 'cause I knocked at yours.'

'Erm, yes. The boys are at school and Vinny's at work. Brenda's with Viv and Lenny. But it'll have to be a quick chat as Albie could come home at any time.'

Freddie smiled. 'A quick chat is all I need, Queen. I won't chew your ear off again, I promise.

Back at Macca's flat, Vinny felt more chilled than he had in weeks. Their shopping trip had been fun and he'd come home with some real good clobber. Macca had even treated him to a classy shirt.

It had felt weird sitting in a posh restaurant in the West End, eating steak and drinking wine. The wine had tasted far worse than the beers Macca had given him, but Vinny had sipped his slowly and it had made him feel good about life. Macca was right. Who wanted to end up in prison? It was far easier talking shit to perverts, male or female.

Knowing he had Vinny in the palm of his hand now, Macca suggested they have a beer and sit on his bed and have a man-to-man chat.

'Yeah, OK,' Vinny grinned. He'd had a wonderful day, didn't really want it to end. Sometimes when he woke up of a morning, he had reservations about what he was doing. But when he thought of the early starts he'd had to roll out those barrows for peanuts and the dosh he was currently earning, in his heart he knew he was doing the right thing. His mum had ordered a new carpet for the front room with the dosh he'd given her so far.

'You ever smoked cannabis, Vinny?' asked Macca.

'Erm, no.'

'You need to try some. That's what I smoke when I go to my aunt's parties. It chills you out, makes everything you do seem far easier. It makes you feel horny an' all.'

Suddenly feeling uncomfortable again, Vinny stood up. 'Best I be going now, mate. My mum sometimes needs me to look after me brothers and sisters. Thanks for me shirt and the meal though.'

The son of infamous bank-robber Teddy McCartney, Macca wasn't stupid. He'd done his homework on Vinny, he'd had to in case his old man was a villain or he had older brothers who were liable to turn nasty if the truth came out. 'We need to talk, mate. Sit back down.'

Feeling anxious, Vinny did as he was asked.

Macca turned to his prey. 'I know you lied about your age, Vin. You're fourteen, aren't you? Not sixteen.'

Feeling stupid, Vinny put his head in his hands. 'I'm sorry I lied, but I really needed this job to help me mum out. She works so hard herself and we struggle to pay the bills most weeks. My dad's useless. He earns peanuts and most of that he gambles or drinks away. I'm the oldest son, so it's me who should help out. I'm the only one that can.'

Macca put a hand on Vinny's back. 'It's OK. I understand. But my aunt wouldn't. She'd go mad if I told her, would sack you on the spot. She won't employ underage boys, says it's asking for trouble.'

'Please don't tell her, Macca. She don't have to know, does she? I look so much older than my age, I always have done. All the lads in my class looked like little kids compared to me. I towered above the lot of 'em.'

'I get what you're saying, but if my aunt finds out I knew, she'll sack me an' all, Vin. She normally wants to see proof of anyone's age before employing 'em. She didn't with you, because I vouched for you and told her I knew you were sixteen. You've put me in a difficult position, if I'm honest. It also explains why you seem so uncomfortable around the clients.'

Vinny looked Macca in the eyes. 'Please don't grass me up, mate. I seriously do need this job. I know I've acted a bit mongy about parts of it. But I've had time to think now and I'm happy to go with the flow. Within reason, like.'

Macca sighed. 'I dunno, Vin. I think my aunt will end up guessing unless you man up a bit. I take it you're still a virgin?'

Vinny felt his face redden. 'Yeah.'

'And you can stay a virgin. You haven't got to have full-blown sex with anybody, Vin. My aunt ain't running a brothel. All you need to do is bits and bobs, nothing bad. You don't have to have sex with people to put a smile on their faces. There's other ways.'

Having never even kissed a girl, Vinny didn't have a clue what Macca was talking about. 'What have I got to do then?'

'It's probably best I show you rather than tell you. You trust me, don't you?'

Vinny nodded. He was desperate to bring home his next wage packet.

Macca grinned. 'I like you, Vinny. You remind me very much of myself at your age. I'm not gonna grass you up to my aunt. You're my mate, so I'm gonna teach you some tricks of the trade instead. Take your jeans off and get in my bed.' Macca turned his back as Vinny got undressed and rolled a joint. He lit it up, placed it in an ashtray and then took his own jeans off.

Vinny had never felt more awkward in his lifetime. He was shaking, but he couldn't lose this job. It paid too much and his mum needed the money.

Macca got into the bed next to Vinny and handed him the ashtray. 'Smoke some of that.'

Vinny nearly coughed his lungs up with the first puff, but every time he took another he felt calmer and somehow more in control.

Macca waited until they'd finished the joint before putting his hand inside Vinny's pants. His penis was big for a lad of fourteen and immediately became rock hard. 'This is all you have to do, mate, to earn fortunes. Not too bad, is it?' Macca said softly.

Having never felt the urge to masturbate before, Vinny didn't know if he was coming or going. Until he actually came that was. It felt explosive, awesome, unreal. But so very wrong at the same time.

Totally unaware her pride and joy had just been tossed off by a twenty-six-year-old man, Queenie yelled, 'Cooee, that you, Vinny?'

'Yeah.'

Vinny took a deep breath. He could not look his mother in the eye. It felt like, if he did, she would guess what he'd been up to. 'Yeah, I'm fine,' he lied. 'Apart from having a dodgy stomach all day.'

'Let me make you up an Andrews powder. That'll sort you out. Did you not go shopping in the end?'

Feeling a little dizzy, Vinny flopped on the sofa. He'd run out of Macca's flat so swiftly, he'd forgotten his shopping bags. 'Yeah, I went shopping.'

'You've not been drinking, have you? Your eyes look glassy.'

'No, Mum.'

Queenie handed her golden boy his Andrews. She was sure he had been bloody drinking. He looked as white as a sheet. 'Get that down your hatch and take it from me, alcohol is a slippery slope, boy. You've only got to look at your father.'

'Don't worry. I'm nothing like him.'

'So where are your shopping bags then?'

'Round my mate's. I forgot 'em.'

'See! You have been drinking. I knew it!'

Knowing his mother would throttle him if she had any inkling he was stoned, Vinny thought it best to own up to being a bit tipsy. 'I had two beers and, if you must know, I hated the taste. But because I was with my mate from work, I thought I better drink 'em 'cause I don't want him guessing my real age. I bought you something, and Roy, Michael, Bren, Champ and Auntie Viv.'

Queenie softened. Vinny had already admitted to her he'd lied about his age to land the job in the posh hotel. 'You're a good boy, you are. Do you know what, I always knew you were special from the moment you were born. I'm glad you've made friends at work and I'd love to meet Macca. Why don't you invite him round for tea?'

Vinny didn't know if it was the Andrews powder hitting the back of his throat or the thought of his mother meeting Macca that made him spew his guts up all over her carpet.

CHAPTER TWENTY-SEVEN

Queenie got out of bed, checked on Brenda, who was still asleep, then marched down the stairs. She'd heard that drunken bum of a husband of hers come in after midnight and he'd made an awful racket. 'Gawd stone the crows! You've broken me fucking mirror. How did ya do that? You stupid bloody fool.' The mirror in question was hung on the wall. It was attached to a big silver chain. The chain was still there and part of the mirror, but most of it lay smashed on her new carpet.

Albie lifted the blanket from over his throbbing head. It was all coming back to him now. He'd tripped up and gone head first into the poxy mirror.

Queenie looked at the gashes on her husband's head in horror. He was covered in congealed blood. She immediately looked down at her new carpet. 'Oh no. Look what you've done, you bleedin' imbecile! There's blood on my new carpet our son worked his bollocks off to pay for. I'll never forgive you for this, Albie Butler, not ever. Seven years' bad luck you've cursed us with and you've ruined my lovely carpet.'

'I'm sorry, love. It was an accident. I tripped.'

'Don't lie! You were legless, you dirty, stinking old tramp.' Beside herself with anger, Queenie picked up one of Albie's slippers and began clouting him around the head with it.

Hearing shouting, Vinny and Roy ran downstairs. 'What's going on?' asked Roy.

Vinny burst out laughing as he witnessed what his mother was doing.

Queenie gave her husband one last clump, then pointed to the mirror, then the carpet. 'Look what he's done, the pisshead. Broken my mirror and got blood on our lovely new carpet.'

'Stop it! What you doing?' Roy shrieked when Vinny grabbed his father around the throat.

Michael appeared and tried to grab hold of Vinny, then Brenda ran into the room and began screaming.

'Do you know how hard I worked to buy that fucking carpet?' Vinny hissed, shaking his father's neck as though he were throttling a chicken. 'Well, do you?' he bellowed.

When Vinny swung around and pushed Michael away with such force he fell on his backside, Queenie stepped in. She could understand Vinny's anger, but he was scaring her. She knew he had a temper on him, but never had she seen him like this before. His piercing green eyes looked manic. 'Enough,' Queenie yelled. 'Stop it, now! You're scaring the kids.'

Vinny punched the wall, sank to his knees, put his head in his hands and breathed deeply.

Albie held his throat. He was in shock, could barely breathe. His eldest son had actually tried to kill him.

Brenda put her little arms around her father's ankles and clung to them. She was frightened.

Michael sat next to Albie. 'You OK, Dad? Shall I get you some water or something?'

Roy said nothing. He just stared at his older brother. Vinny had changed since he'd left school and started work. They spent little time together these days. Vinny also said very little about this new mate of his he was hanging out with. He never spoke about his job much either, just got off on flashing the cash at the end of the week.

Queenie took charge of the situation. She looked at the dishevelled state of her husband and actually felt quite nauseous. Albie might not be a violent drunk like her father had been, but she couldn't stand drunks nevertheless. 'This is all your own doing, Albie. I think it's best you go and stay round Bert's for the weekend. Let Bert and Ivy put up with you dripping blood all over their carpets, 'cause we've had enough of it 'ere. Especially my Vinny, who paid for it. You need to apologize to that boy.'

Albie stared into the eyes of his so-called wife and, not for the first time, truly wished he'd never married her. She was a materialistic, frigid cow who was enough to drive a saint to drink. No wonder he found solace in alcohol and Fishy Fanny these days. As for Queenie's parenting skills, she was doing a bloody good job of leading her own sons up the wrong path. Only God knew where Vinny was getting all that money from, but it certainly wasn't your average bellboy's wage. Far bloody from it.

Albie ruffled Michael and Brenda's hair then stood up. No way was he apologizing to Vinny. His own flesh and blood had nearly strangled him.

Shuffling out of the room, Albie put on his suit jacket and said nothing as he left the house. Neither the house nor the kids felt like they belonged to him any more.

*

Queenie stood up and wiped her hands on her apron. 'Got it all out. Look!' she said to Vinny. 'You can't see any bloodstains now, can you?'

'Well done, Mum,' Vinny smiled. He knew why he'd lost his rag. It wasn't just about the carpet; he was het up because he was dreading Auntie Marnie's party. 'Mum, I've got to work late tomorrow, really late. So I'm gonna stay round my pal's rather than come home.'

'Erm, I don't think so, love. I haven't even met this friend of yours yet. Why have you got to work late anyway?'

'There's a private function, and I've offered to be a waiter. The money's good and, apparently, I'll get loads of tips. It's all rich people there. It don't finish until the early hours.'

'I'd still rather you came home, Vinny. I don't mind any of youse boys kipping over mates' houses that I know, but not strangers' houses. Tell me more about this mate of yours. I don't even know where he lives.'

Vinny glanced at the clock. 'Not now, Mum. I gotta be somewhere in a bit. I'll talk to you later.'

Albie banged on his brother's front door. No answer, so he looked through the letterbox, then put his hand inside.

'Can I help you?' a woman asked abruptly.

Albie spun around and for once felt ashamed of his drab appearance. He'd slept in his strides and, not being the best material, they were creased like no tomorrow. Thankfully, he'd had the sense to hang his suit jacket over the banister. But he hadn't had a wash or shave. 'It's all right, love. I ain't no burglar. I'm Bert's brother.'

'Ivy and Bert have gone away for the weekend. I saw them leave this morning. They're visiting Ivy's sister.'

'OK, thanks.' Albie walked dejectedly away from the

house. Bert and Ivy wouldn't leave a key on a string inside the letterbox, they had no kids so the two of them had the house to themselves.

Knowing he wasn't welcome back home, Albie looked in his wallet. He had a ten-bob note and a bit of loose change. Debating whether to pop round Fishy Fanny's as he usually did on a Friday afternoon, for once Albie decided he couldn't be bothered. He was in no frame of mind to get his leg over. After the morning he'd had, all he wanted was another drink and his local would be open now.

'You're late. You not going to work today?' Viv asked her sister.

'No. I rang that posh bitch up from the phone box around the corner and told her I have a sickness bug. She wasn't happy, but tough shit. Just a shame it's the day I get my wages, but I can manage without 'em until Monday, thanks to Vinny. As for bleedin' Albie,' Queenie hissed, before explaining what had happened earlier. 'So I sent him round his brother's, told him to stay there a couple of days. But I tell you, Viv, I'm worried sick about my Vinny. Something ain't right with this new job of his, which is why I thought we'd take a trip up town today, go to Soho and track him down. I wish he was working with the Kelly brothers or somebody I knew. At least I could be certain he was safe then.' Queenie had even debated getting in touch with the O'Leary brothers to see if they knew where Vinny was working. But had decided against doing so for one reason or another.

'I dunno, Queen. Lenny's had a bad cold. I'd prefer to keep him in the warm today. It's a bit nippy out there.'

Hearing his name mentioned, Lenny skipped into the front room with his beloved toy monkey in his hand.

'Hello, Auntie Queenie,' he beamed, planting a big kiss on his aunt's lips. 'Give Zippy a kiss too,' he urged.

'He looks well enough to me, Viv. Please? I would do the same for you.'

Viv sighed. She wasn't in the best of moods. Bill had been coming home earlier of a night, but he never wanted to make love to her any more. Viv knew why. Bill was too scared to have any more children with her, in case there was something wrong with them too. 'OK. Lenny, go and wash yourself and don't forget your ears – no carrots and onions, boy. Oh, and put the flannel round your dingle-dangle too.'

As bad as her day had been so far, Queenie could not help but smile. 'Dingle-dangle! I've heard it all now, Viv.'

Viv raised her eyebrows. 'I made it up. I had to. You know how vocal he is. I took him round Mum's yesterday afternoon and she had the bible-punchers there. Lenny walked in and shouted out, "We're late because my mum wanted to wash my cock!" I felt ever so embarrassed, Queen. He can wash it his bleedin' self from now on – and we've renamed it his dingle-dangle.'

Queenie chuckled. 'He's such a funny little character.'

Vivian pursed her lips. 'Shame his father doesn't think so.'

With none of his usual cronies in the Grave Maurice, Albie downed his brandy then wandered along to the Blind Beggar to see if there was anyone in there he could ponce a few drinks off.

'Hello, Albie. What can I get you?' asked Big Stan.

'Erm, I'll have a pint of bitter and a brandy chaser, if that's OK, Stan? I won't be able to buy you a drink back, mind. I'm a bit short on readies until tomorrow.'

'No worries. Can you get me another rib of beef joint

for tomorrow? Handsome, that last one you sold us. Her indoors cooked it slowly and it melted in our mouths.'

Albie's pal Tom owned a butcher's shop and it had been Tom's idea that Albie sell his meat in local pubs. It wasn't the biggest earner, but along with the fags and booze he flogged, paid a wage at the end of the week. 'Yeah sure, mate. I'll be popping in 'ere usual time tomorrow.' Albie would cart the meat around in a wheelbarrow – a clean one, of course. It was far too heavy to carry.

''Ere, don't look round, but your old mate you fell out with has just walked in. He came in 'ere the other day as well, asking after you.'

'Shit,' Albie mumbled. It could only be Micky One Ear as he hadn't fallen out with any of his other friends. Albie had heard a few months ago that Cilla had left him, then not long afterwards, Micky had left the Hoop and Grapes.

'He's spotted you, mate,' Stan hissed.

Albie waited until Micky tapped him on the shoulder before turning around. Micky looked a shadow of his former self. He'd lost a load of weight, was unshaven, his clothes were crumpled and far too big for him and he had bags under his eyes as though he hadn't slept for a week. 'Whaddya want, Micky?'

'To talk. Please, Albie. Alone.'

Having never been to Soho, Queenie and Viv were both in shock. Vinny had described the area as posh, but it was as seedy as hell. There were lots of strip clubs, many advertising 'French Lessons'. Queenie dreaded to think what that might mean, but doubted it involved learning the French language.

'Look over there, Queen. It's a coffee bar,' Viv pointed out.

Outside the coffee bar there were lots of trendy young men and women and the inside was packed solid. 'That would shut down in a week round Whitechapel. I don't know anyone who drinks coffee, do you?'

'Nope,' Vivian replied, clutching Lenny's hand tightly.

Queenie marched over the road. 'Excuse me; I'm looking for a posh hotel. My son works there. I'm sure he told me the name of it was Valentino's. Do you know whereabouts it is?'

'No,' replied a couple of the girls.

A flash-looking lad dressed in bikers' leathers piped up: 'I told my mum I was working in a posh hotel here too. She'd have killed me had she known I was working in a strip club. My guess is your son is having the time of his life, lady,' he laughed.

As a few of the other lads and girls started to laugh too, an embarrassed Queenie marched back over to Viv. 'Ignorant little bastards. I feel like giving 'em a piece of my bleedin' mind. I swear to you, Viv, if Vinny is lying to me, I'll kill him stone dead.'

Unaware that his mother and aunt were on the prowl nearby, Vinny was entertaining Geoff, one of the regulars, who always made a beeline for him.

Seeing Geoff's glass virtually empty, Vinny topped it up with champagne. That was one of Marnie's rules: top the client up so they ended up spending more. Another rule was never ask any awkward questions. It was against protocol to enquire about work, family, where the client lived, etc. But it was fine to chat about current affairs, TV, radio, sport or any other subject the client wished to speak about.

The thing that had shocked Vinny the most was how

open some of the men were. Macca reckoned lots used false names, but a few had spoken openly to Vinny about having a wife and kids.

Geoff was in his late forties, medium height, thin, with straight grey hair. He wore glasses and spoke in a posh accent. He liked to ramble on about politics and was often moaning about how stressful his job was and how coming to the club, chatting with Vinny and sharing a bottle of bubbly, helped him unwind after another stressful day at the office. Geoff had never mentioned what job he did, but by the way he spoke Vinny knew it was something dead important.

Geoff put his hand on Vinny's knee and squeezed it. He was clearly besotted, waxing lyrical about Vinny's fabulous green eyes and adorable cockney accent. 'I have an idea, Terry.' Apart from Marnie and Macca, Vinny had never disclosed his real name to anyone at the club, not even the other lads who worked there.

'Go on.'

'How about I buy us another bottle of bubbly and we take it to one of the private rooms with us?'

Even though Macca had showed him what to do, Vinny had yet to go inside one of the private rooms, and he had no intention of doing so. Just the thought of being mauled by some old perve made him feel physically sick. 'I'm sorry, Geoff. It's not that I don't like you. I do. You're wonderful company and a true gent. But I haven't been working here that long and I'm a bit shy when it comes to all that.' Macca had told him what to say in situations such as this: 'Keep 'em hanging. Be nice and always let 'em think they're in with a chance in the future. That way, they'll keep coming back,' were Macca's exact words.

Geoff stroked Vinny's left cheek. 'I promise you, we

don't have to do anything you're uncomfortable with. I know you're only eighteen and I myself was still a virgin at that age. Even if we only have a kiss and cuddle, I'd be over the moon. Please, Terry? Name your price. Fifty pounds? A hundred?'

Vinny patted Geoff's knee. 'Not tonight, Geoff. I'm sorry. But never say never, eh?'

'Oh my gawd! To your right, Viv. Look discreetly,' hissed Queenie.

'Gawd stone the crows! She's got legs like a bleedin' rugby player and her face needs a shave.'

Both Queenie and Viv were transfixed. Neither had been aware transvestites even existed, let alone seen one in the flesh. The individual in question was dressed in a mini skirt, high stilettos and was wearing a blonde wig whilst clutching a red handbag. 'Is she drunk?' Viv questioned.

'He!' Queenie spat. 'Ain't a bleedin' woman, is it, ya silly cow. Not sure if he's drunk or just can't walk in those heels. I'd struggle walking in them. Must be six inches.'

'Ask her. I mean him! Everyone seems to know him round 'ere. Lots are saying hello.'

'Ask him what?'

'Where Vinny's hotel is of course.'

'Mum, I need a wee-wee,' Brenda announced.

'In a minute, love. Excuse me,' Queenie shouted out. The transvestite didn't turn around, so Queenie ran towards him and tapped him on the shoulder. 'Sorry to bother you, but do you by any chance know where the hotel Valentino is?'

'Never heard of it, darling. Sorry.'

'Mum, is that a man?' Brenda asked in her loudest voice.

318

'Shut up!' Queenie hissed. 'Do you know the area well? Only my son has told me he works in a posh hotel in Soho and nobody seems to have heard of it.'

'That's because it doesn't exist, sweetie. Seriously, if I had a shilling for every mother that had asked me a similar question round 'ere, I'd be stinking rich. Gotta dash. Got a client waiting.'

Queenie's face turned white. 'Come on, Viv. We're going home.'

Albie wasn't one to hold grudges, and as Micky spilled his guts, he couldn't help feeling a tad sorry for the bloke who'd once had more than most and had now lost everything. To top it all, his mum had recently died.

'Cilla knew my mum was a dying woman. How could she just fuck off like that, Albie? I truly loved her ya know. She didn't even give me an inkling anything was wrong. We had sex a couple of days before she left. Not even a note. What type of woman does that to a man, eh? I had to hear through the grapevine she'd moved away with her new geezer to Ilford.'

Albie rolled his eyes. There was a lot he could tell Micky about Cilla Watkins, but it was pointless rubbing salt in the wounds now. Micky kept crying as well, that's why they'd left the Blind Beggar and walked back to Micky's latest abode, a horrid little bedsit in Stepney Green. Albie was actually glad he'd bumped into Micky, as at least he had somewhere to stay tonight.

Micky unsteadily poured another two large brandies. 'I'm sorry, Albie, selfishly rambling on about meself and me own problems all day. How's Queenie and the kids?'

'If you want the truth, Micky, I should never have married Queenie. You were right all along when you said she weren't my type. She's as hard as bloody nails, the woman. Don't get me wrong,' Albie slurred, 'I will always be grateful to her for looking after my mum, but she's raising our boys wrong, Vinny especially. D'ya know he tried to strangle me today in my own home?' Albie undid his shirt. 'Can you see any hand marks? The boy ain't the full shilling and it's all Queenie's fault, I'm telling ya.'

'It might not be Queenie's fault,' Micky slurred. He was far more drunk than Albie, had been supping spirits since first thing this morning to ease his heartache. In fact, he hadn't had a day off the booze for over a month. 'Another reason I came to find you, I looked for you a few times, weren't just to apologize, Albie. I wanted to warn you about Vinny's new friends.'

'What new friends? Queenie tells me sod all. I know Vinny's working now, but I don't believe that posh hotel bullshit.'

'Vinny's hanging out with Marnie McCartney's nephew. He lives above that new launderette that's opened near Old Jack's cafe. The lad and Marnie are running all Big Macca's brothels and nonce clubs in the West End. Big Macca got a twenty-year stretch. I know you hate me, but once I heard Vinny was hanging around with that mob, I had to warn ya, Albie. Their world is seriously seedy. Your Vinny is working in a poofter's bar.'

'You what!'

'Vinny is working in Marnie's poofter bar in Soho. Don't worry, I ain't told a soul, Albie. I wouldn't do that to ya.'

'Nah. That can't be right, Mick. My Vinny might be a lot of things, but he ain't no iron. Who told you this?'

'A friend of mine, who shall remain nameless, is a queer who goes to that bar. He recognized your Vinny. He calls himself Terry inside the bar and entertains the poofters. Not saying Vinny touches 'em or anything untoward happens, but you don't want him working in that environment, do you, Albie?'

Albie had never been more gobsmacked in his life. Queenie would go ballistic like never before, that was a dead cert. 'No, Micky. I fucking well don't.'

CHAPTER TWENTY-EIGHT

'Come in for a beer, Vin. I need to have a chat with you about tomorrow night,' said Macca.

'OK,' Vinny replied. Nothing had happened between himself and Macca since *that* night, neither had the experience ever been spoken about again. That suited Vinny as even though Macca had only been showing him the ropes, it hadn't felt right afterwards. It had made him feel sordid.

Macca handed Vinny a beer. 'Right, tomorrow, there's a lot of money to be earned at that party. There'll be loads of rich old birds there, many of whom are desperate for a bit of fun, if you get my drift? It would also please my aunt if you joined in a bit more than you do with the geezers. Whaddya say?'

Feeling his heartbeat increase, Vinny shrugged. 'There's loads of lads there, you said. Can't I just chat to the women, be nice to 'em like I am to the men at the club?'

'Didn't you listen to a word I just said?' Macca retorted sharply.

'Yeah, but what do you want me to do, like? I ain't fucking old women.'

'You don't have to fuck 'em. You ever fingered a girl?'

'No.'

'Well, it's easy,' Macca said, explaining to Vinny what he had to do. 'And if they want to give you a wank or a blowjob, just gratefully accept. It's good experience for you and, most importantly, it'll earn you dosh and make my aunt a happy woman. I actually think Aunt Marnie might make a beeline for you herself. She's always raving about how good-looking you are,' Macca chuckled.

Vinny began to feel nauseous. Aunt Marnie must be the same age as his mum or Auntie Viv. 'How much money will I earn if I finger a few?'

'All depends if you make 'em come or not, I suppose. Most of the ladies tip well. I earned over a hundred and fifty quid at the last party.'

Vinny's eyes bulged. 'Hundred and fifty quid! Really?'

'Yeah. I wouldn't lie to you. So, you up for it or what?'

Thinking of all the things he could buy with that money, Vinny rather reluctantly nodded his head. 'I'll give it my best shot, but I know I'll be nervous.'

'No, ya won't. We'll have a couple of drinks and a joint before we go there. That'll take the edge off. You'll be fine. I got every faith in you.'

Queenie was twiddling her thumbs waiting for her first-born to arrive home. Her other three were upstairs in bed. She'd grilled Roy earlier and he'd sworn he knew nothing of what Vinny was really up to. Queenie could usually tell if Roy was lying, so was fairly sure he was telling the truth.

She stared at the rosary beads Mrs O'Leary had given her. Her dear friend had been a big believer in life after death: 'Whenever you look at those beads, you'll think of me, Queenie. Please don't be sad, because I'll be creating fecking mayhem upstairs, and when I'm not I'll be looking down on you. You talk to me through those beads and I'll guide you.'

Queenie sighed. 'I could do with your help right now, Mary. I miss you so bloody much. You always knew what to do in a crisis, didn't ya?'

She jumped as she heard the front door open. She'd already planned what she was going to say. 'All right, boy?' she asked chirpily.

Vinny sat on the arm of the shabby sofa. He'd already bought his mum a carpet and a TV. If he could get through tomorrow night, he would hopefully earn enough money to buy her a new sofa. But he was dreading it. The thought of even going to that party scared him shitless. 'I'm gonna go to bed, I think. Knackered, I am.'

Queenie studied her son when he handed her a tenner of his wages, as he did every Friday night. He looked worried. 'How was work?'

'Yeah, OK. Bit boring today, if I'm honest.'

'What's the name of your hotel again? One of the neighbours asked me and I couldn't bleedin' remember it.'

'Valentino's.' There was a restaurant near where he worked with that name, which was why Vinny had chosen it. It was easy to remember.

'And whereabouts is it in Soho?'

'Erm, just off Wardour Street. Why?'

Queenie's tone changed from nice to nasty. 'Because me and your Auntie Viv walked all around Soho today looking for it and we were laughed at like two silly old bats and told by numerous arseholes that it didn't bastard-well exist.'

'Yeah. It does,' Vinny stammered.

Queenie leapt off the sofa, grabbed hold of Vinny's right ear and twisted it like she used to when he was naughty as a child. 'Don't fucking lie to me, boy. You know I can't stand liars. Now I want to know where you're really working – and don't be making up another load of old crap 'cause I will be visiting Soho or wherever you are to be checking your story out next week.'

Vinny rubbed his ear as his mother let go of it. 'I'm working in a club, but it ain't dangerous or nothing, Mum, and we need the money.'

Queenie clapped her hands together, twice. 'I knew it! I bloody well knew it! You're working in one of those strip clubs, ain't ya? You can't pull the wool over my eyes for long, boy. As soon as I realized your hotel never existed, I knew you were working in one of those places where all those perverts flock to. Disgusting!'

Vinny breathed a sigh of relief. This was much better than his mum knowing where he was really working. He held his hands up. 'I surrender. You're right. But I'm only working on the door, Mum, with a couple of other geezers. I chuck out all the nonces that get out of hand. I only lied to you 'cause I didn't want you to worry,' Vinny lied.

Queenie flopped on the sofa. For obvious reasons, she despised nonces. 'Have you clumped many of the filthy bastards?'

'Yeah, about ten. That's why the money's so good.'

'So, this mate of yours does the same job as you?'

'Yeah. He got me the job. Please don't come down there though, Mum. You'll make me look a right idiot – they think I'm eighteen. They won't let you in anyway, as it's in a downstairs basement. It's men only, apart from the strippers. They're bound to guess I'm not eighteen if you and Auntie Viv turn up, then I'll be sacked on the spot and we'll have no money again.'

Queenie was deep in thought. The money Vinny was bringing home was more than bloody handy. They could barely survive without it. 'OK. You can keep the job. But, now I know the truth, I want to meet this friend of yours. Bring him round for lunch one day, or Sunday roast.'

Vinny forced a smile. 'OK. I'll ask him. Don't forget I got a late one tomorrow night. It's much easier if I can just stay at my pal's gaff.'

'I'd rather you come home 'ere no matter what the time.'

Knowing he might be pissed and stoned, Vinny nodded. 'I'll do my best to get home, but I don't know what time the private do finishes.'

'Don't you dare touch any of those dirty tarts, Vinny. They'll be riddled with disease, I'm telling ya. Has any of 'em come on to you yet? I bet they have, with your looks.'

'One or two, but obviously I told 'em where to go. I wouldn't touch 'em with a bargepole.'

Smiling, Queenie squeezed Vinny's hand. 'You're a good boy. I'm very proud of you, sorting out those perverts. That lad of Old Jack's needs a good bleedin' hiding too.'

'Jack who owns the cafe?'

'Yeah. That son of his is a pervert. Been touching up young girls.'

'I don't think he's the full shilling, to be honest.'

'It doesn't matter! They're more dangerous than most, the nonces who ain't the full shilling.'

'OK. I'll have a word with him and give him a dig if necessary. I'm going to bed now, Mum. Love you,' Vinny said, kissing her goodnight.

'Night, boy. Oh, before you go, what does "French lessons" mean?'

The following day, Vinny felt sick to his stomach until he met up with Macca and had a few beers and a joint.

'Feeling better?' Macca asked. He knew Vinny was incredibly nervous.

'Yeah. I am,' Vinny grinned. He couldn't actually think straight at present, which felt good. He was calm, the best he'd felt all week. 'So, what do we do when we first get to your aunt's?'

'Mingle. I'll introduce you to some of the women, then we'll separate and chat with whoever takes our fancy.'

'What am I gonna do if your aunt makes a move on me though?'

Macca smirked. 'I was winding you up, ya nutter. You were so nervous, I thought I'd prepare you for the worst, then you'd feel better tonight.'

'Thank God for that. Don't get me wrong; she's a nice-looking lady, your aunt. But she's old like my mum and she scares me a bit.'

Macca laughed. 'She scares me an' all sometimes, trust me. I weren't lying when I said Aunt Marnie thinks you're a cracking-looking lad though. You are, especially with your hair greased back. It suits you. Aunt Marnie thinks her friends are gonna love you, and they will. You're charming, funny, handsome, what's not to like? You're also fresh meat, which means if you play your cards right, you can make a bundle tonight. Some of the women are only in their late twenties, early thirties.'

Vinny took another gulp of beer. 'Are they married?'

'Some are, some aren't. Most women are whores at heart, Vinny. Never forget that. A lot of these women you'll be meeting got hitched to rich older men, who are pig ugly and they probably don't want to fuck 'em. Some of the men probably can't even get it up any more. There's some widows amongst 'em, lost their husbands during the war. But I'd say the majority are married. Remember the rules though; they're the same as at the club. Don't be asking any awkward questions, eh?'

'Nah. Course not. Can we have another joint before we go?'

'No, mate. You look a bit stoned as it is. The drinks'll be flowing there, so please don't hammer 'em too much. Aunt Marnie'll go mental if you get plastered. Just be yourself and enjoy it.'

'OK.'

When Vinny stood up, Macca noticed he looked a bit dishevelled. Aunt Marnie had paid for his suit, shirt and tie. Her rich clientele didn't like casual, they liked smart. 'Come 'ere, your tie's all wonky. Let me do it up properly for you.'

Vinny looked into the eyes of the man who looked so much like Elvis Presley and smiled as he sorted his tie. 'Cheers for everything, mate. I'm gonna buy my mum new furniture with what I earn tonight.'

Macca held Vinny's face in his hands and kissed him on the forehead. 'Good lad. Right, time to make tracks.'

Albie had been grafting hard. He daren't go home to Queenie with no money and thankfully it had been a busy day. Three trips he'd made to his butcher pal and two to his tobacco supplier.

Desperately trying to remember everything Micky had told him last night, Albie put his key in the door.

'That you, Michael?' Queenie yelled.

Albie nervously smiled as he walked into the lounge.

'Oh,' it's you. Bleedin' state of you. Bert not got a sink or razor? I didn't think Ivy would put up with you for long. Been slung out already, have ya?'

'Bert and Ivy are away, Queen. I haven't seen them.'

'Where you been then?'

'Grafting. I had a busy day. Ere you go,' Albie said, handing his wife three pound notes plus a handful of loose change. He'd had a tip on a horse earlier that had romped home at 10-1, so he'd kept those winnings for himself.

'Where did ya sleep? Rough? State of those bleedin' trousers, Albie. I hope none of the neighbours clocked you coming home. Thank Christ it's dark.'

'I bumped into Micky One Ear. Well, actually he came looking for me. That's where I stayed, at his bedsit. We need to talk. It's about Vinny. Micky told me some pretty disturbing stuff, Queenie.'

'I already know what Vinny's been up to. Got it out of him meself last night. I thought you hated Micky?'

'I did. But it was good of him to come and see me. Where's Vinny now?'

'At work.'

'What! You let him go back there? Are you mad?'

'We need the money and Vinny's assured me he's in no danger, Albie. I was fuming when I first found out. Viv and me went to Soho to check out his story, as I was becoming more and more suspicious. As soon as I found out the hotel didn't exist, I guessed he was working in one of them seedy bloody strip clubs where all those dirty, disgusting nonces hang out. But he's working on the door, chucking out the—'

Albie waved his hand. 'I'll stop you there, Queenie. Your beloved boy is a good bloody liar, I'll give him that much.'

'Whatever do you mean?'

Knowing how much this was going to upset Queenie, Albie sat next to her and held her hand. 'Now, try not to go too ballistic, as me and you both know Vinny ain't no iron.'

'What! You been on the sauce again?'

'No. I bloody ain't. Vinny is working in a poofters' bar, love. Obviously, it's just for the dosh. From what I've been told, he don't touch 'em or nothing like that. But that's where he's working. Oh, and he don't use his real name there. He calls himself Terry.'

Queenie dug her fingernails into Albie's arm, then froze. 'Nah. No way. Not my Vinny. There must be some mistake.'

'There's no mistake.' Albie stood up. 'Stay there. I'll pour us both a brandy, I think we need one. Then we'll work out what we're gonna do next.'

Queenie couldn't speak. Her firstborn. Her Baby Blue. For once in her life, she was completely lost for words.

Marnie McCartney's mansion was on the outskirts of West London and as soon as Vinny walked inside, he felt like a rabbit caught in the headlights. Never had he seen such an opulent property, not even in the films he'd seen at the cinema. Huge chandeliers hung from the ceiling and there was a stuffed moose's head hung in the hallway.

Smartly dressed young waiters were walking around with trays of champagne. Macca grabbed two glasses and handed one to Vinny. 'Just sip it, OK? You mustn't get plastered,' he reminded Vinny.

'What's them things?' Vinny pointed to the small items of food on trays. He had barely eaten all day and now felt ravenous.

'Hors d'oeuvres, my aunt calls 'em. I'll grab us some. You need to eat. Your eyes still look glazed.'

Spotting her nephew and Vinny, Auntie Marnie walked towards them, beaming. 'How are my two favourite gents this evening? You look very dapper, I must say.' Marnie locked arms with both lads. She had a good little earner out of her parties. The first couple of drinks she would provide for free, then the guests would buy their own. Most drank champagne or fine wine, which Marnie got for peanuts off a friend who sold the finest bootleg booze. She also stocked the best spirits and her prices were not cheap.

Even when Marnie had paid her lads, the waiters and jazz band, she'd clear over five hundred pounds per party. She wasn't a mean woman either. Any tips her staff made, she allowed them to keep for themselves.

'Don't forget, Vinny. When you greet the ladies, you peck them on both cheeks and no asking any awkward questions, OK?'

'I won't, Auntie Marnie,' Vinny replied. Marnie liked all the lads to refer to her as their aunt.

Marnie smiled. 'OK then. Let me introduce you to some of our lovely ladies.'

Vinny gulped the rest of his drink and snatched another off the tray. This was it. Shit or bust time.

'Sit down, Queen. You'll wear your new carpet out, pacing up and down like that,' urged Albie.

Queenie's brain was working overtime. 'When I find out where that club is, I'll rip that pervert of a woman's head off. I'll give her fucking Marnie, the dirty whore. How dare she employ my fourteen-year-old son to entertain a bunch of fucking queers?'

'You said yourself he lied about his age, Queen. You can't go up to Soho creating havoc if Vinny lied.'

'I can do what I bastard-well like. You might be gutless and ballless, Albie, but I bleedin' well ain't,' Queenie bellowed.

'As you said earlier, love, Vinny can look after himself. He'll be home soon and we can have it out with him then.'

'But he might not be home soon, that's what I'm worried about. There's some private party going on tonight. I wish I knew the bloody address. I'd be up there like a rocket and drag him out by his poxy hair. Then I'd give every pervert in there what for.' Queenie sat on the sofa and put her head in her hands. Her own awful experience came flooding back, how that dirty bastard had tricked her and then done what he had. 'Say they get him drunk, Albie? Or drug him? If anyone touches my boy, I'll kill 'em with me own bare hands. I swear I will.'

'Don't cry, love.' Albie put an arm around his wife's shoulders. 'I've got an idea. Why don't you ring your friend, the copper, Freddie Angel? I'm sure if you mention the name Marnie McCartney, he'll be able to get an address and bring Vinny home for us.'

'No way! We never mention this to anyone, Freddie included. Can you imagine the shame if the neighbours and locals were to find out where Vinny is working? I'll never be able to hold my head up high round 'ere again. We know Vinny is only working there for the money, but the gossip-mongers won't see it that way. The boy's life will be over before you know it, and I've always had such high hopes for him – still have. Think again where that dirty hag Marnie's nephew lives. Think of his name an' all.'

'I honestly don't think Micky told me his name. I know he said he lived locally though, but I can't remember where. What I'll do is pop round to Micky's first thing tomorrow and find out everything he knows.'

'Don't say nothing in front of Roy and Michael when they get in. We just act normal, OK?' Brenda was already in bed.

'Of course, love.'

'And you mustn't slip up when you're on the piss with your mates, Albie.'

'I'm hardly gonna bring up the fact our eldest is working in a poofters' bar, am I, Queen?'

'No. I suppose not. I'm not gonna tell Viv. The less people that know about this, the better.'

'I agree. And that's why you mustn't go to Soho and make a scene, Queen. Not only might you find yourself in danger, some bastard is bound to find out and spread the word.'

Queenie squeezed her husband's hand. 'Yes. You're right, for once. It's your mate Micky I'm worried about the most, mind. He could spout his mouth off to anybody. Might have already done so.'

'Micky only found out a few days ago and he swore to me he hasn't told a soul. He won't say nothing, honest. I'll make sure of it, love.'

'How?'

The doorbell saved Albie from answering.

'Get that. I can't be talking to anyone,' Queenie said.

Hearing Albie cry out, Queenie felt her legs tremble as she stumbled out into the hallway. Fully expecting to see a policeman at the door, she was surprised to see Mr Sharples standing there. Albie had his hand over his mouth, tears in his eyes. 'Whatever's wrong?' Queenie couldn't help but fear the worst. Something must have happened to one of her boys.

'It's Micky One Ear. He walked out in front of a bus along the Whitechapel Road. I gotta pop round there, Queenie. It's not long happened.'

'Oh no, that's awful, Albie. Go on, you go. Thanks for letting us know, Mr Sharples.'

Queenie poured herself a brandy and held Mrs O'Leary's rosary beads. She pressed them close to her chest. 'Thank you, Mary. Nobody survives being run over by a bus, I doubt. One more favour now, please. Ask that Saint Anthony you swore by to bring my Vinny home safe and sound for me.'

Back at the party, Vinny was buzzing. He'd felt slaughtered earlier, had been unsteady on his feet like his dad was after a few too many. That was until Macca had dragged him into his aunt's study and made him snort some white powder. When Vinny had asked what it was, Macca had told him it was 'Aunt Marnie's special party medicine'. It had most certainly worked, much better than the Epsom Salts that his mother gave him when he felt rough.

The women at the party were all friendly, but Vinny didn't find any attractive, not in a sexual way. They all looked really old to him. The more they drank, the louder they got and Vinny was surprised by how coarse some were. They might speak posh and be stinking rich, but some of the things they came out with, even the commonest women down The Waste wouldn't say.

'Excuse me, ladies. I need to borrow this gentleman for a minute. I promise I'll bring him back to you though,' winked Macca.

'Oh please do,' shrieked the older of the two, pinching Vinny's bum as Macca led him away.

'What's up?' Vinny asked.

'Just helping you out. Brain damage, those two. They don't tip well either. Don't waste your time with 'em. How you feeling now?'

'Brilliant. That medicine was proper.'

'Good. Now I want you to do me a favour. Aunt Marnie wasn't happy with you earlier. You were staggering all over the place, Vin, and she hates all that. But you can definitely redeem yourself. Lady Rose, that posh blonde you were chatting to earlier, wants to have some time with you in one of the bedrooms. She's a good tipper. You OK with that?'

Vinny gulped, then feeling he had little choice, nodded fearfully.

CHAPTER TWENTY-NINE

Queenie lay awake all night. Vinny hadn't come home and she was beside herself. The thought of what might have happened to her firstborn filled her with dread, so much so, she'd been sick twice and had a bad case of the trots.

Albie had come home in the early hours, pissed as a newt. She could barely make sense of what he was saying, but had got the gist. Micky One Ear was dead and Albie was blaming himself.

Brenda was still asleep, so Queenie tiptoed out the room and down the stairs. Albie was the only one who could now tell her where Marnie's nephew lived and that would be her first port of call. She'd even decided if Vinny wasn't home by late afternoon, she would ring the police station; if Freddie wasn't on duty, she would leave a message for him to pop round urgently. She would hate Freddie knowing Vinny had got himself mixed up with perverts, mind. She would hate anybody knowing. It was shameful.

Albie was snoring like a pig on the sofa. Queenie podded him. 'Wake up,' she hissed. Albie didn't even flinch, so Queenie filled a glass with water and slung it all over his head.

'What the hell! What you doing?' Albie sat up, startled.

'Waking you. Now think and think carefully. Vinny still isn't home and I need to find him. Where did Micky say Marnie's nephew lived?'

Albie put his wet head in his hands. 'Micky's dead, Queen. Walked straight out in front of that bus. Eyewitnesses say he did it on purpose.'

'Yes, I know. You told me last night. But at this precise moment, I'm more worried about our eldest son, who could be any-bloody-where. Think, Albie, think,' Queenie spat.

'Let me wake up a bit and then I'll have a think.'

'No. You'll think now! Our Vinny could be in all types of danger and all you're worried about is that piss-pot Micky.'

Albie looked at his wife in horror. 'Don't speak about him like that. The man's brown bread.'

'And so might our son be, for all we know,' Queenie shrieked. 'Get your sodding priorities right and use your brain, for once.'

Vinny woke up in Macca's bed feeling as rough as a badger's arse. He had no recollection of the journey home or getting undressed. He remembered throwing up though, all over Lady Rose. She went mental at him, like a woman possessed.

Macca propped himself up on his elbow. 'How you feeling?'

'Like death warmed up. How did we get home?'

'My aunt got a friend to drive us. You were sick in her motor. You proper let yourself and me down last night, Vinny. How much did you drink? I warned you before we went not to get sloshed. Lady Rose was fucking livid.

My aunt weren't best pleased either. You got a lot of making up to do, you have.'

Vinny swung his legs over the side of the bed and put his thumping head in his hands. Thankfully he still had his pants on. 'She was horrible, that Lady Rose.' It was all coming back to him now, what had happened at the mansion.

'Whaddya mean?'

'She didn't want me to finger her, like you told me to. She wanted me to do something else to her. Something really vulgar.'

'Like what?'

'I don't wanna talk about it. I ain't never going to one of *those* parties again though. Not ever.'

'Chances are you'd never be invited again, mate. My aunt's fucking fuming, if you want the truth. You're the first lad ever to sick your guts up over one of the guests.'

'Will I still be able to keep my job at the club?' Vinny asked.

'I dunno. We'll have to see. I'll put in a good word for you once Aunt Marnie calms down a bit. Don't turn up there tomorrow though. Take a couple of days off while I try to clear the air for ya.'

Vinny was worried. He'd earned nothing last night, not a bean. 'What's the time? I'd better get going soon. Me mum'll be worried.'

'She'll be even more worried if you go home like that. You stink of booze and your eyes look like pissholes in the snow. It's only early, not even seven yet. I'll get you some headache tablets. Go back to sleep for a couple of hours. You'll look and feel much better for it.'

Vinny lay back down. His head was spinning and he felt queasy again.

When Macca jumped out of bed, Vinny was surprised to see he had no pants on. He turned on his side and shut his eyes. He couldn't wait to feel better, then go home to his mum.

Queenie was in the kitchen cutting some bread for Brenda's breakfast. Roy and Michael had gone off to Petticoat Lane to earn a few bob.

Albie darted into the kitchen. 'The launderette, Queenie. The launderette!'

'What launderette? What you on about?'

'That new laundry that's opened, nigh on opposite Jack's cafe. That's where the nephew lives. Above that.'

Queenie felt her pulse quicken. 'You sure?'

'Positive. I remember Micky telling me now, God rest his soul.'

'Right, you look after Brenda while I go round there.'

'I don't want you confronting the lad alone. I'll come with you, love.'

'Right, one of the neighbours can look after Brenda then.'

Queenie put on her coat and grabbed the meat knife from the kitchen. If any of those perverts had touched her precious boy, she'd personally cut their bits off.

Macca gently shook Vinny. 'I made you a cuppa. How d'ya feel now?'

Vinny yawned and put a hand on his forehead. 'A bit better, I think. What's the time?'

'Half nine.'

'I'll get up soon. Me mum'll be sending out a search party.'

'Not just yet,' Macca said, getting back in bed. 'I've

been thinking, how to save your bacon with Auntie Marnie. I know you need the money you earn at the club. But I got a feeling she'll sack you after last night. Obviously, we're mates and I don't want that to happen. Who else am I gonna travel to and from the club with?' Macca grinned.

'What you gonna say to your aunt then?'

'That you're gonna up your game. Get my drift?'

Vinny felt awkward. He'd got himself out of his depth and he knew it. 'But I ain't a queer, Macca.'

'Neither am I. But I jerked a fair few off before I ran the gaff. You ain't gotta kiss 'em or even look at 'em. Just give 'em a wank. Most of 'em are that frustrated, they come within a minute or two. It's such easy money, Vinny. Seriously.'

'I don't think I can do it. I'm sorry, Macca.' Vinny had never even wanked himself off. His mum reckoned boys who touched themselves down below in that way, went blind.

Macca put his hand on Vinny's penis. It immediately sprang into life. Macca then guided Vinny's hand onto his own, which was already rock hard. Both lads were lying horizontal on the bed, not looking at one another. 'You need another lesson, Vin. Just follow what I'm about to do to you, on me. OK?'

Vinny was relieved when a hammering at the door downstairs saved him from even more embarrassment.

'That'll be Auntie Marnie,' Macca said, putting a towel around his waist to cover his nakedness. 'Stay where you are. If she thinks you're a queer, that will calm her down and help explain what went wrong last night.'

Macca ran down the stairs, opened the front door and instead of his aunt, was confronted by a shortish woman with blonde hair and a face like thunder, and a man in a crumpled suit. 'Hello, love. How can I help you?'

'Erm, hello,' Albie stammered. 'We're looking for—'

'Shut up, you.' Queenie punched her husband on the arm and forced a smile. 'I'm an old friend of Marnie's. You're her nephew, I've been told. Could you pass on a message for me, please?'

'Erm, yeah. OK. Oi! What the fuck d'ya think you're doing?' Macca shouted, as the woman ducked under his arm and ran up the stairs. Unfortunately for Macca, he then stubbed his toe and stumbled.

'Queenie, wait for me,' shouted Albie.

'Mum!' Vinny shrieked, raising his knees to his chest, while pulling Macca's posh black silky bedspread under his chin. 'Dad.'

'Get up, boy. Now! You're coming home with me.' The bed was a double. Queenie was horrified, but relieved Vinny still had his pants on as he scrambled around, his face as white as a sheet, hunting for his clothes.

Albie turned his head. 'Jesus wept!'

Having a penchant for younger lads, Macca had been in a similar position to this in the past. 'I'm so sorry. I didn't realize you were Vinny's mum and dad. I would never have sworn if I had.' Macca smiled and held out his right hand. 'Vinny's told me lots about you, but I don't know your actual names?' he lied.

Queenie glared at Macca with hatred. He had black hair, a dishevelled quiff and was far older than her Vinny. 'Often have young boys sleep in your bed, d'ya? You dirty, disgusting, fucking pervert.'

'You got the wrong end of the stick, Mum. I was drunk last night, that's why I slept in Macca's bed. He looked after me,' Vinny panicked.

'Vinny's telling the truth, ma'am. We worked late last night and Vinny was slightly worse for wear. I thought it was best to bring him home here. I put him to bed and I slept on the floor.'

'Shut your bastard cakehole, you,' Queenie spat.

'It's true, Mum,' Vinny said, struggling to tie up his shoelaces. His hands were shaking like never before.

'You go downstairs, Vinny. There's a good boy,' Queenie seethed.

When she heard her son's footsteps run hell for leather down the stairs, Queenie pulled the meat knife out of her sleeve and pointed it at Macca, who backed away from her. 'Fourteen, he is. Fucking fourteen! If you or your disgusting whore of an aunt ever go near him again, I shall kill the fucking pair of ya meself. Under-fucking-stand?'

Wanting to get rid of this mad knife-wielding mother sharpish, Macca nodded his head. 'Yep. Understood. Fully.'

'Right, give him a bleedin' clump, Albie.'

'Erm, I think he's already got the message love.'

Queenie glanced at her useless husband in despair, before picking up a lamp and walloping the onyx base around Macca's head.

Macca yelped, fell to the carpet, head clutched in hands as the blood began to pour. 'You're mental, you are.'

'And you're a fucking pervert. People like you disgust me. You ever speak to my son again, you'll be pushing up the daisies. Come on, Albie, we're going home now.'

PART FIVE

'The course of true love never did run smooth'
William Shakespeare

CHAPTER THIRTY

I walked around like a zombie over the next couple of days. I couldn't eat, sleep, or concentrate at work. I even dropped one of Mrs Huntingdon-Brown's crystal vases and was threatened with the sack.

Vinny refused to talk about what had happened, would not speak about his job or tell me anything. But finally on the Tuesday evening, after I had put Brenda to bed and was alone in the house with my eldest son, he broke down and opened up to me.

I cringed when he explained his job had been to chat up mainly old homosexual men and encourage them to spend money by pretending he was interested in them. Vinny swore he'd never gone into a private room with any of the men like some of the other lads had, but I was still appalled. What must those other lads be feeling? Being groped and Christ knows what else by these old men? And what type of woman runs such an establishment? A vile, disgusting, heartless bitch, that's who. I knew there and then that I would somehow make sure Aunt Marnie got her comeuppance. I had

345

to. 'Write down the address of that club for me,' I demanded.

I knew exactly who to go to for help.

Two days later, I put on my best red frock, smart black shoes, and black coat I only wore for special events and funerals, then I jumped on a train to Covent Garden.

I hadn't seen Patrick or Daniel O'Leary since they cleared Mary's house out. In fact I'd completely lost touch with them, so I had to ask Freddie Angel to get me the address of their club he'd told me about. Turned out they'd done very well indeed for themselves. It wasn't any old club. It was a jazz club.

On the train I thought about Mrs O'Leary. 'If you are ever in trouble, you go to my boys. I have given them strict instructions to help you in whatever way you need' were Mary's words to me. But I couldn't help but feel uneasy all the same. The thought of seeing Daniel again after all this time filled me with dread. I wasn't about to disclose too much about Vinny, for the sake of his future, I'd already decided that. I'd tell them just enough to get the job done.

Patrick O'Leary greeted me warmly. 'What a joy it was, getting a phone call from you yesterday, Queenie,' he smiled.

I was gobsmacked at how flashy the club was inside. Real leather sofas and armchairs, huge chandeliers, flashy glass tables and it had the jazziest of wallpapers. 'Wow! Your mum would be so proud of you, Patrick,' I told him. The club wasn't open, but I could imagine how glamorous it would look when full of people. There was a big stage and photos of jazz musicians hung on the walls. I had no idea who most of them were, but I recognized Ella Fitzgerald, so presumably the rest must have been just as famous.

'This was my scatterbrain of a brother's grand idea, but in fairness, it's worked. Credit where it's due,' Patrick chuckled.

'How is Daniel?'

'As crazy as ever. I told him you were popping by today and he apologizes for not being able to be here. Daniel has woman trouble, as always.'

'Is he still with Dolores?'

'Bejesus, you're way behind. He was never really with Dolores. She wasn't Daniel's type. She gave birth to a daughter, then moved back to Ireland, same as Bridie did. He's been married again since then and is now getting another divorce. He must like wedding cake. Mum would marmalize him, as you cockneys say, if she were still around. Anyway, enough about him, how you doing? I would take your coat, but I can see you're cold. Nippy out there today, isn't it? I'll pour you a brandy instead. That'll warm you up.'

I downed the brandy, then told Patrick about Marnie, her nephew, the club they ran, the private parties, and the way they exploited young lads. I didn't mention that Vinny had lied about his age, I left that bit out, along with finding Vinny in bed with Macca.

'To take advantage of young lads in such a way is appalling, Queenie.'

'My Vinny's not been himself since he opened up to me. I know he looks older, but he's only recently turned fourteen. Your mum loved Vinny and she hated nonces as much as I bloody well do. She told me if I ever had any trouble I was to come to you, Patrick. So I hope you don't think I'm taking liberties rocking up here like this. That Macca only lives around the corner and I'm scared Vinny hasn't seen or heard the last of him. It keeps me awake at night.'

347

Patrick ran his fingers over the stubble on his chin, deep in thought. 'Mum told me I was always to help you, Queenie. She loved you dearly. You were most certainly the daughter she never had and you cared for her like a daughter when she was ill. Myself and Daniel could never have done what you did. You're family to us; of course I'll sort this for you. No word to anyone, mind. I mean not Vinny, Albie, Viv or anybody – no one must know. Have you already told them you were coming to see me?'

'Goodness, no,' I exclaimed. 'I've told nobody. You can trust me, Patrick. I would never betray my Mary and I won't betray her sons. You boys were her world.'

'Good girl. Give me a few weeks, tops, and this'll be sorted. Don't ring me or come here again any time soon though. You can never be too careful. I'll visit you, in time.'

I stood up. 'Thank you, Patrick. I'll be off now. Give my regards to Daniel.'

Patrick hugged me. 'You take care, Queenie.'

My eyes welled up as memories of the past came flooding back. 'I often hold your mum's rosary beads in my hand and ask her advice on things. I know deep down she's still with me.'

'That's lovely. My mother was certainly a one-off, that's for sure. Father Michael will never forget her, especially after she called him a pervert that time. One day – not in the near future, for obvious reasons – I will take you to Ireland, show you where Mum grew up. And you can visit her grave. Would you like that?'

I dabbed my eyes with a handkerchief and smiled. 'Yes. Thank you. That would be absolutely wonderful.'

It was approximately ten days after my visit to Patrick when Vinny thrust a newspaper my way. The headline read: *AUNT AND NEPHEW MISSING. POLICE FEAR FOR THEIR SAFETY.*

'This ain't got nothing to do with you, has it, Mum?' Vinny whispered.

'Don't be so stupid,' I said calmly. I'd already heard the news on the radio a couple of days beforehand. Marnie and Dave McCartney had been ambushed outside Marnie's nightclub in Soho by four men wearing balaclavas and dragged into a van the police were unable to trace. Neither had been seen since.

'Do you reckon they're dead? I hope they are,' Vinny said bitterly.

'No idea, boy. Perhaps they messed with the wrong boy, eh?'

Vinny looked at me quizzically. 'You sure you never had something to do with this, Mum?'

A promise is a promise and I would never break mine to Patrick. 'Don't be so stupid. I'm hardly a gangster's wife, am I? I married your bleedin' father. But good riddance to bad rubbish, son. Bloody good riddance.'

Marnie and her nephew were never found and they were never mentioned by either of us again.

Eighteen Months Later

Spring 1961

A baking hot June day, it was Queenie's idea that she and Viv skip going up the Roman and instead pack a picnic and take the kids over Vicky Park. Brenda was six now, Lenny five and they were more like brother and sister than cousins.

The park was packed and it wasn't long before Lenny insisted they put his radio on. Vinny had bought it for him recently and along with Zippy the monkey, Lenny took the radio everywhere, even slept with it next to his bed. Music mad, Lenny was. He knew all the words to his favourite songs and loved to dance.

Viv switched the radio on and turned to Queenie. 'I still can't believe we can now listen to music outside with no electric. Some brainy people about, ain't there? You know, these scientists.'

'I know. Marvellous, ain't it? We only had *The Archers* to look forward to once upon a time. I couldn't do without me TV now, could you?'

Viv shook her head. 'Imagine how boring our lives would be without *Dixon of Dock Green*, *Opportunity Knocks*, *Come Dancing* and *Saturday Night at the London Palladium*. Oh, and *Coronation Street* of course.'

Queenie smiled. *Coronation Street* was a soap that had started last year and she and Viv were addicted to it. 'You forgot to mention *The Benny Hill Show*, *This Is Your Life* and *The Avengers*. We got it bloody good these days, Viv. Come on leaps and bounds since the war days, technology. Our kids don't know how lucky they are. We had nothing growing up, did we?'

A serial earwigger, Lenny piped up. 'And us kids got *Blue Peter*, *Crackerjack*, *Watch with Mother*, *Andy Pandy* and *Juke Box Jury*. It ain't all about you, ya know.'

Queenie burst out laughing. 'Who you talking to, ya cheeky little monkey!' Lenny might not be like other children of his age, but he was certainly a one-off. Everybody who met him fell in love with him.

'For your information, young man, *Juke Box Jury* isn't a kid's programme. And if you don't tidy up that bedroom of yours and put all your toys away, like I asked you to earlier, I won't let you watch it any more,' Viv piped up.

Lenny chuckled. 'Yeah. You will.'

'I'm starving, Mum,' complained Brenda.

'Me too,' Lenny added.

Viv rolled her eyes at Queenie. 'Picnic time it is then.'

Flicking through a local paper while eating a bacon sandwich in a cafe in Poplar, Vinny turned to page nine and could barely believe his eyes.

Scottish Pat slurped the rest of his tea and glanced at his watch. 'We better be making tracks, Vinny. Time's ticking on and we've still got a fair bit to do today.'

Transfixed, Vinny read the article in full. It was definitely him, standing there as large as life with his wife and two children.

'Earth to Vinny,' Scottish Pat joked, waving a hand in front of Vinny's face. 'What's up? You look like you've seen a ghost.'

Vinny ripped the page from the paper, downed his tea and stood up. 'I have. A ghost that's gonna come in handy. Very fucking handy indeed.'

'What you cooking for dinner tomorrow then, Queen? Is Albie gonna be eating with us too? I wonder what she's like, this Yvonne. I can't wait to meet her.'

Queenie pursed her lips. Vinny was now working for Willy Almond, a friend of the Kelly brothers. Willy was in the long firm game and, even though Queenie didn't particularly understand how setting up a long firm worked, she got the gist of it. A company would be set up, would build up its credit rating, then go in with a massive order and shaft the suppliers. Vinny's job was to collect the money for goods they sold. It was mainly electrical goods such as TVs and if people didn't pay up on time, Vinny and the Scottish lad he worked with would give them a dig. The money was bloody good; so much so, she had saved a fair bit, as had Vinny. But ever since meeting his first girlfriend just over a month ago, Vinny hadn't stopped spending. He was forever buying the girl gifts, and Queenie wasn't happy about it.

'We're having beef and I dare say Albie will stagger home when the pub shuts at lunchtime. As for Yvonne, I obviously want to meet her, to see what she's like, but Vinny's head's gone and I don't want him getting serious with any girl at his age. He's only bloody fifteen for Christ's sake. He should be out spending his hard-earned wages on himself. A gold locket he bought for her last week, Viv. It's too much too soon, in my opinion.'

'He looks much older than fifteen though, Queen. He's so tall an' all.'

'Over six foot now and, yes, he looks older because he dresses smart in his suits. But he's still only fifteen and I don't want some bloody girl trapping him.'

Vivian squeezed her sister's arm. 'She might be a very nice girl, Queen. At least meeting her will put your mind at rest.'

'I suppose so,' Queenie replied unenthusiastically. She had never told Viv about Marnie, Macca, or the club Vinny had been working at. She'd told her sister he was working in a strip club on the door.

'Does Yvonne work?' Viv asked.

'Yeah. In a hairdresser's. She better not practise on Vinny and balls up his lovely hair. I'll cut her bleedin' hands off if she does.'

'Whose hands you gonna cut off, Auntie Queenie?' asked

Lenny, in a voice so loud, the people sitting nearby all turned around.

'Nobody, earholes,' Viv snapped. 'Shall we make a move, Queen? Brenda's half asleep.'

'Yeah. Got a headache, I have. Dunno whether the sun's given it to me, or it's the thought of Princess bleedin' Yvonne spending all my son's hard-earned dosh.'

The following morning, Queenie unpacked her best china that she rarely used and kept wrapped in newspaper in a box for safekeeping. Whatever Yvonne was like, she wanted to make a good impression.

'You've got to give the girl a chance, Queen. She might be just what Vinny needs to keep him on the straight and narrow, and he does seem smitten with her,' Albie said.

'I was smitten with you once and look where that bleedin' well got me. If it wasn't for Vinny we'd have no TV or telephone and still be living in the dark ages. Unlike you, my Vinny is a good catch, Albie, and I ain't having any little madam getting her claws into him. He's fifteen, not twenty-five.'

Knowing there was no point arguing, or pointing out he wasn't *her* Vinny, but *their* Vinny, Albie nodded, said goodbye and set off for his singing gig in the Prince Regent. Sunday was his favourite day of the week. Not only had Albie missed singing in pubs, it brought back memories of the good old days, before he'd got lumbered with Queenie.

Viv arrived at lunchtime with a face like thunder. Bill was up to his old tricks, hadn't come home all night.

'You already know my opinion, Viv. I've told you this many a time over the last few months. I'd have kicked Bill's arse into touch when he first started staying out all night. My Albie might not be much use to me, but never has he stayed out all night. Not unless I've kicked him out. I wouldn't put up with it. If a man randomly don't come home, they're with some old tart. I'd put money on it.'

Pretending to watch TV, but earwigging at the same time, Lenny ran out to the kitchen. 'My dad ain't with an old tart. He loves me and Mummy.'

Viv glared at Queenie. 'I know he does, boy. Auntie Queenie wasn't talking about your father. She said she's gonna make you some jam tarts in the week. They're you're favourite, aren't they?'

'One of my favourites.'

'Why don't you and Brenda go outside and play for a while? It's such lovely weather, you don't want to be cooped up in here all day,' Viv suggested.

When her son and Brenda left the house, Viv snarled at Queenie. 'I wish you'd watch what you say in front of him. I've told you before he's at an age now where he understands every bloody thing.'

'All right. Keep your hair on. It ain't my fault you married a womanizer. I warned you he was a wrong un when you first got with him.'

'And I warned you Albie weren't for you, but you still married him, didn't ya? Pot calling kettle, Queen. At least Bill supports us and I don't have to go to work like you do.'

'Cooey. The door was open,' said Molly Wade.

'Smile and act normal,' Queenie hissed.

Viv greeted their mum warmly, so did Queenie. She rarely came around for Sunday dinner and it was nice she'd made the effort for once. Then Roy bowled through the door. 'Oh, it's you, Roy. I thought it might be Vinny and his young lady.'

'Nah. Sorry to disappoint you, Mum. Just me.'

'I didn't mean it like that, you daft ha'porth.' Queenie gave her middle son a hug. 'How was work? Michael not with you?'

'Work was fine and Michael's walking home the bird who works in the chicken-slaughtering factory. She smells horrible, like death, but she's pretty. She's fourteen an' all,' Roy said, aiming to shock. Ever since he could remember, he'd had a feeling that Vinny was his mum's favourite. But the past eighteen months or so, ever since Vinny had got kicked out of school and started working in proper jobs, he'd felt like even more of a spare part. He always gave his mum some of his money from his meagre earnings, but she never seemed that grateful any more. Michael was her baby boy, so he could do no wrong, Vinny was most certainly her golden boy, especially now he was bringing home lots of cash, and Roy felt like piggy in the middle.

'Why is Michael walking the girl home? Is there something wrong with her?'

Roy grinned. 'Nah. I think he's hoping to get his leg over with her. By all accounts, she's shagged half the market.'

Queenie felt annoyed. Roy had to be winding her up surely. 'Shush. Your nan's in the kitchen. Don't you be talking filth in front of her or Vinny's girlfriend. Go and get washed and changed, smarten yourself up a bit before you meet Yvonne.'

'Too late. I've already met her. Vinny brought her to the pet stall earlier and bought her a kitten.'

'Ooh, what's she like?'

Roy was about to answer when the front door opened and Vinny walked in smiling. 'Mum, meet Yvonne. Yvonne, meet my lovely Mum.'

'Hello,' Yvonne giggled. 'Meet my beautiful little kitten Vinny bought me,' she giggled again, opening the lid of a box.

Queenie glanced at the tiny white blue-eyed kitten, glared at Vinny as he giggled like a dickhead, then sized up Yvonne. Tall, leggy, scantily dressed, looked far older than sixteen and was clinging to Vinny's arm like a limpet. Queenie forced a smile. 'Hello, dear. Welcome to our home.' She didn't mean it, not one little bit. She hated the tart on sight.

The dinner was Queenie's worst nightmare. Albie arrived home partly sozzled, bragging how he'd sung his first ever Frank Sinatra song and got a standing ovation. Then he'd proceeded to sing it – much to her mum and Viv's delight; they both clapped him until their hands must have hurt.

Michael didn't arrive home until dessert, with barely any apology and a big grin on his face. Brenda was ratty, complaining she had an earache and Lenny wasn't his usual bubbly self either. He kept demanding to go home as he missed his dad and kept whinging there were no jam tarts.

Roy was the worst behaved out of everybody. He kept coming out with lewd comments about Michael and the girl who smelled like death. Queenie knew that smell. Everybody who purchased those chickens off Petticoat Lane did, and she could smell it on her baby boy. Michael was only bloody twelve. Surely he didn't know about the birds and bees already? She would have to ask him later, or get Albie to do the honours.

The worst part of the day for Queenie, though, was the interaction between Vinny and his silly, giggly girlfriend. Vinny was clearly besotted with her, but in Queenie's opinion Yvonne was brainless.

When Roy came out with another lewd comment while they were eating the rhubarb crumble Queenie had carefully prepared, Queenie could not help but clout her middle son around the head and tell him to, 'Get your arse up them stairs before I brain ya.'

Appalled, Molly stood up. 'Thanks for the lovely dinner, Queenie. I must be going now though. I will call you and Viv in the week.' Molly kissed Vinny's cheek and Yvonne's. 'I wish you two all the happiness in the world. You make a lovely couple.'

Queenie saw her mother out. 'Thanks for coming, Mum.'

'Don't be inviting me again anytime soon, Queenie. It's too hectic round yours for me. As for Roy, he needs his mouth washing out with soap. I can't listen to filth like that. It's vulgar.'

Wanting to remind her mother of the horrendous childhood herself and Viv had endured, Queenie chose not to bother. Her mum lived in her own little cocoon these days; she seemed to have lost her marbles since she started hanging out with her bible-punching pals. 'OK then. Bye, Mum.'

Molly turned and stroked Queenie's cheek. 'I will always love you and Vivvy, no matter what. I pray to God every night for you and your children.'

'Thanks, Mum,' Queenie smiled. 'Means a lot,' she added, not meaning a word of it. She was about to crack a funny and ask her mum if she could have a word with God regarding Albie getting a proper job, but Queenie bit her tongue instead. Her mum didn't get her jokes any more. Never had done really.

An hour later, the only two people left in the house, apart from herself, were Vinny and Yvonne. Albie was back down the pub, Roy and Michael had gone out with their pals and Viv had taken Brenda home with Lenny to save Queenie dropping her off in the morning before she went to work.

Queenie made a pot of tea, put some biscuits on the tray and was horrified as she walked into the lounge to see the kitten running riot all over her new Dralon sofa. 'Erm, get that cat off my couch please, Vinny. Look! There's white hair all over it.'

Yvonne giggled. 'Sparkle. Come to Mummy. There's a good boy,' she said, cradling the kitten in her arms.

Queenie was bemused. 'Sparkle! That's not its name, is it?'

'Yes, Mum. Yvonne chose it,' Vinny grinned.

'But it's a boy. You can't call a boy cat Sparkle.'

'I like sparkly things, you see,' Yvonne explained.

'Oh well. Don't be moaning to me when it gets laughed at and bullied by all the other cats. Never gonna find a girlfriend, is it? Not with a name like Sparkle.'

Vinny gave his mum a warning look, then squeezed Yvonne's hand. 'I told you my mum was funny, didn't I?'

'Yes,' Yvonne said, putting the cat back in his box, so she could hold Vinny's hand.

'So tell me more about yourself, Yvonne. Vinny told me you work as a hairdresser. I take it you live with your parents. What area do you come from?'

'Bethnal Green, and I live with my mum. She and my dad are divorced.'

'Oh right. Why's that then? Did your dad cheat on your mum?'

'Mum!' Vinny hissed.

'What? I'm only trying to get to know more about Yvonne.'

'My mum left my dad for another man actually, but she's not with him any more. It's just me and my mum now, and Sparkle,' Yvonne giggled.

'That must be tough. Does she work then, your mum?' enquired Queenie.

'Yes. She works on a fruit and veg stall on Whitechapel market.'

'Really! What's her name? I must know her.'

'Alice. She's blonde like me and very bubbly. Everyone knows my mum.'

It was at that point, Queenie choked on her tea. Everybody knew Slack Alice, for all the wrong bloody reasons.

CHAPTER THIRTY-ONE

Once Queenie had a bee in her bonnet, she found it hard to dislodge it, therefore spent the following day at work, fuming. Slack Alice was a buxom blonde with a mouth like a foghorn. She was also a notorious tart and had gone through more American servicemen during the war than Queenie had had hot dinners.

Having laid awake most of the night, Queenie remembered other things too. She was reasonably friendly with Jeanie Thomas, who also worked on Whitechapel market, and Queenie was damn sure Jeanie's son Trevor had got engaged to Slack Alice's daughter not that long ago. Jeanie hadn't been happy about it, wasn't struck on the girl, but Queenie could not remember why. She'd bloody find out why tomorrow though when she paid Jeanie a visit.

'Queenie! You're slacking again. Come into the parlour now, please.'

Queenie threw down her feather duster and rolled her eyes. 'Coming, Mrs Huntingdon-Brown.'

Vinny walked into a pub in Bow and ordered himself a neat brandy. Suited and booted these days, Vinny never got questioned about his age. He wore his black hair Brylcreemed back and at over six foot could easily pass for eighteen.

Sauntering over to an empty table, Vinny took a sip of brandy. It burned the back of his throat. He didn't really like alcohol, hadn't touched a drop since knocking around with that perve Macca. But today he'd been on tenterhooks and was hoping the brandy would calm his nerves a bit. His mother had drummed it into him at an early age via her bedtime stories that if an opportunity arose, especially if a wrong un was involved, he should stampede all over that person.

Vinny took the newspaper article out of his pocket and read it again. The meeting started at seven p.m. and was being held in Poplar Town Hall, which was actually situated in Bow. Ever since the war had ended, due to the loss of so many homes, the local councils had been building tower blocks of flats. His mum hated them, said she'd never live in one, but lots of people liked them because they were brand spanking new and modern. That's what the meeting was about. A couple of new tower blocks had recently been built in Poplar and local councillor Jeremy Johnson was chairing the meeting which would eventually decide who moved into those properties.

Studying the photo of Jeremy Johnson, his wife Katherine and their two children Oscar and Felicity, Vinny couldn't help but smirk. He knew Jeremy Johnson well, of course, but not under that name. He knew him as Geoff, the man who'd always made a beeline for him at Marnie's club.

Vinny glanced at his watch, then downed the rest of his brandy. It was time to reacquaint himself with Jeremy. His mother needed a better house.

*

Vinny sat at the back and kept his head bowed as Jeremy rambled on. There was a projector screen showing stills of the inside of the flats and Vinny could understand why lots of people were interested in them.

The bathrooms were immaculate and modern, as were the kitchens. The front room and bedrooms were a decent size too.

The elderly woman next to Vinny nudged him. 'Bigger rooms than in my tinpot house and how lovely it must be to have an inside toilet and a proper bath. I'm still using a tin bath and me toilet's outside. I'm putting my name down for one, are you?'

'Not sure yet. It'll be up to my mum,' Vinny replied politely.

The meeting lasted another forty-five minutes, as many raised their hands to ask questions. Then finally it was over and those who were interested were urged to queue on the left to put their names on the list.

There was a small queue of people wanting to speak to Jeremy himself, so Vinny sidled past them and waited for Jeremy to finish. He then tapped him on the shoulder and said, 'Hello, Geoff. Remember me? Long time no see, mate.'

The colour drained from Jeremy's face as recognition hit home. He frantically craned his neck to see where his wife was before grabbing Vinny's elbow and leading him outside the building. 'What do you want?' he hissed, once out of earshot.

'That's not a very nice greeting, is it, Geoff?' smirked Vinny.

'Just get to the point, please. Is it money, is that what you want? Because if you blackmail me, I will go to the police and have you arrested.'

'Nah, you won't and I don't need your money, thanks.

362

Here's the deal. My mum's currently renting privately – a two-bedroomed property in Whitechapel.'

Jeremy glanced around nervously to check nobody was watching. 'You want a flat, I can sort you a flat.'

'Nah. My dear old mum don't like flats. But she would like a nice council house in Whitechapel. A new-build that's modern with more bedrooms.'

'I can possibly sort something in Poplar. Whitechapel isn't my area.'

Vinny patted Jeremy on the back. 'Best you make it your area, you must know whoever runs it. Tell 'em you need a favour. Only I would hate to have to tell Katherine, Oscar and Felicity you're as bent as a nine-bob-note.'

Jeremy took his business card out of the inside of his pocket and handed it to Vinny. 'I'll make some enquiries first thing tomorrow. Call me after lunch on that number. But that's it, Terry. Don't come back to me for more favours. Otherwise I will have no alternative but to go to the police.'

Vinny held his hands up. 'That's all I want, I promise. Anybody who knows me will tell ya I never go back on my word. Oh, and my name ain't Terry, by the way, neither am I a poofter. The name's Vinny. Vinny Butler.'

The following morning, Queenie met Viv in old Jack's cafe. Jack was in his early sixties and he ran the cafe with his wife Ethel, who was only a couple of years younger than him.

Queenie leaned towards Viv as Jack and Ethel's weird son Peter walked past with his school satchel. 'No wonder he's a nincompoop, that boy. Didn't they have him late in life? Makes you wonder if he's adopted.'

'Nah. He looks like Ethel. Got her sloppy mouth and double chin. We ain't heard about him flashing or touching up young girls any more since your Vinny had a word with him eh.'

'Nope. Vinny did threaten to chop his hands off if there was a next time, mind,' Queenie smiled.

'Right, Jeanie's on her own now. You sure you don't want me to come with you?'

'No. You wait 'ere and I'll tell you all the gossip afterwards. Oh shit, she's got more customers now, look. Bloody nuisances.'

'Not to her they ain't, Queen. The woman's trying to earn a living.'

Queenie grinned. 'Sorry about Sunday, what I said about Bill and stuff.' Whenever she and Viv argued, they always made up quickly. Each one looked on the other as her rock; it had been that way since they were kids.

'No worries. Everything you said was more than likely true anyway. Bill still hasn't told me where he was. I'm sorry for what I said to you too. Bill had arrived home Sunday evening, inebriated, and all he would say was that he'd got drunk the night before and stayed at his pal's house. No apology or anything.'

'Is Lenny still liking the nursery?'

'Loving it. He's mixing ever so well with all the other kids too. I'm so pleased and it's made my mind up. I'm not sending him to no special school, Queen. I shall put his name down at Brenda's school and he'll start there in September.'

'Good for you. If Lenny gets any grief, Brenda will stick up for him. Right, Jeanie's on her own again. I won't be long.'

'Morning, Queen. Your hair looks nice. You had it done different?' smiled Jeanie Thomas.

Queenie and Viv both wore their hair the same. Straight, shoulder-length and dyed blonde. 'No. It's the same style, but Viv and I have found a new hairdresser. Alan has a shop in Roman Road, the Bethnal Green end.'

'Oh right. I'll have to give him a try. How's Albie and the boys?'

'Albie's Albie and it's the boys I want to speak to you about – well, one of 'em anyway.'

Jeanie put the tops she was holding on a rail, then turned to Queenie. 'What's up?'

'Does Slack Alice have a daughter called Yvonne?'

'Yeah. Yvonne got engaged to my Trevor. Broke his heart when she called the engagement off. Not the first time she's done it, by all accounts. She's been engaged to two other blokes an' all. One was twenty-seven.'

'Really! How old was she when she got bloody engaged to these other blokes then?'

'Dunno, love. I'm glad things ended with Trevor though. I never liked her much. Can't stand her bleedin' mother either. It was horrible seeing my boy so upset, and he still ain't over her I don't think. He is dating another girl now though, Mandy. It's early days, but Mandy seems nice. Comes from a decent family too.'

'Aah, I hope your Trevor'll be happy with Mandy. Yvonne has now got her claws into my Vinny and I ain't happy about it at all. Vinny's besotted with the dopey mare and I don't see the attraction. I met her for the first time on Sunday. All she did was bleedin' giggle.'

'She's a bit old for your Vinny, ain't she?'

'Only a year. Vinny's fifteen now.'

'Yvonne ain't sixteen, Queen. She'll be eighteen this year, love. I know it's only a three-year gap, but it's a lot when the boy's only fifteen, ain't it?'

'Lying little slut!' Queenie spat. 'Right, tell me any other dirt you got on her please, Jeanie. I won't say a word where I got the info from. I just want that girl out of my Vinny's life.'

'OK. But don't mention me or my Trevor. Your Vinny's got quite a name for himself now as being handy with his fists. Trevor's been through enough as it is, Queenie.'

Thrilled that people were seeing Vinny as handy with his fists, Queenie crossed her forefinger over her face and chest like Mary O'Leary used to. 'You have my word, Jeanie. On my kids' lives.'

Queenie was indoors with Viv debating what to say to Vinny when the phone rang. 'What you up to, Mum?' asked Vinny.

'Eating shit with sugar on it.'

Vinny chuckled. 'Meet me at Jack's cafe at five. I've got a surprise for ya. Oh, and come on your own please.'

Queenie hated surprises at the best of times. 'This better be nothing to do with Yvonne, Viv. She best not be there with him, I'm telling ya,' Queenie raged. Her conversation with Jeanie hadn't unearthed anything too shocking, but she'd learned that Yvonne was a slapper like her mother, as she'd once told Trevor she thought she was pregnant, which turned out to be a false alarm. It was blatantly obvious Yvonne was a ponce too as she was forever pointing out things she liked to Trevor who then bought them for her, just as Vinny was now doing.

'I wonder what the surprise can be?' Viv pondered. 'I hope he ain't bastard-well proposed to her, Queen.'

'I'll throttle him if he has, believe me.'

'What you gonna say to him about her?'

'I can't say much that Jeanie told me as Vinny'll know

it's come from her and Trevor. The only things I can say is she's lied about her age, been engaged three times and had a boyfriend of twenty-seven. I can also tell him what a slag her mother is.'

'Do you think that'll be enough to put him off?'

'Dunno. Keep your fingers crossed. I'm gonna take a slow walk round to the cafe now, before I wind meself up any more. We'll have our sprats when I get back. The kids and Albie can have ham, egg and chips.'

'OK. I'll cook tonight.'

When she arrived at the cafe, Queenie was relieved that Vinny was standing outside alone.

'Where we going?' Queenie asked, as Vinny took her by the arm and turned off the Whitechapel Road.

'You'll soon find out. We've only got a short walk ahead of us.'

'Where to though? Just tell me, Vinny. You know I hate bleedin' surprises.'

Beaming from ear to ear, Vinny put an arm around his mother and kissed her on the top of her head. 'Oh, you'll like this surprise. I can promise ya that much.' He'd been buzzing ever since viewing the property earlier. It was brand spanking new as the previous house on that site had been bombed.

'How's Yvonne and the cat?'

'Dunno. Not spoken to her today. I'll be seeing her later on. You did like her, didn't ya, Mum?'

'Yes,' Queenie fibbed. 'But I know her mum, love. She's an old slapper who Viv and I call Slack Alice. She's got a terrible reputation for hawking her mutton.'

'Oh well, horses for courses. As long as Yvonne don't hawk hers, we'll be OK.'

'Another thing, I've known Slack Alice for years, Vinny, and I'm sure Yvonne must be older than sixteen. I think she might be lying to you about her age, love.'

'It was me that lied about her age, Mum. Yvonne's seventeen. I'm sorry, but I was desperate for you to like her, not think she was too old for me. Anyway, forget Yvonne. We're here now.'

'Who lives 'ere then? Done a nice job doing these up, haven't they?'

Vinny opened the front door and gestured for his mum to follow him inside.

'What you doing with a key?'

'It's our house, Mum. Well, it will be as soon as you sign this bit of paper,' Vinny grinned, waving an envelope at her.

'But these belong to the council.'

'Yeah. Then the council rent them to people like you. Look at the bathroom, Mum. It's ever so posh.'

Queenie put her hand over her mouth. The bath, toilet and sink were a lovely apple green. The walls were tiled in white and green. 'Oh, Vinny, it's beautiful and so spacious. But it can't be ours. I took my name off the council list after they only offered us flats that time.'

Vinny took the contract out of the envelope and showed his mother her name on it.

'But how did you get it? I can't believe it. Oh, look at the beautiful kitchen. And the garden! It's a proper garden, where I can plant flowers.'

'I meet many people in my line of work, Mum. I know a bloke who knows a bloke who can pull some strings and I was owed a favour.'

As the reality hit home that this beautiful home actually was hers, Queenie could not help but burst into tears.

Vinny hugged her close to his chest. 'You deserve this. You're the best mum in the world. You raised me right. Now it's time for me to pay you back.'

Queenie arrived home on cloud nine. Vinny had left her outside the property. He was meeting Yvonne from work.

Viv was astounded by the fantastic news. 'Oh, Queen. I walk past those houses often, have watched 'em go up. How the hell did Vinny pull that one out the bag? They're gorgeous.'

'Vinny knows a man who knows a man who can pull some strings,' Queenie replied proudly.

'How many bedrooms?'

'Three. The boys can have the biggest, I'll have the middle one and Brenda can finally have her own room. The rent's much cheaper than what we're paying here an' all. I'll take you round there tomorrow, show you the inside.'

'When can you move in?'

'Anytime I want. There's no carpets down though. Vinny wants me to choose the carpets tomorrow and he'll pay for them. I have saved some money meself, but he told me to save that for other things I might need. He's such a good boy, Viv. I don't know what I'd do without him.'

'All the more reason to get rid of Yvonne.'

'Oh, yes. Apparently, it was Vinny who lied about her age. He didn't want me to think she was too old for him. He didn't seem overly concerned when I told him about Slack Alice either. I'll suffer their relationship for now, I'll have to. I won't rest until I've found a way to get rid of her though. Just gotta bide me time. Girls like Yvonne usually end up digging their own graves anyway.'

CHAPTER THIRTY-TWO

Three Months Later

Summer 1961

Queenie relaxed in her deckchair, drinking her cup of tea. It was a lovely September day, warm, sunny, but with a slight breeze.

Smiling as a couple of robins nibbled at some bread-crumbs she'd put out earlier, Queenie screamed as that bastard kitten appeared from out of nowhere and pounced. 'Get away, you little bastard. Go on, shoo.' The birds thankfully flew off unharmed and the cat scarpered when she threw the dregs of her tea at him.

Queenie put her cup down and shut her eyes. She loved her new garden with a passion. Her old garden was more like a back yard, not a proper garden like this where you could plant flowers and listen to the birds sing.

These days, Queenie liked her own space. She wasn't one to invite the neighbours indoors, but she would stop and chat to them in the street. She already knew most of them from the local market and shops.

Next door lived sprightly old Ivy Harris, a true East Ender. Queenie liked her very much and often popped in Ivy's for a cuppa and a natter. The only neighbour Queenie wasn't particularly struck on was the woman who lived opposite. 'Nosy Hilda', Ivy called her and Queenie soon found out why. She was a proper curtain-twitcher and was always prying or spreading idle gossip.

The house itself was beautiful, so posh and modern. The kitchen was tiled in green and white and it was lovely to have posh cupboards. Even the larder was double the size of her previous one.

The rest of the house was painted apple green, including the bedrooms. That pleased Queenie as it was ever such a modern colour. It also matched her mustard Dralon sofa, although Queenie had decided that in future she would like patterned wallpaper in the lounge to jazz things up a bit.

The boys all loved their new home too. The bedroom they shared was bigger than the last one. Brenda had settled into her little room too. At first she'd been scared sleeping alone as she'd never done so before, but after Lenny stayed over a couple of nights with her, she soon adapted to her new surroundings.

The move had been a huge success. It was a lovely street with decent neighbours. The only sour note had been losing her rosary beads when they cleared out the old house – her mother had donated them to a church jumble sale by mistake, the stupid woman. Mary O'Leary had been twice the mother Molly Wade had been. Much to Viv's displeasure, she wouldn't apologize for her outburst, neither had she visited nor phoned her mother since the rosary beads ended up at the jumble sale.

Queenie just couldn't forgive her. Losing the beads felt

like losing Mary all over again. She couldn't explain to Viv why she was so upset. She wouldn't understand. Nobody could.

Another thorn in Queenie's side was that bastard kitten Vinny had bought Yvonne. Three days after moving into her new home, Vinny had turned up with it in a box and begged her to look after it for the time being as Slack Alice was allergic to it.

Queenie hadn't been best pleased, but seeing as Vinny had wangled her such a beautiful home, had agreed to feed the thing provided it lived in its own little home in the garden and didn't come inside the house.

Within a day of the kitten's arrival, Queenie guessed Slack Alice had lied about her allergy. It might look like butter wouldn't melt, with its pure white fur and piercing blue eyes, but it was pure evil. It kept attacking Queenie with its horrid sharp little claws. Vinny got it in the ear when he came home from work that night. 'Slack Alice is about as allergic to that cat as she was to all those American servicemen her bucket fanny swallowed up during the war. You've not bought a normal cat, ya silly bastard. That's one of them wild animals they sell down the Lane. It's probably come from the bleedin' jungle,' Queenie ranted.

The loathing she felt for the cat was nothing compared to her hatred of its owner, mind. The more Queenie saw of Yvonne bloody Summers, the more she could not stand the tart. She was leading Vinny up the garden path financially and otherwise. Twice in the past month her son had been involved in fights over his girlfriend. Queenie had now come to the conclusion Yvonne wasn't quite the giggly simpleton she came across as. She was clingy, manipulative and false. Queenie was that desperate to get rid of her, it had even crossed her mind to ask Patrick O'Leary for help. But what could she say? She could hardly ask Patrick to make her son's girlfriend disappear without a valid reason. And even if she had a valid reason, she very much doubted Patrick would put the frighteners on any eighteen-year-old girl. Queenie didn't want her dead; she wasn't that callous, just wanted her as far away from her son as humanly possible.

Queenie's daydreaming ended with the arrival of Viv and Lenny. 'Why aren't you at school?' Queenie asked, as Lenny clambered on her lap.

'He was sick this morning, so I kept him home,' Viv replied. Lenny had started the infant school Brenda attended a couple of weeks ago. There was one lad who'd been a bit nasty to him, but other than that he'd settled in well.

'I got a smack, Auntie Queenie, 'cause I ate all the biscuits.'

'Yes, he did. No wonder he was sick, Queen. Scoffed his cereal as though he hadn't eaten for a week, then I caught him polishing off me Garibaldis. Vomited all over the bleedin' carpet, the greedy little sod.'

Queenie laughed and cuddled her nephew. He was slightly overweight for his age, loved his grub.

'Where's Vinkle, Auntie Queenie?'

'Out roaming somewhere. Little bugger was trying to kill my birds earlier.' Unbeknown to Yvonne, Queenie had changed her cat's name. She still referred to it as Sparkle in front of the prat, but no way was she shouting that out in front of the new neighbours. The bleeding thing wouldn't answer to Little Vinny, so Vinkle it was. Queenie had told the neighbours Brenda and Lenny had named it after their favourite nursery rhyme. 'Wee Willy Winkle' but couldn't pronounce it properly, so she didn't look a fool.

'We need to talk, Queen. About Mum,' Viv said.

'Why? What's the matter?'

'I bumped into the vicar on my way round here. Mum's vicar. Apparently, she's distanced herself from him and all her church friends since you kicked off at the jumble sale. The vicar's worried about her, reckons she's too embarrassed to face them. Whatever did you say and do, Queen? Mum's told me very little apart from you swore like a fishwife.'

'I was so angry, I can't really remember. To be honest, I don't want to talk about it any more.'

'Well, I think we need to. I know we've never particularly understood Mum's involvement with the church crowd, but she made a new life for herself and seemed happy, until you kicked off. I know you were close to Mrs O'Leary and how upsetting it must have been to lose her beads. But I don't want Mum becoming a hermit. Imagine if something happened to her and you two weren't talking. You'd never forgive yourself, would you?'

Feeling a bit emotional, Queenie stood up. 'I'll make us a cuppa and I'll think about what you've said later. But drop the subject for now please, Viv. I really ain't in the best of moods today.'

Queenie's mood changed for the better when Vinny arrived home at teatime just as she was dishing up her mince and onion pie. 'You're home early again, boy. Everything OK?'

Usually, Vinny met Yvonne from work weekdays and would spend hours with her before coming home around ten in the evening. This was the third day on the trot he'd arrived home early and Queenie was hoping her prayers had finally been answered.

'Fine. What's for dinner?' Vinny looked and sounded glum.

'Mince and onion pie, and we're starving, so hurry up, Mum,' Michael grinned, nudging his pal Kevin.

'I don't like pie,' Brenda reminded her mother.

'You've got mince and baked beans, young lady. So has your father. That'll teach him to stagger home pissed and show me up in front of the new neighbours,' Queenie replied carefully watching Vinny's reaction. Usually he'd chuckle and comment, but not today.

'I ain't hungry, Mum. I'm knackered. It's been a long day at work. I'm gonna go upstairs and get me head down for a bit.'

'You all right, bruv?' asked Roy.

Wanting to show off in front of his best pal, Michael said what everybody else was thinking. 'What's the betting the lovely Yvonne's blown him out?'

Without thinking, Vinny clumped his eleven-year-old brother so hard around the face, his head hit the wall.

Roy leapt up and pushed Vinny in the chest. 'Don't you dare hit him like that. What's the matter with ya? He's only a kid. You've changed since you got with that bird of yours.'

Vinny grabbed Roy in a headlock. 'Birds are things that fly in the sky. Her name's Yvonne. Show some respect.'

'Stop it! Enough! You're upsetting your little sister,' bellowed Queenie. 'I've raised you to watch one another's backs. You *never* fight with one another. Do you hear me? Never! Shake hands and apologize to one another at once.'

Over the next couple of days, Vinny continued to come home from work early, face like a smacked arse on him. He admitted to his mum that Yvonne and himself had had their first row, but wouldn't go into any more details. That alone hurt Queenie. They'd always been so close and, as a rule, Vinny would tell her everything. Had Yvonne told him to keep schtum about what had happened? Queenie fumed, winding herself up that Yvonne was purposely coming between herself and her son.

It was on the Thursday, as Queenie was ambling along The Waste overloaded with shopping bags, that Jeanie Thomas called out to her.

Queenie walked over to Jeanie's stall and put her bags down to give her aching arms a rest. 'You all right, love?'

'No. Hang on, let me serve this woman and I'll explain.'

'What's up?' Queenie asked a minute later, hoping for some gossip regarding Yvonne.

'You gotta promise me you won't breathe a word of what I'm about to tell ya, Queen. Not to anyone.'

'On my kids' lives. I won't even tell Viv, I swear.'

'Your Vinny and Yvonne have had a falling out and that little mare has been reefing round my Trevor again. Trev swears there ain't nothing going on, but he got done up like a dog's dinner before meeting up with her last night. I don't want him anywhere near the girl. I've tried warning him that if Vinny finds out, he'll knock seven bells out of him, but it's like talking to a brick wall. Trev won't admit it, but I can tell he's still besotted with her. Why though, I don't know. Has Vinny said anything to you?'

Queenie felt adrenaline pumping through her veins. Obviously she'd have to come up with a plan, but was this the chance to finally get her son away from that manipulative little bitch? It was Yvonne's eighteen birthday next month and Vinny had already put a deposit on an eternity ring for the prat. If she could get rid of Yvonne before then, it would save her boy a fortune. 'All Vinny's said is they had their first argument. He clammed up when I pried.'

'I know what the row was over. Vinny beat up a lad outside Barry's dance hall in Mare Street on Saturday night. Beat him up real bad, by all accounts. This is what she does, Yvonne. She flirts with other lads all the time. She got my Trevor into a fight once. I think she must get off on it, having two lads fight over her. Apparently though, Vinny scared the living daylights out of her on Saturday. He grabbed her around the neck and threatened her an' all.'

'Good. Serves her bleedin' right. Do you think she's trying to get back with your Trevor?'

Jeanie shrugged. 'I pray she ain't, but I know Trevor would take her back in a heartbeat. I was wondering, should we arrange a meet-up with us two and the boys? Surely if we explain she's playing 'em both, they might see sense.'

'I don't think that's a good idea, Jeanie. My Vinny's so fiery of late, unpredictable. He started a fight with his brothers the other evening, so I dread to think what he might do to Trevor.'

'Yeah, you're right. Vinny's so tall an' all. My poor boy wouldn't stand a bleedin' chance. What do you suggest we do then?'

A plan already forming in her mind, Queenie picked up her shopping bags. 'Leave it with me and I'll have a think about it.'

'Don't tell Vinny that Yvonne's seen Trevor, though, will ya? I think he's seeing her again tonight.'

'Do you know where they go?'

'Out the area. A pub in Barking somewhere.'

'OK. Thanks for the update, Jeanie. I'll pop back and see you soon, lovely.'

Queenie knew Yvonne worked in a salon not far from Bethnal Green tube station, so the following day she took a slow stroll up there. She shuddered as she laid eyes on the station itself. Poor Aunt Edna. Queenie still had nightmares about that horrendous night. The horror of what she'd seen would never truly leave her.

'Queenie!' Yvonne was shocked to see her boyfriend's mum walk in. 'Do you want to have your hair done?' she asked awkwardly.

'No. I think me and you need to have a little chat, love. What time's your lunch break?'

'Erm, not until one.'

'You can take it now if you want, Yvonne. We're quite busy this afternoon, so make sure you're back by half one,' said a dark-haired smart lady who Queenie presumed was the manager.

'Where do you normally go for lunch?' asked Queenie, once outside the shop. She could tell Yvonne was on edge.

'Erm, I bring my own sandwiches and on a nice day like this, I sit on the green down by the church and read my magazines.'

'Let's go there then. What I've got to say to you won't take too long.'

The rest of the journey was walked in silence. Queenie sat on the grass opposite the girl.

'I take it this is about Vinny?' Yvonne asked. 'Did he tell you what happened last Saturday?'

'No. Vinny didn't. However, not much goes on round 'ere that I don't get to hear about. I'm quite well known you see. For instance, I know you've been seeing your last boyfriend, Trevor Thomas, again. A pal of Albie's spotted you with him in a pub in Barking.'

'I'm not back with Trevor or anything like that. We're just friends and I needed someone to talk to.'

'I doubt Vinny would see it that way, would he? I haven't told him, not yet anyway. But my guess would be he'd throttle the bloody pair of ya.'

Yvonne's eyes widened. 'I don't want any trouble, Queenie. Please don't say anything.'

'So, here's the deal. I won't say anything to Vinny, provided you end your relationship with him.'

'But he's my boyfriend. I like him.'

'You're no good for my son, Yvonne. For a start, you're too old. You also make him miserable, not happy. I've got some savings, two hundred pounds. I will give it to you. You can make a fresh start somewhere, with Trevor. He's older, more mature than Vinny. Between you and me, Yvonne, my Vinny has a screw loose,' lied Queenie. 'You must never repeat this to anyone, but the last girl who cheated on Vinny was found floating face down in the Thames. Whatever you do, do not tell Vinny I told you this as he will see you as a liability and might feel he has to get rid of you too. It's your safety I'm thinking of here – and Trevor's. I would hate any harm to come to either of you.'

Hand over her mouth and deathly white, Yvonne mumbled. 'Oh my God! Vinny told me I was his first girl-friend.'

'Well, he would say that, wouldn't he? He's hardly going to mention the one found floating.'

Recalling how scared she'd been when Vinny grabbed her around the throat last Saturday and how badly he'd beaten up her old school friend Timmy Dickins, Yvonne felt a shiver down her spine. 'Where would I go? And what about my mum?'

'You're a hairdresser. You can get a job anywhere in the country, can't you? Your mum can visit you and your friends.'

'I don't know. Trevor's got a job and he's very close to his mum. I'm not going away on my own. I'd be too scared.'

'You've got good enough powers of persuasion. I'm sure if you begged Trevor to come with you, he would.'

'What about Sparkle?'

'You can take him with ya. I can sneak him out the house and bring him to you. I'll just tell Vinny and the kids he's gone missing. They won't be any the wiser.'

'I don't know. Two hundred pounds isn't going to get us far. I'll only be able to take one case with me, so I'll need a whole new wardrobe. Plus there's the train tickets, renting a property and I might not get a job straight away. Same goes for Trevor.'

Knowing Patrick O'Leary was loaded and would lend her money, Queenie was so desperate to get rid of the girl, she said. 'How about five hundred pounds?'

Aware that she was now on to a good thing, Yvonne chewed at her fingernails. 'It's a difficult decision. I know Vinny's only young, but I think I love him.'

'I doubt you'll be saying that when you end up in the Thames like Juliet did.'

'No. You're right, Queenie. Can I have a think about it?'

'There's no time to think, love. It's only a matter of time before Albie tells Vinny you've been seeing Trevor again.'

'OK. Make it a thousand pounds and I'll be gone next week.'

'A thousand!'

'Yes. If you want me out of your son's life, then that's the price you're going to have to pay I'm afraid.'

Queenie looked at the girl with distaste. She'd been right all along. Yvonne was one money-grabbing conniving little bitch.

Patrick O'Leary lent Queenie the eight hundred quid she needed without asking any questions.

Queenie told him it was a family matter, but Vinny was

now earning good money of which she would save ten pounds a week and pay him back a hundred pounds at a time.

'There's no need. Call it a gift, Queenie,' Patrick had said.

'No. I'm not a ponce, Patrick. I will pay you back every penny, I promise.'

'OK. Whatever. But don't bother giving it to me in dribs and drabs. If and when you've got the full amount, you can give it to me then.'

Patrick never mentioned Marnie and Macca, so neither did Queenie. Patrick never mentioned Daniel either and even though Queenie was dying to ask what he was up to, she didn't in the end. Patrick was in a rush to go to a business meeting anyway, so didn't have time for small talk.

After leaving Patrick, Queenie found a phone box. Mrs Huntingdon-Brown had gone into one of her hissy fits when she'd called her this morning and lied she was unable to work as Brenda had sickness and diarrhoea and there was nobody else to look after her. So Queenie called her again, apologizing profusely and promising to do an extra day next week. This time Mrs Huntingdon-Brown didn't slam the phone down, she just issued Queenie with a final warning that if she let her down again, she would be fired on the spot.

Queenie then took the piece of paper out of her pocket and rang the number. Yvonne answered; she'd also feigned illness to get the day off work, and was thrilled when Queenie told her she had all the money. 'When and where shall I meet you?' Yvonne asked excitedly. She'd spoken to Trevor the previous evening and he'd agreed to run away with her. A thousand pounds was a fortune, would set her up just nicely in life. She hadn't mentioned her windfall to Trevor. That was nothing to do with him and if it didn't work out between them, she'd have money to make a fresh start without him.

'I'll meet you at noon tomorrow outside Bethnal Green station. Make sure you have your case with you and you're ready to leave immediately, Yvonne. Only, if you try to dupe me, I will make sure *you* end up floating down the Thames. Understand?'

'Erm, yes. Don't mention this to anyone as I haven't told my mum and Trevor isn't going to tell his. We're just going to leave and then phone home when we get to our destination. Oh, and don't forget to bring Sparkle with you.'

'Gladly, dear. Have you spoken to Vinny since I saw you yesterday?'

'No. He rang the house, then turned up with flowers last night. My mum told him I wasn't in.'

'Good. Make sure you avoid all contact with him. I will break the news of your departure to him, gently.'

'OK.'

'Oh, and one more thing, Yvonne.'

'What?'

'You don't ever return to this neck of the woods, because if you do I shall tell my Vinny everything. And believe me, when he finds out you traded him in for money that you blackmailed out of me, he will kill you stone dead.'

'I didn't blackmail you, Queenie. You offered me money to leave.'

'No, I didn't, dear. Vinny'll believe whatever I want him to believe. Trust me on that one.'

The following morning, Queenie confided in Viv about Yvonne's imminent departure, but didn't tell her she'd had to borrow eight hundred quid off Patrick O'Leary. 'Snapped me hand off for the two hundred quid, Viv. Just shows you how little she thought of my boy. Vinny can do so much better.'

'You were right all along, Queen. We both were really. I never liked her either. What did you actually say to her to get rid of her?'

Having sworn on her kids' lives to Jeanie Thomas that she wouldn't mention her or Trevor, Queenie made up some white lies. 'I just told her how upset Vinny had been and asked her if she was serious about him. I could tell straight away she wasn't, her eyes lit up when I offered her the two hundred quid I'd saved. She said she wanted a fresh start away from her mother anyway.' Queenie wasn't going to mention the imaginary ex-girlfriend story who ended up dead in the Thames either. Viv might disapprove of that little fable.

'Where's she going?'

'I dunno. Shush, now,' Queenie said, as Brenda and Lenny ran into the kitchen. Queenie took some shillings out of her purse. 'Who wants some sweeties?'

Lenny jumped up and down. 'Me, me, me.'

'Can I have an ice-cream, Mum?' asked Brenda.

'Of course. Off to the shop you go then.'

'So we're not going to the Roman today?' Viv asked, once the kids left.

'Yeah. We'll go this afternoon. I'll get a train to Bethnal Green and meet you at the Roman after I've met the gold-digger. But first we need to catch this bleedin' cat. Vinkle, Vinkle,' Queenie yelled, in her nicest possible tone.

Vinkle was sitting at the bottom of the garden, just staring at Queenie. He clocked the box, the one he hated being put inside. 'Want some ham? There's a good boy.'

Vinkle waited until Queenie bent down, snatched at the ham, scratched her hand, then bolted over the fence into next door's garden. 'Gertcha! Come back 'ere, you little bastard,' Queenie shrieked.

Yvonne was already waiting at the station by the time Queenie arrived. 'Where's Sparkle?' she asked.

'I'm sorry, but I couldn't catch him. He's not a nice cat anyway, he's turned real vicious. Look at the state of me bleedin' hands. Anyway, never mind Sparkle, you can buy a fucking cattery with the money you're getting off me. More importantly, where is your case?'

'Trev's got it. He's waiting for me on the platform. I told him I had to pop to the hairdresser's to pick my wages up and hand my notice in and I wanted to do it alone. I'm not leaving without Sparkle though. We had a deal.'

'You've got to leave, love. Albie told Vinny you're back with Trevor last night and he went ballistic, smashed the house up,' Queenie fibbed. 'Vinny's out looking for you and Trevor now. I tried to restrain him, but I've never seen him so angry.'

Yvonne looked scared. Very scared. 'Give me the money then.'

Queenie handed her the envelope. 'Remember the deal we had. You're not to come back to the East End, OK?'

Yvonne nodded, snatched the envelope and bolted inside the station.

That was the last time Queenie ever saw Yvonne Summers. But more importantly, she had her boy back.

CHAPTER THIRTY-THREE

Eight Months Later

Spring 1962

Albie Butler whistled as he walked towards home with a spring in his step. He'd earned a nice few bob today, selling some china that had fallen off the back of a lorry and he'd also got his leg over with the lovely Maureen, whom he'd been chatting up for a while.

Fishy Fanny didn't do it for Albie any more. She never really had, if he were honest. But up until she'd let herself go and started living up to her nickname, she'd been a handy booty call. Meeting Maureen had been the tonic Albie needed. They'd met in the Black Boy in Mile End and there'd been an instant attraction. Fortunately, Maureen lived in Upton Park, so Albie would meet her down her neck of the woods to woo her. His wooing had obviously worked. Today, Maureen had dragged him back home while her twelve-year-old twins were at school, and had given him the best shag he'd had in donkey's years.

'You all right, Albie?' shouted Big Stan.

'I'm good thanks, mate. You and the missus, OK?'

'Yep. We're fine. A word of warning, Queenie was looking for you earlier, came in the Blind Beggar. She didn't look happy. What you been up to?' chuckled Stan.

Albie felt the elation drain out of him. Surely she couldn't have found out about Maureen?

'See you tomorrow, Stan,' Albie said, before quickening his pace. He just hoped Fishy Fanny hadn't opened her big gob because he'd binned her.

Queenie poured Viv another brandy and paced up and down the front room like a woman possessed. 'He was never good enough for you. I knew he weren't to be trusted from day one. It wouldn't even surprise me if it was him who got my Albie mugged that time. Slippery bastard, he is,' Queenie ranted.

'I hate him, Queen. Nobody makes a fool of me. I want nothing from him in the future, not a fucking bean. Let him spend it on *her* kid.'

'Don't talk about my dad like that,' Lenny shouted.

'Shut up!' Vivian spat. 'He's never been a dad to you. I've been your mum and your bleedin' dad.'

'Your mum's right, Lenny,' Queenie added.

When Lenny burst into tears, Queenie gave Brenda a pound note. 'Go and get him something to eat. That'll cheer him up,' she ordered.

'Whatever's wrong?' Albie asked his daughter, having arrived in time to see Lenny bolt out the front door and run past him, sobbing.

'All right, Dad?' Brenda said calmly. 'You're not in trouble. Today Mum and Auntie Viv hate Lenny's dad.'

Breathing a sigh of relief, Albie bowled inside the house.

'Everything all right? I just saw Lenny crying.' he said innocently.

Queenie picked up her umbrella and clouted her husband around the head with it. 'How long you known about Bill Harris and his fancy piece?'

Albie clutched the left side of his head. 'I dunno what you're talking about, love.'

'Don't "love" me, you lying good-for-nothing bastard. How long you known? And I know you know, 'cause I was told earlier you know.'

Albie flinched as Queenie picked up the umbrella again. 'I had an inkling, but I wasn't sure.'

'Cobblers! You were too scared to say anything in case Bill gave you a wallop. Once a coward, always a coward,' hissed Queenie.

At that precise moment, Vinny strutted in. 'What's going on?'

'Bill Harris has been knocking off Brassy Barbara who works behind the ramp in the Beggar. It's been going on for the past six months or so, but your father failed to tell us, Vinny. Viv's packed Bill's clothes up in sacks. She don't want no more to do with him, son.'

'I didn't know, not for sure. I'd heard rumours, but that was all. I never actually saw them together,' Albie gabbled.

Vinny walked up to his father and stared him in the eye. It beggared belief they were father and son at times. They were so different. Vinny poked Albie in the shoulder. 'Why don't you sod off down the pub and get rat-arsed like you usually do, while I sort out Mum and Auntie Viv's problems like I usually do.'

Later that evening, Queenie and Viv marched inside the Blind Beggar carrying Bill's belongings in sacks. Unfortunately,

Bill was nowhere to be seen, but Brassy Barbara was behind the bar serving.

'That's her.' Viv nudged her sister. Dyed blonde permed hair, tits like footballs, massive earrings, draped in jewellery and done up like a dog's dinner with a skirt up her arse. It was no wonder Brassy Barbara was her nickname. It suited her perfectly. What hurt Viv the most was that Barbara had a son who was a similar age to Lenny, and Bill had been spotted playing happy families with his bit of fluff and the lad. Not once had Bill wanted to go anywhere with her and Lenny, and that cut deep.

'I'll do the talking,' Queenie said, strutting up to the bar like she owned it. 'You Barbara?'

'Yes. That's me. What would you like to drink, sweetheart?'

Queenie ordered a pint of Guinness and the second it was placed on the bar, she slung the lot straight at Barbara's over-made-up face. She pointed at Viv. 'This is my sister, whose husband you've been wrapping your legs around, by the way. Ya dirty no-good whore.'

Some of the blokes in the pub cheered, some laughed. Barbara didn't look so glam with all her mascara running down her cheeks. 'I'm sorry,' she mumbled.

'Oh don't be. You've done me a big favour, actually. Bill's a terrible husband and an even worse father.' Viv lifted the first sack up and slung it at the slapper. Queenie followed suit with the others.

The last sack was particularly heavy, so Queenie and Viv lifted it between them, then slung it with force. 'That's all his clobber. He's all yours now, darling. Good luck, 'cause believe me, you're gonna fucking need it. Come on, Queen. Let's go.'

As the two sisters walked out of the pub far more

gracefully than they'd walked in, some of the men gave them a round of applause.

'OK?' Vinny asked. He'd offered to go inside the pub with his mum and aunt, but they'd insisted this was something they wanted to do alone.

'Yep. All fine. I feel better now I've got that off me chest and all his crap outta my house.'

Vinny put an arm around his aunt's shoulders. 'Good for you. You don't need that tosser in your life, Auntie Viv. I'm earning enough now to help you out financially.'

Vivian smiled at her smart, tall, handsome nephew. He had been in pieces for months after Yvonne Summers had left the East End, but seemed to have got his act together again now. 'You're a good lad, Vinny. Me and your mum love you dearly, don't we, Queen?'

Queenie linked arms with the apple of her eye. He'd cried like a baby over that bitch Yvonne, had gone into his shell for weeks afterwards. But finally he was smiling again, happy in himself. 'We sure do love him. He's our very own hero.'

Vinny grinned. 'Well, in that case, I will meet you two up the Roman tomorrow and take you out for a few drinks and a bit of grub. How's that grab ya?'

'Do we have to go the Roman again? It's boring,' Brenda sulked the following morning.

'Why don't I look after the kids today, Queen? You and Viv can have a bit of peace then, if you're going out for lunch. I'll rustle the kids up some grub 'ere.'

Queenie looked at her husband with suspicion. Every Saturday, without fail, he would spend most of the day in the pub, playing cards, gambling on horses and drinking himself into a stupor. 'Are you ill?'

'No. Why d'ya say that?'

'Because you always go to the pub on a Saturday.'

'An old pal of mine is having a birthday party tonight. Custom House he lives, so I thought I might go to that instead,' Albie fibbed. The real reason he wanted to go out tonight was because Maureen had invited him over for dinner. The twins were spending the weekend with their father, so he'd certainly get his leg over again.

'You're up to something.'

Albie felt himself twitch. Was it that bloody obvious? No. It couldn't be. 'Whaddya mean?'

'I bet it's free booze at the party, ain't it?'

Feeling relieved, Albie chuckled. 'You know me far too well, Queenie.'

Vinny met his mum and aunt outside Woolworths. 'Give us your bags. I'll carry those,' he insisted. 'What the pair of ya bought?'

'We'll show you in the pub,' Queenie replied.

'What d'ya fancy to eat? I'll take you somewhere posh, a nice restaurant if you like?'

Viv turned up her nose. 'I dunno about you, Queen, but I quite fancy our usual, pie and mash.'

'Me too. Shall we have a couple of drinks first though? I'm not overly hungry at the moment.'

'Suits me,' Viv agreed.

'Christ, you two are easy to please. The pub it is then,' Vinny laughed.

The pubs in the market were packed, so Vinny led his mum and aunt along to Fairfield Road and they got a table straight away in the Caledonian Arms.

'Hello, Vinny. How's tricks, mate?'

'Yeah. All good, thanks, Bob. Just treating me mum and

aunt to a few drinks and a bit of grub. You can't beat spending time with the family eh, mate.'

'Most certainly not, and what a beautiful mother and aunt you have,' Bob smiled, lifting Queenie's hand up to kiss it and then Viv's.

'Who's he?' Queenie asked her son.

'Bob the Bookie. OK, he is. Comes from a family of villains. His father is inside for murder.'

When a couple more men came over to shake hands with Vinny, Queenie was as pleased as punch. Her boy wasn't even sixteen yet and already he was making a name for himself.

'Bleedin' old pervert,' Viv said.

'Who?'

'Him. The hand kisser. I'm going a toilet, wash me hands. Could be lice in that moustache of his.'

Queenie roared with laughter as Viv left the table. 'What's that?' she asked when Vinny put her and Viv's drinks down.

'Gin and tonic.'

'Oh, we've gone off that. We prefer a sherry now.'

'I'll get you a sherry instead then.'

'No. Sit down. Not gonna waste the gin. We'll have a sherry next. What you got with your orange juice?'

'Nothing. I've got a date tonight, so will probably have a couple of drinks then.'

Queenie's heart sank. She'd only managed to save just over three hundred quid so far, to pay Patrick O'Leary back. She couldn't be borrowing any more if this tart turned out to be a nightmare as well.

Viv returned to the table. 'That's better.'

'Vinny's got a date tonight, Viv.'

'Oh, that's good. Who with? Do we know of her?'

'You sure do. She lives in the same road as us. Bonnie Tarbuck,' Vinny smirked.

Queenie was dismayed. 'Oh no, not the Tarbuck girl. You don't wanna be taking the likes of her out, Vinny. She's got an awful reputation among the neighbours for being easy. She's older than you as well. Have you learned nothing from that Yvonne turnout?'

'Actually, I have, Mum. That's why I asked Bonnie out,' grinned Vinny. 'I've heard through the grapevine she's a bit of a goer an' all, so rather than waste me time with another Yvonne type, I thought I might as well get something in return.' Vinny had been that furious when he'd found out that Yvonne had run off with Trevor Thomas, he'd clumped a couple of Trevor's pals to try and find out where they were. At the time, he'd wanted to hunt them down and drag Yvonne back home, but since finding out she wasn't the vestal virgin she'd pretended to be, he was glad to be rid of the slag.

'If you're gonna, you know, make sure you use protection, boy,' Viv wisely advised.

'Yeah, course I will.'

'Don't be spending your bleedin' wages on her either, taking her up the Lane, buying her gold, clothes and kittens. I'm still stuck with that bastard cat you bought for the last one, chasing all me birds away.'

'I can assure you, I won't be buying no more scrubbers any presents, Mum. Just a few drinks to loosen 'em up a bit. Then when I'm bored, I'll dump 'em.'

Queenie felt relieved. 'Good boy. I'm glad you've learned your lesson.'

Queenie and Viv weren't regular drinkers. With kids to care for, dinners to cook and homes to keep spotless, they were always far too busy to get sloshed. However, today the sherry was going down rather nicely and they were currently on their fourth drink.

'Can you believe that bastard ain't been home or even rung me?' Viv raged. 'I bet he stayed at that slapper's last night.'

'You're well rid, Auntie Viv. Wait until I see him. He'll get a dig all right. When you gonna show me what you bought today then, ladies,' Vinny asked, thinking a change of subject was needed.

Queenie delved inside her shopping bags. 'I bought these pretty summer dresses for Brenda, but you know what a tomboy she's becoming. I bet she won't bloody want to wear 'em. I got meself these flat shoes for work. They're not nice to look at, but they're ever so comfy. Oh, and I got your father a couple of shirts. Gone all grey round the collar, the white ones he's got. Now I've got me posh house, he ain't showing me up, Vinny.'

Vinny smiled. He was thrilled his mother was happy in her new home. So much so, he'd decided it was worth the shitty experience he'd gone through with Macca and Aunt Marnie, to get his mum the property. 'What about you, Auntie Viv?' Hearing loud laughter coming from behind him, Vinny turned around. Teddy boys didn't seem to be the in thing any more, bikers were, and there were two sitting behind him. He treated them to his special stare when he wouldn't blink, then turned back to his mum. 'They laughing at us?' he asked.

'No. I don't think so,' Queenie lied. She could sense the bikers were laughing at them, but there were two of them and only one of her son. They also looked older, in their early twenties.

Feeling a bit merry, having let her hair down for the

first time in ages, Vivian took her new dress out the bag, stood up and held it up against her. 'Well, Vinny, what do you reckon?' she asked, swaying her hips. 'Will this pull me a better man than the tosser I've just sent packing?' Viv joked.

'I doubt that very much, darling,' Vinny heard a voice say behind him.

'Vinny, leave it,' Queenie urged, as her son leapt up to confront the bikers.

Vinny stood in front of the pair who were now laughing their heads off. 'That's my mum and aunt you're laughing at. Apologize. Now!' he demanded.

'Yeah, right cocker. I love your suit by the way,' the ginger one replied, much to the amusement of his pal. 'Very posh.'

'We reckon you'd look better in that dress, than her,' the dark-haired one chuckled, nodding towards Viv.

'Vinny, no,' Queenie screamed, as her son picked up both the biker's drinks.

'You're hard, ain't ya?' laughed the dark-haired imbecile. His drunken mate then giggled like a five-year-old child.

Seconds later, neither of them was laughing as Vinny shoved the pint glasses in their ugly faces.

'Oh, Jesus,' Viv mumbled, as blood spurted everywhere, including all over her new frock.

'Vinny, come on. Let's go,' Queenie panicked.

'We're going, Mum. And believe me,' Vinny pointed at each and every customer in the pub. 'If any of these grass me up, they'll have more than a slashed face to deal with. I can't stand rats.'

'They won't, Vinny,' shouted a very impressed Bob Morten. 'I'll make damn sure of that, lad.'

Vinny took a last look at the bikers. One was rolling

on the carpet, screaming that he couldn't see properly. As for the ginger one, he was crying like a baby.

Vinny smirked as he sauntered out the door. That'd teach the pair of them to insult him and his family. They got what they asked for. End of.

CHAPTER THIRTY-FOUR

'Hello, Queenie. I don't arf miss you and our wonderful chats. How you doing, sweetheart?'

I couldn't believe my eyes. There, right in front of me, was Mrs O'Leary, showing no signs of the disabilities she had in her later life. She looked beautiful and vibrant, wearing the silk scarf I bought her from Cohen's. 'Mary, is that really you?' I whispered. 'It is you, isn't it? Oh Mary, I miss you so much. But you're looking so well.'

'All mended now. Vinny did well today. Those bikers were fecking arseholes. Nobody will grass him up, so don't be worrying about it.'

'You were there?' This was madness. Was I awake or was I dreaming, I wondered.

'I'm always there, looking over you. I'm your guardian angel. Told you to look out for a sign from me, didn't I? Vinny will go from strength to strength now, mark my words. That Yvonne was wrong for him. You did well getting rid of her,' smiled Mary.

I started to cry. It was so surreal. Here was my best friend ever, dead fourteen years now, chatting away to me as though she was still alive. It seemed real, but very *confusing. 'I'm so sorry I lost your rosary beads. My mum sold 'em at the jumble sale.'*

'Yes. I know. They went to a good owner. Religious, yet fecks and blinds like me. You mustn't blame your mum. She didn't mean to sell them. You need to make things right with her.'

I was laughing and crying at the same time. 'Are you able to see your boys all the time too?'

'Yes. Patrick helped you out, didn't he? I was pleased about that.'

'How's Daniel doing, Mary? I haven't seen him for years.'

'Still nutty as ever. I have to go now, Queenie, I'm being called back. You take care, my darling friend, and keep a close eye on Vinny. He's your nutty boy – he'll always need you by his side.'

'Mary, Mary,' I shrieked. But she was gone, like a genie in a flash of smoke.

I woke shortly after, and sat bolt upright. It must have been a dream, but it seemed so real. I remembered every word Mary said to me, so I wrote them down. I felt comforted, happy. Dream or no dream, I would treasure my visit from Mary for ever.

Two Months Later

Queenie was dozing in her deckchair, when she felt something attack her leg. She leapt up shrieking. 'Gertcha, you horrid bastard creature! Get off me leg.'

Viv let herself in Queenie's house. 'Cooey.'

'Help! Help me, Viv,' Queenie screamed, kicking her leg in the air in the hope of dislodging the kitten, but it was clinging on to her like a psychotic leech.

Viv slung a glass of water over Vinkle and he scarpered.

'Ooh, that did hurt. Look! He's scratched me to shreds and bitten me. Poxy thing. Next time it comes back, I'm gonna drown it in a bucket of bastard water.'

Viv couldn't hold it in any more. She burst out laughing.

'It ain't funny, Viv. I'm bleeding to death 'ere. I wouldn't mind, I ain't seen the horrid little creature for over a fortnight. It's obviously moved in with some other poor bastard family. It only pops back to kill me birds and attack me. I always fed it regularly an' all,' Queenie said in earnest. 'And gave it milk.'

Viv was hysterical by this point, holding her crotch to stop her from wetting herself. 'The sight of you hopping around with Vinkle stuck to your leg is a sight I'll never forget, Queen.'

'Well, I'm glad you find it amusing. Now make yourself bleedin' useful. Get me TCP out the medicine box. I need to bathe me wounds.'

Vinny Butler wasn't having much luck getting his leg over Bonnie Tarbuck. Sucking her tits was as far as she'd let him go, and that did nothing for Vinny. In fact, it left him cold.

A beautiful June day, it had been Vinny's suggestion he organize a picnic and they take it over Vicky Park. He'd asked his mum to rustle one up, but told her not to push the boat out. 'Just sandwiches and a few sausage rolls is fine, Mum. I ain't splashing the cash on this one,' he'd added, much to his mother's delight.

'What you brought a blanket with you for?' asked Bonnie.

'It's a picnic blanket. In life, if you're gonna do something, you gotta do it in style, girl.'

Bonnie leaned towards Vinny with another of her kisses,

which he hated. She liked to shove her tongue down the back of his throat. 'Are we officially boyfriend and girl-friend now, Vinny? Only I don't see you much. You're always busy lately.'

'If you want nice things in life, you gotta work hard to attain 'em, Bon. One day, when I have kids, I wanna be able to give 'em everything,' Vinny lied. He loved his little sister and Champ, but couldn't imagine ever having kids of his own. He knew what soppy birds liked to hear though. That slut Yvonne had taught him that much.

'So, are we boyfriend and girlfriend then?' Bonnie giggled. She totally adored Vinny. All her friends were terribly jealous she was dating him, he was fast getting a hard man repu-tation and she was dying to tell them they were officially a couple.

Having brought the blanket with him for different reasons than he'd admitted to Bonnie, Vinny winked. 'I'll have a think about it and let ya know before we leave the park.'

Taking this as a yes, Bonnie clapped her hands together like Champ often did when excited.

Vinny forced a smile. Considering she was eighteen, Bonnie was so immature. She was pretty, had a good body, but all Vinny wanted from her was a wank and a shag. He'd be sixteen this autumn, his only sexual experience so far had been with Macca. He needed that memory to be wiped once and for all, which was why he'd chosen Bonnie. The most attractive, single, local bike.

'Oooh, I know what I meant to tell you,' exclaimed Queenie.

'What?' Viv asked.

'Two things. Vinny bumped into that bloke the other day, that Bob.'

'Bob who? I know about six Bobs.'

'Bob the Bookie, from that pub where Vinny glassed those bikers in. He was the one who kissed our hands and you rushed to the loo.'

'Oh, that tashy-faced pervert. And?'

'Well, we know nobody grassed Vinny as we never had the Old Bill round. But Bob found out about the bikers. I dunno how, 'cause they were obviously too scared to snitch too. Turns out, one lost the sight in an eye and I think they had about a hundred stitches between 'em.'

'Oh well. Serves 'em right for taking the piss out of us, Queen.'

'Exactly! And me other gossip comes from the Huntingdon-Browns.'

Viv had never met Queenie's employers, but loathed them anyway. They spoke to her sister like shit, she knew that much. But Queenie insisted she needed the money. Viv couldn't think why, given that Vinny provided for her so well, but then she had no idea that Queenie was still saving to pay Patrick O'Leary back the eight hundred quid she'd borrowed. 'Go on. No, let me guess. The old man's having an affair?'

'Nope. Even better than that. I told you that brat of a daughter of Pearl's had vanished off the face of the earth, didn't I?'

'Yeah, about six weeks ago, wasn't it?'

'Yes. Well yesterday, I came across a letter. I wasn't prying in drawers or nothing like that. It was lying on top of the desk in Basil's office.'

'And?'

'Training to be a vet, my arse. Only got herself up the spout, didn't she? They've carted her off to one of those mother and baby homes. Bound to get it adopted to save face.'

Viv clapped her hands. 'Brilliant!'

'Ouch.'

'What's a matter?'

'It's my leg. It's hurting me, Viv.'

Viv laughed. 'You were attacked by a kitten, not a bleedin' tiger, Queen.'

Back at Victoria Park, Vinny was still getting nowhere fast.

'Drink some more of that champagne, darlin'. That's not the cheap stuff, ya know. It's proper. Only the best for you,' Vinny lied. It was actually Pomagne, but he'd ripped the label off, pretending it was the nuts and had fallen off the back of a lorry.

'I've drunk most of it, Vinny. You have some now,' Bonnie took a gulp and then handed the lad she'd already decided she wanted to spend the rest of her life with, the bottle.

Vinny took a couple of sips, then handed it back to Bonnie. 'I've got some important business meetings tonight, so I can't turn up sozzled. That's why I can't take you out tonight.' Vinny had no meetings, but he'd arranged to play snooker in the club near their home with Roy and his pals.

'You haven't answered my question yet.'

'What question?' Vinny asked, as if he didn't know.

'Are we boyfriend and girlfriend now?'

Vinny pulled the blanket over himself and Bonnie. 'I'll tell you soon, but we need a cuddle first.'

Vinny put up with her dodgy kissing for a minute or so, before grabbing Bonnie's hand and shoving it on his cock. He was as hard as a rock.

Bonnie rubbed her hand against Vinny's penis and then quickly pulled it away. Nobody apart from her mother knew about the back-street abortion she'd had to endure, and her mother had told her afterwards, if she ever got pregnant again before marriage, she would disown her.

'That felt nice. Carry on, babe,' Vinny groaned, undoing the zip of his trousers.

Bonnie wanted to, she truly did. But her mother had given her another talking to over Vinny. 'You've got a good un there, Bonnie. That lad is going places in life. Don't balls it up. Lads such as Vinny Butler won't marry slags. Keep your hand on your ha'penny and two legs in one stocking, girl. Once you've got his wedding ring on your finger, the world will be your oyster.'

Vinny sat up. 'Whatever's wrong with you? I thought you liked me.'

Bonnie had to follow her mother's advice, could not repeat her past mistakes. 'I do, Vinny. I truly do like you. But I'm not that type of girl and we're not even in a proper relationship yet. You refuse to come to dinner at my house and you've never invited me to yours to meet your family properly. You won't even admit I'm your girlfriend. I'm confused.'

Vinny was also confused. How comes she'd spread her legs for a couple of lads he knew, yet wouldn't even toss him off. 'OK. Say I invite you round me mum's for Sunday roast tomorrow. Can we sort of move on a bit with our relationship then?'

Bonnie was totally thrilled to be invited round Vinny's for dinner, could not wait to tell all her friends. But unfortunately for her, she didn't look at the bigger picture. 'Yes. Of course. I like you far more than any lad I've ever dated in the past.'

'Nice one,' Vinny grinned.

*

The following morning, Viv made her way around Queenie's earlier than usual. She didn't miss Bill, but for some strange reason, Lenny did at times. Today was one of those days. He'd been crying his eyes out all morning.

Viv found Queenie in the garden bathing her wounds. 'Go put your music on then, boy,' she told Lenny before informing Queenie he'd been upset over his father this morning.

'What, the father who couldn't give a toss about him and don't give you a penny for his bleedin' upkeep?'

Viv rolled her eyes. 'He don't understand at his age, does he? I'll always be indebted to your Vinny for helping me out, Queen. If he didn't pay my rent, me and Lenny'd be out on the streets.'

'Don't be so daft. You'd always be welcome to move in 'ere, you know that. Might be a bit squashed, but we'd manage. I'd get one of them garden sheds and Albie could live in that,' Queenie chuckled.

'Did you ring Mum last night?' Viv asked hopefully. She visited their mum every other day, but Queenie rarely did. They were on talking terms again now, so that was one good thing.

'I did ring Mum and, rather surprisingly, she agreed to come round for dinner today.'

'Oh, that's great, Queen,' beamed Viv.

'What I didn't know at the time was that Vinny's invited that Tarbuck girl. Last time Mum came for dinner was when Vinny introduced us to Yvonne Summers – and look how that turned out.'

'I didn't think Vinny was into the Tarbuck girl.'

'He isn't, so he says. We'll soon see the way he acts around her.' Queenie stared at her injured leg. 'Does it look red and swollen to you, Viv?'

'No. You've just got a bit of sunburn. I'm beginning to think you're obsessed with that cat,' Viv laughed.

'That'll be the bleedin' day.'

'I'm sure he thinks he's Buddy Holly, your son,' Albie joked, poking his head around the back door. 'Morning, Viv. You all right, love?' Albie had seen her only last night. She was like a permanent fixture in his home these days.

'Yep. Fine, thanks. You off to work?'

'Albie doesn't work, Viv. He sings for peanuts, like a performing monkey.'

When Viv rolled up in fits of laughter, Albie glared at both her and Queenie. Neither ever had a good word to say about him. Witches, the pair of them were. 'I'll be home later today, Queen. They're having a lock-in at the pub for one of the regulars 'cause it's his birthday, and they're gonna pay me extra to sing for longer.'

'Christ, you'll need to take the wheelbarrow you lug your meat about in to carry home all your wages,' Queenie cackled.

Viv roared.

'Bollocks to the pair of ya,' Albie said, before walking off in a huff. He wasn't really singing all day. He was going round Maureen's for dinner and leg-over. She was his saviour, was Maureen. She gave him something to look forward to in his otherwise miserable life.

'Been lovely weather this past week, hasn't it?' said Molly Wade. She always felt uneasy around Queenie, never quite knew what to say.

'Yes. Meant to be nice this coming week too,' replied Viv.

'Listen to this one, Nanny,' Lenny ordered, as he began jigging about and singing to Jerry Lee Lewis's 'Whole Lotta Shakin' Going On'.

Molly chuckled. 'Isn't that the musician who married his young cousin?'

'Yes. The pervert. Thirteen years old, she was, should be bloody ashamed of himself. I wouldn't buy his records and put any money in the dirty bastard's pocket out of principle,' snarled Queenie.

Viv stared out the window on tiptoes, craning her neck. 'Vinny's on his way, Queen. She's with him.'

'Can I sit on your lap, Nan?' asked Brenda.

'Of course, darling. Where are Roy and Michael, Queenie?'

'Working down the Lane, then they're playing snooker. I'll warm their dinners up later.'

Queenie took off her apron and checked her hair in the mirror.

'Hiya all,' Vinny said. 'This is Bonnie. Bonnie that's my mum, my Aunt Viv, me nan, my little sister Brenda and this little groover 'ere is Champ.' Vinny grabbed his nephew in a playful headlock.

'Thank you for allowing me to come to dinner. It's a pleasure to meet you all,' beamed Bonnie.

As soon as dessert was over, Vinny and Bonnie left.

'I'd best be making a move now too. I've got lots of bits to do in preparation for next weekend's bazaar.' Molly had reconciled with the vicar and her church friends, but was still thoroughly embarrassed Queenie had bellowed the F and C words in the church hall, of all places. Her friends and the vicar had never mentioned the incident since and neither had she. She doubted her friends had forgotten about it, mind. She never would.

'Thanks for the lovely dinner, Queenie.'

Queenie politely kissed her mother on the cheek. 'I wrapped a piece of apple pie up for your supper.'

'Oh, that's kind of you, love. Thank you.'

When her mum left, Queenie sat next to Viv. 'You can tell Vinny don't like Bonnie much. He was entirely different with that Yvonne, wasn't he?'

'Yes. Entirely. He spoke to her like shit a couple of times and you could see he was in a rush to leave an' all.'

'He's arranged to play snooker with his brothers, that's why. Bonnie was better than I expected, to be fair. Shame she's hawked her mutton so much. Lads will only see her as a slut now, Vinny included.'

'I liked her. She's very pretty, polite and seems to have a sweet nature. Oh well, she might grow on Vinny, ya never know.'

'I know my own son, Viv. All Vinny's after is a leg-over,' smiled Queenie. No way did she want a daughter-in-law who'd been around the block.

The following day, Queenie was working at the Huntingdon-Browns. Unusually, Basil was at home. 'Try not to make too much noise today, Queenie. Basil is in bed, poorly,' Pearl had snapped the second she'd arrived. The posh bitch never greeted her with a 'Hello'; her arrival was always greeted with, 'Oh, it's you.'

Queenie was cleaning Basil's office when she knocked her poorly leg against his desk. The letter had gone, she'd noticed. 'Sod that,' Queenie cursed, limping over to the big leather armchair that Basil used for reading his newspaper in peace, so she'd been told.

Having been told never to sit on any of the furniture, Queenie ducked down behind it to inspect her leg. Seconds later, Pearl walked into the room and tried the safe.

Queenie had no idea why she did what she did, but something urged her to stay hidden behind the chair.

'Four, four, two, nine,' Pearl mumbled, before saying 'Damn! What's the code? Oh, I remember. Four, four, three, nine. Bingo.'

Queenie heard a click as the safe opened. Pearl took something out and left the room.

As soon as the coast was clear, Queenie darted into another room.

'Have you been skiving again, Queenie? Only I popped into Basil's study, and there was all your cleaning equipment, but no sign of you,' Pearl questioned.

Queenie never skived. She worked bloody hard, always. 'I'm sorry, Mrs Huntingdon-Brown. I had to use the toilet and now I need to get my handbag and use it again, I'm afraid. Women's problems,' lied Queenie.

Pearl turned up her nose. 'Oh please! Spare me the details, just do what you've got to do. You know where *your* toilet is.' The house had four toilets, but Queenie was only allowed to use the one Pearl referred to as the 'staff toilet'.

Queenie shut the toilet door. 'Don't you have periods then, ya prat,' she mumbled. She then took a pen out of her handbag, wrote the safe code on a piece of toilet paper and hid it in her cigarette packet.

Queenie lay in bed that night, deep in thought. She knew there'd been a few burglaries recently near where the Huntingdon-Browns lived as Pearl had told her she must be more vigilant and make sure any windows she opened were closed and locked afterwards. The posh prat couldn't even pronounce the word cockney. 'Basil's policeman friend reckons it is a bunch of cockerknees responsible, Queenie. You know, your people,' she'd said, a look of disdain on her clock.

Queenie knew that Pearl and Basil were going on holiday in a couple of months as Pearl had told her she wouldn't be needed that particular fortnight. Usually, Pearl would brag about the vacations they took, but this time she'd said very little. Queenie reckoned that was around the daughter's due date and they must be taking her off to recuperate after giving birth to a child she'd be forced to give away.

As a throbbing pain similar to a toothache shot through her leg, Queenie forgot all about the safe code. She was in too much pain to concentrate on anything.

The following morning, Queenie took a slow walk down to the Waste.

'Queen,' yelled Jeanie Thomas. Queenie had felt slightly guilty for Jeanie's son moving so far away; she would be fuming if her sons ever moved too far for her to visit. But Jeanie seemed to have accepted the situation now. Trevor was happy with Yvonne apparently, and Jeanie had been to visit them recently. The money Queenie had bunged Yvonne had thankfully never been mentioned. Queenie guessed Jeanie hadn't been told about it. She wouldn't put it past that slippery bitch Yvonne to have left Trevor in the dark and kept the grand for herself.

Leg still throbbing, Queenie hobbled over to Jeanie. 'You all right, love?'

'I'm gonna be a grandma,' Jeanie beamed.

'Oh, how lovely. I'm glad their relationship worked out, for your sake, Jeanie. If our kids are happy, we're happy, aren't we, darlin'.'

'Well, I gotta accept her now, Queen. I ain't got no choice if I want to be part of my grandchild's life.'

'True.'

'What you done to your leg, Queen? It looks mauve and ever so sore.'

'That poxy cat that Vinny bought for Yvonne bit and scratched me. I've been putting TCP on it, but it kept me awake last night.'

Jeanie crouched down. 'That's infected, Queen. Cats carry germs where they kill mice, rats and birds. You should go to the quack sharpish with that. I know a man who got bitten by a cat, left it like you have, and ended up having his leg cut off.'

Queenie felt the colour drain from her face. She'd rather be dead than have one leg.

Queenie felt nostalgic as she hobbled round to her doctor's surgery. Kids didn't know how good they had it these days. Back in her day, if you couldn't afford a doctor, chances were you'd die. There were no ambulances when she was growing up either.

'Hello, Queenie. How you doing, sweetheart?'

'Hello, Violet. I'm OK, thanks, apart from a gammy leg. Been a while since I've seen you. You been OK?'

'I was living in Dagenham for a couple of months, Queen, with me poor Daisy. She was devastated after her Charlie died, still is. Which is why I've come to the decision to move to Dagenham and live with her. We're both widows now and the company'll do us both good.'

Violet was a lively sixty-six-year-old Queenie had known since she was a small child. She hadn't seen her twin Daisy for years, but imagined they still looked identical. 'I'm sure you're making the right decision, Vi. Life's too short to be lonely.'

'You'll never be lonely with those kids of yours, Queen. Your Vinny adores the ground you walk on. I saw him last week and he spent ten minutes singing your praises. Making a right name for himself round 'ere lately, an' all. Another few years, he'll be up there with the likes of Ron and Reg.'

About to reply, Queenie saw a familiar figure leap over the doorstep Violet had been scrubbing and lovingly rub against the woman's legs. 'Ahh, there you are, boy,' Violet said, picking the horrid creature up and kissing him on the lips.

Queenie was that stunned, she was temporarily lost for words. It was definitely Vinkle. There weren't many pure white cats around Whitechapel and she'd recognize those evil blue eyes anywhere.

'Queenie, meet my boy I named after your son. He was ever so feisty when he first turned up on me doorstep, but I've tamed him. Loves a bit of chicken and ham for his dinner. I call him Little Vinny. Ain't he a cutie?'

Queenie locked eyes with the monster. 'You taking him to Dagenham with you?'

'Of course. I asked around, he's definitely a stray. We're moving on Friday, aren't we, Little Vinny?'

'Brilliant. Well, I wish you well in your new home, Violet. Gotta go now. Me leg's killing me and I'll be late for me doctor's appointment. Love to Daisy too.'

'Bye, Queenie. It's been a pleasure knowing you all these years, my darlin'. Keep well. Those boys of yours will look after you, I know they will.'

Queenie hobbled away as fast as she could. She would miss bumping into Violet from time to time, but not that bastard cat. She wanted to forget that thing existed.

The following Saturday, Vinny got up with a spring in his step. He might not be into Bonnie that much, but he couldn't wait to get some action and he was sure tonight was the night. All week she'd been making the right noises, raving about him and his lovely family. He was also planning to tell her she was his girlfriend tonight, just so he got what he wanted. He might not even dump her straight away, not if she was any good at it. Even his youngest brother Michael had got a wank off the bird who worked in the chicken factory down Petticoat Lane, so Vinny was desperate to be the first lad in his family to get laid.

'Morning, Mum. How you feeling today, sweetheart?'

'Better than I was thanks, boy. The pain's subsided now, thank God. Never felt pain like that in me life before, and I never want to experience it again.' Queenie had spent the past three days in the London Hospital. The infection in her leg had been that bad, she'd been on a drip and all sorts.

'I've only got to pick up a few bob today, Mum. So you rest up and I'll sort out breakfast.'

Queenie smiled. She had hated being in hospital away from her boys. 'Thanks, Vinny. You're a diamond.'

'All right, treacle? You look nice,' Vinny said, pecking Bonnie on the cheek. He never picked her up from home as he had no interest in being introduced to her parents. He always arranged to meet her outside the snooker hall instead.

Bonnie stood on tiptoes and wrapped her arms around Vinny's neck. She felt like the luckiest girl in the world this week. Her friends had all been so excited to hear about her going round Vinny's for dinner and meeting his family. They'd insisted he must be really serious about her.

'I thought we'd do something special tonight, girl. I booked a nice restaurant to take you for a meal.'

Bonnie felt like the cat that had got the cream. She'd been so worried that Vinny had been going off her recently, but her mum had been right all along. On the odd occasion he'd taken her out of an evening, Vinny had only ever taken her to pubs outside the area. So a meal was very special. A turning point in their relationship.

'Right, we're heading to Whitechapel station and jumping on the rattler.'

Bonnie beamed. Was he going to propose to her? she wondered.

'Thanks for a lovely evening, Vinny. That is the nicest restaurant I have ever been to. My chicken was out of this world. I do feel a bit tiddly though. I'm not used to drinking that much,' giggled Bonnie.

Good, Vinny thought. If she was sloshed she should drop her drawers easily. 'The night ain't over yet, darlin',' Vinny said, leading Bonnie down the side of the snooker club where they usually said goodnight. It didn't smell too healthy as it was where the dustbins were kept, but it was secluded, and the snooker club was now shut.

'I'm so happy you asked me to be your girlfriend tonight, Vinny,' Bonnie said, draping her arms around Vinny's neck.

Vinny felt his penis leap into action. It was literally throbbing. He kissed Bonnie, holding the back of her head with one hand and undid his zip with the other to flop his member out.

'No, Vinny. Stop it!' Bonnie ordered, when he put his hand up her dress and began pulling her knickers down.

'I wanna fuck you badly,' Vinny mumbled, putting Bonnie's hand on his cock.

'No. We mustn't do this. Not now, not here.'

'Yes, we must. You're my girlfriend now,' Vinny said, ripping the side of her knickers so they fell to the floor.

'You're scaring me, Vinny. Please stop,' Bonnie pleaded, genuinely frightened. Vinny had a manic look in his eyes, a look she'd never seen before.

Overcome by lust, Vinny pushed Bonnie to the ground, parted her legs and rammed his throbbing penis inside her. 'Don't play the innocent with me, Bon. You've fucked other blokes, so now you can fuck me.'

Crying her eyes out, Bonnie had no choice but to let him do what he wanted. Vinny was far too strong for her. She tried to scream for help, but no sound came out of her mouth.

'I bought you an expensive meal. You owe me, bitch,' Vinny groaned, before shooting his load inside her.

Bonnie was in shock. The man she had been in love with and wanted to marry was a rapist. How could she have got Vinny so wrong?

'Get up and sort yourself out,' Vinny ordered, zipping up his trousers.

Bonnie's legs were trembling that much she couldn't get up, so Vinny yanked her up, pushed her gently against the wall and put his hand around her throat. 'You say nothing about this to nobody, OK? No one would believe a slag like you anyway. Do we understand one another?'

'Yes,' Bonnie croaked. Vinny let go of her and she slid down the wall next to the overflowing rubbish bins. So much for her dreams of a proposal and pretty wedding.

When Vinny walked off, Bonnie stopped crying and tried to compose herself. Her mother would be waiting up when she got in to hear all about the date she'd been so excited about going on.

Bonnie brushed herself down. The new dress she'd

bought especially for tonight was now filthy. She'd have to tell her mother she'd got drunk and fell over, Vinny had had a go at her, then they'd split up. Lying was the only choice she had.

CHAPTER THIRTY-FIVE

'If everything is to your satisfaction I'll be off now, Mrs Huntingdon-Brown.'

'Yes. You can go. No more time off sick though, Queenie, otherwise I'll have to replace you. You left me totally in the lurch last week. It's completely unacceptable.'

'I was in hospital,' Queenie reminded the posh unfeeling cow.

'Yes. Well. You can go now. I'll see you on Wednesday, bright and early.'

Queenie left the house and headed towards the station. She wasn't even supposed to be back at work yet; the doctor had told her to rest up for a week.

'Queenie. It is you, Queenie, isn't it?'

Not recognizing the voice, Queenie turned around. She looked beautiful, far more glamorous than she used to, and she was stunning back then. She reminded Queenie of a movie star in her oversized dark sunglasses, big floppy hat and designer clobber. 'Doreen! Oh my God!' Queenie put her hand over her mouth, genuinely shocked to see her. Queenie hadn't seen Doreen Laine, her old work colleague, since the day she left Cohen's and verbally abused her.

Doreen greeted Queenie warmly, embracing her in a hug. 'Queenie, it's so wonderful to see you. How are you?' She sounded far more posh than she used to, thought Queenie.

Queenie felt ever so drab beside her. She'd been sweating like a pig at work and was wearing a tatty dress and her flat work shoes. 'I'm fine, thanks, and who's this little one?' she asked, gazing into the poshest Silver Cross pram she'd ever seen.

'This is Barnaby, our new addition to the family. I only live around the corner. Please say you'll come in for a cup of tea?'

Queenie felt she couldn't refuse. She owed Doreen an apology for the terrible way she spoke to her all those years ago.

The house was amazing. Big and trendy with every mod-con going. Queenie was envious, but not jealous. She couldn't begrudge Doreen happiness.

After introducing her to two older children who were just as gorgeous as Barnaby, Doreen ordered the nanny to take them to the nursery so she could have a catch up with a dear friend she hadn't seen for years.

Queenie felt guilty. 'I am so sorry for the way I spoke to you that time, Doreen. I said some awful things to you and I shouldn't have. I didn't mean it. I was in a temper.'

'Forget it, Queenie. We were only young back then. I remember saying some hurtful things to you too in the past. We're older now and wiser.'

Queenie smiled as Doreen handed her a cup of tea in a posh cup and saucer. Fine china. 'I still keep in touch with Eliza from time to time. I know a wonderful restaurant in the West End. The food is superb. We should all meet there for lunch. It'll be fun, just like the old days.'

'Yes. That would be nice,' Queenie replied, not meaning it. Doreen and Eliza were both wealthy women. She wouldn't be able to afford such luxuries. Paying Patrick back what she owed was her priority, not dining in fancy restaurants that cost a bloody fortune.'

'Tell me about your life, Queenie. Why are you in these neck of the woods? And how is Albie, and your children?'

Queenie plastered a smile on her face and made her marriage and life sound as glamorous as she possibly could . . .

On the journey home, Queenie made up her mind. She owed the Huntingdon-Browns nothing. Pearl in particular was an awful person who had done nothing but look down her pointed nose at her since day one. Queenie knew whatever was in that safe would be worth a small fortune and even though she was considered to be reasonably well off in her neighbourhood, thanks to Vinny, she wanted more.

Queenie didn't want to work or worry about money for the rest of her life, she wanted what Doreen and Eliza had. Queenie would love to walk into that posh restaurant, and match her old friends pound for pound. She also wanted to give Vinny a leg-up in life. He was already going places, but she yearned to push him even further up the ladder to achieve his dreams and hers. He'd learn to drive soon, would need a posh car to swan around in.

Queenie was still deep in thought as she got off the train and walked towards home. Her daydreaming of a better life was diminished the moment Bonnie's mother rushed out of her house and collared her. 'Hello, Mrs Tarbuck. Everything OK?' Queenie asked. She knew Vinny had binned her daughter. He'd told her yesterday.

'No, Queenie. Everything is not OK. My Bonnie came home in a terrible state on Saturday night. Her new dress was ruined and she's refused to leave her bedroom since. She won't eat and also refused to go into work today.'

'Young love,' Queenie replied. 'I think your Bonnie and my Vinny had a tiff and split up. Shame. I thought she was good for him. Such a lovely girl,' Queenie fibbed.

Mrs Tarbuck shook her head. 'No. You don't understand, Queenie. Something happened that night, something that Bonnie won't tell me about. I think she was attacked, or worse.'

'My Vinny's a gentleman, I'll have you know. I raised him that way,' Queenie snapped abruptly.

'I've searched everywhere for the underwear Bonnie was wearing, but couldn't find her knickers. She also has bruising around her throat. I'm not blaming Vinny, Queenie, but could you talk to him? I need to know exactly what happened and where Vinny left her. I threatened to call the police and Bonnie went ballistic. I know my own daughter. Something traumatic happened to her that night.'

Queenie felt herself go cold; a shiver ran right down her spine. Memories came flooding back: the drive down that bumpy track, herself running across fields, desperate to get away from *him*. That vile man who she refused to think about any more. Instinct told Queenie that Vinny was responsible for whatever trauma Bonnie suffered. He'd been acting differently since Saturday night, but she wasn't about to admit that to Mrs Tarbuck.

Giving the woman's arm a squeeze, Queenie told her, 'I'm so sorry if what you're saying is true, my love. But Bonnie is probably just upset over breaking up with Vinny. He's only a child still, not even sixteen yet. But I will talk to him tonight, find out what happened, I promise. I'll give you a knock tomorrow daytime.'

'No. Don't knock. I don't want Bonnie's dad or brother to know anything is wrong. I've kept this from them. My hubby is very over-protective of Bonnie and I don't want trouble. Thank you, Queenie, and please call me June in future. Can we meet in Jack's cafe? At noon, say? I don't want Bonnie to know I've spoken to you either. She begged me not to.'

Queenie squeezed the distraught woman's arm once more. 'OK, June. I'll see you at noon tomorrow, lovely. I do hope Bonnie is feeling better soon. I'm sure she will be.'

Queenie rushed home, feeling sick inside. She needed to confront her firstborn and get the truth out of him, for his own bloody sake.

Vinny arrived home late. Gone 11 p.m. by the time he rolled in. Roy, Michael and Brenda were all in bed. Only Albie was still out and, frankly, Queenie couldn't give a toss where he was.

'I've decided, Mum. I love that snooker club so much, one day I'm gonna buy it, when I'm rich enough,' Vinny grinned. 'It's got great potential.'

'Sit down, boy,' Queenie said sternly. 'We need to talk.'

Vinny sat on the armchair opposite. 'What's up?'

Queenie decided bluntness was the only way to deal with this particular situation. No point beating about the bush. 'I know you attacked Bonnie on Saturday night. Don't panic, nobody else knows. But I need you to tell me why you did it. What you tell me will stay between us. But I need to know what possessed you to do such a thing?' Queenie could not bring herself to mention the word 'rape'. That word had always disgusted her.

419

Vinny got to his feet and began pacing the room. 'What's that slut said to you? Only, she better not've been telling lies about me, for her sake.'

'Sit your arse down now,' Queenie hissed. She stared her son in the eye. He didn't blink, a dead giveaway he was either lying or angry. 'Bonnie has said nothing to me. Apparently, the poor girl is in pieces, won't come out of her bedroom. Her mother collared me. She knows Bonnie was attacked, so best you tell me the truth, boy, so I can smooth things over. You're going places, got a good reputation round 'ere. Just tell me what happened and I'll sort it. Did she lead you on?'

Vinny put his head in his hands. 'I had sex with her, Mum, but she asked for it. She dressed like a tart every time I took her out. The dress she was wearing on Saturday barely covered her minge and her lils were hanging out. I know a couple of lads who've shagged her – she's easy. I took her out for a meal, treated her proper nice. She came on to me, then went all weird.'

'Did she try to stop you when you – ya know? Did she say no to you, Vinny?'

'Well, yeah, but I didn't believe her. She was always asking me to play with her tits and stuff. She even made me do that when we went for that picnic over Vicky Park. What was I supposed to think?'

Queenie patted the sofa next to her. She didn't want to believe her number one son was a rapist. He might look older, but he was only fifteen, going through his adolescence, and it was common knowledge that Bonnie Tarbuck was the local bike. Lots of the neighbours had told her that soon after Queenie had moved in. 'A right little hussy', Nosey Hilda described Bonnie as.

Vinny sat next to his mum. 'Son, you were led up the

garden path, but what you ended up doing was wrong. Very wrong indeed. I need you to promise me, in future, if a girl says no to you, she means no and you're to do as she says. You've got so much going for you, you don't want to get a reputation for, ya know.'

'But you always drummed it into us, never look a gift horse in the mouth, take the opportunities. Bonnie led me on, I'm telling ya.'

'Don't you be blaming me. I know it's difficult to understand, but girls are different to men.' Queenie sighed. It was clear Vinny couldn't comprehend what he'd done wrong. That made her furious, yet she had to help him out regardless. 'Listen, I will speak to Mrs Tarbuck tomorrow and vouch you were home early, OK? What time did all these shenanigans happen?'

'Around half eleven, I think.'

'Well, you came in at midnight, so I shall say you were back here at half ten after having a row with Bonnie. Did you walk her home?'

'No. I left her by the snooker club.'

'Well, if Bonnie does open her trap, you're just gonna have to deny it. I'll back you up.'

Vinny grinned. 'Cheers, Mum. Serves her right. She shouldn't have dressed like a whore,' he said brazenly.

Appalled by his lack of empathy, Queenie walloped Vinny hard around his head. 'You never force yourself on any female again, no matter how she dresses or acts. Do you hear me, boy? It's wrong. Very wrong.'

'All right. Sorry, Mum.'

Queenie looked into her son's eyes. He wasn't sorry at all, she was sure of that. But it wasn't entirely his fault. His involvement with Marnie, Macca and then Yvonne, had obviously damaged him in some way, left him with issues. 'I think it's best you stay away from girls for the time being, Vinny, until you're older and wiser. Little tarts like Yvonne and Bonnie will only bring you down, son. You're going places. Girls aren't worth the grief of ruining your future.'

'Yeah. You're right, Mum. I'm gonna give girls a wide berth and concentrate solely on earning money from now on.'

'Good boy. You know it makes sense. Actually, I've got a proposition for you. You swear to me you will never again do what you did to Bonnie, and I'll give you the details of a job that could set us up good and proper.'

Vinny's eyes lit up. 'I swear on my life, Mum, I'll never do it to another girl. What's the job?' he asked excitedly.

Queenie explained about the Huntingdon-Browns' imminent holiday and all the gold, diamonds and cash she presumed they kept in their safe. 'I can draw you a plan of the easiest way to get into the house, but you'll have to break a window and bash the safe up afterwards. The safe needs to look like it's been jemmied open, rather than opened with the code, otherwise they'll suspect me. The whole thing needs to look like a robbery, boy. There's been burglaries round that area recently, so if you do it right, nobody will think I had any involvement. Upturn some drawers, that kind of thing.'

Vinny beamed from ear to ear. 'Don't worry, Mum. I know exactly what to do. A piece of piss, this sounds. I'll take Roy with me as my lookout.'

Queenie smiled. 'Perfect.'

Vinny wrapped his arms around his mother. This was exactly the break he needed. 'You know what, you're the best mum in the whole wide world.'

*

The following lunchtime, Queenie met June Tarbuck in Old Jack's cafe. 'Hello, love. How's Bonnie today? Feeling better, I hope. I got you a mug of tea. Is that OK?'

'Yes. Thanks. No. Bonnie's no better. She wouldn't go to work again today. I had to ring in sick for her, lie she'd been up all night with a bad tummy bug. I'm at my wits' end, Queenie. Did you talk to Vinny?'

Queenie and Vinny had spoken some more about Bonnie last night, come up with a concrete story. 'Yes, I did. Vinny says he took Bonnie to a posh restaurant on Saturday night in Stratford and he wasn't too happy because Bonnie got a bit tipsy. Vinny isn't a drinker, you see. He's too young for all that lark, and seeing my Albie roll home drunk over the years has left a mark on him. Apparently, after they left the restaurant, Bonnie was staggering and fell over a couple of times. That's probably why her dress was ruined. She acted up on the train also, was sick, and Vinny was embarrassed by her behaviour. They had a few cross words and Vinny packed her up after they got off the train at Whitechapel. Bonnie got upset, cried, and refused to let him walk her home. She went off in the opposite direction. What time did Bonnie get home, June?'

'About half twelve. I wish Vinny hadn't left her, seeing as she was so drunk, Queenie.'

'My Vinny was home by half ten and I said the same to him last night, June, that he shouldn't have left her. He said he did go after her, but she started swearing at him, so he gave up and came home. To be honest, June, I think it's a blessing in disguise they've split up. Bonnie is far too old for Vinny. She wanted him to do things over the course of their relationship that Vinny didn't feel entirely comfortable about. Bonnie needs to date lads her own age in future. Vinny's inexperienced when it comes to girls, and Bonnie is a young woman.'

June Tarbuck was mortified. Bonnie had sworn to her she hadn't done anything with Vinny other than kisses and cuddles. She was obviously up to her old tricks again. 'OK, Queenie. Thanks. I'll get to the bottom of what's happened, don't you worry.'

'You not going to drink your tea, dear?' Queenie asked, when June stood up.

'No, love. I have to be somewhere. You drink it,' Embarrassed beyond belief, June Tarbuck couldn't get out the cafe quickly enough.

CHAPTER THIRTY-SIX

Two Years Later

Autumn 1964

I only needed a few bits – sugar, flour, suet, a tin of Spam and a tin of sardines – but was tempted to do without when I saw the length of the queue. All I wanted to do was get home and sit in my beloved garden. The weather had been crap all week, but it was unusually warm that day.

'Come up to the front, Queenie love,' shouted Maura, the shop owner.

Heads turned towards me. I received nods, looks of admiration and numerous 'Hello, Queenies'. The only two who looked at me with hatred were Freda Smart and Old Ma Bloggs. I disliked both women as much as they disliked me. Freda was as mad as a hatter, the other was a well-known shoplifter.

'No need to pay me, Queenie,' Maura said as I went to open my purse. 'Send mine and Colin's regards to Vinny and Roy. Love to the rest of the family too, sweetheart.'

'*How comes we gotta stand 'ere like a bunch of lemons, while she gets to go to the front of the queue?*' *bellowed Freda Smart.*

The shop fell silent, that quiet you could almost hear a pin drop. I winked at Maura, picked up my goods, turned around and locked eyes with Freda. '*She is what you call the cat's mother, darlin', and I'm that all right. Thanks to my boys, I'm the cat that got the cream.*'

Most of the queue started to laugh and I winked at them. Freda loathed my sons, everyone knew it. She never stopped banging on about them. Probably because her own son Terry was such a bloody loser.

Freda started to rant, just like I knew she would. Every time I bumped into her, a similar situation would occur. '*I ain't scared of you, or those villainous sons of yours. Who do you think you are, eh? Coming in 'ere, giving it the high and mighty. It weren't so long ago you had nothing, like the rest of us. Dirty money, that's what you've got now. So best you get off your high horse.*'

I chuckled, thanked Maura again, nodded politely at the rest of the queue and calmly left the shop.

On the way home, I couldn't stop chuckling to myself. Freda was a card. Credit where it's due, mind, she certainly wasn't scared of me or my boys.

She was right about one thing though. It wasn't so long ago I had nothing. But thanks to that robbery I set up at the Huntingdon-Browns, things had changed.

My good mood evaporated when I bumped slap bang into June Tarbuck. '*Hello, my lovey. How you doing?*' *I asked. June looked terrible. She had lost so much weight since everything went wrong for her. Firstly, with Bonnie, and then her old man ending up in the loony bin.*

June explained she was moving and I squeezed her arm.

I liked her. She was a decent woman. 'I reckon you're doing the right thing, sweetheart. Where you moving to?'

'East Ham. Moving back in with my old mum. It'll do Adam good to start afresh. Life round here isn't the same for him without his sister. I can't wait to see the back of Whitechapel. Not brought us much luck, has it?'

I gave June a hug, wished her well for the future, then said goodbye to her.

Truth be told, I was glad to see the back of the woman. Reason being, five months after that fateful last date with my Vinny, Bonnie Tarbuck hung herself . . .

Queenie fed the birds, sat in the deck chair and shut her eyes. Her heart went out to June Tarbuck, it really did. There had been a rumour that Bonnie had been pregnant when she'd hung herself, but Queenie chose not to believe that. She would hate to think the poor girl was traumatized because she was carrying Vinny's child.

Vinny had shown no emotion whatsoever when Queenie had broken the news of Bonnie's death. He'd shrugged, mumbled, 'Shit happens' then swiftly changed the subject. Oh well, thought Queenie. Now June was moving they could put the whole sorry saga behind them and forget Bonnie had ever existed.

Since that unfortunate episode, Vinny had kept to his word. As far as Queenie was aware, he'd never dated another girl. He'd recently turned nineteen and had given up the long firm. Roy was now seventeen and he and Vinny worked together, ducking and diving. Her eldest two were so close these days, and that pleased Queenie immensely. Her boys had one another's backs and that's what family was all about.

The robbery Queenie had set up for the boys had set

the ball rolling. There hadn't been as much in that safe as she'd hoped there would be – turned out a couple of Pearl's diamond necklaces were as fake as she was. But there were also real diamonds, Basil's collection of expensive watches and plenty of other valuable stones and gold. The Kelly brothers introduced the boys to a diamond dealer who'd bought the whole haul off Vinny, including Basil's watches.

'All right, Mum?'

'What you doing, home so early?' Queenie asked. Her youngest son Michael would be sixteen later this year and was working in a local garage. Tinkering with cars and motorbikes was his passion in life. That and girls. Queenie dreaded to think how many girls he'd lured with his cheeky grin and charm. But she never worried about Michael dating, nor Roy. With Vinny things were different.

'My boss gave me the rest of the afternoon off 'cause he's going to a funeral. Starvin', I am. What we got for dinner?'

'Shit with sugar on it, and don't you dare sit on my furniture with those dirty overalls on, ya little grease monkey.' Michael wasn't little by any means. He'd shot up this past year or two, was nearly as tall as Roy who was six foot. Vinny was the tallest at six foot two.

'Me and Kev got a hot date tonight with two Mod birds we met. My one's a right little cracker,' Michael grinned.

'Be gone with you, you evil boy,' Queenie chuckled. Mary O'Leary used to say that when addressing Daniel back in the day.

'How much we got?' Roy asked Vinny. They'd robbed a container-load of TVs last week, hijacked the geezer driving the lorry at gunpoint, then tied him up and left him somewhere rural.

428

'There's a grand in that pile and eight fifty in this one,' Vinny pointed.

'I still think we should have asked more for 'em, Vin.'

'Nah. Best to get rid of 'em sharpish, especially seeing as they were hot, what with the robbery having been mentioned on the radio. The fact they're now up north suits us down to the ground.'

'Shall we go and put our new offer in then?' grinned Roy. They'd been trying to buy the snooker club for a while now, but Dick who owned it was asking a bloody fortune.

'Nah. The Kelly brothers are gonna visit Dick today, put the squeeze on him. Anyway, I gotta be somewhere,' Vinny replied, glancing at his watch.

'Where you off to?'

Vinny tapped his nose. 'To do a favour for Auntie Viv.'

Jeremy Johnson was already waiting in the car park when Vinny arrived. He was petrified. He was well aware that Vinny was a true force to be reckoned with these days. He'd even heard people at work talking about his exploits.

Vinny got out of his shiny black Jaguar Sedan and grinned as he got in the passenger seat of Jeremy's cheap car. Jeremy looked as scared as he had sounded on the phone when he'd finally managed to get hold of him yesterday. 'Good afternoon, Geoff. Oh, sorry, I meant Jeremy. How you doing, me old mucker?'

Desperately trying to stop his hands from shaking, Jeremy clenched them together. 'What do you want, Vinny? We had a deal when I gave you the keys to your mother's house. You said you were a man of your word and you wouldn't pester me again.'

'I'm not pestering ya and I am a man of my word, which is why I'm giving you this.'

Jeremy stared inside the envelope. It was filled with bank notes.

'There's two hundred and fifty quid in there. I need a favour for my dear Auntie Viv, you see. The old girl who lives next door but one to my mum croaked it the other day. My aunt would love that house. She's got a son with learning disabilities and she'd be made up to live so close to Mum. Her old man left her, ya see. Dumped her like an old bag of unwanted rubbish, a bit like Felicity would dump you if she ever found out you bat for the other side. So, do we have a deal?'

Jeremy handed the envelope back to Vinny. He had morals, unlike some, didn't take back-handers. 'I don't want your money, Vinny. I just want you to leave me alone. If I get you the keys for the house, will you promise never to contact me again?'

'Yep. You get me those keys and I swear on my dear mother's life, that'll be the last you see or hear of me.'

'OK. I'll do my best.'

'You need to do better than your best, cocker. Only I got my heart set on surprising my aunt with that house and when I don't get what I want, I get angry. You wouldn't like me when I'm angry.'

Jeremy gulped as Vinny got out of his car. His whole body was trembling as he drove away. A minute down the road Jeremy's bowels loosened and he shat himself. He rued the day he'd ever met Vinny Butler. The man was a menace.

'Don't you be making a fuss of him, Queenie. He's a dirty boy,' Viv fumed on her arrival, clouting her eight-year-old son around the head.

'Oh dear. What ya done now, Lenny?' giggled nine-year-old Brenda.

'Don't laugh,' Viv hissed. 'It ain't funny. He said he wanted a wee, I told him we'd be home soon and what does he do! Flops his dingle-dangle out and pisses in Old Mother Taylor's evergreens.'

Queenie laughed. She couldn't stand Old Mother Taylor. Her curtains were black and even her children looked frowsy.

'It ain't bleedin' funny. He'll get a reputation like that weirdo Peter, Jack's son, if he ain't careful. Have you heard what Peter did to young Lucy Potter, Queen? Saw her mother earlier. She called the police. She was livid, poor mare.'

The Potters lived down Queenie's road. A nice clean family and Lucy seemed a sweet girl. 'No. What happened?' Queenie asked, praying the poor girl hadn't been raped.

'Peter put his hand inside poor Lucy's knickers and then made her do things to him. Ya know, dirty things.'

'Lenny, Brenda, go and play in the garden for a minute, please.'

'No. Don't want to,' Brenda replied.

Brenda was the next to get a clout around the ear. An obstinate child who was becoming far too cocky for her own good of late. 'Get out there now,' Queenie said through gritted teeth. 'Else there'll be no tea for you and no TV.'

'Don't care,' Brenda retorted, grabbing Lenny's hand and running out in the garden before she received another clout.

'What did the police do?' Queenie asked Viv.

'Same as they always do: took Peter down the station, cautioned him and then let him go. Fucking disgusting, if you ask me. You should have a word with Freddie Angel. That boy needs locking up before he rapes or kills, the horrible dirty bastard.'

Queenie pursed her lips. Viv was right. It was only a matter of time before Peter did worse. He reminded her of a younger version of her own attacker. Awkward, clumsy and both were definitely not the full shilling. 'This can't go on, Viv. Poor Lucy. I'm gonna have a word with Vinny later. The police are useless. Vinny'll sort this out.'

Viv nodded. 'Good.'

Albie Butler grinned at his fancy piece and lit them both a cigarette.

'You better get dressed and make a move, love. The boys'll be home from football practice soon,' said Maureen.

'OK, sweetheart. We still on for Saturday night?'

'Yes. The boy's dad will be picking 'em up around lunchtime, so you can come round in the afternoon if you like. Ring me first like you usually do, mind, to check they're gone.' All the neighbours must know she had a man around regularly, but so far she'd managed to keep Albie and her sons apart. The relationship suited herself as much as Albie. The sex was great and Albie was good company. Maureen didn't want to remarry, liked her independence these days.

Albie stubbed his fag out and gave Maureen a kiss. What he didn't realize as he left the gaff, was that that kiss would be the last they'd ever share.

'How do I look, Mum?'

Queenie smiled. Both Vinny and Roy wore sharp suits from Savile Row and their hair Brylcreemed back. Michael had his own style though. He was a Mod, dressed in tonic suits, had sideburns and wore his hair flicked forward. 'You look very dapper, son.'

'Thanks. Right, I'll be off. Wish me luck. I think I'm onto a winner with this little Doris.'

'Behave your bleedin' self,' Queenie laughed.

Vinny and Roy walked in minutes later. 'You still giving your job up tomorrow, Mother?' asked Vinny. He'd been on at her for ages to tell her employees where to shove their poxy job as he was in a position to support her now.

'Yes. I shall be leaving 'em right in the lurch. I can't wait to see Pearl's face. Viv's coming with me. It's gonna be great entertainment.'

Vinny laughed. 'Make sure you're back 'ere in the afternoon. I got a surprise for you both.'

'What? We don't like surprises, do we, Queen?' Viv replied.

'Nope. We don't.'

'Have I got a surprise too?' enquired Lenny.

Vinny picked his nephew up and swung him in the air. 'You, Champ, had enough out of me last weekend when I took you and Brenda shopping.' Vinny grinned at his mother and aunt as he put Champ back down. 'I can assure you, you will like these surprises, won't they, Roy?'

Roy smiled. He was over the moon that a deal had finally been agreed for the snooker club. That miserable old bastard Dick had been asking four grand for it, but after a visit from the Kelly brothers had dropped his price to two and a half. Tomorrow they were picking the keys up and Vinny was also picking the keys up for the house next-door-but-one for their aunt. Vinny had somehow wangled that one on his own.

'Tell 'em about Lucy,' urged Viv.

Queenie ordered Lenny and Brenda to play outside again, then explained to her eldest two what Peter had done to Lucy.

'Fucking nonce,' spat Roy.

'That boy needs to be dealt with once and for all, Vinny. He gives me and Viv the willies when he leers at us in the cafe. As Viv said, it's only a matter of time before he murders a little girl.' Queenie purposely didn't mention the word rape.

'Don't worry, Mum. Peter will be dealt with good and proper this time. He's had his warning. I can assure you, by the time me and Roy have finished with him, he won't be noncing no other girls.'

'Good,' said Viv.

Queenie smiled. 'That's my boy.'

Later that evening, Queenie lay in bed unable to get June Tarbuck's haunted face out of her head.

She got up, put her hand inside her mattress and took out the envelope with the four hundred quid Patrick O'Leary had made her keep. Patrick hadn't wanted to take back any of the money she'd borrowed, he'd said it was a gift, but Queenie wasn't a ponce and after a playful argument, she'd paid him back only half the money.

Queenie opened her handbag and took out a pen.

To June
   A little something to help you settle into your new home.
   X

She knew June was skint, but didn't want the woman to know it was from her. She might see it as guilt money.

Queenie put her coat on over her nightdress, slipped her shoes on and walked down the road. There wasn't a soul about, it was nearly 3 a.m.

Queenie

Lifting June's letterbox so it wouldn't make a noise, Queenie popped the envelope through and walked away feeling a weight lifted from her shoulders. Giving June that money was the least she could do.

CHAPTER THIRTY-SEVEN

Vinny was with Roy, chomping on a bacon sandwich, when Harry Mitchell and his sons sauntered in the cafe. The Mitchells were out of Canning Town, another firm with a good name, who had their fingers in many pies.

Vinny nudged Roy, leapt up and shook hands with Harry, Ronnie, Paulie and Eddie. Roy then did the same.

The sons plonked themselves down on the next table while their dad ordered their grub. 'So what brings you out to our neck of the woods?' enquired Eddie.

'Don't worry. We ain't nicking any of your boozers,' Vinny laughed. 'Me and Roy have been to see a pal of mine, Nick. We got a bit of business he's interested in.' It was common knowledge that the Mitchells ran a pub protection racket in their area.

'A little birdy tells me you've bought the snooker club just off Whitechapel High Road,' Eddie smirked.

'Jesus wept! Good news travels fast, eh Roy? We ain't even picked the keys up yet.'

'Whaddya plan on doing with it?' grunted Ronnie.

Vinny liked Ronnie the least out of the Mitchell family. He was a known pisshead and had a reputation for being a pain in the arse. Eddie was the youngest out of the three brothers and, in Vinny's opinion, was more savvy than the other two put together. Vinny explained his and Roy's plans for the club, but not in huge detail.

'Cushty. You need any protection, you know where to come,' sneered Ronnie. He didn't like Vinny Butler, saw him as a kid who was becoming far too big for his boots.

'How's your mum doing, Vin?' Eddie didn't particularly know Queenie, but knew how close Vinny was to her. His own mum had unfortunately died when he was young.

'Yeah, Mum's good, thanks. Me old man don't change, mind. Still a drunken tosspot.' The dig was actually aimed at Ronnie. Vinny could tell he didn't like him.

'Nothing wrong with letting your hair down, cocker,' snapped Ronnie. 'You should try it sometime. I often see your old man in a boozer I drink in with his fancy piece, the lovely Maureen. Looks as happy as Larry to me.'

'Shut it, mouth almighty,' hissed Eddie.

Vinny stared Ronnie in his gloating eyes and leaned forward. 'Tell me more about my father and the lovely Maureen, please. In fact, tell me all you fucking know.'

Queenie travelled, deep in thought, to her employers' house for the very last time.

Pearl and Basil had been livid when they'd returned from holiday that time to find their safe ripped open and their beloved home ransacked. Queenie had worked round there the following Monday and Pearl was literally spitting feathers. 'Cockerknee scum! If I get my hands on those thieving toerags, I will chop their fucking hands off,' she'd raged.

How Queenie hadn't laughed that day she would never know, especially when she'd seen the Chesterfield furniture

Pearl had only recently bought, slashed to pieces. Her boys had even slashed up Basil's reading chair. Talk about do her proud!

Queenie was never suspected of having anything to do with the break-in. Pearl had no idea what her beloved sons were capable of. Queenie doubted she even knew their names. Vinny insisted a few months later that she give up her job, but Queenie decided to stick with it. She didn't want to ponce off her boys, liked to earn her own money.

Just lately, things had changed, though. Working for Pearl had become even more unbearable since her awful mother had moved in with her. The posh old hag treated Queenie like a slave rather than a cleaner. The batty cow literally followed her around the house barking out her orders, screaming this and that hadn't been cleaned properly.

'You're quiet. Not having second thoughts are you, Queen?' asked Viv.

Queenie chuckled. 'Not on your nelly!'

Tonight the Huntingdon-Browns were holding an extremely important dinner party for the old crow of a mother. All their posh friends were invited. After the years of misery she'd endured working for them, today was going to be so much fun. It truly was.

Pearl yanked open her front door so hard it nearly flew off its hinges. 'Over two hours late! Two hours and a quarter, to be exact, Queenie, on one of the most important days of my social calendar. How dare you do this to me! It's totally unacceptable.'

Pearl's eyes were blazing angrily just as Queenie had told Viv they'd be. 'And who is this, erm, woman?' asked Pearl, nodding her head towards Viv.

'Sorry for being late, Mrs Huntingdon-Brown, but as I told you on the phone my youngest was spewing her guts up last night,' Queenie lied. 'This is my sister. She's a cleaner too, so seeing as I know how important tonight is to you, Viv offered to help me. Two pairs of hands are better than one, so they say.'

Pearl looked Viv up and down as though she was something nasty she'd trod in. 'I hope you don't expect me to pay her?'

'Of course not, Mrs Huntingdon-Brown. Now do you want us to come in and clean, or stand like two eels on your doorstep all day?'

'Start in the kitchen, please. It's messy. I've been busy all morning, making my mother's favourite sherry trifle.'

'Fine. Is Mother not here then?' Queenie asked, her voice laden with sarcasm.

Viv nearly laughed, but covered it up well with a coughing fit. She had never met anyone like Pearl in her lifetime. The woman was far worse than Queenie had described.

'Basil's taken Mother out for the day, shopping in the West End. It's a surprise party, as I told you the other day.'

'Best we get cracking then, eh Viv?' said Queenie.

'Yep,' Viv replied, immediately overcome with the urge to laugh again. Somehow she managed to cover it with a coughing fit once more.

As Viv and Queenie walked inside the hallway, Pearl grabbed Queenie's arm. 'She isn't carrying any terrible diseases, your sister, is she? Nothing contagious, I mean.'

'No. She suffers badly from asthma,' lied Queenie.

Vinny Butler was raging. Not only had Ronnie Mitchell mugged him right off, it also turned out his father was mugging his mother off.

Vinny paced up and down inside the snooker club they'd just picked up the keys for. It now officially belonged to them. 'This should be one of the happiest days of my life, bruv. Our lives. He needs knocking spark out, does that cunt, Ronnie. So does the old man.'

Roy poured himself and Vinny a large Scotch on the rocks. Dick had wanted to hold on to the club for another week, so he could find a buyer for the worn-out snooker tables and shitty wooden furniture. Desperate to surprise their mum today, Vinny had refused and ended up giving him another two hundred quid to sign the papers immediately. 'I bought this bottle for us and the sherry for Mum and Auntie Viv to celebrate later, Vinny. Sit down, for Christ's sake, will ya? You can't go starting a war with the Mitchells. Ronnie is a prick, everyone knows that. As for Dad, don't do anything daft. He and Mum haven't even slept in the same bedroom for years.'

'That ain't the point, Roy.' Vinny drank his Scotch in one fell swoop. 'Dad ain't only making a fool of Mum parading his fancy piece around Upton Park and East Ham; he's making a mug of us an' all. Everyone knows how much we love Mum, so why are we letting that happen? I'm going to find Dad now. This needs to be dealt with immediately. No way is he seeing that Maureen again. If the old man needs to get his leg over in future, best he goes outside the area and shags brasses like I fucking do.'

'Queenie! The kitchen really isn't up to your usual standard. Who cleaned it? You or your sister?' screamed Pearl.

Queenie winked at Viv. 'I'll go over it again now, Mrs Huntingdon-Brown. We both cleaned it, but the house looks so dirty today, we thought we'd better get cracking on your other rooms, seeing as you have guests coming.'

'Dirty! What do you mean by dirty? My house is always clean. I don't live in the slums you pair come from.'

'Right, that's it,' Queenie said quietly. She threw her feather duster down and gestured to Viv. 'That's the vase – supposedly it cost thousands. Wait until I shout out to you, then you drop it on the fireplace and smash the bastard. In the meantime, I'm going back to the kitchen to do even more damage. I've already spat in Mother's favourite sherry trifle for an extra treat.'

As her sister left the room, Viv held her sides. Today had been so funny, she ached from laughing.

Knowing all his father's haunts via the grapevine, Vinny finally caught up with him in The Artichoke in Stepney. His dad was doing his usual Friday lunchtime thing, selling fags and tobacco to earn his beer money, the loser.

Albie was at the bar supping a pint when his eldest son tapped him on the shoulder. 'Me and you, outside now,' were Vinny's exact words.

Thoroughly embarrassed, Albie excused himself from the men he was talking to and warily trotted outside. He had a feeling he'd done something wrong, as not only did Vinny have a face like thunder; he never usually bothered with him these days. Albie could not even remember the last time they'd had a proper conversation. 'You all right, boy?'

Vinny grabbed hold of his father and slammed him as hard as he could against the pub's brick wall. 'You and Maureen are over, under fucking stand? Because if any more of my mates see you out with that slapper, I will not only kill her, I will fucking kill her kids an' all. You don't mug me off like that, nor my brothers, and especially our mum. You are a useless piece of shit, you always have

441

been. No father of mine, you ain't. But I'm lumbered with ya, aren't I? So in future, you do as I say, OK? If you need to get any action for that shrivelled up old cock of yours, you go out the area and go to a brass. You never disrespect my name again.'

'Butler is my name too,' Albie replied bravely. 'And nothing is going on with me and Maureen. She's just a mate who I have a drink with. I swear to you, boy, she's only a friend. I miss female company. Not as though your mother ever wants to come out with me any more, is it?'

Vinny put his hand around his father's throat and gripped it tightly. 'Friend or lover, you never see Maureen again. 'Cause if you do, you'll regret it big time. My mum is my world; you've never been a dad to me. In fact, I hate you, you skinny-gutted tosser. You do as I say.'

Albie looked into his son's evil unblinking eyes. They were bright green just like his, but unlike his own, held no warmth. Always the coward, Albie took the easy path. 'I get the message. I'll stay away from Maureen, lad.'

Vinny kneed his dad as hard as he could in the nuts, leaving him crouched on the pavement in obvious distress. 'I'm glad we understand one another, Daddy Dearest. Enjoy the rest of your day.'

In agony, clutching his privates, Albie looked up as his son strutted off. This was all Queenie's fault. Vinny was a monster and she'd made him that way.

On the train going home, Queenie and Viv were in such hysterics, all the other commuters were looking at them and some were laughing too.

'Let's have one in the pub, Queen, before we go back to yours,' Viv suggested as they got off the train at Whitechapel.

Queenie wasn't one to venture into the pub usually, but today had been so funny, she felt full of beans. 'Those prawns we hid will start stinking by tonight, Viv, in this hot weather,' she chuckled. 'As for Mother's sherry trifle, I hope it goes down well. We'll have one in the pub and then get home 'cause of the boys. I wonder what surprises we have in store?'

Viv chuckled. 'Whatever it is, it won't be as much of a surprise as when I smashed Pearl's favourite vase to smithereens. The look on her face was fucking priceless.'

'You all right, ladies? Ready for your surprises?' Vinny grinned.

'You ain't sozzled, are ya?' asked Roy. His mum and aunt were giggling away like two silly teenagers.

'We had a couple in the Grave Maurice, but only to celebrate,' Queenie chuckled. 'You should have seen Pearl's face when I told her to shove her shitty job up her arsehole, just after Viv purposely smashed her favourite vase that was apparently worth thousands. The house ain't even clean, boys. Viv and I only cleaned a couple of rooms. We created havoc. It was Viv's idea to shove the prawns down the back of her new sofa and the guest's beds. They'll be chucking up by tomorrow, let me tell you.'

Wetting herself with laughter, Viv punched Queenie playfully on the arm. 'Oh and it was your mother's idea to spit in the sherry trifle.'

'You didn't spit in the trifle, Mum?' Roy asked, shocked.

Vinny smiled. He felt OK now. Roy was right. Starting a war with the Mitchells over Ronnie's comments wasn't worth it. The main thing was, he'd found out the truth. Since he'd confronted his father, he was on a high again. The high he should have been on all day. 'That's a classic,

Mum. Serves the posh arseholes right for treating you with disrespect all those years. Now, are you two ready for these surprises? They're the nuts, trust me,' Vinny teased, dangling two sets of keys.

Brenda and Lenny leapt up. 'Can we come too?' they asked in unison.

'Pinky and Perky, you two are. Come on then,' Viv said, unsteadily standing up and cuddling her son. Those sherries had gone straight to her head.

Vinny gestured his mum, aunt, Roy, Champ and Brenda to follow him. Michael was still at work in that shitty garage. He wouldn't be working there much longer, mind, as Vinny had other plans for him.

'What we doing 'ere?' Queenie asked, as Vinny opened the door to Eva's house. Queenie hadn't been close to Eva, poor woman had been off her rocker. She'd only died this past week.

The house was a new build, same as Queenie's. Vinny handed his aunt the keys. 'Welcome to your new home, Auntie Viv. It's all yours, sweetheart.'

Viv and Queenie were still emotional when Vinny and Roy led them away from Viv's new home towards the snooker club.

'I can't believe it, Queen. I really can't. It's the home I've always dreamed of, and we'll be neighbours.'

Queenie squeezed her sister's hand. 'My boys are the best. I raised them right.'

'Will Dad know where we are in our new house, Mum?' asked Lenny.

'Yes. If Daddy wants to find us, he'll still be able to,' Viv replied patiently. Her son was doing OK in school, but it was clear that his mental age wasn't up there with the other children. That's why Viv had decided to wait until Lenny was older to tell him the truth about his father. Hopefully then he would understand.

'Why you bringing us in 'ere?' Queenie asked, as her son opened the door to the snooker hall around the corner.

Vinny urged his brother to pour the drinks, like they'd planned earlier. They'd even purchased bottles of ginger beer, knowing the kids might be with them.

Roy handed his family their drinks and urged them to raise their glasses.

Vinny grinned as they did so. 'Thanks to you, Mum, and the way you raised us, today Roy and I finally achieved our dreams. We've bought this gaff and we're gonna turn it into a proper palace. It's gonna be blinding.'

Queenie's eyes welled up, just as Viv's had done earlier when she'd been shown around her new home. She stood on tiptoes and hugged both her boys around the neck. 'My babies. My boys. I can't tell you how over the moon I am. You've cracked it.'

Later that evening, Vinny and Roy were plotted up in a cheap green van they'd purchased via the Kelly brothers. Thanks to Brenda, they'd known the best place to wait to capture their prey. Apparently, of an evening the pervert hung out with another weirdo who lived in the opposite direction.

''Ere he comes,' said Roy.

Vinny checked the coast was clear before grabbing hold of Peter Davidson and shoving him in the back of the van.

Peter was stunned. 'What you doing, Vinny?'

Ordering Roy to drive, Vinny tied up Peter's arms and legs.

Knowing what Vinny was all about, Peter started to panic. 'I'll never do anything wrong again, I promise ya. I just wanna go home to my mum and dad now. Please let me go. What am I meant to have done?'

'Lucy Potter ring a bell to ya, does she?' Vinny spat. 'You're a wrong un, lad. My sister and her pals ain't safe around the likes of you.'

Realizing he was in big trouble, Peter started to whimper like an injured dog. 'But I ain't even touched your sister, I never would.'

'Shut it,' Vinny hissed, as he punched Peter in the side of the head.

In the driver's seat, Roy was feeling wary. 'Take it easy, bruv.'

'I am gonna do what is right this time, Roy. This scumbag isn't someone we want living on our patch.'

'I'm gonna walk round to Mum's, Queenie. She weren't in when I popped round hers yesterday and I must have rung her ten times today and she isn't answering her phone.'

'Probably out preaching with those fruitcake mates of hers,' Queenie snapped.

'Don't be nasty. You might not be in touch with Mum much, but I bloody am. She's always in on a Thursday afternoon when I go round there. I'm afraid something ain't right.'

Queenie downed the rest of her sherry. Today had been one of the best days of her life. She'd told Pearl where to shove her job and not only had her boys achieved their dreams, they'd achieved hers too. Vinny was the instigator in purchasing that club, she knew that much and was so bloody proud of him. 'OK. I'll come round Mum's with you. There'll be sod all wrong with her though. There never is.'

Vinny pulled the tape off Peter's mouth. They were now in a nice secluded lock-up, thanks to the Kelly brothers helping him out.

'Please don't hurt me,' Peter sobbed. 'I will never touch any girls again, I swear.'

Vinny grabbed the lad by the throat. 'I warned you once, didn't I, Peter lad, and you disrespected me by not taking my advice.'

'I'm sorry, Vinny. I'll never disrespect you again, I promise. Please can you just take me home to my mum and dad now? They'll be worried where I am.'

Violence was a turn-on for Vinny. He could feel his cock starting to stir.

'What you doing, Vin?' Roy asked. He was still sitting in the driver's seat.

Vinny punched the lad again. He was on a roll now. 'Can you swim, kiddy fiddler?'

Fifteen-year-old Peter was petrified. 'No. I can't swim. Please take me back to the cafe. I beg you.'

Vinny grabbed the lad's neck and had a full-blown erection as he tightened his grip and watched the life seep out of him.

'For fuck's sake, Vin. Enough's enough,' warned Roy.

Ignoring his brother, Vinny kept on squeezing as the lad's face turned beetroot. He didn't release him until he stopped choking and went still.

Roy was in bits by the time Vinny jumped back in the van. He'd watched in the interior mirror as Vinny checked for a pulse, then lugged Peter's lifeless body out. 'What the fuck! You've killed him, ain't ya? I don't think Mum and Auntie Viv meant us to do that. We can't leave him here.'

Vinny squeezed his brother's arm. 'Mum and Auntie Viv meant exactly that. You've got a lot to learn, bruv. Let's leave him 'ere tonight, come back tomorrow, weigh the nonce-case down and chuck him in the Thames. Job done. Don't feel bad about it, Roy. The streets'll be a lot safer for the likes of our Brenda and her friends.'

Vivian pulled the key from under her mother's plant pot. She'd knocked on the door again and there'd still been no answer. 'You ready, Queen?'

Queenie nodded.

The two sisters walked inside the house hand in hand. Molly Wade was dead in the armchair with her knitting still in her hand.

'Mum. Oh, Mum,' sobbed Vivian.

Queenie hugged her sister. She felt none of the raw emotion she'd experienced when Mrs O'Leary died. She couldn't even cry.

CHAPTER THIRTY-EIGHT

'You OK, my dear? What a lovely send-off for your dear mum. She's gonna be sorely missed down this street, let me tell ya. Molly had such a good heart, was always bringing food for me and a lot of the older generation. Since I lost my Peggy, there's many a day she'd turn up at the door with a roast dinner on a plate or a slice of her wonderful date and walnut cake. An angel, she was. I couldn't fault her,' said Mr Shipton.

Queenie smiled politely, patted Mr Shipton's arm and walked over to where Vinny and Roy were. Today was the day of her mother's funeral and it had been Viv's idea to hold the wake back at her mum's house. The house that held so many dreadful memories for Queenie, especially after Mary had died. She'd hated going round there. It reminded her of Aunt Edna, her drunken bully of a father, the hardship during the war years. Very few happy memories had been made there.

Vinny put a strong arm around his mother's shoulders. 'You all right, sweetheart?'

'Yeah, feet are bleedin' killing me though. Gonna take

these new stilettos back to Blind Keith. He's definitely got the size wrong. I've crippled meself.'

Vinny chuckled. 'What have I warned you about buying hooky goods off Blind Keith. Not only do I believe he can see better than me and you, I know for a fact he changes the sizes in stuff. I've seen him do it with me own eyes. I'll take the shoes back for you tomorrow and get you a refund plus compensation.'

'Thanks, boy. Where's Michael?'

'He shot off half an hour ago. Got another little dolly bird on the firm. As soon as he grows out of this wanting to shag the arse out of every girl he meets, Roy and I will take him on as a partner at the club. I know it's early days, but we've already spoken about it. I'm determined to turn the snooker club into a proper little drinking den, a classy one. It's gonna take me time to save up for the proper furniture I want. I plan to get the club up and running first, have a big opening night in a couple of weeks, then move upwards from there. We'll get Christmas out the way, build up the custom and by this time next year, that club will look the bollocks, trust me.'

Queenie stroked her number one son's cheek, 'I got every faith in you, boy. Ever since you said your first words, I knew you were going places.'

Roy walking over spelled the end of the intimate moment between Mother and her firstborn. 'I'm gonna shoot off, Mum, if that's OK? I got a date tonight.'

'Yes. Fine, love.' Queenie patted her second eldest's arm. 'And thanks for helping out today.' She and Viv had cooked and prepared all the food and the boys had brought it round to her mum's in Vinny's car. The boys had also bought all the alcohol and soft drinks. They'd seen her mum off in style.

Vinny snarled, 'This is the third time this week he's seen this Alice bird. I've told him to concentrate on the club, but does he listen? Nope. You need to talk some sense into him, Mum, like you did with me that time. We need to put our all into this new business venture. Birds are nothing but an unwanted distraction.'

'You ain't my keeper, Vin. I am allowed a social life an' all. She's a nice girl Alice, but I ain't planning on proposing to her, if that's what you're worried about.'

Queenie squeezed both of her sons' hands. 'Now is neither the time nor the place for disagreements, boys. Not at your nan's wake.'

Mr Ricketts walked over to Queenie and her sons. 'You did your mum proud, Queenie, it was a lovely send off. The sun shone for her too. Molly loved the sun, would spend hours in her garden knitting and crocheting when the weather was warm. I have to make a move now, lovey. My Nora can barely walk these days. I can't leave her for too long.'

'Sorry to hear that, Mr Ricketts. Give my love to Nora and thanks for coming today,' replied Queenie.

''Ere, they still ain't found Old Jack's boy, Peter. Been nearly a week now since the lad went missing. The cafe's shut for the time being, but I bumped into Jack round the Paki shop. In bits he was, had tears streaming down his face. Such a shame. Not looking good though, is it?'

Roy glanced at Vinny, who didn't glance back. 'It must be very worrying for the family, Mr Ricketts, but sometimes kids do run away, then come home again. I'm sure Peter's OK. Roy and me are gonna join up with the search the neighbours have organized tomorrow to try and find the lad.'

Roy looked at Vinny in horror. This was the first he'd

heard of this. How could Vinny even contemplate joining up with the search?

'That's very good of you, lads, giving your time up like that. I know how busy you two are these days,' smiled Mr Ricketts.

'My boys are never too busy to help a family in need. That's the way I raised them,' Queenie replied.

Roy glanced at his watch. 'I really do have to dash now.' He glared at Vinny. 'I'll speak to you later.'

When Roy and Mr Ricketts left, Queenie started chatting to Vinny about her trip to the school to see the headmaster. Brenda was turning into a proper little tomboy. She'd had a fight with a boy who'd stolen Lenny's school bag and had broken the bully's nose.

'Serves the lad right, Mum. Brenda did good. A chip off the old block,' grinned Vinny.

Queenie smiled. She had no idea what her sons had done to or with young Peter, and she had no wish to know. As long as the perverted teenager wouldn't be attacking any other young girls, that's all that mattered.

An hour later, Queenie said an awkward goodbye to the vicar and her mother's church friends. She could sense they saw her as Molly's awful foul-mouthed daughter, but they were polite nevertheless.

'Sing Molly's favourite song, Albie. She would love that, and you sing it so beautifully,' shouted Lily Turner.

When Albie began belting out 'You Are My Sunshine', Vinny rolled his eyes at his mother. 'That's me outta here. I can't be listening to him for the next fucking hour or so.'

'Me neither. Once he starts singing, he never knows when to bleedin' stop. Let's just listen to this one song, mind. It'll look bad if we walk out, seeing as the old goat is singing it for your nan.'

Albie got a rapturous round of applause at the end of the song, so sang 'Daisy Daisy' next.

Queenie walked over to her sister. 'I'm gonna make a move, Viv. Brenda's tired and me feet are bleedin' killing me. Vinny's gonna drop me home. You want a lift too? Been a long old day, hasn't it?'

Vivian looked at her sister in amazement. 'We can't just leave. There's several people still 'ere. And how can you say it's been a long day? This is our mother's wake.'

'I didn't mean it like that, Viv.'

'Oh yes you did. From the moment Mrs O'Leary moved across the road and you became friendly with her, she became a mum to you and you stopped loving your own. You make me sick at times, Queenie. You're so bloody selfish. Go on, sod off home. I don't want you 'ere and neither would Mum.'

The following morning, much to Roy's dismay, Vinny insisted they must join Peter's family, friends and their neighbours in the search for him. 'Look, this is the third search and if we don't turn up again, it'll look weird,' Vinny explained.

'But I can't face his parents, not after what you did. I can't look 'em in the eyes, Vin.'

'I think you mean what *we* did. What did you think was gonna happen when we snatched him off the street? Did you think we were gonna give him ten whacks on each hand with a fucking ruler or something? You need to man up, bruv. We're going on the search whether you like it or not, so best you get your act together, sharpish.' Queenie knocked at Viv's house. The boys had moved her and Lenny into their lovely new home a few days before their mum's funeral. There was no answer so, deep in thought, Queenie walked towards The Waste.

She had barely slept last night. She hated rowing with Viv. She also felt a tad guilty. Would it really have hurt her to stay at the wake until the end?

It had been a weird time for Queenie since finding her mother dead. Viv had been tearful, but she hadn't cried at all until a few tears had finally run down her cheeks during the actual service yesterday. Her mum's death had brought back memories of Mary's death, and Queenie had been reminded of that awful sense of loss, knowing she would never see or speak to Mary again. Mary had never appeared to her in her dreams again. That was a one-off. It certainly hadn't been a figment of her imagination though, Queenie was sure of that. She hadn't mentioned anything about that experience to Viv or the boys. It was too personal. But she felt bad about speaking to her mum the way she had and showing her up in front of her friends. Her mum hadn't meant to sell the bloody beads, it had been an accident and she'd felt awful about it afterwards.

'Hello, Queen. So sorry to hear about your mum, love. I hope you received my condolence card? And my flowers arrived OK yesterday?' asked Freddie Angel.

'Yes. Both arrived, thank you. Beautiful words you wrote in the card, Freddie, and that wonderful arrangement of flowers must've cost you a fortune.'

'I wanted to attend the funeral, but we've been so busy at work, searching for young Peter Davidson, that today is my first day off since the lad went missing.'

'My Vinny and Roy are helping with the search today. Hopefully the lad will turn up safe and well soon.'

'I'm not sure he will, Queenie. Peter's behaviour toward

young girls had unfortunately made him quite a few enemies. I hope we get some closure though, for his parents' sake.'

'Me too,' Queenie lied.

'Are you busy today, Queen? Only I could really do with some advice from a friend and I can't think of anybody better to spill me guts to than you.'

Wanting to take her mind off other things, Queenie told Freddie she wasn't busy.

'Brilliant. How about I pick you up and we go for a nice lunch somewhere? Just as friends, I promise,' Freddie grinned. 'There's a new lady in my life now, one whom I'm very fond of, which is why I need your advice.'

'Lunch sounds fine, but don't pick me up from home, Freddie, and we'll have to drive away from the area somewhere. You know how people talk round 'ere. I'll jump on the tube and you can pick me up outside Bow Road station at twelve. That all right?'

The real reason Queenie wanted to keep their lunch undercover was because she knew Vinny would kick off if she was spotted out with Freddie. Vinny didn't like her being friendly with him, had ordered her to knock that particular friendship on the head because it didn't look good, his mother associating with the filth.

It had actually occurred to Queenie to tell Vinny that Freddie had once saved her from a long prison stretch, but she'd kept her gob shut. Betraying Freddie's trust would be unforgivable and knowing how her eldest's brain ticked, she wouldn't put it past Vinny to use any knowledge he had about Freddie to his own advantage.

'Hello, Jack. How you holding up, mate?' said Vinny, greeting the father of the boy he'd murdered.

Jack's eyes welled up. 'Not good, lad, if I'm honest. The

wife's in bits, spends all day looking out the window expecting Peter to walk in. She's adamant he's still alive, but I'm not. I can't help but fear the worst. Peter would never worry us like this. It'd be totally out of character for him to have run away.'

'Well, let's hope we get some answers on today's search. Sorry Roy and I couldn't make the last two. We've just bought the local snooker club and we're trying to knock that into shape so we can open it.'

'I understand. It's good of you to be here today, lads.'

'I wouldn't be thanking them,' piped up Freda Smart. She pointed at Vinny. 'Wouldn't surprise me if he had something to do with Peter's disappearance.'

'Oh, 'ere she goes, spouting shit as per usual. We hardly knew the lad, ya nutter,' said Vinny.

Having been unable to look Peter's father in the eye, Roy decided he'd better say something too. 'We only knew Peter from the cafe. Vinny and me are here 'cause we wanna help find the lad.'

Freda pointed at Vinny again. 'You don't fool me. I know you better than you think, Sonny Jim.'

Vinny glared at the woman. 'You don't know me at all, darlin'. Show some respect for Peter's friends and family who are worried sick about him. Your conspiracy theories are a figment of that notright imagination of yours.'

'Yeah, shut it, Freda. Vinny and Roy are busy lads. It's good of 'em to help us,' shouted Ronny Tobyn, a drinking buddy of Albie's.

Others who liked, feared or respected Vinny and Roy, also backed them up.

'Why don't you go home, Freda? Jack don't need all this nonsense you've created,' said Ronny Tobyn.

'Yeah. Go home, Freda,' shouted another man.

'Bollocks to the lot of ya then,' Freda bellowed, as she stomped off down the road.

Minutes later, the search for Peter began. Vinny put an arm around his brother's shoulders. 'See. Told you it would be all right, didn't I?' he whispered in Roy's ear.

That was the first time Roy actually wondered if Vinny was mad. It wasn't all right at all. They were about to spend the next however many hours searching for and talking about a lad whose dead body they'd slung in the Thames.

Later that evening, Queenie guessed that Viv hadn't been home since the funeral and was still around their mum's house. She'd let herself into Viv's after getting no answer again and could see no sign of her funeral outfit or Lenny's smart black suit.

Queenie walked towards her mother's, thinking about her lunch with Freddie. He was such a nice man and she was pleased he'd found love with a new lady. He and Sheila Ricketts had never been well suited and her advice to Freddie had been to leave the miserable cow and start afresh with his new love. 'True love is hard to find, Freddie. I should bleedin' well know. Your kids aren't little uns any more. They'll be able to visit you whenever. You deserve to be happy,' Queenie had told him, thinking of Daniel O'Leary.

Queenie knocked on her mum's door. The lights were on, 'Viv, it's me. You in there, love?' Queenie had wanted to speak to her sister in person, rather than on the phone.

Lenny opened the front door. 'Hello, Auntie Queenie. Me and Mum have been sorting all Nan's clothes out to go in the church jumble.'

Viv was sitting on the living room floor, surrounded by boxes. 'Oh, it's you.'

'I was worried about you. Have you not been home since yesterday?'

'Lenny popped home at lunchtime to get us both a change of clothes. I wanted to get Mum's stuff sorted. Not like I've got a sister who'll help me, is it?' Viv snapped.

'I'm sorry about yesterday. You were right; I shouldn't have left you at the wake. I just hate this house, Viv, and all the bad memories it holds. I would've helped you sort Mum's things out though. You shouldn't be doing this alone. Let me give you a hand.'

'No point. I'm nearly done. It's not just you who has bad memories of this house, ya know. I grew up here too.'

'I know and I'm sorry.'

Viv delved inside her handbag and handed Queenie a letter. 'Mum left us one each. I've already read mine.'

Queenie stared at the envelope as though she was looking at her mother's ghost. 'What did it say, yours?'

'Just said how much she loved me and Lenny, and how proud of me she was for kicking Bill out and raising Lenny alone. She also said she wished she'd had my strength and kicked our dad out so our childhoods could have been happier.'

'Why did Nan say that about my dad?' piped up Lenny.

'Because she knew he was a useless, womanizing tosspot,' hissed Viv. She refused to fanny around painting a pretty picture of Bill any more. Lenny was old enough now to be told the bloody truth. Not once had his father ever tried to make contact with Lenny over the years. The man was a scumbag as far as Viv was concerned.

'You gonna open it then?' Viv asked her sister.

Queenie's hands trembled as she took the letter out of its envelope.

Dear Queenie,

By the time you read this letter, I will no longer be with you in person, but I want you to know I will always be with you in spirit, my darling daughter.

Firstly, I want to apologize to you for the awful childhood you endured. I was a terrible mother, putting you and Vivvy through that, but I was a weak woman. My main concern was we'd never manage financially if I chucked your dad out. I also knew he would always roll back like a bad penny. Looking back, I know I made the wrong decision and I hope one day you will find it in your heart to forgive me.

Queenie took out her handkerchief and blew her nose. She then continued to read on.

I always loved you Queenie, so very much. I knew you always saw Mrs O'Leary as a mother too and I can fully understand why you loved her more than me. I was hurt by that at first, very upset. At times I felt as though Mrs O'Leary had stolen my daughter, but as I write this letter I am glad you had your other mum in your life too. She turned you into the wonderful strong woman you became. Not me. I'm grateful to Mrs O'Leary for teaching you everything that I couldn't. She was somebody you could look up to in life, unlike myself. I'm very sorry for feeling envious of your relationship with her. It was only when I started going to church that I realized envy is one of the seven deadly sins.

I know you never understood why I turned to the Church. The truth is, I was never that religious, but the vicar and my new friends in the church brought a comfort to my life that had been missing until then. Also, the Church taught me to believe in life after death. I was determined not to go to hell, as I'm sure that's where your father will be. So every Sunday I would pray for forgiveness in hope I would be allowed in heaven instead. I was desperate to see Edna again, you see. Hopefully, by the time you read this letter, Edna and I are together having a singsong and knees-up, just like the good old days. I will do my very best to send you a sign, Queenie, so you know I'm with Aunt Edna and we're both OK. I know how much it would mean to you to know Aunt Edna is all right.

Please send my love to Vinny, Roy, Michael and Brenda. I wish all of them happy and healthy lives. Also give my regards to Albie, please. Whatever your thoughts on him, Albie has a good heart.

There is so much more I want to say to you, darling, but if I carry on writing, it will turn into a book and I don't want to bore you.

Therefore, my final words to you are, try to remember the good times if you think of me in the future. Our hop-picking days in Kent, the laughs we had at the beach in Southend. Think of the pre-war days, my love. The good old days.

Stay healthy and be happy, my beautiful firstborn.
Your loving Mum, Molly xx

PS I forgot to mention Mrs O'Leary's rosary beads. I am so sorry I lost those for you. Never in a million years would I have done such a dreadful thing on purpose. Please forgive me for that mistake too. I don't expect you to love or cry over me. But if you

Queenie

could forgive me for all my sins, I would be a very happy lady looking down on you. Xx

Tears streamed down Queenie's cheeks. She might not have looked up to her mother, but she realized now she had loved her, deeply.

CHAPTER THIRTY-NINE

I still felt dreadful when I woke up the following morning. Try as I might, I couldn't get that letter out of my head. Mum had obviously seen herself as totally worthless. I'd have given anything to spend one more day with her, make her feel special; tell her how wonderful and loved she actually was. But I'd left it too late. Years too late, in fact. I felt gutted and empty inside.

I waved Brenda off to school and made myself a cuppa. I was just about to drink it when Vinny came bounding in like a bull in a china shop. 'Whatever's the matter?' I asked.

Vinny smashed his fist so hard against the kitchen worktop, some of my tea slopped out of the cup. 'I know you've been out having romantic lunches with a pig, I thought I told you to stay away. Shagging him are ya, Mother?'

'Don't talk so bleedin' daft. Freddie is a friend. He needed some advice, that's all,' I said. I couldn't believe we went all the way to Barking for lunch and I was still caught out.

Vinny was raging, his eyes glinting dangerously as he

approached me. 'Don't you fucking lie to me. I've seen the way he looks at you, reefing around you like a lovelorn puppy. Now tell me what's really going on. Why you sneaking off to Barking with him?' Vinny snarled.

For the first time in my life, I felt wary of my own son. 'I'm not lying to you. I bumped into Freddie yesterday morning. He's met a new love, wanted my advice on what he should do, so I agreed to go for lunch with him. That's it. I swear on my life.'

Vinny punched the wall right next to my head. 'Now listen to me and listen to me good and proper. It really don't look good on me when pals of mine tell me my mother is out gallivanting with Old Bill. Straight Old Bill, might I add. I'm telling you now – and I mean this with all my heart – if I hear you've been out with your boyfriend again, I will kill the bastard.'

I flinched as Vinny produced a small handgun and began waving it under my nose. 'Don't you dare threaten me or Freddie,' I seethed. 'I'm your mother, show some respect. You've got a bloody short memory, Vinny. Think of all the things I've done for you over the years. All the alibis I've given you. I even set up the burglary at the Huntingdon-Browns to give you and Roy a leg-up. As for covering for you over Bonnie, d'ya know how hard it was for me to look June Tarbuck in the face after what you did? Even more so when the poor girl hung herself. She was rumoured to be pregnant, an' all. Bet you didn't know that, did ya?'

'Like I give a shit about Bonnie fucking Tarbuck. Good riddance to bad rubbish is what I say.'

'Have you got no feelings?' I slapped him hard around the face. 'You disgust me at times, d'ya know that?'

'Well it was you who raised me to become what I am. Remember all those bedtime stories, Mother? King of the

jungle, king of the wilds, king of the East End, king of the fucking castle. You mapped out my future from the cradle, a future that would benefit you.'

'What do you mean by that?' I bellowed. 'Everything I've ever done, I've done it for you.'

'And you,' Vinny smirked nastily. 'Got a nice house, lovely furniture, plenty of money and a good life now, ain't ya? You don't even have to pay for your shopping when you get called to the front of the shop like royalty. That's what you always wanted. You can't kid a kidder, Mother.'

I could feel the tears running down my cheeks. Vinny had never spoken to me that way before. I was in shock, and utterly disgusted with him.

'You can stop with the waterworks, Mother. I ain't getting the violin out. Hard as nails, you. You didn't even cry when Nan died. You don't fool me.'

'Get out!' I screamed. 'Get out of my house and don't come back. You and I are finished, boy.'

Vinny put his face close to mine. His breathing was heavy. I could smell whisky. 'Good. About time I cut the apron strings from you, Mrs Manipulative. But believe me; if I ever catch you even talking to that pig again, those kids of his will be fatherless. Got me?'

Sobbing, I slid down the wall and put my head in my hands. 'Just get out,' I repeated.

As the front door slammed behind him, I could only sit there, broken-hearted and helpless.

For the first time it occurred to me that Albie might be right. In raising Vinny the way I did, I'd created a monster.

Queenie spent the rest of the morning and early afternoon in deep shock. The awful things Vinny had said were not only upsetting, they were totally untrue. From the moment

Vinny was born, she'd only wanted the best for him. Same as her other three. It had never crossed her mind to raise her children for her own personal gain.

As for Vinny spouting off about Freddie Angel, the troubling thing was, she would have to avoid Freddie like the plague in future. She had no doubt that Vinny was capable of carrying out his threat and she'd never forgive herself if anything happened to the poor man or his kiddies. Freddie had risked his own livelihood to save her, and she'd never forget that.

Queenie poured herself a sherry. Manipulative and hard, that's what Vinny had called her. Well, if she was hard it was because life had made her that way. She had nothing to be ashamed of on that score.

'Cooey.'

The tap on the window made Queenie jump. It was her neighbour, Nosy Hilda from the house opposite, the last person she fancied talking to today. She yanked open the front door, glass in hand.

'Ooh, drinking in the daytime. Something wrong?' pried Hilda.

'No. Whaddya want? Only, I'm busy.'

'No need to be snappy with me. I just thought you'd want to know the police have found Peter Davidson's body. Murdered, by all accounts. He was fished out the Thames a couple of hours ago. Poor Jack and Ethel. I'll start a collection tomorrow for some flowers.'

'OK. Sorry to hear the bad news. Send Ethel and Jack my regards if you see them. Bye, Hilda.'

Queenie shut the door and leaned against it. The gossip-mongers were bound to be out in force, speculating how Peter had ended up in the Thames. She could do without listening to their tittle-tattle.

An idea forming in her mind, Queenie searched for the number of Patrick O'Leary's club. A trip to Ireland to visit Mary's grave might be just the tonic she needed.

That evening, Queenie felt a bit better as she packed a small case. In her whole life she'd never been further afield than Kent, for hop-picking, or Southend. She couldn't wait to see the country Mary was raised in and pay her friend a long overdue visit at her graveside.

'I can't believe you're going all that way,' Viv said. 'I'd be too scared, me. You going because you rowed with Vinny?'

Queenie had admitted she and Vinny had argued, but only over her going to lunch with Freddie. She couldn't bring herself to repeat the horrendous things her eldest had said to her, not even to Viv. 'Partly. But I was also thinking about all the gossip that's bound to be doing the rounds now Peter's been found. I can't be arsed listening to all that. On top of that, Mum's letter's been playing on my mind. I think a break might do me good.'

'I ain't 'arf gonna miss ya.'

'I'll only be gone for a few days, Viv. Four at the most. Patrick's got some business to attend to out there, so I'll be looked after. I'll be home before you know it.'

'Will Daniel be out there?'

'I don't know if I'll see him,' lied Queenie, feeling that usual fluttering in her stomach. 'He is living in Ireland, and apparently he's got himself into a bit of bother. That's why Patrick is going over there – to sort it out.'

'I see you're taking all your posh frocks just in case,' chuckled Viv.

'Bren, Lenny, answer that door,' shouted Queenie. Roy and Michael were both out on dates.

'It's Vinny,' shouted Lenny.

Queenie pursed her lips. 'Wait there,' she ordered Viv, slamming her bedroom door. 'Get in the front room and shut the door,' she told Brenda and Lenny.

'But I wanna see Vinny,' Lenny argued.

'Do as I say. Now!' bellowed Queenie.

Vinny had a massive bouquet in one hand, chocolates in the other and a sheepish look on his face. 'Mum, I'm sorry. I didn't mean—'

'Save your fucking breath,' spat Queenie, as she pushed him out the door. 'And you can stick the flowers and chocolates up your arsehole. You hurt me, boy, more than you'll ever know.'

Vinny had tears in his eyes. 'But, Mum, please, let me explain.'

'Nope. Fuck off! And don't you ever darken my doorstep again. You're no longer my son. You're dead to me.'

Queenie totally dismissed Patrick's suggestion they fly to Ireland. She had never been on a plane in her life and had no wish to. Buddy Holly, Ritchie Valens and more recently Patsy Cline had all died in aircraft crashes. Their deaths had put the fear of God into Queenie, so she'd asked if they could go by boat instead. Patrick had sorted all the travel arrangements. They'd driven to Liverpool in the early hours of the morning and taken the ferry across.

Glad to be off the ferry, Queenie spent the rest of the journey gazing out of the window, taking in the scenery. Ireland was very green and pretty in comparison to the East End. Cows, sheep and horses grazed in fields. It was idyllic.

'Here we are, Queenie. I'll get your flowers out of the boot, show you Mum's grave, then leave you to it.'

'Thank you, Patrick. Not just for this, but for all the

other things you've done for me. I really do appreciate your help and kindness.'

'My pleasure, Queenie. You were my Mum's rock. You cared for her like no other.'

Queenie arranged the bouquet in a vase next to Mary's grave, then touched her dear friend's headstone. It was beautiful, a massive piece of marble with a carving of Jesus. It really stood out among all the others nearby. 'Hello, Mary. It's me, Queenie. I finally got to visit you and I have lots to tell you, darling.'

Queenie spoke for ages about her life, Viv, her children, Lenny, then chuckled as she told the story of leaving the Huntingdon-Browns in style. 'Pearl rung me up the Monday after the dinner party, threatening to have me arrested if I didn't pay for the vase Viv had broken. I told her if she called the police, I would knock on every neighbour's door down her road and tell them her daughter had got herself up the spout and they'd had the baby adopted. She soon changed her tune then, Mary. It was so funny. I know you would've done the same.'

Queenie went on to remind Mary about some of the laughs they'd had back in the day, like when Mary's husband had turned up on her doorstep serenading her drunk late one night and Mary had opened the window and slung a bucket of piss over his head.

'And what about when you chased Ada O'Brien down the road with your rolling pin and she fell flat on her face and her false teeth flew out and rolled down the drain,' laughed Queenie. 'Oh, and then there was that Christmas when you dragged me to the Blind Beggar and poured Mr Higgins' beer over his head because he'd clipped your Daniel round the ear. "He's my fecking son, therefore if he's a little sod, tell me and *I* will clip him round the ear. You lay another finger on my boy and I'll be punching you on that horrible pointy nose of yours,"' Queenie said, mimicking Mary's Irish accent.

She also told her old friend about her new home and the neighbours. By the time she finished her account of that pervert Peter Davidson being fished out of the Thames, almost an hour had passed.

Realizing Patrick would be waiting for her and it was time to leave, she steeled herself to tell Mary the thing that had been tearing her apart for so long: 'It's been lovely visiting you, Mary. But unless I have to come to Ireland again for a reason, which I very much doubt, this will be my one and only visit. I will always love you, treasure the times we spent together and will always be indebted to you for your kindness, help and advice. But I've been riddled with guilt since my Mum's funeral and I know it's the right thing to keep you in my heart, and my mum in my head. Like yourself, Mum was a big believer in life after death and I know she'll be looking down on me. I'm going to get her the best headstone and make sure her grave has fresh flowers every week. Mum loved flowers and I feel that's the least I can do for her.'

Tears rolled down Queenie's cheeks. 'I've also got a confession to make. I did something bad, but please don't hate me for it, Mary. I always wanted to tell you. I even tried to a couple of times, but I couldn't. I didn't want to risk you thinking badly of me.'

A voice piped up from behind her: 'Mum knew. Everything. She wasn't silly. She could never hate you, Queenie. Not in a million years.'

Queenie managed to stand up even though her legs were like jelly. 'Daniel,' she croaked, her voice no more than a whisper. She turned around and there he was. The only man she had ever truly loved.

Daniel walked towards Queenie and held her in his arms. 'I thought I'd surprise you. It's been ages since I've seen you. Too long.'

Queenie looked up at him. She could barely believe her eyes. His aftershave smelled gorgeous and, unlike Patrick, he still had pure black, wavy hair without a trace of grey. It was slightly longer than when she'd last seen him, and he looked older, with crow's feet around the eyes and a few lines on his forehead, but he was still so bloody handsome. 'It's great to see you, but I have to leave now. Patrick's meeting me in the car park. What did you mean when you said your mum knew everything?'

Daniel grinned. 'Patrick isn't picking you up. He knows I planned to kidnap you for the day. We need to talk, catch up properly. I got things I have to say to you.'

'I thought you were avoiding me.' Queenie's heart was beating like a drum. She so hoped he couldn't feel it. She felt a silly teenager all over again.

Daniel tilted Queenie's chin. She was a lot shorter than him. He kissed her on the forehead. 'You say your good-byes to Mum, then I'll take you out for lunch. I'll take a slow walk, give you some privacy.'

Queenie didn't know if she was coming or going as she bent down to say goodbye to Mary. 'I'll never forget our last conversation. You asked me, "Is there anything you want to tell me?" Is this what you meant, Mary? Were you encouraging me to open up to you? I'm so sorry for not telling you, but I know you knew I was always in love with Daniel. It was a weak moment, Mary, when you was in hospital that time. In fact it was a few weak moments in the end. But if what Daniel said is correct, you knew about it and didn't hate me, I'm so relieved. Such a special person you were. A legend, in my eyes. My boys wouldn't be in the position they are today, if it wasn't for your sound advice. I owe you so much, I truly do.' Queenie stared at the headstone for the last time, then bent down and planted a kiss on Mary's engraved name. 'Until we meet again, my guardian angel.'

The weather was perfect, sunny with a nice breeze. Queenie was relieved she'd got her hair coloured and cut recently, painted her nails and worn her pretty red and white polka-dot dress.

'I know a nice quiet little pub, Queenie. The surroundings are pretty and the food is wonderful,' Daniel grinned.

Queenie put on her dark sunglasses and smiled back. He still had that cheeky lopsided grin, the one that had melted her heart even as a child.

Daniel did most of the talking on the journey. He spoke about Queenie's mum, said how sorry he was to hear that she'd died. Then he asked about the family.

Queenie kept her answers short. She couldn't wait to get inside the pub and have a couple of drinks to calm her jangling nerves. Daniel had a lovely suit on and expensive shoes. When he'd put his sunglasses on, he looked like a film star.

The pub was beautiful, a proper little countryside pub. The homecooked food smelled amazing, but Queenie wasn't hungry. Seeing Daniel had totally killed her appetite, so she asked could they just have a drink now and perhaps eat a bit later.

After a couple of drinks, Queenie felt brave enough to ask some questions herself. 'Are you in touch with Bridie at all?'

'No. Bridie turned into the bitch of all bitches. She smashed my car up with a sledgehammer, cut up all my suits, poured paint over my expensive shoes and generally behaved like a lunatic.'

'Well, they say hell hath no fury like a woman scorned. Do you see your kids? They must be all grown-up now like Vinny and Roy.'

'Yes. But not as often as I'd like to. Bridie remarried and they treat their stepdad as their real dad, which upsets me. I think Bonkers Bridie tried to poison their minds against me. I'm always here for them though if they need me. When they do, it's usually for money.'

'Do you see the child you had with Dolores?'

'Nah. Dolores seemed to disappear into thin air soon as she moved back to Ireland. No idea where she is, or my kid.'

'Oh, that's a shame.'

'I think I would've settled, had I married the right girl. I need a feisty lady, one who'll keep me on my toes. Bit like yourself.' Daniel looked straight into Queenie's eyes and she felt like a teenager again.

Blushing, Queenie changed the subject. 'I thought you got married again? I'm sure Patrick told me you were engaged.'

Daniel ran a hand through his thick wavy hair. 'Siobhan. The cause of all my current troubles. Patrick warned me not to get involved with her because of who her father and brothers were. But me being me, I didn't listen.'

'What happened? Who are her dad and brothers?'

'The McCarthy family are a proper heavy mob out of Cork. They run their manor and nobody messes with them, not if they want to live. Siobhan and I were OK at first. She fell pregnant quite early on in our relationship, so I did the honourable thing and proposed. Her dad organized the wedding on the hurry-up, 'cause he didn't want people to notice she had a bun in the oven. Then, a fortnight before we were due to marry, she miscarried the baby.'

'Oh, I'm so sorry, Daniel.'

'I should have been a man and insist we postpone the wedding for the time being, but Siobhan wanted to go ahead with it. By this time I knew I didn't love her. The night before I was due to marry her, I went out on a heavy stag do, didn't roll home until six in the morning. I began to panic, sweat, shake at the thought of having to walk up that aisle. So I didn't show, and I've been in hiding ever since. Understandably, her father and brothers want to kill me. Patrick's going to see them tonight, see if he can sort the mess out.'

'Jesus! Your mum always said you don't do things by halves. It was very wrong of you to leave Siobhan at the altar, Daniel. You do know that, don't you?'

'Of course. I'd do it again though. There's only one girl I ever truly wanted to marry and that's you, Queenie.'

'Oh, don't be daft. You don't mean that. I know you're full of blarney. You always were,' laughed Queenie.

'Not this time.' Daniel held Queenie's hands. 'My mum forbade me to get involved with you. She reckoned I would ruin your life and you deserved better. She made me promise her and swear on the Bible that I wouldn't make a play for you. You were like a daughter to her, Queenie, and she knew I was bad news. I never stopped loving you though, that's why I never turned up at your wedding. I couldn't watch you marry another man. I've never been able to talk to anyone like I can with you. And, Queenie, when we finally got it together, it felt so good, so right.'

Queenie's heart was beating so fast she could barely

breathe. 'Oh, Daniel. You've always had a place in my heart too. You always will have. I know Mary was against it, but I didn't know she'd warned you off.'

'Mum knew there was something real between us. I denied any wrongdoing, but Mum wasn't stupid, was she? She could sense the change in us, how we acted towards one another after she came out of hospital.'

'Did Patrick know?'

'No. He's never said nothing to me, anyway. He used to joke you had a crush on me when you were a kid, that was all. Mum knew though and when Vinny was born, that confirmed her suspicions.'

'What d'ya mean?'

'Oh, come on, Queenie. You only have to look at the boy. Vinny's not Albie's son. He's mine.'

CHAPTER FORTY

'Hello, Queenie.'

'Mary, what are you doing here? I'm in a bedsit in Ireland.'

'Yes. I know. Thank you for my lovely flowers. They're gorgeous.'

'You've got my scarf on again. You look so beautiful.'

'So do you, sweetheart. I loved your dress.'

'Thank you. Oh Mary, it's so good to see you again.'

'And you. But what you gonna do about our Daniel, eh? I know he loves you and you love him. But it's a gamble, Queenie. He's not reliable. Never will be. But on the other hand, you've never loved, Albie, so what you got to lose? Not like your kids are babies, is it? Daniel could be your one chance of finding true happiness.'

'Mary. Mary—' I cried out, but she'd gone. I woke up, my heart pounding. I knew it was only a dream, but like the last time Mary appeared in one, it seemed so real. She seemed so real. Was my unconscious mind trying to tell me something?

My brief yet passionate affair with Daniel felt as though it were only yesterday. I'd often relived it in my mind.

Not when having sex with Albie – that would have tainted my most wonderful memory. Daniel and I didn't just have sex, we made love. Passionate love.

The affair lasted four days, to be precise. It ended when I saw Bridie and Daniel kissing at the hospital. I'd been in my own little bubble up until then, but seeing that kiss burst it. It brought me back to reality. So I went home to Albie, did my best to act normal, and carried on with married life. We were newlyweds. I should've felt guilty, but I didn't. The only guilt I felt was towards Mary. I'd made love to her son six times over the four-day period while she was laid up in hospital.

Weeks later, it was confirmed I was pregnant. Albie wasn't suspicious because we'd made love lots of times, such was my desire for a son. Inwardly though, I wanted my son to be Daniel's. That was the only way I could always hang on to a part of Daniel. I'd also have a part of Mary.

When Vinny was born with a mop of black curly hair, I was sure he was Daniel's. I never told a soul obviously, but from the moment I laid eyes on him, Baby Blue was my special boy and he always would be.

Vinny's hair straightened by the time he started school and as he grew up all three of my boys looked reasonably alike. Albie also had black hair and striking green eyes, and in all honesty, there was just as much chance, if not more, that Vinny was Albie's son. But I didn't want to believe that. Not really.

A tap on the door put an end to my reminiscing. 'Half an hour suit you to go down to breakfast, Queenie?' asked Patrick.

'Yes,' I replied. 'See you downstairs.'

I glanced at myself in the small mirror. I had bags under

*my eyes. I must have dozed off to have dreamed of Mary.
But up until that point, I had not slept a wink. I'd lie
awake for hours thinking of Daniel O'Leary . . .*

Queenie spent the next few hours with Patrick. He showed
her his mum's old house that he, Daniel and Seamus were
raised in, the church his mum and dad got married in,
and his old school. He pointed out many other milestones
and Queenie loved seeing the places Mary had talked
about.

They stopped at a pub, but yet again, Queenie wasn't
hungry. Patrick recommended the Guinness, so she had a
couple of halves to calm her nerves. She knew she'd be
seeing Daniel again soon.

'Right, I'll drop you at the cottage. Don't let Daniel go
out, Queenie. He shouldn't have risked going out yesterday,
but he was adamant he wanted to surprise you. I'm gonna
pay a visit to a couple of blokes I know, see if we can
get this crap with the McCarthys sorted out once and for
all.'

'Wouldn't Daniel be safer back in London?'

'They'll only come to the club, and we don't want no
trouble there.'

Queenie said no more, just spent the rest of the journey
looking out the window. It was very remote, wherever
they were going. She hadn't seen another car for over ten
minutes, only fields and livestock. She felt sick at the
thought of spending time alone with Daniel in his cottage,
yet excited at the same time.

Patrick drove down a dirt track and right at the bottom
was a pretty little cottage.

'Wow! This is gorgeous. Who does it belong to?'

'Me,' smiled Patrick. 'But apart from Daniel, nobody

knows that. We call it our secret cottage. It used to belong to an old aunt of ours who was a bit of a hermit.'

Daniel opened the front door with a big grin on his face. 'Top of the morning to you.'

'It's afternoon now, ya nutter,' laughed Patrick.

'Welcome to our secret cottage, Queenie.'

'I don't know how long I'll be as I might have to pay the McCarthys another visit an' all. I also need to catch up briefly with an old friend. But I won't be too late. That OK with you, Queenie?'

Queenie's stomach was churning. 'That's fine, Patrick.'

'Don't worry. I'll look after her,' smiled Daniel.

'You better. Or else,' warned Patrick.

As Patrick's car pulled away, Daniel took Queenie in his arms. 'Let me make love to you,' he whispered. 'I want you so much.'

'No. We mustn't,' Queenie protested, but her body was telling her otherwise.

When Daniel kissed her again, then led her into the bedroom, Queenie had no protest left in her.

Daniel lit up two cigarettes and handed one to Queenie. They'd made love twice, in quick succession, and it was wonderful. 'So what happens now?' he asked.

'I don't know, Daniel.'

Daniel propped himself up on his elbow. 'Divorce Albie and marry me. We've wasted far too much time as it is.'

'I can't just divorce Albie for no reason. I've got the kids to consider, and my lovely home. It's a new build. I'm not moving out of that and I can't just chuck Albie out on the bloody streets. He's the kids' dad.'

'He's not Vinny's dad though, is he?'

'I don't know, Daniel. I doubt we'll ever know for sure.'

'We will if Vinny has a blood test. My blood group's unusual.'

'I can't go home and ask Vinny to have a blood test.'

Daniel leaned across to the bedside cabinet and took two photos out of his wallet. One was of himself as a baby, the other was a photo of Vinny that his mum had given him. He pointed to the one on the left. 'That's me.'

The resemblance took Queenie's breath away. They could have been photos of the same baby.

'Now deny Vinny's mine.'

'I'm not denying anything, Daniel. But my head's all over the place.'

'Understandable,' grinned Daniel. 'You gonna tell him?'

'Tell who?'

'Vinny. You gonna tell him I'm his dad?'

'Goodness no! Then again, he'd probably like that. Vinny is no fan of Albie's. Never has been.'

'There you go then.'

'Don't rush things, Daniel. Please.'

'OK, my love, let's do less talking then . . .' He wrapped Queenie in his arms and kissed her passionately. 'Did you come earlier?'

'I beg your pardon!'

'Did you have an orgasm?'

Queenie felt flushed and also embarrassed. 'I don't know.'

'Well, you would if you'd had one.' Daniel put his cigarette out.

'Whatever are you doing?' Queenie asked as Daniel put his head under the sheet.

'You'll see,' Daniel mumbled.

'Oh no, Daniel. You can't do that. It's not normal!'

Queenie soon changed her tune when Daniel's tongue connected with her clitoris. She thought she'd died and gone to heaven.

Daniel handed Queenie a brandy. 'You all right?'

Queenie was still in shock. She had never known such sexual positions existed. As for an orgasm, she certainly knew what one of those was now. She'd nearly shot through the roof. 'Yes. I'm fine. Just thinking,' Queenie smiled. They were dressed again, and sitting in the pretty back garden.

'What you thinking about?'

'Your mum. I had a dream about her last night. She was talking to me.'

'What about? Can you remember?'

'Yes. You.'

'Did she tell you to marry me?'

'I can't really remember what she said. I wish I'd written it down. I think she told me to take a chance on you though. Oh Daniel,' Queenie put her hand over her mouth. 'Say your mum was looking down on us when we were, ya know?'

Daniel burst out laughing and put an arm around Queenie's shoulders. 'I'm sure Mum wouldn't want to watch. She would've shut her eyes. You're a funny one, you are, Queenie. And that is why I love you. You're not like any of the other women I've met. You're unique, just like Mum was.'

Queenie beamed from ear to ear. She felt like that silly schoolgirl who'd had a crush on Daniel all those years ago. Not a grown woman with four kids who was nearing her forties.

'So where do we go from here? I'm definitely moving

back to London. I wanna be close to you. Will you meet up with me? Regularly?'

'I don't see why not.' Queenie wouldn't shit on her own doorstep, but could meet Daniel in the West End. Vinny liked Daniel, so even if she was spotted out with him, she knew Vinny wouldn't kick off. Nobody could say anything really, what with Daniel being Mary's son.

'I know some lovely restaurants and hotels I can take you to. We can have early lunches, then spend the after-noons in bed,' Daniel said with a twinkle in his eye.

'You've got it all planned out, haven't you, Daniel O'Leary? Your mum always said you could charm the birds from the trees. No wonder the women fall for you,' joked Queenie. She was ever so excited though. The thought of having a passionate affair with Daniel in London filled her with joy. Life was too short to not take chances; especially the way Daniel made her feel. He brought her alive in more ways than one.

'You know what you were saying earlier about Vinny and Roy opening their club? I'd love to be there. Can I come?'

'Oh, I dunno about that. The whole family'll be there, Albie included.'

'I'll behave, I swear. Patrick'll come with me. Everyone knows how close you were to Mum. Nobody'll blink an eyelid.'

'I'll think about it.'

'I don't want you to go home tomorrow. Can't you stay a bit longer?'

'No. I must go back with Patrick. You got a phone here?'

'Yeah.'

'I'll give you my number. Don't ring until after ten of

an evening. Brenda's in bed by then and the boys and Albie are usually out.'

The rest of the day passed quickly. Too quickly. Talking to Daniel was so easy, the conversation flowed like running water.

'Patrick's back,' Daniel sighed, peeping through the curtain.

'Don't you say anything to him, Daniel. It's early days and I don't want anybody to know.'

'You've told me that about fifty times already.'

'And I'm telling you again.'

'You're sounding like Mum now.'

Queenie playfully punched his arm. 'Now act normal.'

'How'd it go?' Daniel asked his brother.

Patrick shrugged. 'So-so. I've told old McCarthy we'll pay the total cost of the wedding, plus give him five grand on top for his trouble.'

'Did he shake on it?'

'No. He demanded ten, the canny bastard. Then Siobhan's brothers turned up mouthing off, so I came away. We'll sort it, don't worry. The old man's definitely calmed down. You stay holed up and I'll come back next week with whatever dosh he fecking wants. Then you can travel back to London with me.'

Daniel winked at Queenie. 'Can't wait to get back to London. I'm bored here.'

'Did you two have a nice catch-up?' asked Patrick.

'Yeah. Apart from Queenie begging for my hand in marriage, Patrick. I told her no, I've already been married too many times,' chuckled Daniel.

Queenie felt herself blush. 'Take no notice of him.'

'I never do, Queenie. Jesus, you got far too much sense to ever get tied up with him.

'Cheers for sorting stuff with the McCarthys, Pat. I'll settle up with you when I get home.'

Patrick rolled his eyes. 'And owe me the rest, I dare say.'

Daniel laughed. 'Yeah. Something like that.'

Patrick glanced at his watch. He was starving. 'You ready to make tracks, Queenie?'

'Yes. Ready when you are.'

'You got enough food to last you another week?' Patrick asked his brother.

'Yeah. I'm sick of eating tinned crap though, I need some proper meat inside me.'

'You'll be home soon. Just keep your head down, OK?'

Queenie felt awkward when Daniel hugged her in front of Patrick. 'Bye then. It was lovely catching up with you, Daniel.'

'Same 'ere. Thoroughly enjoyed it. Until the next time,' Daniel kissed Queenie on the cheek and watched her walk down the path, never taking his eyes off her.

Queenie arrived home from Ireland in a daze and spent the next few days walking around as if in a dream.

Daniel rang her as they'd arranged. They chatted for ages every night, until Albie or one of the boys came home and she had to end the call.

Queenie knew Daniel was the love of her life, but the sensible side of her was wary. She wasn't about to jump from the frying pan into the fire, not when she had the children to think about, but she couldn't wait to see him again.

Queenie's latest daydream was interrupted by Viv. 'What's a bleedin' matter with you? That's the second time today you've forgot to put sugar in my tea,' complained her sister.

'Sorry, give me your cup. I ain't been sleeping well, if you must know.'

'What, over that Peter? Don't be losing sleep over him, Queen. He got what was coming to him, love,' snapped Viv. The whole area was talking about what might have happened to the lad.

'No. Not over Peter. I still feel guilty over the letter Mum wrote me. I want to visit Mum in the morning, apologize to her for the way I made her feel. Mary was my dear friend, but you only get one mother, Viv. So from now on, Mum is the only one out the two I shall talk about. Would you come to the grave with me?'

Viv squeezed her sister's hand. 'Of course I will. You'll feel better once you go there too. Tell Mum what you've just told me. We'll take her some fresh flowers an' all.'

'Thank you,' smiled Queenie.

'You sure there's nothing else you ain't telling me? You've lost weight. And you came back from Ireland glowing with happiness. Did you by any chance see Daniel while you were over there?' Viv was well aware of the crush Queenie had had on Daniel when they were growing up.

'Only briefly. He don't change. Left a girl standing at the altar recently. Her family are seething, and they aren't people to be messed with, so Daniel's lying low. That man has spent that much time in hiding, he might as well have been sent down for a ten-stretch!'

Viv laughed. 'He was always one for the girls. A proper heartbreaker. 'Ere you know who he reminds me of? Your Michael. He's another Daniel. You sure you two have never had an affair in later life and you forgot to tell me,' joked Viv.

Queenie smiled. Her sister was close, but had the wrong

son. She would usually tell Viv all her secrets, but what had happened between herself and Daniel was sacred. Never to be spoken of to anyone. That's how special it had been – and still was.

Albie Butler trudged dejectedly towards home. Since calling it off with Maureen, he had nothing to look forward to. Nothing whatsoever. He was even debating whether to get in touch with her again, but Vinny's threats to kill her kids had chilled him to the bone. It wasn't fair. A son was meant to be scared of his father, not the other way around.

Having had nothing but beer money the past few days, Albie had finally earned enough to buy a small bunch of flowers to leave outside the cafe for Peter. He could only afford the cheapest bunch, so had nicked a few from the graveyard to bulk up a bit. He didn't want to look tight or skint.

The police had announced yesterday that Peter had been strangled before he'd been dumped in the Thames. The whole community was in shock. The lad had had a bit of a dodgy reputation for flashing and touching up young girls, but even just looking at him you could see he wasn't the full shilling. He was like an older version of Lenny, Albie thought.

There were lots of people milling about outside the cafe, including Jack and Ethel, Peter's parents, who were reading all the lovely cards left with the flowers.

Albie laid his bunch, shook Jack's hand, hugged Ethel and said how sorry for their loss he was. As he turned to leave, he saw Vinny standing there with a huge arrangement, smirking at him.

Albie went to turn on his heel, but Vinny grabbed his

shoulder. 'You ever cheat on Mum again, you'll end up in the Thames an' all,' Vinny whispered in his ear.

Albie looked at his monster of a son in horror. He guessed there and then that Vinny was responsible for Peter's murder. 'I won't, I promise.'

Vinny winked. 'Sensible decision.'

After numerous phone calls from her son, begging forgiveness, Queenie decided to allow him back inside the house. He'd stayed upstairs at the snooker club ever since their argument and seeing as the opening night at the club was on the horizon, Queenie felt it was time to listen to what he had to say. She also had a lot to say to him too.

Vinny arrived at 8 p.m., as she'd told him to. Brenda was round Viv's, watching TV with Lenny. She'd slung Albie out, given him some money to go back down the pub, and Roy and Michael both had dates this evening.

Vinny had a posh carrier bag with him which he put down in the hallway. Queenie guessed this was another gift for her, but she didn't want buttering up, she wanted a proper apology.

'Thank you for allowing me inside the house, Mum. How was Ireland? Did you have a nice break?'

'Yes thanks,' Queenie snapped. She was still so hurt over the way Vinny had spoken to her and was determined not to make this easy for him.

'I've barely slept or eaten since our argument. I am so sorry, Mum. I don't know what came over me, I love you so much – too much, perhaps. I've had a long, hard think and know in my heart that nothing is going on between you and Freddie Angel.'

'Oh, you've seen sense at last, have ya? That's good,' Queenie replied, her voice laden with sarcasm. 'You know full well Freddie has always been a friend of the family. He made a fuss of you, Roy and Michael when you were growing up. How dare you accuse me of shagging the man! Yes, he once had a soft spot for me, but that was donkey's bloody years ago. He asked me out before I met your father and I didn't want him then. What makes you think I'd want the man now?'

Vinny looked at his feet like a naughty schoolboy. 'I was wrong. I know that. Honestly, I can't apologize to you enough.'

'I am so disappointed in you, Vinny. Since the day you were born, boy, I've had your back. Look at all the times I stuck up for you and gave you alibis. You cried on my shoulder after that Yvonne Summers turnout and I drummed it into you that *your* future was all that mattered. Then I dug you out of a massive hole when you attacked poor Bonnie Tarbuck. I even looked her mother in the eye and lied so you could keep your reputation intact. My heart went out to Bonnie's mum after that girl hung herself, but I did it for you. Everything in my life, I've done for you. Yet you have the front to accuse me of being manipulative and raising you the way I did for my own gain. I wanted you to make something of your life for you, not me. I didn't want to see you working in some poxy factory or ending up a useless bum like your father.'

'Please forgive me, Mum. I was jealous. I couldn't bear the thought of Freddie wooing you, touching you.'

'But he didn't do any of those things, you silly bastard. I told you that. We're friends.'

'I know that now. I saw him out shopping with his new lady a couple of days ago. They were holding hands.'

'Oh well, at least Freddie took my advice – something you're not very good at.'

'Please, Mum. Look at me. Without you, I'm nothing. I take back all I said, every single word. I was so angry that morning, I drank half a bottle of Scotch and my mouth ran away with me. You are the reason I've bought that club. You've made me into the man I am today. I swear on my life, I will never treat you or speak to you again in such a way. I was bang out of order and I know it. I also know I have issues that I need to sort. I think I'm damaged goods. All that shit with Macca, Marnie, Yvonne, Bonnie – it's had a lasting effect on me. I ain't the full shilling, I know I ain't.'

Queenie softened. 'There's nothing wrong with you. Come 'ere, give me a hug.'

'Do you forgive me? The club opening won't be the same if you don't come.'

'Yes, I forgive you. But I swear to you, Vinny, you ever speak to me like that again, that's the end of me and you. I mean that, an' all. I also want you to bring me that gun you were waving around the other day. I will look after it for you. You're not in a good frame of mind and I don't want you doing anything stupid.'

Vinny smiled. 'Good idea. I bought you a present to wear at the opening night. Wanna see it?'

'Go on then.'

When Vinny pulled the jacket out of the posh carrier bag, Queenie stared at it in awe. Nobody down her street had a real fur jacket. 'Oh, it's beautiful, Vinny. I love it!'

'Try it on, Mum.'

Queenie did as asked. It fitted perfectly. 'Thank you. I love it.' She did a twirl before looking at herself in the mirror.

Vinny grinned. 'Only the best for my mum. Roll on Friday week for the grand opening. I can't bloody wait.'

'Me neither. Oh, and by the way, I've invited Patrick O'Leary. It was very nice of him to pay for me to go to Ireland and visit his mother's grave. He's bringing his brother with him.'

'Great stuff. I always liked Patrick and Daniel. Top blokes.'

Queenie smiled, then looked at the clock. Daniel would be calling her soon. 'You get off now, Vinny. Thank you again for my lovely fur coat. It's truly beautiful.'

'My pleasure, Mum. I'll nip round to the club and bring the gun straight back to ya.'

'Erm, actually I'm tired, boy. It's been a long day. Drop the gun round to me in the morning and in the meantime, I'll think of the perfect hiding place. That OK with you?'

'Yeah, sure.' Vinny held his mother close to his chest. 'Thank you so much for forgiving me. I know I don't deserve it.'

Queenie stroked her firstborn's cheek. 'No. You don't. But that's what loving mothers do. Oh, and by the way, whenever Peter's funeral is, we'll need to attend together, you know that, don't you?'

Vinny smiled. 'Yeah. No worries.'

Daniel O'Leary rang at ten on the dot. 'I'm missing you so much. I can't wait to see you again. Patrick's coming back to Ireland with the McCarthys' dosh next Thursday, so we'll travel to London early Friday, then come to the club opening together.'

'I can't wait to see you either. Please act normal at the club though. Viv isn't silly. She picks up on most things. We need to give it a bit of time – I think I've made my decision, Daniel, it's just my boys – you know.'

'I won't let you down, I promise. I'll act like you're just

a family friend at the party. Then how about I book a hotel room for us the following day? We can have a bit of lunch, spend some quality time together.'

Queenie had butterflies again. Daniel sounded so genuine and she felt exactly the same way. They could make a life together, it felt so right.

'OK. I usually go shopping with Viv on a Saturday, but I can pretend I'm meeting up with Doreen, an old friend of mine.'

'Cushty. So when we getting married then?'

'Don't start all that again,' laughed Queenie.

'I'm not joking. I mean it.'

'You're a very impatient man. Anyone ever told you that?'

'Yeah. My mum. I'm not joking though. I let you go once – big mistake. I'm never letting you go again.'

Queenie felt a warm glow inside her. It might have taken her many years, but finally she knew what being in love felt like.

EPILOGUE

I'm singing along to the radio as I pack my little case. I'm ever so excited; feeling on top of the world. Tonight, I will proudly watch my eldest two open their first club. Then tomorrow, I will be spending the day with Daniel. I've told the family that Doreen Laine has invited Eliza and me over to her posh house for a meal as her husband is away and we'll both be staying over.

I've always hated liars, but I'm getting quite good at living a lie. Case of having to, really. The chance to sleep with and wake up with Daniel for the first time ever is an opportunity too good to miss. I can't wait for him to hold me again and to feel him inside me. Just the thought of it sends shivers down my spine. Daniel has woken something in me that I never knew existed in the first place.

'I didn't know you liked Herman's Hermits, Mum,' laughs Michael.

I'd never been a fan, it's true, but their latest, 'I'm Into Something Good', reminds me of Daniel. Same with the Honeycombs' 'Have I the Right', the Searchers' 'When You Walk in the Room', the Kinks' 'You Really Got Me', and Jim Reeves' 'I Love You Because'. So many songs in the current top forty could have been written for me and Daniel.

'Stop singing, Mum. You're doing my head in,' complains Brenda.

I smile. Nothing can dampen my mood today. My boys have achieved their dreams and for the first time in my life I am head over heels in love. Viv is suspicious, she knows there's something up. I haven't let on, I keep insisting I'm happy because I have finally made peace with Mum.

'Don't just barge in. Knock first,' I scold Albie. I am sitting at the dressing table in my underwear, putting my make-up on. I bought some new undies this week. Not sexy – I would feel silly at my age wearing anything too provocative, so I purchased pretty ones instead.

Albie sighs. 'I've only come in to get me suit. You ain't got nothing I've not seen before, love. I am your bleedin' husband.'

Not for much longer, I think to myself. I must've spoken to Daniel on the phone for fifty or more hours since leaving Ireland and I've made a pact with him. If he treats me right and I feel I can trust him, in six months' time I will ask Albie for a divorce.

'Cooey.'

'Up 'ere, Viv,' I shout.

Lenny runs into my bedroom clapping his hands.

'Been driving me mad all day, he has. Overly excited about tonight. He wants to get there early,' Viv says.

'Can we go now, please? Please, Mum?' Lenny shrieks, jumping up and down.

I stand up to put my dress on. I've brought a new one: black, calf-length with silver embroidery around the neck. Very classy and quite sexy in comparison to all my other frocks.

'*Jesus wept, Queen! You really need to start eating more. You're beginning to resemble a skeleton. You sure you ain't ill?' asks my sister.*

'*No. I'm fine. I've just been excited, what with the boys opening the club and all. I'm also still grieving our mum. Why don't you go on with Lenny. I'll meet you down there in a while.'*

'*Mum, I'll see you later. I'm going to meet, Kev,' shouts Michael from downstairs.*

'*Bye, love.'*

'*I'm off too. Gonna pop in the Maurice for a pint or two first,' says Albie. He's dreading tonight, is positive that Vinny murdered young Peter Davidson. He doesn't want to celebrate with Vinny. He hates the man his son has become.*

Having always had a dream of making a late grand entrance on my own to the opening of my sons' first club, I urge Viv to go on alone with Lenny. 'I'm nowhere near ready yet,' I lie. I need to gather my thoughts and have a sherry or two to calm my jangling nerves. I wonder if Daniel will already be there when I arrive. I'm sure I look more glamorous than he's ever seen me before.

I put on my paste diamond earrings and bracelet, then go downstairs and pour myself a drink. Roy Orbison's 'Pretty Woman' is on the radio. It's the current number one and I can't help but twirl around, singing. After years of feeling plain and drab, this is another song that reminds me of myself and Daniel. Nobody has ever made me feel so desired before, but he does. I actually feel like Roy Orbison is singing about me.

When the song ends, I down my sherry and pour another. I'm calmer now. I wonder how Vinny and Roy are feeling. Vinny's expecting a huge turnout, has a live singer on. I know the Kelly brothers will be there, and they're bringing a group of their friends. 'The more faces the merrier, Mum,' Vinny told me earlier. 'Word gets around then, our club's the new place to be. That's how the business works,' he explained.

I put my fur jacket on, my present from Vinny. I smile. The Queenie who dressed in shabby clothes and skivvied for the Huntingdon-Browns seems a stranger to me now.

The phone rings. Vinny has had a callbox installed in the club reception area and I wonder if it's Daniel.

'Hello.'

My heart leaps at the sound of an Irish accent. 'Daniel, is that you?'

'I'm afraid not. Is that Queenie I'm speaking to?'

The voice sounds very much like Daniel's. 'Yes,' I reply. 'Who is this?'

There's a pause. 'Robbie O'Callaghan. Not sure if Daniel has ever mentioned me to you, but—'

'How have you got my number? I interrupt. My heart is pounding. Something's wrong. Instinct tells me.

'Daniel gave me your number recently, just in case anything went wrong. I am so sorry to have to inform you of this, Queenie, but Daniel and Patrick were both shot dead earlier today. They were ambushed on their way to the ferry.'

'Nah, that can't be right. Who are you? Some joker? Daniel and Patrick are meeting me soon, they'll be at the opening of my sons' club. In fact, I bet they're already there. You're one of that family, aren't you? The McCarthys?'

There was another pause. 'I'm not one of those McCarthys, believe me,' replied the man. He sounded choked up. 'There's no doubt the McCarthys are responsible for what happened today – and believe me, Queenie,

I will be gunning for revenge. Daniel and Patrick were two of my oldest friends. I was very close to Mary too.'

Tears are streaming down my face. This can't be happening. It feels like a nightmare. But I know it is true, can feel it in my bones.

'Queenie, Daniel left me strict orders. If the worst was to happen, I was to call you and tell you that he loves you very much and he always will.'

I drop the phone on its cradle and collapse to my knees. 'Not Daniel. Not my Daniel,' I cry. I don't even think about poor Patrick. All I can think about is the love of my life.

The phone rings again. 'Mum, hurry up,' urges Vinny. 'It's mobbed 'ere, exactly as I predicted it would be.'

I know that man on the phone wasn't joking, but I pray that he was. 'Are Patrick and Daniel O'Leary there yet?'

'Don't think so. Not seen 'em. Just hurry up, will ya? I'm gonna do a speech soon and you gotta be 'ere for that.'

I slam the phone down and burst into tears. I take off my fur coat and look in the mirror. I don't look beautiful any more. I don't feel it either. Who was I kidding, thinking I'd finally found love and happiness? I've always been cursed. Well, from the moment I was raped as a child anyway.

I drink some more sherry. I can see Daniel's face, smell his gorgeous aftershave. I can't live without him, I know that much. I want to be wherever he is.

I put my hand inside the cupboard below the kitchen sink, lift up the loose floorboards and take out Vinny's gun. It takes me a few minutes to work out how to load the bullets. I have never used a gun before.

My hand shakes as I position the gun at my temple.

How can I not leave the kids a note? And Viv? I must write those first, I decide.

The front door bursts open and I hide the gun under a tea towel.

'Mum, whatever's wrong? You put the phone down on me.'

I tearfully explain about the phone call from Ireland. 'I can't come to the club, Vinny. I can't face it. Mary's sons were wonderful men. Why is life so unfair?'

'Fucking hell, Mum. That's awful. Who shot 'em?'

'It's a long story. I can't talk about it right now. You go back to the club, boy.'

'No. Not without you. I'll call Roy, explain what's happened. He'll have to hold the fort.'

'But it's your big night. You have to be there. You've worked so hard for this.'

'Mum, you're my world and if you ain't there, it's pointless anyway. Most of my speech is about you. I know I said some shitty things recently, but this is the truth. I love you so fucking much. Everything I do, everything I achieve, it's all for you. I wanna pay you back for being the best mum ever. You're the strongest, finest woman I know. So tonight, I'll stay 'ere with you.'

I lock eyes with Vinny and I know in that split second that, if I were to kill myself, it would be the end of him too. The others would survive, but not my Vinny. He needs me too much, has always been a mummy's boy.

I down the rest of my sherry and repair my tear-stained mascara. I put my fur coat on and touch up my lipstick.

'You coming to the club?' *Vinny asks, surprised.*

I force a smile. That same smile I've had to force for most of my sad, sorry life. I'm used to wearing a mask, putting on an act. I can't let my boy down.

When Vinny nips upstairs to use the toilet, I quickly put the gun back in its hidey-hole.

Vinny smiles when he sees me. 'You look stunning tonight. Truly beautiful, Mum.'

I close the front door and link arms with my eldest. Daniel might be dead, but I'll always have a part of him. In Vinny we created something special. Something very special indeed.